WINGS

SUBVERSIVE GAY ANGEL EROTICA

Edited by Todd Gregory

Rough Trade

Blood Sacraments

Wings: Subversive Gay Angel Erotica

WINGS

SUBVERSIVE GAY ANGEL EROTICA

edited by

Todd Gregory

A Division of Bold Strokes Books

2011

WINGS: SUBVERSIVE GAY ANGEL EROTICA

ISBN 13: 978-1-60282-565-9

This Trade Paperback Original Is Published By
Bold Strokes Books, Inc.
P.O. Box 249
Valley Falls, NY 12185

First Edition: September 2011

Credits
Editors: Todd Gregory and Stacia Seaman
Production Design: Stacia Seaman
Cover Design by Sheri (graphicartist2020@hotmail.com)

This is for all my real-life angels

Contents

Mead-Sweet

Jeff Mann

The English pour down the hill in clouds of hoof-raised dust. Hot September sun flashes on their helmets; their sharp spears and swords gleam like ice. They are a surprise, and most unwelcome. We thought them far south of here. We should not have come. We should never have left Norway. A journey needless and for naught. And we should never, never, despite the heat of the day, have left so many of our mail shirts on the ships.

My mail shirt I wear, however, and my sturdy helmet, for in a dream last night a troll-woman gave me warning, which I now see I was wise to heed. My axe Gut-Reaper is honed and ready, as am I, and so, as we Vikings retreat, hearing behind us the screams of slaughter, our first line of warriors falling beneath the English swords, I ask the king a favor. He knows me better than I would prefer. He knows, without Eirik, I have only my hollow life left to lose. And so he nods and passes on, leading our army's remainder over the narrow bridge, toward the east, where the ships wait, with our mail shirts and our reinforcements.

I stand upon the bridge. Today is the day I will die. So it occurs to me, but without regret. I rub the Thor's hammer amulet hung about my neck, murmur a strength-prayer to Sky-Father and Storm-Lord, pat the iron mesh that coats me, then in both hands heft my axe. The river flows below, a surge of gray, pearl-white where it tongues the stones. I must hold this place as long as I am able.

It will be a pleasure to kill them, the damned English, who brought down my brother-in-arms Eirik during a raid last spring, in a village we had plundered and burnt. I heard the deep, sharp sound, like the thump of axe-blade swung down into wood, turned in the midst of our flight, saw the arrow embedded in his chest. I carried Eirik to the ship.

Stubborn, he lived halfway across the deep swan-road, the cold expanse of sea between England and Norway. I smoothed the golden hair from his brow, wiped away blood-gush from his blond beard. The men who once had mocked us, mocked how close we were, until our strength taught them better, taught them a respectful silence, they rowed, and they mourned as they rowed, they held their tongues and rowed under the guiding stars, while I cradled Eirik and Eirik smiled up at me, and I kissed him, there before the men, and I sobbed—most unmanly, true, though I hope my courage since has redeemed me from any charge of womanliness. In my arms, Eirik gasped his last. We brought him home, we piled his pyre, we raised a stone above him and etched his name in runes.

We will not lie together in earth's grave-grasp, as once we lay together, body upon body. He will lie there, on the ridge-top above the fjord; I will lie here, in some rank English midden. Today is the only future. Today is the promise of eternal honor. Today is the day I own. And I do not intend to cry.

So, as my foes approach, here in this foreign land where my bones will bleach far from his, I think of Eirik, I remember how he and I made blood-brotherhood, our slashed forearms bound together, life-blood mingling; the way we made love in secret—in quiet caves and isolated moor-huts, dense woodland and scree-slope, misty mountaintops far from village or clan—taking turns as the man, as the woman, and how our shame diminished, if not disappeared, after a decade of brotherhood, and we came to know manliness together, lying upon and lying beneath, then lying afterward side by side, sticky hands stroking beards, hairy breasts, the scored crescents of battle scars. I think of Eirik as the English form in lines of battle upon the river's western bank, determined to dislodge me. I think of him as I grin, gnash berserker teeth, swing my axe at the first lunging fool, bring him down, spit on his twitching corpse, and swing again. I can see their fear, and they do well to fear, for I am great in body, a head taller than any of them, my beard like the lord Thor's, a bush of red fire, my hair the same hot hue, hanging to my shoulders, those shoulders the hard expanse Eirik so loved, my arms and torso like oaken boughs and oaken trunk, swollen with strength, and I remember how Eirik loved me to force him, to hold him down and force him, the violence we spread in battle there too in the deep way we made love, half-hurtful and half-tender, like two brute bears of the forest-firs, yes, I see him grinning beside me, wiping blood from his braided yellow beard, as the next English falls and then the next—my axe cleaves helmets the way a ship's prow cuts the star-spattered whale-road, their flimsy English javelins bounce off my mail coat like trifling hail—and then the next falls and the next, till there is a heap of them at my feet, and I am shouting and laughing, drool dripping off my chin, sweat staining my face, beckoning on the next man to die, and our army is, with the gods' help, far from here now, and my name, my name, Thorir Egilson, will be remembered as long as bards sing, or if not my name, then at least my deed, and who knows how long this goes on, bless the Valkyrie that brings me such a breeze, for sweat seeps down my chest and back, and this is the fortieth, I think, and then from below, a sharp stab, beneath my mail shirt, between my legs, from whence came such a craven blade, my strength seeping fast, and I bring down another five before, here, night-helmet slipping over my vision, and I drop my axe, I lift my wet hand from my groin—it is a river, black, unstoppable as any flood-flow, a mead-horn spilling irretrievables—and I fall to my knees and remember Eirik's full lips framed by golden hair and his great hairy breast and his great hairy sex dripping rapture and his bones blackening within the pyre-fire and the deep-cut harbors of home and the forests of mist and moss where we met and loved, and I fall onto my side, my great limbs like thistledown now, the scud of clouds, mere feathers now, useless, I am useless at last, and I pray to Odin, come to me, Father, lift me up, make me strong again, send me eagle or raven, lift me up, and now foe-shadows fall across me, what's left of the sky flashes with foe-swords, so I close my eyes and smile, for I know I will be remembered.

❖

The voice that speaks my name is low and deep. It sounds like home. "Wake, Thorir," it says. In the sound is the faint beat of wings.

I open my eyes; I look out again upon the world. Below me, a rainbow's arc is fading, a rain-squall is passing. Above me perches an eagle. An eagle, all black. I lean against the ash-trunk and look up at it, its golden eyes, its hooked beak. Then I look down, and here is my great body yet, naked, moist with raindrops, though younger than I recall, for the scars I bore, the scars Eirik used to stroke, are gone.

I wipe wet from my eyes. Smoke is the cause; it stings my sight. "Look there, Thorir," says that familiar voice, and I do, peering down across a distant moor, where a pyre burns, and another, and another, a plain of fallen bodies. I bend forward, and I see the king, and many, so many comrades, lying on piles of flaming wood. Then upon a pyre I see myself, naked, a tangled mass of maimings, pale skin and blood-gash and even a glimpse of hacked bone, broken axe laid upon my chest. I wipe my eyes again, more unseemly tears, and then the wind shifts, sparks leap heavenward, and smoke covers my face, this living face here, that dead face there, and I close my eyes and cough.

The smoke is black feathers, teasing my brow and lips. I brush the soft touch away, but it returns, so I open my eyes again, and there he is, white teeth and red lips gleaming, eyes gray-blue, long-lashed, and laughing, as young as when we met, golden beard braided, golden hair bound back. He's clad in a cloak of black, cloak open to reveal the glistening nakedness I so love.

"Eirik?" I say, throat tight. Eirik is smiling as he brushes his cloak's edge against my face, playful as he used to be after lovemaking. The cloak's woven of pyre-smoke, black feathers, eagle feathers, fire-flicker. Flicker and feather tickle my nostrils and lips.

"Eirik," I say again. I sneeze; I clear my throat. The smoke pours over his shoulders like storm-waves, like forest cascade. His torso is thickly hairy, as it was in life, a great muscled expanse, a silver Thor's hammer to match mine glittering in the blond fur curling upon his breast, the charm I gave him when our blood first mingled. His belly's lean, as are his hips. And there, between his burly, pelted thighs, is his man-sex, half-hard, which filled and fulfilled me, which gave me such bliss for so many years. I want to reach out and take his flesh in my hands, as I have hundreds of times in our past, but I am afraid, truly afraid, for the first time since he died. I am afraid he is not real, has not returned.

Pulling my gaze from his body, I stare into his blue eyes. He smiles, lifts his hand, tickles my nose yet again with his black fire-and-feather cloak. His aroma, oh so familiar, so long ached for after we were parted, washes over me—animal musk and seashore and the black earth in which forests root.

"Are you real?" I ask, pushing a strand of hair off my brow. I look down at my own form, as muscled as his, as young, coarse red fur coating me from neck to ankles, gilded in firelight. The stray silver with which age had dusted my chest and belly is nowhere to be found. "Are you real? Am I?"

"Yes," says Eirik. "Yes." He touches me now, very softly, fingertips brushing my chest. "Red-gold," he says. "The hue of Yule-fire, of dragon-hoard. Bloody and golden, my brother Thorir. Odin and I, we bid you welcome."

I seize him by the shoulders and slam my lips against his. His beard's soft; it smells of honey and beer. I grip him by his bound-back hair and shove my tongue into his mouth. He laughs, grips my arm till it hurts, bites my lip till I taste my own blood. "Hold on to me," he says, in between rough kisses, "and I will carry you farther." Then his arms fold over me, the black feathers and flame-points engulf me, and what's left of what's solid drops beneath my feet.

❖

Golden leaves fill my sight. Gold's all I can see, awash in sunset wind. Eirik's muscle-hard arm rests upon my shoulder. I'm weak suddenly, my knees buckling. "Easy, brother, easy," Eirik murmurs, helping me sit in a pile of glittering leaves.

"Glasir. So is called the tree." He shoulders off the eagle-cloak; it drops into the leaves and disperses, a few dark puffs of smoke the wind carries off. Naked, he sits by me.

"Sick," I grunt, my head swimming, my limbs of a sudden feverish and shaking.

"Here, brother," says Eirik, arranging my bulk as if I weighed nothing. My head's in his lap now, the leaves drifting over my limp limbs.

"Why are you so strong?" I mutter. "In our last life, I could lift you into my arms with ease. Remember?"

"I remember," says Eirik. His palm rests on my forehead. His face hovers over me, blue-sky eyes and sun-gold beard, sun-gold hair, cascade of honey and wheat. "Here." He lifts my head and holds a drinking horn to my lips. I sip, and then I gulp. Ale—foaming, bitter, tinged with herbs. "Good," I sigh, licking my lips. Eirik shares long draughts with me. His fingers fondle the hair around my nipples, then the nipples themselves. When they harden, he gives each a fond pinch.

"I have missed you, big bear. Missed the musk of our bodies grappling together, missed the feel of your flesh inside me and my flesh inside you. When you're ready, Thorir, we will enter the hall. The All-Father has sent me to fetch you in. Drink now, drink more."

"More," I say. "Yes. You want my mind addled with drink so that you might vanquish me and bind me and take a turn atop me, eh? As you used to do. I know you, Eirik Fairhair, Eirik Man-Raper. I know your tricks. The wrestling hold, the blade held to my throat, the slipknot about my wrists, the grease rubbed between my nether-cheeks, and then the brutal taking." As I grumble the memory, my cock hardens despite myself.

Eirik laughs. "Sweet memories indeed. And more to come." He strokes my cockhead with a fingertip. Again he lifts the horn to my mouth. When I gaze into its amber depths, I find it as full as when we began.

"This drink will clear your head, hero, not addle it. It will give you strength to rise. You must rise soon, for we must not be late for battle."

"Battle?" I take a last gulp, then, grimacing, roll onto my belly, hoist myself up on elbows, then knees. I gain my footing. "Never late," I say, swaying. "Lead on. Whatever's needed. The bridge? I thought I fell. Will you help me hold the bridge?"

"The bridge you held is gone, brother. You held it long. Oh, fear not, you were magnificent." Eirik chuckles. "But that time is no more. You fell, the king fell, the English triumphed, and then they themselves, mere days later, were swept away by other foemen, and the years passed, mead-halls fell, the great stones crumbled, and Weird changed the world. You and I, we are out of time. We have passed on, over a new bridge, and now we move toward other battles."

Eirik rises. Glorious nakedness, he stands before me. Between my thighs my cock bobs at the blessed sight of him. Grinning, he takes my sex in his fist and leads me, stumbling after him, beneath the golden tree, through drifts of yellow leaves high and shifting as sea-dunes, and into the dark fir-forest beyond.

❖

It's a mead-hall, the greatest I've ever seen, with a pitched roof of shields overlaid like golden shingles, with high-horned wooden gables that fade in and out of low cloud. "You know its name," Eirik says, dropping my cock and gripping my hand. He leads me around it. Inside the quiet of this woodland glade are wafts of other worlds: loud men laughing and singing, the shriek of sea-eagles, the break of surf on craggy ness, the sough of wind in pine boughs, the greedy crackle of fire, the tiny patter of rain on tarn, the distant spear-shake of thunderstorm. Here, high above the entrance, is a wolf carved into the gable-end, and there, on the far gable, a carven eagle.

"Valholl," I whisper. "Is it true? I have made it, then?"

"You have!" Eirik slaps my shoulder. "Think, Thorir! How you fought beside me all those years, how you held the bridge. What better sword-wielder is there? Who above you would Val-Father summon here?"

"And he sent you." I squeeze Eirik's hand.

"I come for those who fall. That is my reward. That, and time out of time with you."

"I have heard tell of women who…"

"Yes. Valkyries, my sisters, white-armed helmet-maidens. Swan-skins, not eagle-cloaks, but no less ruthless or war-like for all that, sweeping the battlefields like flake-dusted winds, choosing those who fall. So one came for me on that day."

"That day in the ship, yes." I take Eirik's head in my hands, run my fingers over his face, tug gently on his braided beard. "When I saw you die, blood bubbling around that damned Englishman's arrow, blood bubbling on your lips… And you smiled as you left me."

"I did. Because I knew you would not forget me. Because I could hear her wings as she bent to fetch me home. Because I knew we would meet again. Here. Where fallen warriors dwell."

A fine mist is rising, droplets gleaming in Eirik's hair. Somewhere nearby, a river's torrent roars. Inside, a horn sounds, and the deep voices of men, and then the great door is thrown open, and out they stream, the great mob of Odin's army. Scruffy and dirty, hairy and glorious, they are laughing, shouting curses and blessings, clad in bronzy helmets and byrnies, brandishing axes and cudgels, spears and swords.

I step back, gaping. "There must be hundreds," I gasp. They pass by, they pass by, they pass by. The earth shakes beneath their tramp.

"They are too many to count," Eirik says. "Every day further swells their ranks. We choose them and we find them, curled broken and panting in their earth-ends. As swan, eagle, hawk, or raven, we bend to them and lift them up. Strong men they all are, but to us they are so light, fragile as the new-born.

"Here, Brother Bear-Might, Wolf-Rage, Thorir Man-Killer." Eirik holds up a metal glint. It's my axe Gut-Reaper. And chain mail. And helmet. "Here where everything begins anew and warriors are rewarded, I have these gifts for you. And, if you are strong enough to take them, a bloody prize or two."

❖

The noise is deafening—the clash of sword on shield, the smash of mace on helmet, the cries of the wounded, the trumpeting of horns, the cheering of the victorious. Eirik leads me over the plain, past snarling clots of men swinging weapons against one another. Through a stand of trees, a bank of fog, and suddenly we are on a narrow ness, a short spit of rock thrust out into wave-beat and wind-claw and the lowering drizzle. There, at the end, stands a man. He is young, pate-shaven, slight of build, weak of chin. His face is not familiar. He cowers, clutching shield and spear, wide-eyed, staring at us.

"He is yours." Eirik steps back. "Yours to kill as often as it pleases you. He will fall today; he will rise tomorrow, a fresh toy on which to whet your rage."

"But who is he?" I wipe rain from my brow, lick rain from my lips, striding further down the ness, axe-heft sweet in my grip. "I don't know him."

"He knows you. He is the English poltroon who slew you. On a barrel the carl floated beneath the bridge. With that very spear, through the bridge-slats he stabbed you beneath your mail shirt and opened your blood-flood. He boasted of your death for years after. Cowards often make up with cleverness what they lack in courage, do they not? Here on the plains of Asgard, at the end of earth-time, such cravens, for our pleasure, are lent us from Hel. They are condemned to spend their days as sword-food, axe-fodder, raven-feast, fallen beneath the hands of those who lived bravely, who died in valor."

The wind picks up now; the sea smashes against rocks, heaving up great gouts of white foam. "Here, hero," Eirik says, binding my long hair behind me with a leather thong. "Is it not needful and beautiful, to create the death of one we hate, one who has harmed us or ones we love? Vengeance is one of Valhalla's rewards."

I appraise the carl's bony form, thin arms, quivering hands. I lick my lips. "This is too easy." Grinning, I stride forward. "You, *boy*!"

He starts at my shout; he brandishes his spear. Behind him the sea heaves, splashing the land-spit with cold foam. "Stay back, Viking!" he yells, voice shaking like aspen leaves.

"We have time yet till tonight's feast," says Eirik behind me. "No rush. Savor your sport."

"I will, never fear." With a war-howl, I charge. The boy screams, a shrill, womanish sound. Again and again he feints with his spear, again and again he tries to dash past me, but I am nimbler now than I was before, so each attempt at escape I block with ease, my axe-edge hacking his shield. He falls to his knees beneath my blows, scuttles off, makes another run for it, is cut off once more. Soon I have cornered him at ness-end, in the lash of wave-spume and rain.

"Get back!" he pants, waxy face peering over his shield like a moon cresting a hill. The boy is so small, so weak, so terrified that I might almost pity him. Laughing, I move closer. Perhaps I will simply pummel him cross-eyed and leave him crumpled in his own piss, shit, and abject prayers. But then, as I raise my axe, with what last nerve he has he thrusts his spear. Aim more of luck than of skill, but true nonetheless. I snarl as the sharp iron sinks into my calf.

Bending, I seize the spear. Gritting my teeth, I pull out the flesh-lodged blade, jerk the haft from his grasp, snap it in half over my knee, kick the shield out of his hands. I grasp him by the throat, lift him into the air, squeeze his windpipe.

"So you boasted of my end, boy?"

Eyes bulging, tongue flailing, he's in no position to answer. I drop him onto his belly. Crabwise, he tries to crawl. I plant my foot on his back and raise my axe.

❖

His body, nudged over the edge, is wave-meal, shark-snack, fish-feast. His head I bring to join the others.

Eirik and I stand on a hill, among acres of pike-mounted heads. "Beside this one," says Eirik, gesturing. On the pike he points to is the head of an ugly man, with short hair like a gray skullcap, thin lips, hollow cheeks, and heavy bags, bruise-gray, under staring, angry eyes. I look into the bitter countenance and grimace.

"Who is that?" I say, juggling my severed English toy from hand to hand.

"The archer who shot me. Sometime soon, if it pleases you, you may slaughter him, while I enjoy carving the blood-eagle on the scrawny slave who slew you."

"Oh, yes!" I spit in his sour face, the man who stole my lover from me. Then I shove my killer's neck-stub onto the sharp end of the nearest pike. The eyes are clenched shut; the slack lips drool.

Beyond the forest, there are the blasts of horns and the excited whoop of men. "The feast begins," say Eirik. Taking my hand, he leads me down the hill of heads, around a mere, and into the shadow of the firs. All about us, fallen warriors are grinning, gripping one another's hands, helping one another to their feet. I turn back once, to see a flock of black birds descending upon the hill of heads.

"Ravens," says Eirik with a faint smile. "They are very hungry. They start with the eyes."

❖

Attendants—fair-eyed maidens and hard-limbed boys—take our weapons to clean and polish, wash blood from wounds already half-healed, help us into tunics, lead us in to the crowded mead-hall. Spears rafter the roof; in huge hearths wood-fires leap. On the walls, mounted swords flicker with violet flame, casting light on the scene.

"He is there," Eirik says, pointing up the long rows of groaning boards to the head of the hall, where, on a throne atop a dais, a great-muscled man with a gray beard and a patch over one eye holds court. A raven perches on each shoulder; two wolves sit at his feet, occasionally treated to scraps of meat. The hoard-lord smiles over the clamoring, hungry men; he sits back, lifts a jeweled cup to his lips, bends to speak to a thick-armed, red-bewhiskered man at his side.

"The Gray-Eyed One. The Father of the Slain. And his son, the Thunderer. Thor is back from thrashing trolls in the east."

Maidens lead us to our places near the front of the hall. "Our seats are good ones, thanks to your bravery on the bridge," Eirik says. "Nearer the All-Father than most." Side by side, we sit, surrounded by burly-breasted and boisterous men who laugh and talk, swapping battle boasts and bawdy speech, displaying new but fast-fading scars, swilling cups and horns of drink.

"It is as the Eddas said," Eirik explains. "We *einherjar* fight all day; we rise from our new hurts and heal; at night we feast."

"All night?" I say, slipping my hand beneath the table to massage Eirik's sex. Inside my touch he is in mere seconds hard.

Eirik grins. I stroke his shaft. As a serving platter's passed, he stabs a fire-charred chunk of roast boar with his dagger, dropping it onto my plate. Next he fills my empty cup with beer, my empty horn with mead. "Not all night. Drink up, eat up, blood-brother. You will need your strength for the evening I have in mind."

Harp music strikes up. I give Eirik's cock a last stroke, then with both hands we tear into boar meat and roast fowl, into great loaves of black bread, rounds of salty cheese, sweet bilberries and honey. For hours, we eat like starving men stranded on a skerry. For hours we drink, hornfuls of the sweetest mead, huge mugs of hoppy ale. We laugh, lick foam from our mustaches, and pour ourselves more.

By the time the Sky-Father and his flame-bearded son retire, the hearth-fires are low, and men are staggering out, or wrapping themselves in blankets to snore on the floor. When I rise from my empty trencher, I grow dizzy. Eirik chuckles, wrapping an arm around me. "Sword-sharer, you are as yet unaccustomed to Valholl's strong ale and mead. Lean on me." I obey, swaying as we pick our way through the drunken sleepers toward the great arch of the mead-hall door.

Outside, the glade is silent. Above us glint tiny shards of stars. "Come here, Thorir," says Eirik. With no effort at all, he lifts my warrior-bulk, one arm beneath my legs, one beneath my back. His eagle-cloak has returned, curling about us its smell of smoke and tickle of feather. Normally I would protest, a man of my age and might being cradled like a child, but instead, drunk and happy, I relax in his embrace. We rise, in a gust of wind, in a beating of wings. I want to lie back, close my eyes, and sleep, but Eirik says, "Look now," so I do.

Stars stream above us, and the seething curve of comets, and twilit clouds stained wound-red with last light. Below us flash night-moors, and the great expanse of glaciers, sighing their moonlit breath, and the flat black of lakes, moon-spangled and reed-edged, and dense forest after forest, and sparse hamlets, with their tiny gleams of candle- and hearth-light, and lace-flecked seashores, with their breaker-boom, and unbroken sheets of snow-fields and Arctic ice, where only gods can dwell.

Frigid air whistles in my ears. About me, Eirik's arms are warm. Now we descend, through scuds of cloud, into the farthest forest, into scents of pine needles and loam. Bump of feet on earth, and Eirik's eagle-flight becomes wolf-lope, the embrace about me shifts from feather to fur. Tree trunks flash by; banks of mist part.

Creak of a door. Eirik releases me, and I fall into softness. I roll over, face brushing the texture of woven wool. It is a low bed, in a low-ceilinged hut. Nearby, a small fire crackles. I give a groan of pleasure, and then hands are ripping off my moist tunic, and Eirik's naked weight is upon me.

"Ha! I knew it!" I shout. We wrestle, long and fierce, but he is stronger than he was in life, and soon he has me on my belly on the bed, one arm wrenched behind my back, a knife at my throat. When I give him further fight, "Surrender, brother," he snarls, and the blade nicks me, drawing blood. Now I have the excuse I need to save face, to go limp and let him do what we both want.

"Always the dagger, damn you," I pant. "Yes, I surrender. Do it, Eirik Man-Raper. Do what you please."

Within a minute, Eirik has my hands bound behind me with rough rope. I flex, testing the cord; it does not give. Eirik is as good with knots in Asgard as he ever was in Midgard. I thrash around, rolling onto my back, trying to kick him. He sits on me to subdue me, stilling me long enough to trap my feet in circles of rope and bind my ankles.

Finished, he sits on the bed by me, wiping sweat from his brow. I lie back, helpless, sex-hard, heart hammering my breastbone. Wind's rising outside, soughing in firs. A wet gust slaps the house. A hard rain begins its tattoo.

"Storm's coming," he says, rising. "You always did give me a damned good fight." He stokes up the fire; from a bedside table, he lifts a goblet and sips.

"Always, brother," I mutter between clenched teeth. "Always."

Beneath me, I twist my hands in their bonds, straining till my wrists burn. Both of us are grinning now, eager for what is to come. The hard shaft of flesh between my thighs is nigh hurtful with blood-throb. "Fighting you always made me feel mighty. Even when you won, even when you overcame me, through force or through trickery."

"Ah, you are mighty even bound. You are beautiful. Here, brother, struggle makes men thirst. Drink. This is heaven's hot mead—rich as man-milk, sweet as bard-song. Drink."

Eirik tips the horn; I take a gulp. My tongue sears, my brow burns. Forked fire flickers along my veins; the flames of my heart-hearth leap.

Gasping, I lie back. Sweat beads my temples, wets the cleft of my chest. Smiling, Eirik straddles me. His erection bumps my face, fat-headed pole rising from a wiry bush of gold.

"Gods, you are even larger than…" Staring, I lose my words in a hungry lapping of lips.

"In life? Another of Valholl's gifts." He gulps more mead, then dips his cock in the goblet. "Will you suck me, brother?" The dripping head nudges my chin.

I am given no time to answer. With an impatient thrust of his hips, Eirik shoves his cock between my lips. He tastes of honey and smoke, sea-salt and bread. The shaft's stone-hard as the rock I raised above his ashes; the taut skin's soft as orchard petals, tender as cloudberries. From his slit I can already taste a briny drooling.

Groaning with gratitude, I work his cockhead with my lips and tongue, then slide my mouth farther down the shaft. Our gazes interlocked, Eirik fucks my face, slow and deep. He sighs, sips from the cup, strokes my hair, and impales my throat. I choke and chuckle, gurgle and slobber till my beard's wet. Setting down the cup, he rides me harder, both hands gripping my head, pounding my gullet, while I sputter and suck and fight for breath.

"Drink, brother," Eirik pants. His cock drives home, his crotch-hair tickling my nose, my throat crammed full with flesh. One last jerk of his hips, and his sap floods my mouth. Man-mead, gulp after gulp after gulp. I swallow, greedy as a bear in a thicket of berries, in a broken honey-hoard.

Eirik lies astride my face, softening slowly. Pulling out, he rests his cockhead on my lips. Happily I lick off the oozy aftermath. The storm comes back to me now, battering the roof, the rain's softer sounds shifting to the click of sleet, and the crackling fire, eating resinous twigs.

"In Asgard there are many kinds of feasts." Eirik slips into bed beside me, tugging a blanket over us. He pulls me against him, my back pressed against his chest. With my roped hands, I brush his belly-hair. His fingers tug on the fur between my buttocks. "This hut is our home. Is it enough?"

"Yes," I sigh. "Oh, yes."

"Are you warm enough?"

"Yes, Eirik. I lost all warmth when you left my life, but now…"

"Do you want me to take you? To ride you as I once did?" His cock, sword-stiff, bumps my bound hands.

"God, brother," I groan, fondling him. "By Odin, yes. It has been…"

"Long months, yes. Long and bitter seasons."

"But how are you already hard?" I ask, amazed, squeezing his shaft. "How are you hard so soon after spending your seed in my mouth?"

"Yet another gift waiting for warriors here at the end of time." He spits in one hand. A moist finger brushes my ass crack and circles my hole, probing gently. "Fucking as endless as the fighting and the feasting," Eirik whispers in my ear, his cock pressed against my buttocks. "The sword aches for the sheath; the sheath aches for the sword. Will you not open for me, lover? Will you not let me inside, where you are so tender, so hot and tight?"

I cannot bring myself to speak. Instead, I nod, nestling my eager ass against his loins. Flushing my face is the same shame I suffered on earth, most bitter in our first years together, those nights of wrestling when Eirik would win, forcing me down and binding me tight, when, freed by my own powerlessness, I would wax wild and forget warrior-pride and beg him to use me and would know myself, in the white-hot minutes of our coupling, as much a man in the being taken as in the taking, only to wake in morning's aftermath, burning with the same damned doubts, feeling both blessed by him and entirely unmanned.

Eirik laughs. "I know your thought." His fingertip teases my nether-gate, slips inside. "How desire battles against shame. That is what we Vikings were taught, were we not? That such a lust—to be taken from behind, to be ridden like a steed—was the abject and passive desire of a whore, and certainly nothing a warrior should feel."

Eirik pulls out, licks his forefinger, dips it in the bedside goblet. "Gods, your hole is mead-sweet." I tremble as his finger's length slides inside me, moistening me with heated honey as thick, sticky, and warm as blood.

"It was a secret…what I wanted…I kept from all other men…save you," I manage to gasp as Eirik pulls out, only to replace one finger with two. "Had they known—"

"We would have been killed or driven into exile, yes. As effeminates and cowards, yes, as outlaws. Does not such shame seem—here, in Asgard's cold clarity—the stupid and misguided fear of a child, of a boy, not a man, a boy who does not know who he yet is, who cannot yet comprehend or come to terms with his own desires? I promise you, Thorir," Eirik says, adding a third finger, pumping my hole gently, opening my nether-gate further, "gods and *einherjar* know better. I also promise," he adds with a broad smile, "by night's end you will take your turn on top."

Roughly he rolls me onto my back. As he finger-fucks me harder and deeper, his beard rubs my face, his mouth finds mine. We feast on tongues and lips, probing and licking, chewing and wounding till both blood and spit tinge our mouths and stain our beards.

Four fingers are jammed inside me now. Eirik's mouth abruptly leaves mine, falling onto my chest. He finds a nipple, licking and biting as he did in life, hurtful and hungry as a wolf-whelp. I groan, I bleed and buck beneath him, straining against my bindings. Suckling, he holds me down with one burly forearm, then moves to the nipple's twin, growling low like a beast. I whimper and shake, arching my chest against his lips.

Suddenly his fingers leave my hole, and I'm thrown onto my side. I barely have time to catch my breath before Eirik's arm is locked around my neck from behind and his cockhead's nudging my wet asshole.

"Oh, gods," I croak. I can barely breathe. Eirik's biceps-bulge digs into my windpipe.

"Ready, lover?" Eirik says, pushing his cockhead inside me. "Oh,

I know you are." With a sharp, quick thrust, he's embedded to the hilt. I give a loud moan, not of pain, as I used to when he forced me, when he was overeager and took me too fast, but of pure pleasure. "Like that?" Eirik kneads my torso, fingernails digging into the hairy mounds of my chest. When I struggle, putting on the show of resistance we both so relish, he forces me onto my belly, his weight pressing me into the pallet. When I groan again, Eirik's hand claps over my mouth.

"Shuuusssshhh!" Eirik pulls my head back, kisses my cheek, and gives my hole a vicious cock-prod. "Behave now. You always were parlously loud." Pulling entirely out, he slams home again, then commences a violent ass-pounding, big hand gripping my face. I spread my thighs wider, as far as my bound ankles will allow, and with my hole-muscles clench his cock. He slams up into me; I slam back onto him.

"You like this, lover? You like this?" Eirik pants. "We can last as long as you like. This is Asgard. This is eternity."

I give a vigorous nod, and Eirik kisses my shoulder. Now the only sounds are Eirik's ecstatic sighs, my own hand-muffled whimpers and snorts, and Asgard's icy rain beating the roof of the hut.

❖

First he is eagle. I clutch one taloned foot, determined to hold on. His black wings batter my face; his hooked beak slashes my shoulder. About the room I stagger; he flaps and tugs, uttering sharp cries. It's like wrestling a thunderhead, enduring the claws of lightning.

I am surrounded by smoke. His form slithers from my grasp. Now the acrid cloud clears, and he is wolf, hackles high, snarling and snapping, darting around me. I lunge, seizing a back leg. We thrash about the hut. His fangs surge toward my throat; I shove my forearm between his teeth, pop him between the eyes with a fist, clutch his black-furred throat, force him to the floor.

Smoke fills the room again, and a sweaty, naked man is heaving and cursing beneath me, long golden hair in disarray, doing his best to writhe from my grip. I wrap one arm around his neck, another around his waist. We roll about, till he slips from my hold, tries to rise. I shove him backward. He falls onto the bed, and I leap upon him. Seizing his wrists, I force his arms above him, trap his legs between mine, crush him beneath me.

We lie there, face-to-face, heaving breast to breast, straining and panting, my red hair mingling with his gold. "Yield!" I gasp, digging my elbows into his biceps.

Eirik licks his lips, wriggling his wrists within my sweaty grasp, his arms bulging with effort as he bucks beneath me. Then, suddenly, he gives a great guffaw. With that, his struggles cease.

"I promised you your turn, yes. Do what you will."

"Good man." I kiss him roughly. Then, with the cord with which he'd bound me, swiftly I tie his wrists above him and anchor them to the headboard. He sprawls on his back, unmoving, offering no resistance. Rising from the bed, I take a great draught of mead, then I study my flushed captive, his wide blue eyes, the tangled golden-blond hair, the honey-blond fur framing his smile and matting his chest and belly, and his cock, harder and larger than ever, jerking with the tide of his blood.

Sleet spatters the hut; the hearth spits sparks. "By Odin, you are so noble, so well formed, so strong," I whisper. Taking a mouthful of mead, I bend over him, cup his head in my hand, and kiss him, wine trickling from my tongue onto his.

Eirik chuckles, swallowing the mead. "What now, warrior? This, perhaps?" He rolls onto his belly and positions himself on his elbows and knees, presenting the hairy wonder of his ass.

"To worship a body for millennia, that is the greatest gift here. To know a beloved for all time. To exist inside him," Eirik mutters. Head down, he angles his buttocks higher and spreads his legs wider. "Give as I gave; take as I took."

I climb onto the bed, kneeling between his legs. The thick hair between his buttocks gleams like sunrise streaking a wind-stirred sea. I run a hand over the hard-muscled plain of his back. He gives a little grunt as I nuzzle his crack with my chin, brushing his hole with my beard's coarse hairs. He gives a long groan as I lick his nether-gate, another groan as I tongue-dig deep. I grip his hips, wet his crack with heated honey-wine, rub my sex-head against him, and against his tight treasure gently push.

"Oh, gods," Eirik sighs, as he opens for me, as I slip inside.

"Tell me if I pain you, brother." I bend, kissing his shoulder. "I will wait till you are truly ready."

In answer, Eirik's flesh grips me from inside. So I begin to thrust, but then Eirik begins to sob.

"What?" I say, slowing. "Brother, am I—?"

"No hurt," Eirik whispers. "These are the tears of the blessed, the fulfilled. Even here, outside of time, I have waited long. I have wanted this, wanted you. I have wanted you home."

Bending, I wrap my arms about his torso and press my cheek to his back.

"No more farewells," Eirik gasps. "Praise Odin."

My eyes are wet. I cannot speak. Hugging him, I ride him harder.

❖

The fire's dwindled into embers; the room is cold. Pale dawn glows in the hut's windows. Outside, in the fir-forest, a dove is cooing.

I yawn and stretch. I pull Eirik closer.

"How many honeyed centuries have we been here?" I press my face into the musky-furred nest of his armpit, loosen the rope about his wrists.

"Fifteen, if you must know." Eirik rises to stir up the fire and fetch us food. I lie back, watching the sway of his long hair and limp cock, the way muscles move beneath the skin of his back and ass. Breakfast's more mead, sweet milk, cloudberries, honey-topped brown bread, a hunk of herby cheese. We eat side by side in bed. Beyond the window, all is white.

"The long snows have come. I must fetch more fallen warriors home," Eirik says, feeding me a chunk of bread.

I tweak his beard. "No farewells, you said. Shall I fight today, then?"

"If you choose, hearth-sharer. You and I, here in Asgard we will part only long enough for longing to flare higher, to sharpen itself like spear-head or axe-blade. Absence is only a whetstone."

"Are you not my greatest reward for a life of valor, Eirik? You, and the feasts of Valhalla?"

"Yes, that's true. Why?"

Taking the goblet of mead, I dribble a bit in Eirik's dense chest hair, smearing it over his nipples. We both watch as our cocks lengthen, first Eirik's, then mine.

"Would the All-Father mind then, if, for my first full day in His kingdom, if perhaps…" I nibble a nipple. With a mead-wet finger, I anoint Eirik's cock. Bending, I take the head in my mouth, sucking tenderly.

He trembles and closes his eyes. "Yes, today, my swan-sisters might complete what's necessary. If that is your wish, hero."

"It is," I mumble, mouth half full of him. "Tomorrow," I say, giving his sex a last lick before rising on one elbow, "I will gladly swing swords with the best of Valhalla's warriors. And I will slay with infinite pleasure the homely carl whose arrow brought you down. I will make the blood-eagle; I will lift out his lungs. Today, though, what I want is not the delight of carnage but more mead-sweet fucking."

I straddle Eirik's waist, rubbing his groin with my ass. Moistening my hair-hole with mead, I spread my rear cheeks. Silent, we gaze into each other's eyes. Slowly, my nether-gate opens; slowly, I slide onto him. I grip his wrists, spread his arms, hold him down. Bending, my long hair tenting his face, I brush his beard with mine. We rock together, one man inside the other, as the thick snows of heaven heap Asgard's forests and moors, falling upon the sea's gray waves and the mountains' sharp spines. Wind beats the hut, whistles through the eaves, soughs through the firs.

"They are coming. Together we shall share them—the final snows, the final fires, the final battle," my lover whispers, thrusting softly. Black smoke's rising from him again, swirl of eagle feathers and thundercloud. About us the hut's walls smolder and burst into flame. The roof is gone, and then the charring timbers, sucked up into a great whirlwind. I look up into rushing clouds, violet and gray, and shifting sheets of snow, and the emerald shimmer of the northern lights. I look down at Eirik, and suddenly, in this fire-heart and wind-heart, I am again afraid. He smiles up at me, his cock driving deep into me like a blazing brand. The honey-gold hair across his breast begins to spark, then catches fire.

"Hold on, brother," he says, yellow flame framing his face. "Be not afraid. I give you my word: we are safe, we are god-fuel, we are past all good-byes. Soon come a new Wind-Home, a new morning, with new gods and new sun and new green rising from the sea."

Snowflakes sting my forehead. About us the circle of fire, streaming red and white, rises into a roar. Soon my own body will ignite, for I can feel his cock-heat funneling up my spine, feel my heart-hammer glow and my bones flicker like piney kindling. I grip Eirik's wrists harder, staring into his blue eyes. I bow down to kiss him, from his gold-bearded mouth drink in the bonfire of his breath.

Landfall
Jeffrey Ricker

Did you hear that?"

Morgan prodded Chad's shoulder. Chad mumbled something incoherent and turned over. Before long he was snoring again. *He probably could sleep through a nuclear war*, Morgan figured, *and wouldn't hear anything above his own snoring.*

When they'd moved to this house in the place Morgan affectionately called left of the middle of nowhere, he thought the quiet would be what got to him. It wasn't; it was the noise. Crickets, birds, the slithering rustle of leaves, the wind itself. Even quiet had a sound, a heavy, echoing emptiness that thudded against his eardrums. The cacophony kept him awake their first night in their new home, when he should have been out cold. He'd lost track of the number of boxes he'd hauled that day, but he remembered Chad had him reposition the sofa eight times. Then he was sore in places he hadn't realized could be sore.

As quietly as possible (as if anything could have woken Chad), Morgan slid out of bed and grabbed his bathrobe. One thing he'd discovered about the country: it was always chilly at night, even in the middle of May.

Even though they'd been there three months already, a few boxes remained to be unpacked. Morgan skirted around these in the living room and made his way into the kitchen. A nearly full moon hung in the sky and bathed the kitchen in blue light bright enough for Morgan to see nothing was out of place. Maybe he'd actually been asleep for once and just dreamed the noise.

He had turned around and headed for the stairs when he heard something again, something outside. Morgan went back to the kitchen and stood at the back door. Across the yard stood the old barn, the feature Chad had used to convince Morgan that moving out to the country was the Best Idea Ever.

"This will be perfect for your ceramics studio," he'd said when they walked in, clearly seeing beyond the cobwebs, the three missing wallboards Morgan had counted, and the dirt floor. "We fix it up a little and it'll have plenty of room for your wheel, the kilns, everything."

"So…you're saying I can have my own pottery barn?" Morgan asked. Chad smacked him in the shoulder for that.

Since the move, Morgan hadn't done much work in the studio. He said it was because he had his hands full getting the new house in order, and he still hadn't found a contractor to fix the woodwork and install some basic heating. In reality, he was avoiding the place. He told himself there was still too much to do around the house (this, of course, did not prevent Chad from going to work each weekday like a normal person). The truth was, his inspiration had fled as soon as they unpacked his equipment. How was he supposed to work *here*?

He heard it again, and a crash from inside the barn made him jump. He grabbed the flashlight they kept by the door and, holding it like a bludgeon, he went outside.

This is stupid, he thought as he walked barefoot across the gravel driveway. *This is like every horror movie where the dumb blonde goes out by herself and gets her head chopped off. I should go back inside. We should own a gun. Why did I agree to move out here?*

The barn door was ajar. They never bothered to lock it or much else out here. They used to live in a loft, with neighbors on all sides. Their nearest neighbors now, as far as Morgan had seen, were a small herd of cows in the adjacent pasture. At that moment, shivering in his robe as he pocketed the flashlight so he could grab a shovel, Morgan really wished they were back in the city.

As swiftly as he could, Morgan yanked the door open and raised the shovel above his head.

It was lighter inside the barn than it should have been. Morgan's eyes were drawn first to the ceiling, where a jagged hole let the moonlight in, then to the floor, where a man lay sprawled.

Still holding the shovel in front of his chest, Morgan crept closer. So many things about this seemed wrong that his mind couldn't settle on which detail seemed the most impossible. How could anyone plummet through the roof of their barn when there was nothing above them except sky? There was no sign of anything like a parachute—*that would have been big and noticeable, right?* he thought—and he registered the absence of a parachute at the same time he noticed the man's total absence of clothes. Why had a naked man crashed through the roof of their barn? The floor around him was littered with feathers, as if he'd taken out a pigeon on his way down.

And what was that smell? *Flowers?*

Morgan had no idea what to do first. He wanted to go back to the house and drag Chad out of bed, but he knew also that he should probably see how badly hurt the man was. *I should call 911 too*, he thought. *How long will it take them to get out here?*

The man groaned. Morgan yelped and jumped back. Feeling foolish at being afraid of a naked, clearly injured man, Morgan lowered the shovel but still kept it in his hands as he edged closer again.

"Hey," he whispered, then wondered why he was whispering. "Are you all right?" *Don't be an idiot, of course he's not all right.* Morgan dropped the shovel and knelt over the man, trying to ignore his nakedness. That, and the fact that he was very good looking. Neither of these points was easy to set aside, as he had a full head of hair the color of freshly cut straw and an ass that looked like it was carved from rock. And he smelled like a rose garden.

Morgan placed his hand on the man's back. The stranger turned over and briefly gave Morgan a bird's-eye view of the works, which were a sight to behold. Morgan could have even sworn he heard the man's dick slap against his belly, which was ridged and perfect. Morgan couldn't remember the last time he'd had abs like that because he'd never had them, ever. He resisted the urge to touch this man's now to see if they were as firm as they looked, and instead took off his bathrobe and threw it over the man's shoulders. After looking him over without finding any visible injuries—the man didn't even appear to be bruised—Morgan hooked his hands under the man's arms and hoisted him up. The belt of the robe wasn't tied, and it quickly became inadequate at keeping the man covered. Morgan's best efforts threatened to send both of them tumbling back to the ground. He gave up, averted his eyes, and together they hobbled toward the house.

Their progress across the yard was painfully slow. Morgan tried shifting the man so he could successfully carry him some way other than like a sack of potatoes. (*Hot potatoes*, he thought, before he could stop himself.) It didn't make the load easier to bear, but it did jostle the man long enough to rouse him. He looked up at Morgan, his expression vacant, and said, "Who am I?"

"Who the hell is that?" Chad, now uncharacteristically awake, asked when Morgan finally made it into the kitchen with the man.

"Help me get him to a chair," Morgan said. Barefoot on the tile floor with his burden barely standing on his own, Morgan felt his own feet sliding with every step. Chad took an arm, and together they steered him into a chair.

"Where did he come from?" Chad asked, his tone half-accusatory. He scratched the bald spot on his head, which he did whenever he was irritated with Morgan. Morgan hadn't let on that he'd noticed this pattern—and wasn't about to, either.

"He came through a hole in the roof of the barn, as far as I can tell," Morgan said. The man had passed out again. His head lolled to the side, and his whole body listed as if he were about to keel over onto the floor. Morgan pushed him upright again, positioning him so he was leaning against the table. Looking at him for a moment, as if he were a vase of flowers needing arrangement, he carefully tied the belt on the robe.

"I don't get it," Chad said. After a moment of silence passed, he asked, "There's a hole in the barn?"

"There is now. Do you think we should call nine-one-one? He could have internal injuries."

Chad seemed to not hear the question. He shuffled over to the back door and squinted, as if from there he could have seen the hole in the barn roof. His eyes suddenly widened.

"What the hell?"

Morgan left the stranger and stood at Chad's side. In a line from the barn door to the house, the same line along which Morgan had dragged the stranger, from the hard-packed ground a lush stripe of grass had sprung, and the branches of the sycamore had unleashed a profusion of leaves.

They both turned back to the stranger, still slumped against the table.

He snored.

From the kitchen table they moved him to the sofa. They slept in shifts, so one of them would always be awake if the stranger came around. Chad took the first shift, but Morgan couldn't sleep. He got out of bed but didn't go back downstairs immediately. He looked out the window at the tree, now lopsided in green, the yard bluing in the pre-dawn gloom. A sensible person would have taken the stranger to the hospital. Called an ambulance. Or the police. Morgan wanted to ask where the hell the stranger came from—but he already had an idea.

When he couldn't stand staring at the ceiling or gazing out the window anymore, Morgan went downstairs to find the living room transformed into a jungle. The ficus tree that had languished in the corner near the rocking chair now brushed the ceiling. The philodendron scaled the wall and obscured the picture window facing the driveway. The African violet on the windowsill rioted with purple flowers.

The stranger was still unconscious on the sofa. The room smelled like a bouquet. Chad slumped in the recliner, also snoring. At first, in the gloom, Morgan thought his eyes were fooling him. When he tiptoed closer, he realized he wasn't seeing things. Chad's bald spot had vanished beneath a thatch of wavy brown hair.

As Morgan leaned over the back of Chad's head to get a closer look, the stranger rolled over and tumbled onto the floor. Chad woke with a start and darted out of his chair, right into Morgan's chin.

"Are you all right?" Chad asked, leaning over Morgan where he lay on the floor. Morgan's teeth tingled where they'd smacked together and his chin throbbed. Chad rubbed his head, his eyes going wide when he felt the new-grown hair.

Still, when Morgan told him his theory, Chad had doubts.

"You can't be serious."

"How else do you explain the barn roof? And the feathers?" They argued in hissing whispers on the porch so they wouldn't wake the stranger, who'd slept through his tumble off the sofa. *Would nothing wake him?* Morgan wondered.

Chad frowned. "I can't explain it. But an angel? Come on, you don't even believe in God."

Morgan looked away from Chad and stared at the tree. If they hadn't argued about that, they would have found something else to argue about. Most of their conversations the past year had culminated in clipped tones, half-swallowed digs, and redirected glares. It was safer than saying the things they really thought.

Morgan pointed at the tree with its lopsided crown of leaves. "How do you explain that, then? Or your hair? Or our living room jungle?"

Chad touched the back of his head and peered through the greenery in the living room window.

"Hey, he's awake."

The stranger stood in the middle of the living room taking stock of his surroundings. He examined the furniture and the pictures on the walls with the expression of someone who'd never seen such things before—and also had no sense of modesty. His robe had come undone again and he made no move to tie the belt when Morgan and Chad came in.

"You might want to, um, tie that," Chad said.

"Where am I?" the stranger asked. To Morgan's relief, he tied the belt.

"You're in Augusta, Missouri," Morgan said, though he thought it might have been more helpful to tell the stranger he was on Earth.

"Where's that?" he asked.

"I'm gonna make coffee," Chad said.

Morgan took the stranger upstairs to find him something to wear besides a bathrobe. He was about Chad's size. Morgan handed him a pair of jeans, some underwear, and a T-shirt, then had to turn and leave the room as quickly as possible when the stranger simply took off the robe and started changing right in front of him.

"Did I do something wrong?" he asked when he rejoined Morgan outside the bedroom.

"No, no." Morgan was conscious of the wildfire blazing across his cheeks. "It's just that..." He shook his head. Why the hell was it even necessary to explain modesty? Could amnesia go that deep? "Never mind. So you don't remember who you are or how you got here?"

"No."

They went downstairs. Something about the stranger's voice unsettled Morgan. It wasn't entirely unpleasant, but when he spoke, there was an undertone of musicality, like he had a faint backing chorus. It was pretty. Everything about the stranger was beautiful. Even the way he smelled—the floral scent that tempted Morgan to move close and press his face to the man's skin. It unnerved him.

Chad handed him a mug of coffee and offered one to the stranger. "Do you take anything in your coffee?"

"I don't know." He sniffed the mug and took a drink. "Ow, hot."

"Sip," Morgan said, blowing across the top of his mug and taking a sip to demonstrate. Maybe the stranger was mentally impaired. Given how beautiful he was, it only seemed fair, Morgan thought, immediately feeling guilty for even thinking it.

"So what do we do now?" Chad asked.

The stranger was sitting outside on the porch. Morgan wanted to make him walk around the other side of the tree so its crown would be balanced. "He doesn't seem hurt, but we can't exactly just send him on his way. Not out here in the middle of nowhere."

Chad threw up his hands. "Don't start on that again."

"What?"

"And don't 'what' me either."

Morgan was tempted to say more. Instead, he just sighed and bit back a hateful comment he couldn't say aloud. "At least we have all weekend to figure it out."

"Let's hope it doesn't take that long," Chad said.

While Chad made breakfast, Morgan decided to clean up the debris in the barn and took the stranger with him. They got out the ladder and nailed a blue tarp over the hole in the roof, and stacked the splintered fragments of roof deck on the woodpile. At least they'd be good for kindling.

Morgan looked at his potter's wheel, which the stranger had narrowly missed landing on. A storm strong enough to rip the tarp off would drench the wheel and probably ruin the motor. "Would you mind helping me move this?" he asked.

Together they wrestled the thing into a far corner of the barn, underneath the hayloft, which still had hay in it and probably a few rodents. Although Morgan had to strain to hold up his end, it seemed barely an effort to the stranger—though the veins in his arms stood out while they carried it. They set it down gently. When Morgan straightened up, something in his back seized, and with a sharp intake of breath he bent over, placing both hands on the wheel for support.

"Are you all right?"

"My back—"

"Where does it hurt?"

The stranger seemed to move on instinct, supporting Morgan with one arm around his shoulders while placing his other hand at the small of Morgan's back. Almost at once a warm tingling spread through the knotted muscles, gently persuading them to untangle.

"Is that better?" the stranger asked.

"Much," Morgan said. He was still bent over the wheel, and with the stranger standing behind him, he realized how it would look if someone walked in. His guilty feeling was not enough to keep him from getting aroused, however, which made him feel even guiltier.

He turned around and found himself nose to nose with the stranger, who looked at him with a mixture of guilelessness and concern. "What's wrong?"

"We can't—" Morgan tried to step back but the wheel was behind him. He stumbled, and the stranger caught him before he fell.

"This is wrong," Morgan said, his voice barely a whisper, the stranger's lips hovering before his own, were they even an inch away? He prayed the stranger wouldn't bridge the gap, wouldn't press his body against Morgan's and feel his arousal, which Morgan felt was a betrayal.

"How long have you both been so unhappy?" the stranger asked.

Morgan felt like he was starting to forget who he was. "What?"

"It radiates off both of you," the stranger said. "Yet neither of you does anything about it."

"It's just a bad patch," Morgan said.

"Is it?" The stranger's hip inched forward, brushing against Morgan's erection. Morgan gasped, inhaling the smell of flowers, which woke him to reality. He put his hands on the stranger's chest—even that touch felt like a gamble—and straightened his arms until they were apart. He felt as if he'd just run a marathon.

"I love him," Morgan said.

The stranger shook his head. "That's not in doubt. Why is it so hard for you to show him you love him?"

"I don't know." Morgan closed his eyes, trying to will his breath to even out, his heart to stop racing. He opened them again and glared at the stranger. "How is it you know all of this?"

"I don't know." The question seemed to defuse the stranger's glamour—that was the only word Morgan could come up with to describe the spell-like feeling that had enveloped him when the stranger touched him. It evaporated along with his arousal, thankfully. The sense he'd somehow betrayed Chad in that moment, though, went much deeper.

❖

Morgan retreated to the barn again after breakfast. To his relief, neither the stranger nor Chad followed him. Instead, Chad said he'd drive the stranger into town to see if he recognized anything, or if anyone recognized him.

He sat at the wheel and gave it a kick every so often, sending the wheel head on a lazy spin that put him in a trance. The barn door was open. He stared through it at the house across the lawn, which had greened up considerably the more the stranger walked across it.

Saying he hated the house would have been too strong a sentiment. He just didn't feel like it was home. Chad, on the other hand, had fallen in love immediately. He loved the high ceilings, the wood floors, the plaster and lath walls. It had good bones, he said. Morgan saw it as a skeleton. The old boiler. No central air—how hot would it get come summer? The retro farmhouse kitchen. No dishwasher. Chad didn't mind the commute, and out here Morgan had peace and quiet to get on with his pottery.

Except he hadn't.

Now he wondered whether the problem was the place or their relationship. The fact that a complete stranger came crashing into their lives and suddenly Morgan was flirting with infidelity had to mean something, likely nothing good.

And yet… When he wasn't driving him crazy, Morgan knew he loved Chad, knew it like something that didn't even require thinking, like the way a vase or a pot came into being beneath his hands as if it had always been there only waiting for Morgan to find it with his touch.

Before he realized what he was doing, Morgan had opened his bag of clay and a jug of slip, centered a ball on the wheel, and started working. He did this three times, pausing only to slice and lift the vessels from the wheel and place them on the drying racks. He'd have gone a fourth time if he hadn't looked up toward the house and seen someone standing on the porch.

"He doesn't remember who he is, does he?" the man asked before Morgan even had a chance to ask if he could help him. He was just as beautiful as the stranger, but darker, his hair jet black and his eyes a brown so dark they were almost black too.

"No," Morgan said. He stopped at the foot of the porch steps, unwilling, though he couldn't say why, to come up to the same level as this man. "You know him?"

The man nodded. "Where is he?"

"He's not here. They went into town." The man didn't blink, and it occurred to Morgan this was one of the many things about the stranger that disturbed him too. "What's his name?"

"Mike. Any idea when they'll be back?"

Morgan shook his head. "And you are?"

"Gabe. I'll be in town for a while. Maybe I'll run into them. Or I'll check back later." The way he said it sounded like a threat.

They both turned to the horizon. Distantly, thunder rumbled, even though the sky was clear and blue.

"Gonna be a storm, sounds like," Gabe said. "I'll see you later, Morgan."

It was only after he'd walked around the corner of the house that Morgan realized he'd never told Gabe *his* name. He went after him to ask him how he'd known, even though he knew, when he rounded the corner as well, the man would be gone.

"I kind of want him to leave," Chad said while they lay in bed that evening. No one in town had recognized Mike, though several people had acted strangely around him, Chad reported. The number of people who stopped and stared as they walked down the street was embarrassing, though Mike seemed oblivious to it.

Gabe hadn't returned that day. Morgan told both men about the visit, and what Mike's name was, but only told Chad about how unsettling he'd found the visit from the second stranger.

"'Kind of'?" Morgan asked. He rolled onto his side and leaned on his elbow. Chad looked over at him, then looked away.

"It's hard to explain. He's pretty…"

"Yes, very."

Chad looked over at him and grinned, which was not what Morgan would have expected. More often than not, Chad bristled with jealousy if Morgan mentioned that anyone looked remotely attractive.

"But it's a weird pretty, you know? Like there's something, I don't know…"

"It's like he reads your mind when he looks at you," Morgan said, remembering the barn and feeling a simultaneous wash of shame and desire. The window was open, the night milder than Friday night, and it began to rain gently.

"More like he reads your blood," Chad said.

"That's an interesting way of putting it." Morgan rolled onto his back and felt as if Mike were hovering an inch away from him once again. "When he helped me move the wheel this afternoon I threw my back out again—"

Chad rolled over. "Honey, what were you thinking lifting something like that? You know how your back gets."

"Well, in this case, all it took was Mike putting his hand on it and it was suddenly better. In fact, it feels better than it's felt in a long time."

"You're kidding."

"No."

"I wasn't going to tell you this, but when I was washing the dishes after breakfast I started to feel a migraine coming on, and it was like he could just tell. He put his hands on either side of my face and then it was like I'd never had a migraine before."

"Wow."

"And the way he looked at me freaked me out like you wouldn't believe. I felt, I don't know, naked, like he'd just taken off all my clothes. And yet he was so innocent about it, like he didn't know he had this effect on me."

Morgan sighed. "He told me we were unhappy."

"Me too."

Morgan was surprised they were talking so freely about something so fraught with peril. He was certain now that Chad had felt the same aura of sex emanating from Mike. As he lay in the quiet dark, he thought he could feel it faintly even down the hall in the guest bedroom. He wondered if Mike was asleep.

"So, I kind of want him to leave, but I also kind of don't want him to," Chad said.

"I still wish I knew how he got here. And who the man is who was looking for him today."

"Maybe—"

Chad's words were interrupted by a flash of lightning outside and a simultaneous crack of thunder. The air sizzled. The electrified atmosphere tingled against Morgan's skin as he leapt out of bed and looked out the window.

The lightning had shredded the tree in the front yard, its trunk reduced to splinters and a smoldering black smear on the ground. Morgan wasn't surprised to see Gabe standing in the middle of that scorch mark.

❖

"Do you recognize him?" Morgan asked. He and Mike peered through the curtains in the living room. Gabe hadn't moved. He simply stood in the yard, waiting.

"No." Mike looked at both of them. "Do you think I should go out there?"

"Absolutely not," Chad said. He had found the baseball bat they'd kept beside the door when they lived downtown and now held it in both hands.

Mike took one look at it and said, "That won't do us any good."

"How do you know that?" Chad asked. He lowered the bat but didn't put it down. It was the first time since he'd arrived that Mike had indicated he recalled anything.

"I'm not sure," Mike said. "I just do. He won't go away until I go out there."

"That seems like a bad idea," Morgan said, unsure why he was suddenly filled with an overwhelming urge to protect this strange man.

Mike smiled at him. "You're probably right, but I have to go anyway."

Chad and Morgan followed him out onto the porch. Gabe watched them but still didn't move.

"You know, I really liked that tree," Mike said.

"Be glad I didn't take out the house accidentally," Gabe said. He looked beyond Mike to Chad and Morgan. "You really should stay inside."

"You realize you're trespassing, right?" Chad asked.

Gabe ignored the remark and said to Mike, "Stop this foolishness and let's go. You know you can't stay here."

"Why can't I? How do you know me?" He walked down the porch steps. Chad and Morgan followed, not wanting to be left behind and not wanting to leave Mike at the mercy of Gabe, who didn't seem to have any.

Gabe narrowed his eyes. "You really don't remember who you are?"

"No."

Morgan pointed toward the barn. "He fell through the roof and hasn't been able to remember a thing since he arrived."

Gabe turned to look at the barn, and that was the moment Chad, impulsively, ran headlong at Gabe, brandishing the bat. Before Morgan could ask what the hell he was doing or shout at him to stop, Mike lifted his hand and the bat flew out of Chad's hands and Chad himself flew back and landed on his ass. Gabe turned around in time to see Chad land. Morgan ran over to him, while Mike just stared at his hand as if it were someone else's appendage.

"How did I do that?"

"Second nature," Gabe said. "Now come on."

"Second nature?" Mike grinned, raised his hand again, and blasted Gabe through the barn.

Chad lifted his head dazedly and looked at Morgan. "What happened?"

"The angels are fighting and they're probably going to kill each other. *And* knock down our house."

They looked toward the barn. The force of Gabe's impact had ripped off the doors along with a good chunk of the front. Mike was already headed that way. Morgan helped Chad to his feet, and they hurried after him.

After he'd gone through the front, Gabe also went through the back of the barn. Miraculously, Morgan's wheel was still intact. Out the other side, Gabe got to his feet and brushed off the sleeves of his white button-down shirt.

"Damn it, Mike, why do you always have to be so dramatic about things?" Thunder rumbled distantly, and the drizzle picked up again.

Mike laughed. "This from the guy who blew up a tree to get some attention?"

"Well, it worked, didn't it?"

"Gabe, go away. I'm still mad at you."

Gabe smiled. "So your memory's come back?"

"Enough to know that I'm still pissed. Now *go*."

Mike knocked Gabe back through the hole in the back of the barn, through the fence beyond and into the cow pasture.

"Are you sure this is such a good idea?" Morgan asked. When Mike turned back to him and smiled, it was as if the whole world glowed.

"Trust me on this," Mike said, just before they were all knocked off their feet by a crack of lightning that ripped off the back of the barn.

When Morgan got up, Mike was already standing and so was Gabe.

"You are such a fucking bitch," Mike grumbled. "Is it any wonder I like Danny better than you?"

"Yeah? Well, I've just about had it up to here with your attitude. You come down here, put on this stupid flesh suit, and for what?" As Gabe walked toward Mike, lightning strikes lashed down all around them. Miraculously, they all missed the house, but they set the yard on fire, as well as the pasture. Through the gaping holes at the front and back of the barn, Morgan could see they were surrounded by fire.

"Gabe, you are so self-centered. Look at what you're doing to their home."

"I'm going to do a lot worse if you don't give up this bullshit and come back home."

Mike started to grin a little. "So you're saying you miss me?"

"Of course I do. We all do."

Mike's grin turned into a smile. "Prove it."

Gabe opened his mouth, but couldn't think of anything to say. "Is that really necessary?" Mike just kept smiling, and Gabe sighed. "You really enjoy this, don't you?"

Only a few inches separated Mike and Gabe now. Mike reached out and ran his hands along the front of Gabe's shirt, deftly unfastening the first few buttons with one hand while the other kept traveling down, lingering in places that made Gabe take in a sharp breath. Mike, as if he wanted to capture that breath back, leaned forward and kissed Gabe.

"Tell me you don't enjoy this even just a little," Mike said.

Gabe seemed, to Morgan's surprise, just beyond the power of speech at the moment. Morgan's own attention was split between the tense pairing before him and the encroaching flames. When Gabe nodded mutely, Mike smiled, one hand on Gabe's now bared chest, the other still cupping the front of his trousers.

"See you later." This time Mike sent Gabe flying upward, the force of the invisible impact so great that he kept rising until Morgan couldn't even see him anymore.

"Where did you send him?" Chad asked.

Mike grinned. "He should be somewhere around the moon about now. He'll be even more pissed than ever, but at least it'll take him a while to get back."

"We have a bigger problem at the moment," Morgan said. The flames from the lightning had reached the barn and set both sides on fire. "There's no way out."

"There's one left, actually." Mike took off his shirt, the incandescent beauty of his body still enough to momentarily dazzle Morgan. "I just hope neither of you is afraid of heights."

Even though he'd known they must have been there, the sight of Mike's wings still awed Morgan. He gasped, even more surprised, when Mike shrugged his shoulders and shook his arms, and they unfurled to their full span, at least fifteen feet across. Morgan looked over at Chad, who said nothing but simply stared transfixed.

Mike put an arm around each of them and pressed them close together.

"Hold on," he said.

Morgan expected it to be like the dreams he'd had where he was flying, but the reality was different, and not just because of the flames heating their faces or the blue tarp that flapped in the storm. Leaving the ground was like tripping without falling. They rose up, through the hole in the roof and higher, the house growing rapidly smaller, the barn, quickly becoming engulfed in flames, receding to a spot of light. He held on to Chad as they both held on to Mike and Mike held on to them, the beat of his wings like a pulse that undulated them.

Morgan looked down. They were over the river valley now, their flight path tracing the black ribbon of water below. Chad and Morgan faced each other in a one-armed embrace, their other arms around Mike's neck.

"We could have died," Chad said.

"We still could," Morgan said.

Mike laughed. "I promise I won't drop you, guys."

"Even so," Morgan said, "maybe we could set down someplace soon?"

The rain continued in a steady downpour when they made landfall somewhere along the river. Mike set them down gently on their feet, but remained hovering just slightly off the ground. Though they were safely on the ground, Morgan kept his arms around Chad.

"We're okay now," Chad said. "You can let go."

"I don't want to."

They were still wearing what they'd worn to bed, T-shirts and sweatpants. Gently, Morgan slid his hands underneath Chad's soaked shirt and pulled it over his head. He let his hands roam over Chad's torso and leaned forward, bridging the short distance between them, and kissed him.

It was only when Morgan's hands tugged at Chad's sweatpants, coaxing them down past Chad's erection, that Chad broke their kiss and said, "We're not alone, you know."

"I don't care," Morgan said, kneeling to untangle the sweatpants from Chad's feet. "I don't think he does either."

They sank to the wet grass and Chad pulled off Morgan's sodden clothes. It didn't matter that they were soaking wet and the rain was pouring, that Morgan's knees were muddy as he pulled Chad's ass up to his hips. The grass was soft, the rain was cool, and there was no one for miles except the man with wings who hovered above them, keeping some of the rain off them.

At some point, while Morgan fucked Chad in the rain, the angel began to sing. There were no words, and no melody they could discern, but if either of them asked they would have said they'd never heard any music that could match it.

"Oh, my God," Chad groaned after they'd both come.

"Hey, watch that," Mike said.

"That was—"

"Yeah," Morgan said.

They were both wobbly on their feet when they first stood. Morgan kept one arm around Chad to make sure he stayed upright.

"Where are our clothes?" Chad asked. Morgan picked up a pair of sweatpants and made a face as he wrung them out.

"If you don't want to bother with those," Mike said, "it's only a short trip back home. It's not like anyone will notice in the middle of the night in the pouring rain."

The rain had extinguished the fire by the time they returned, though the wreckage of the barn still smoldered. Morgan looked at it sadly, but the wheel, the kilns, all of that was replaceable.

"I'm glad tomorrow's Sunday," Chad said. "I'm taking a shower and then I'm going to bed."

As recently as the day before, if Morgan had seen Chad completely naked and hugging another man, he would have seethed with jealousy. Watching him embrace Mike, though, it seemed like the most normal thing in the world.

"You're worried about something," Mike said to Morgan as they watched Chad climb the porch steps.

"What if we end up going back to the way we were before?"

"There's no telling what might happen in the future," Mike said.

Morgan frowned. "That's not very reassuring."

Mike laughed and put an arm around Morgan's shoulders. "Morgan, I'm just a messenger. I don't get to pick the messages I send."

"Just a messenger, huh? What about Chad's hair? And the plants? And the tree before it was turned into matchsticks?"

Mike looked behind him and shrugged. "I can only encourage what's already there to grow. That includes love, by the way."

Morgan wrapped his arms around Mike and held him tight, inhaling the scent of flowers one last time. The rain had finally dwindled out, and the breeze, he realized, was from Mike's wings. Morgan reached up and brushed his fingers through the feathers. Although he knew he'd likely never see Mike again, he decided not to be sad about it, and instead was grateful he'd had the opportunity in the first place.

"Thank you," Morgan said.

"I think I'm the one who should be thanking you."

Morgan stood in the driveway until he could no longer make out the shape of Mike as he ascended through the clouds. Before he turned to hustle up the porch stairs and, if he was lucky, join Chad in the shower, he looked at the blackened circle where the tree had stood.

In the center, a sapling had already started to grow.

You Know You Want To

Jerry L. Wheeler

Everything you know about us is wrong. This whole "winged messenger from God" bit is a crock. We're *not* messengers, the wings are artistic expression, and there *is* no God—or rather God is a huge pool of energy that ebbs and flows as life-forces are added or subtracted. But the Jesus-died-for-your-sins-heaven-and-hell crap so many of you believe in is just that—crap.

And angels, like ghosts, are merely larger, stronger life-forces who, for some strange reason, survive the corporeal body that sheltered them in life. Don't ask me why or how because I couldn't tell you. Death doesn't come with a manual. There is no friendly spirit guide to explain how it all works when you die. It just unfolds.

So call me an angel or a devil or a ghost or whatever fits your favorite concept of the afterlife. Doesn't matter. All I can tell you is that I had to get back to Nick. Something compelled me. I couldn't even say *how* I got back to him or how I knew he needed me, but he was on the brink of a big mistake and I had to keep him from doing something he'd end up regretting. That's what exes are for, right?

I'm not sure you could call him my ex, though. I mean, we were perfectly happy together, content with our fund-raisers and Pride parties and being movers and shakers in the local queer community until I fell off a curb and got hit by a bus. And no, he *didn't* push me. At least I don't think so. I guess you could say he survived me, but that makes me sound like lung cancer.

The first time I actually saw Roger, the new boyfriend, he was sitting outside at a sandwich shop on the 16th Street Mall waiting for Nick to keep a lunch date. He held his Reuben in one hand, taking large, meaty bites as he probed the corners of his mouth with his tongue for stray smears of Russian dressing and dipped french-fry bouquets into a paper cup of ketchup with the other.

Nick was running late as usual, for some reason. He always had a reason. Sometimes they were better than other times, but he always had one. I used to tell him he'd be late to his own funeral. He was for mine. Roger was almost finished with his lunch by the time Nick arrived, apologetically offering a pitcher of beer he'd gotten from the bar.

Nick pulled out a chair and sat on its edge, gesticulating his inability to prevent whatever had caused his tardiness. Roger, however, kept a stern countenance, staring directly ahead. Nick made a few more tentative stabs at begging forgiveness, then shrugged his shoulders and left, looking back at Roger once.

I knew exactly what the deal was. He was going back to work. Nick was the grants manager for the local AIDS nonprofit and really loved the job. He had probably missed a deadline or forgotten a meeting or something and spaced out lunch. Things like that happened all the time with Nick. Sure, it was annoying the first couple of times, but he was such a great guy that you learned to look past that.

Roger wasn't at that stage yet. In fact, he seemed ready to kill. A disproportionate wave of negativity rolled off him like an angry tide. He drained his water glass, refilled it with beer, and sat there drinking and sulking. I was about ready to pop into his head—just for a second, you know—to plant a little chill-out suggestion, when this dude in black jeans, biker boots, and a tight black T-shirt sat down at the table opposite him.

Out of either natural inclination or spite for Nick, Roger immediately went into hunt mode—fixing his target with a steady gaze, smiling, and grasping the pitcher of beer, getting ready to join him. Before he could make his move, I made mine.

Head-hopping is easy enough. Most of the time they don't even know you're there. The tough part is planting thoughts, trying to convince the head you're in that the idea you're giving it is original. Otherwise they think they're delusional, and that won't get you far at all. It's always smart to stay unnoticed in the background, working in small, steady steps.

...tap that ass, Roger was thinking. *That'd show the motherfucker he can't stand* me *up. Goddamn...HEY, WHO'S IN HERE WITH ME!?*

I froze—well, that's impossible since I have no body. Rather, I tried to make my presence as small as I could. Exiting would draw more attention than staying put. I hadn't expected him to be so sensitive or aware, and that meant trouble for Nick—trouble because this was a cold, calculating head that had no difficulty making tough decisions or carrying them out. It was a dry, prickly, unwholesome place to be.

Hey, I asked you a fuckin' question—*who are you and what the hell are you doin' in my head?*

Roger certainly liked to get to the point. No use trying to hide. *I'm Michael, Nick's late partner.*

I sensed no shock, no disbelief—only contempt and the odd feeling that I was the one being probed instead of him. Roger's was easily the most challenging head I'd ever been in. *Listen, buddy,* he replied, *I don't know what you think you're doing, but you're dead—D-E-A-D. Why don't you go lie down and leave me the fuck alone?*

You're not good for Nick, I said. *You have to stop seeing him.*

He almost laughed out loud. *Yeah, right...*

I don't want to have to force you.

Roger poured himself a beer and took a long sip. *You can't force me to do* shit. *I give Nick something he couldn't get with you—a little edge. He needs someone to tell him what to do, how to act, who to be. For the money you left him, I'm happy to step up to the plate.*

I'd forgotten about the money.

There's not much you're gonna be able to do about it anyway—and I wouldn't plan on playin' around with Nick's head if I were you. If he starts hearing his dead boyfriend's voice, he'll think he's going off the deep end. And who do you think he'll come running to? Me. So you see, you're pretty much screwed before you start.

You're a real shit, aren't you?

He shrugged and took a long sip of beer. *I've learned to live with it. Now why don't you go back to wherever the fuck you came from and let me drink my beer in peace?*

I hated to leave it like that. I wanted to smack him down, show him he couldn't get the last word in. I wanted a big, blue bolt of lightning to hit him and reduce him to a pile of smug, smoking ash—but as I said, there is no God, and lethal atmospheric pyrotechnics aren't exactly up my alley. In the end, I wound up slinking away mortified but determined to bring Roger to his knees one way or the other, for Nick's sake as well as my own.

❖

I did exactly what I would have done during life. I watched and waited, knowing that one of the keys to winning is picking the time and place of the battle, and I'd have to choose carefully with Roger. I also popped into his head now and then, not saying or doing anything but letting him know I was there. I wasn't sure if it was unnerving or annoying him but either way, he knew I hadn't left Nick to him without a fight.

What did I see as I watched and waited? I saw Roger move in with Nick, sharing the condo on the lake as well as the apartment in the city. Nick, of course, paid all the bills. Roger sat home all day, ostensibly studying for his realtor's license but mostly watching satellite TV and smoking dope purchased with money Nick had given him or he'd taken from Nick's wallet.

But the drugs, the indolence, and the dishonesty were nothing compared to the sheer volume of men Roger went through—a constant parade of tricks culled from Craigslist, reaped online, or trolled for in bathrooms. Roger was insatiable. He was also a consummate liar, able to use his winning grin and wounded puppy-dog eyes to make even the most bald-faced untruth sound palatable.

Worse, Nick seemed to trust him implicitly, which galled me. One of the sticking points in our relationship was Nick's jealousy. I believed in monogamy as firmly as he did and thought I showed that at every opportunity, but whenever I worked late or did something the slightest bit out of routine, I'd get questioned and cold-shouldered until he was satisfied I hadn't been fooling around. It was insulting to see how easily he accepted the lamest excuses from Roger. And he was about to get another one.

A well-dressed guy at the end of the bar was eyeing Roger. I didn't see the attraction, personally. My taste ran to pretty boys like Nick, not trash like Roger with his visible tattoos, longish dark hair, and scruffy beard. In his mid-thirties, he was way too old to be that unkempt. He might not be bad if he cleaned up, but that look appeals to some guys. It was sure appealing to the one in the business suit at the end of the bar. He was practically licking his lips.

Roger worked his bad-boy 'tude, staring up at the big-screen TV on the wall opposite the bar, drinking with a sullen, unsmiling smolder. He glanced at the suit every once in a while, leaving the man's half-grin unreturned as he turned his attention back to the TV. After ten minutes of this dance, Roger caught his eye and held his gaze for a good ten seconds before getting off the bar stool and heading toward the bathroom.

The suit, a clean-cut guy in his late forties or early fifties with salt-and-pepper hair and a firm, trim frame, smiled to himself and followed Roger. By the time he entered the men's room, Roger was already positioned at the trough urinal, a thin stream of piss trickling out of his half-hard dick.

The suit sidled up beside him, nodding as he eased his fully erect cock out of his slacks. Roger watched him stroke it as he shook the last drops from his own, tugging on it a few times for good measure. He put his hands behind his head and let his dick bobble stiffly in the air. The suit reached over with one hand and gave Roger's cock a squeeze.

"Suck it, dude," Roger said.

The suit nodded and sank to his knees in front of the urinal, taking Roger's dick in his mouth. He cupped Roger's balls with one hand while he stroked his own cock. Roger put his hands on either side of the suit's head, steadying it as he started to fuck the man's mouth. "Mmmm, yeah," Roger breathed.

Maybe I could break up this little party—frustrate him and get under his skin—but if I was going to do anything, now was the time. I crept into Roger's head as quietly as I could, unprepared for the intensity of feeling that waited for me. I felt drowned in the silken waves of pleasure pulsing through his brain, the glorious friction of skin on skin and the bitter, illicit scent of the urinal disinfectant. I could even feel the gel from the suit's hair on the palms of Roger's hands.

You like that, don't you? Roger cooed to me. *Don't pretend you're not here, and don't tell me you can't feel that even if you don't have a dick. You've been skulking around my head for weeks now and why? For this. Admit it.*

His orgasm was building up as he fucked the suit's mouth harder and harder, ramming his dick into it again and again. He began to breathe faster, thrusting his hips with panting exertion as his whole body tensed.

This is wrong, I managed to reply, nearly swooning.

His body took over before another thought could assert itself, flooding his head with sensation that pushed him over the edge and he came—*we* came—with a shuddering cry and a death grip on the suit's head. He bucked and struggled to avoid the explosion of come in his mouth, but we held on to his hair and forced him into the edge of the urinal until we were spent.

Roger then grabbed the suit's jaws with vicious pressure. "Swallow it," he commanded. "Don't spit it out or I'll kick your fuckin' ass all the way out to the bar." The man's throat moved and his Adam's apple bobbed, and Roger forced his mouth open to make sure he'd swallowed the load. "Nice," he said, releasing the suit.

He instantly jumped to his feet, rubbing his head. "What the fuck's wrong with you, man?"

Roger shrugged, his attitude intact. "I just don't like to waste it, that's all." He threw his head back and laughed as the suit exited, not even washing his hands. Overcome by shame, guilt, and a host of other emotions, I got the hell out of Roger's head as well.

"Come back any time, Michael," he shouted, his laugh reverberating around the metal and tile of the suddenly cold men's room. "Any fuckin' time!"

❖

"A job interview? Really?" Nick said, sarcastic instead of supportive. "Is that why you're an hour late for dinner?"

His estimate was conservative. The sex hadn't taken long, but with three drinks during trolling time in the bar, he was more like two hours late for dinner. Either way, it was nice to see Nick suspicious for a change.

For his part, Roger rocked the innocent, betrayed look. His face was all confusion and indignation and, even more convincingly, he was able to carry it through with his voice. "I thought you'd be happy for me," he not-quite-whined.

"Which bar was your interview in?" Nick asked. "You smell like a brewery."

"I was a little nervous, so I stopped at the Wrangler before I went."

"I'm sure the interviewer was impressed by the stench."

Roger's mask of hurt indignation never dropped. "Why are you being so mean?" he said. "Did you have a bad day at work?" Nick didn't pull away when Roger put his arm around his shoulder. "That Johnson grant you were looking for didn't come through, did it? Or are you just hearing voices in your head?"

He said the last as a joke, but I knew he was fishing. At least he was taking me a little seriously.

Nick sighed. "No," he replied, "the Johnson grant didn't come through." He put his head down on Roger's arm with a weary smile. "You always know what's wrong with me, don't you? I shouldn't bring work problems home, but three hundred fifty thousand is a lot of money to let slip through your fingers. We could have done so much with that."

"You didn't let it slip through your fingers. I'm sure you did all you could. It's not your fault."

Nick raised his head off Roger's arm and faced him. "I'm glad you have such faith in me," he said. "I'll try to remember that when mine is running low. Sorry to take it out on you—forgive me?"

"Sure." Roger leaned in for a kiss, Nick snaking his hand around Roger's back to pull him close.

And that's when I made my mistake.

I can't say why I chose that particular moment to pop into Roger's head—I'm not even sure it was a conscious decision. Maybe Roger even dragged me in, though that would be giving him far more credit than he deserved. Despite my care, despite my making a point of not entering Roger's head when he and Nick made love, I found myself inhabiting Roger just as his lips met Nick's.

Here, Michael, he said. *I'll even let you drive.*

And he was gone—well, not totally gone. I could still feel his presence, as if he was sitting in a corner watching, but Roger wasn't my focus. Nick was. For the first time in five years, I was kissing the man I loved. I raised Roger's arms and cradled Nick's face in his hands, feeling the comfort of his stubble on Roger's fingers as we engaged in earnest.

His kiss—his humanity—was wonderful and warm after five years of the disembodied existence I'd been used to. I don't know if you can call what seized me passion because I'm not sure energy can actually feel anything, but I filled Roger's being with something. I clutched at

Nick and pressed Roger's lips into his as if I could seal us together forever.

Our tongues began an old, familiar dance whose steps were second nature to us both by now, falling into their alternating rhythm of passionate exploration and languid rest so easily, so naturally, that it was a few moments before Nick opened his eyes wide and broke the kiss off with the sudden shock of realization. His eyes narrowed for a second.

Roger took over in a flash. "What's wrong?"

"Nothing," Nick said, hesitating. "It's just that for a minute, it felt like...*you* felt like..."

"Like what?"

He looked like he was going to explain at first, but then realized any explanation for what really happened would sound crazier than just putting the whole thing down to a bad day, distractions or a simple "never mind." He settled for the latter and Roger knew better than to press the issue.

See, Michael? Roger said. *He's not as strong as I am. If you get inside his head, you'll drive him batshit. And neither of us wants that, do we?*

I left without responding, not knowing what I wanted.

❖

As I said, everything you know about us is wrong—including the assumptions that we are always right and that we know what we're doing. Neither of these is necessarily true, at least in my case. I had no idea what I was doing. Roger was ahead of me at each turn, making me unsure of my own motivations.

What was it to the universe that my former lover was going out with a thieving, cheating, substance-addicted sponge? People have been making that same mistake for centuries, and the world has continued to revolve. What was there about this situation that was so urgent?

It was Nick, of course. He was a sweet, innocent guy who didn't deserve to be taken advantage of, and it was my job to make sure that didn't happen. Or was it? Maybe Nick needed to be chumped. Instead of saving him, I was stunting his experiential growth. Unless that was an excuse for inaction because I was afraid of Roger.

And I *was* afraid of Roger. His confidence and surety of purpose were terrifying. Even more terrifying was the fact that, deep down, I wanted to be like him. I wanted some of his confidence, his surety and, yes, his success with men. I was never too keen in that area when alive. I still don't know how I managed to snag Nick, but part of the reason I was so committed to him was that I didn't want to lose him and have to start all over again.

You'd think since I was dead and part of the "angel" set, my human deficiencies would no longer matter, but some scars run deep enough to show up in the afterlife as well. Your inadequacies follow you even in death, which should be reason enough to try resolving them while you're alive.

Roger's constant hunt for cock fascinated me, despite the fact that each new conquest underscored my reason for being there in the first place—to save Nick. I rationalized it by telling myself I was gathering information and material for one swift killing blow of some sort, but I was awed by his complexity of technique and the balls-out nerve that put him in some bad situations. Like the Craigslist ad that read:

> Rape Me!!!
>
> GL, 32 y/o, DD free gym rat looking for someone to break in and rape me. Must be between 30–50, stealthy and able to scale a privacy fence. Attack dog will be locked up. No fats, fems, pussies or safewords.
>
> If you can give it, I can take it. BB preferred. Burglar mask optional.

Don't do this, I said to him.

Hello Michael, he replied. *I figured this'd get you riled. Nick's working late tonight and I'm by myself—well, except for you, that is. Why shouldn't I do it?*

Because it's wrong.

Look, Jiminy Cricket, I'm not in the market for a conscience.

Doesn't it bother you to cheat on Nick and lie to him?

He laughed, finished typing his reply to the ad, and clicked on Send. *Does it look like it bothers me?*

Okay, think about yourself—this looks dangerous.

What do you care? You don't have to come. But you will.

And, of course, he was right. I stayed in his head, quiet and still, during the drive to the McMansiony part of town, all smooth concrete and trimmed greenbelt landscaped to within an inch of its life. The neighborhood was so fussy, the trees were afraid to drop their leaves in autumn.

Roger parked a couple of blocks away and walked in the quiet moonlight, trying to avoid the pools of light from the lampposts that studded the sidewalk. At last he saw the address given him in the detailed e-mail his "victim" had sent in reply.

The streetlight around back's supposed to be burnt out, so there's a dark spot against the privacy fence. I have to climb over, go through the backyard, and enter through the unlocked sliding glass door.

Oh, I said, *are you talking to me?*

No, I'm talking to myself. You just happen to be in the same room.

Roger slipped around the side of the house to the back, finding the strip of yard along the fence quite dark indeed. He jumped up, grabbed the top of the fence, and hauled himself over, landing awkwardly on the other side. The backyard was as antiseptic as the rest of the grounds, all the trees and flowers potted and perfect, not one piece of dyed gravel out of place.

Dogs barked somewhere in the distance, and the breeze blew a mild chill that stirred the shrubbery. Miller moths beat around a dim patio light that shone down on a gas grill and the sliding glass door. Roger approached it slowly, looking around the yard before peering inside and putting his fingers on the latch tentatively.

Scared? I asked.

Just cautious.

He drew the latch back, eased the door open far enough to slip inside, then shut it. He stood with his back to the door, staring into the room. As his eyes adjusted to the darkness, Roger saw he was in the kitchen. Cutlery and pots and pans hung from a rack over the island in the center of the room, on which sat a lone, unwashed plate with the remnants of a T-bone steak and half a baked potato.

Following the e-mail instructions, Roger crept through the kitchen and down the hall, flooded with a faint bluish-green beam from the small night-light plugged into an outlet next to an open door at the far end.

Goal in sight, he said. *This is giving me such a fucking hard-on.*

He paused outside the door, massaging his stiff cock through his jeans as he surveyed the bedroom. Another nightlight cast a pale green glow inside, illuminating a naked, tanned figure sleeping on his stomach atop the rumpled white sheets. His breathing was slow and steady. The sole of his right foot was flat against his left thigh, forming a dark triangle between his legs and ass crack.

Roger slinked to the edge of the bed, his hand still rubbing his dick, then he sank his knees level with the bed and pushed himself on top of the figure, slipping a stiff arm under the man's throat. "Don't fuckin' move," he breathed into his ear, "don't talk, don't scream, and don't fight me or I'll choke the livin' shit out of you—nod if you're with me so far."

The man nodded.

"Good. Now, I'm gonna let you go. I don't want anything comin' outta your mouth except a few grunts. My hands are gonna be close to your balls at all times, so if you want 'em to stay where they are, you'll play it my way. Got me?"

He nodded again. His eyes were open and full of terror. Was this even the right house? I wondered. I popped out of Roger's head and into his, encountering an overpowering mix of fear and lust so palpable I could feel its sludgy weight all around me. Definitely the right house.

Where did you go? Roger asked when I came back to him. *I wouldn't want you to miss any of this. It's what you came for, right?*

I felt dirtier and more ashamed than I ever had while alive. *Yes.*

Then take half of me over—I know you can do it. If you can get into my head, you can get into the rest of me. We'll both do this. C'mon. You know you want to.

And I did it. I imagined myself fog and simply misted myself throughout his body, feeling the cool air on our skin, the wrinkled bedsheets under our knees, and the nervous anticipation of the body beneath us.

We nibbled the back of the man's neck, running our tongue down the tangy salt of his sweat-soaked back until we reached his furry ass. Roger brought our hands up and spread the man's legs apart, lingering on his taint and playing with his nuts. He buried our nose deep into his crack, nuzzling the musky hair until we reached his hole.

Our tongue darted out, grazing the silken, wrinkled pucker, then lapping at it in earnest, tasting it in long, broad strokes and rubbing our nose deep into its spit-slicked center. We probed his asshole with one hand while Roger used the other to undo his belt and get the front of his jeans open, easing out his hard, dripping cock.

Roger spat into that hand, wetting his dick even more before he finally lowered it into the crevice of the man's ass, sliding it up and down with shallow grunts before he finally slipped it in. The man gasped and whimpered, but Roger slapped his ass sharply.

"Not one fuckin' word," he said, his voice hoarse, "or I'll rip your fuckin' balls off—I swear I will."

Roger buried his cock all the way in the man's tight hole, grabbing on to either side of his ass and thrusting long and slow. The man squirmed beneath us, burying his face in his pillow until Roger reached down, took hold of the man's hair, and dragged his head backward. "Take it like a man," he intoned.

It was a cruel, harsh fuck—no tenderness or passion, only coercion and control. I've heard of mercy fucks, but this was a merciless one. Roger kept driving his dick home, harder and harder with each thrust, and at some point in the heedless, robotic slavery to pleasure, something clicked for me.

And I found I liked it. No, I *loved* it.

I knew you would, he said. *Nick doesn't matter anymore, does he? All that matters is this. Am I right?*

I didn't need to answer. He knew.

Then suddenly, Roger's thrusts increased in intensity and I began to feel the load building up in his balls. His breathing became ragged and short, coming in gasps as he rammed the man viciously.

"Don't come in my ass," the man managed to say.

Roger pulled back on his hair so hard, he screamed. "I'll…come… anywhere…I fuckin'…*want*…to!" He barely got the last word out before he came in convulsive jerks, his dick all the way inside. He held the man's ass tight against his body until he had spurted his last.

Still breathing heavily, Roger pulled his dick out of the guy's ass and again forced a stiff arm under his throat. "Didn't I tell you to shut the fuck up?" he wheezed in his ear. "You just said five more words than you should have, and I ought to kick the holy shit right outta you." He tightened up on the choke hold and held on as the man bucked furiously for a second.

Roger suddenly let go, scrambling off the side of the bed as he zipped up his jeans with a deft, fluid motion. By the time the man was sitting up recovering, Roger was tucked and ready for anything. "You wanna fight, motherfucker, let's do it—I'm just givin' you what you asked for."

Long seconds ticked by before a grin split the man's face. "Ain't that the truth," he said. "You throw a mean fuck, dude. My ass is gonna be sore for a week." He lay back down and covered himself with the sheet, snuggling into the pillow. "Make sure the sliding glass door's closed on your way out."

Roger laughed, but as he turned to leave he saw the man's Rolex on the dresser near the door. He snatched it up on his way out, sliding it onto his wrist. The man didn't even notice. I was so stunned I couldn't say anything until we were well into the kitchen.

Stealing? Really? That's about as low as you can get.

Roger shrugged as he opened the sliding glass door and stepped out into the night's breeze. *Call it the cost of doing business on Craigslist. Besides, I don't care what you think anymore. You're as bad as I am now.*

Right then I couldn't think of anyone I hated more than Roger.

Except myself.

❖

I wasn't the best angel, obviously. But I knew I had a problem and hanging around in Roger's head wasn't going to solve it. The situation was only going to get worse now that I had a taste of Roger's experience. I could see myself sliding into his addiction, and that would serve no one well; least of all Nick, who I was supposed to be rescuing, after all.

But how could I turn my thoughts to my original purpose when recalling last night's experience set my senses reeling again? I'd never felt so powerful or masterful before. That feeling was tough to forget and even tougher to forgo, and if I stayed with Roger, I knew I'd be feeling it again. For my own sake, I had to leave—but I couldn't leave until I'd helped Nick.

I even debated getting into Nick's head again, but Roger was also right about that. He wouldn't be able to stand that strain. It had taken five long years for Nick to move on to someone else, even someone as spurious as Roger. If I got into his head, I might do more damage than good even if I convinced him to ditch the loser. He might become dependent on me and never want me to leave. That wouldn't be healthy, either.

No matter how hard I wished, no resolution magically appeared—just complicating factors. Nick's late night at work was the harbinger of a business trip to rescue another grant situation, leaving Roger and me free to indulge ourselves. I couldn't let that happen. Action had to be taken as soon as possible, whatever that might be.

Nothing presented itself during the trip to the airport. I just listened to small talk between Nick and Roger as Nick checked his bags and they went to an airport lounge for a drink before Nick's flight. It was then Roger did something bold enough to surprise even me.

"I got you something," he said to Nick, grinning over his gin and tonic.

"What?"

"Oh, just a little going-away gift."

Nick beamed. "When could you have done that? I just told you last night—you haven't had a chance to shop for anything."

"Actually," Roger said, "I got this a few days ago. No real occasion. I know work's been stressing you out lately, and...well, I thought now would be as good a time to give it you as any. But you have to close your eyes. I didn't have time to wrap it or anything this morning."

"You shouldn't have," Nick said, closing his eyes, "but I'm glad you did."

Once Nick's eyes were closed, Roger reached into the pocket of his jeans and pulled out the Rolex he'd taken from the trick's dresser the night before. I was stunned. The more I thought about it, the angrier I became. It was a slap not only at Nick, but to me as well. I knew where he got it from, and what's more, he knew that I knew. That smug, motherfucking asshole.

And that's when it hit me.

I had no idea if it would work, but I took the memory of where that Rolex came from and about fifteen or twenty of Roger's encounters I'd been privy to, fixed those images firmly in my mind, summoned up all of my anger and frustration and hatred, focused it all in a narrow beam, and threw it with everything I had at the face of the watch.

"Okay," Roger said. "Open your eyes."

"Oh, Roger, it's beautiful." Nick looked at the watch hanging off Roger's fingers, then he slipped his off his wrist and took the new one. "I'll think of you whenever I check the time."

"I was going to get it engraved, but..."

Nick smiled, leaned over and kissed Roger. "It's wonderful like it is," he said. "I don't know what I've done to deserve you."

And then he put it on.

The smile dropped from his face. He seemed to turn inward for a moment. I didn't know exactly what was happening to him, but with each split second that passed more and more anger and distrust built up in those eyes. I knew the look well, and this was fiercer than any of the ones I'd gotten. The desire to get into his head overwhelmed me, and I tried to enter but couldn't get through. I couldn't get into Roger's, either. Moreover, the airport lounge was growing dimmer. Whatever I had done, it depleted my energy to an extent I didn't know was possible.

Nick, however, was on fire. His face turned from doting love to white-hot rage. "You fucking *liar*," he hissed. "This watch came from a trick, didn't it?"

"What? No, I...I...bought it."

"With what? The few measly dollars you get peddling pot out of my apartment won't buy a Rolex. Tell the truth for once in your life, bitch. How many others? You can't even count them, can you? You can't even fucking *count* them."

"I..."

Before Roger could finish his excuse, Nick threw his drink in Roger's face, the lime clinging to his collar. "Keep this for your next trick," he said, tossing the watch back at Roger. He picked up his briefcase and swung it at Roger, connecting with the side of his head. "We're done. Pack your shit up and get out. If you're there when I get home from this trip, I'm calling the cops."

He strode out of the lounge. I wanted to follow him, to cheer for him, to raise his hand in victory, but the whole scene was starting to swim before me. I felt Roger searching around frantically for me, but he couldn't find me anymore—which was a shame. I would have gloated, I would have laughed in his face, and I would have rejoiced in the power of love, even in the afterlife.

But that was impossible. I don't know if I'd used up all my energy or simply accomplished what I'd intended and needed to go back. The lounge got darker and more indistinct, and Roger's shrill cries to Nick grew fainter until I couldn't hear them anymore, and I felt myself tugged away from that reality. I was going into nothingness or another level or the next step or something. I had no clue. We fly as blindly in death as we do in life. Not a comforting thought, I know, but there you have it. Nick was finally on his own.

And so was I.

Maelstrom

Dale Chase

Dr. Hardy says it's projection but that can't be right. I mean, there's not enough in me to create the kind of maelstrom swirling through my apartment. Imagination can't possibly be that vivid, and emotions, even allowing their power to ruin lives, don't actually break the furniture. Maybe I should stop seeing Dr. Hardy. Maybe I need an exorcist.

It all started the week after Robert left, which was possibly the worst week of my life. I hit bottom, swallowed pills, had my stomach pumped, and spent the required forty-eight hours in a psych ward, released, as the law dictates, to return to my wallow and contemplate a more certain end.

About that time, the atmosphere in the apartment began to change, like a storm was not on the horizon but in the next room. I could feel a cold front moving into my bedroom, never mind it was summer and record temps outside. Lying in bed, curled into a fetal position while contemplating the mechanics of ending it all, I felt a chill slink into the room, get under the covers and wrap itself around me, and honest to God, tug at my dick. The first instinct was to flee but the second was to enjoy it and so I lay still, cock stiffening to what felt not quite a hand. I couldn't help but glance up to see if I'd suddenly been transported elsewhere, to the North Pole or maybe farther, something interplanetary, but all I got were the beige walls of my bedroom, dusty blinds and weak light. Same old same old except I was going to come.

I shut my eyes as jizz shot out of me, and it was a gusher as I hadn't done anything since Robert, couldn't actually, wounded not only in heart but in crotch. But now I was wild with climax, cock firing like it would never run out. And in these glorious throes I felt rather than heard a crash that set the bed moving like a foundering whaler, which got the only possible reaction from this born-and-raised Los Angeles native: earthquake!

I leaped from bed and stood in a doorway even though that has been discounted as the thing to do, but when you're brought up with parents directing you to do just that, it's difficult to try something new. Experts now say to get next to some desk or piece of furniture that will support a falling roof so you'll have a little cave in the rubble. Nice. Then, from the doorway, I noticed the room wasn't shaking, just the bed, and it was still at it.

Keeping my distance, I watched my covers rise and fall, my mattress bounce as if some invisible wrestling match was taking place. The frame began to creak against the floor as it moved a few inches, pushed along by this invisible bout. It was like watching a fight absent the fighters. And then as quickly as it started, it stopped, and I stood in fear and wonderment. And at next day's regular appointment with Dr. Hardy, I mentioned it.

Dr. Hardy was patient, taking it in like some benevolent grandfather. I liked him immensely and he'd seen me through several life crises, Robert the latest. I felt so comfortable with him and he knew everything about me, which nobody else did, not even Robert. So I also told him about the cold front and the hand getting me off. That's when the telltale brow crimped upward and I knew I'd lost him.

"So you came, did you?"

"Yes, but I didn't touch myself."

"What were you thinking of before this began?"

"How to succeed at killing myself."

He blew out a long sigh and I realized he was taking my backslide personally so I hastily added, "just a bad moment," but it was too late.

"Your longing for Robert is creating fantasies in your mind," Dr. Hardy intoned, "and these are translating into actions that you may or may not be aware of. You are projecting, Philip. Of course you worked yourself to climax. You were alone. Well, except for thoughts of Robert. Now what we must do is help you to get past him, for you are more than this man, far more." And from there he went into his positive thinking litany and the apartment storm was forgotten. At least by him.

From then on I approached my abode with a mix of curiosity and trepidation, and for a little while all was quiet. Then one morning I decided to get back on track, get dressed, get shaved, start looking for a job, so I was in the shower when a wind swept in, shower curtain flying not in but out, like the storm was in there with me, and water let loose onto the floor as the curtain remained outstretched like some great flag in a storm. And then the most amazing thing. A cock went up my butt.

Okay, I thought, fuck me. I glanced over my shoulder to make sure I was alone, and of course I was because the apartment door was deadbolted and I'm too high up for burglars. So I'm alone, I thought, spreading my legs to accommodate what felt more like an arm than a dick. I started taking deep breaths and bracing myself against the tile as the cock went deeper into my chute. My own dick was instantly up and ready to fire but I left it alone, consumed by the fuck of a lifetime. A giant prick snaked in and out of me, and holy God I started coming unaided, spraying jizz like the shower and keeping on, like I was making more and more and more until I thought I'd pass out.

My knees weak, the rear assault getting more forceful, it scared the hell out of me when the shower curtain suddenly pulled itself down, taking the rod with it, the whole thing falling with a loud clatter that disturbed me but not the disembodied cock doing me. "What the hell?" I cried. At this the prick pulled out of me, which set my knees buckling, and I collapsed into a heap in the tub while the shower curtain resurrected itself, rod still attached, and flew from the room. Okay, Dr. Hardy. We are way past projection.

I forced myself up to shut off the water, grab a towel, and step cautiously from the tub. A crash issued from the living room followed by silence, which let me creep forward, looking for what I have no idea, but still looking, as if some monster might suddenly appear.

The shower curtain lay on the living room floor like some great expired balloon. I put a toe out to touch it, half expecting it to bite, but it just lay there, once again nothing but harmless plastic. I gathered it into a bundle, rod and all, and tossed it into the bathtub, but as I did so there came the sound of shattering glass and I ran to the bedroom to see Aunt Hilda's antique oval mirror shatter, shards cascading onto the dresser. And not only did it shatter, it leaped from the wall where it had hung for a decade and flew across the room, crashing into the closet door where it left a sizeable scratch.

"What is this?" I demanded even though nobody was there. But somebody obviously was there, although "body" might not be right.

Some something was there, maybe two somethings, because it seemed my apartment had become a battleground although all was now quiet. I pulled on shorts and went to the kitchen, where I poured a tumbler of wine and drank like it was water. As I stood gulping, I thought of how I would relate this latest incident to Dr. Hardy. Yes, the shower curtain pulled itself down and flew from the room. And the mirror broke all by itself, then jumped off the wall. This would likely get me another forty-eight hours in the loony bin.

So I didn't tell Dr. Hardy about it, which gave our session a decadent sort of feel, and as we discussed my need to gain perspective about the breakup, I saw the good doc in a new light, for he was a handsome man, gray hair so thick I wanted to get my hands into it, eyes so vivid I suddenly understood steel blue. He was well built and a tuft of chest hair was visible above his pale yellow shirt. I listened to him as never before, and when it was time for me to speak, I felt like an actor onstage, more animated than usual. I also let my eye travel down to Dr. Hardy's crotch, where I could see a nice bulge. We could fuck, it suddenly occurred to me. All this privacy made me want to get naked and do things.

I managed to get through the session with the doctor-patient relationship intact but had to hit the men's room and jerk off, and it was as I unloaded in the stall that I felt something move behind me. I turned, mid-come, spraying jizz all down the wall, but nobody was there, even though it felt like somebody was humping my ass.

Washing up, I found myself confused because Dr. Hardy had gotten into my maelstrom and we weren't even in my apartment, plus the disembodied something that shared my shower had come out into the world with me.

When I got home I tried to take charge of my life by going online to look for a job. Robert had been my sole support for six years, insisting I quit work to care for him while pursuing my painting. I'd willingly sacrificed and now paid the price, trolling Craigslist for clerical work while aware it was futile because hundreds would apply for each position. On this reasoning, I cruised to my favorite porn site, undid my pants, and settled in for a solo session. Ever since the atmosphere had changed in my apartment, I'd been horny as hell, but I didn't question this newfound state, I just enjoyed it. Stroking my cock, I was just getting into things when there came not a climax but a crash in the living room. I halted my stroke but didn't let go of my dick because I was learning that whatever force now lived with me was a chaotic sort, and as it had the power to break things, I didn't get in its way. Following the crash were muffled thumps, like someone bouncing on the sofa, a good thunk, then all quieted. Too distracted to continue the solo session, I zipped up and ventured from the bedroom.

The bookcase was on its side, books scattered. Sofa pillows were on the floor and the tranquil painting over the sofa was askew, the little canoe at its center looking as if it was sinking. "Oh, come on," I said aloud, for I often spoke to the force even though it never responded. I sighed, righted things, sat down and clicked on the TV. And nothing happened. The little red light on the cable box was lit but the TV stayed dark. I wondered if the silent forces were at work again but decided the cable company, also unseen, was far worse. Clicking every button on the TV, cable box, and remote was futile, so I gave up and called them. After futile attempts to reset things, they said they could have a man out next day. We made the appointment and I settled down to contemplate the pros and cons of continuing my life when the doorbell rang.

"Who is it?" I called.

"ViaTel Cable."

Odd, I thought, since they'd been so adamant about next-day service, but who's to quibble? Something was finally going my way. I opened the door feeling buoyant. "I wasn't expecting you today but welcome. I appreciate your getting here so fast."

He stepped inside and paused, as if he expected me to give him the once over—which I did because he was probably the most handsome man I'd ever seen. Thick, dark curly hair enhanced a wide forehead, dark brown eyes, long lashes, straight nose, full lips smiling around stunning white teeth, and a chin so perfectly chiseled it belonged on a superhero.

"ViaTel at your service," he said, moving toward the television. He carried a small red toolbox and wore black work pants and shirt. The yellow ViaTel logo was above one shirt pocket, his name the other: Magnus.

"It just wouldn't come on today," I explained. "Worked fine last night, then today all I get is the red light, and the service desk said it looked fine from their end."

Magnus fixed on me like he was enthralled with my every word.

"Sometimes it's just a glitch in the box," he offered. "We'll have a look."

He approached the TV, clicked it a couple times, then set down his toolbox, and before he squatted down to get to business, adjusted his package. And it wasn't just some quick getting his parts comfortable, it was a lingering grope that announced he had something to offer besides cable service. My own cock, already at attention from the first sight of him, began to throb.

"Sometimes these things just need a little hands on," he said as he did nothing beyond what I had, fiddling with buttons on the box. "But then don't we all," he added.

"True," I squeaked.

"Do you suppose I might have a drink of water?" he asked as he stood up. I sprinted to the kitchen for a bottle, which he drank like some cowboy in from the range while I looked again at his crotch. His handsome face merited attention, but I couldn't bring myself up from between his legs, where a snake seemed to have crawled.

"You thirsty?" Magnus said when he'd drank half the bottle, and when I said no, he said, "Hungry?" And with that he unzipped his pants.

"Kneel," he commanded and I complied, already quivering at the sight of his massive cock. He didn't handle it but stood hands on hips as I crawled to him, mouth open, tongue out. I reached up and began sucking so furiously that I forgot my own erection, and in seconds I was swallowing more come than I'd ever known one man to produce, so much I almost gagged, and it wasn't the usual salty taste, it was something vaguely familiar. I swallowed and swallowed and when at last I sat back, wiping my mouth, I recognized the taste of my favorite maple sugar candy.

"Every man's fantasy," Magnus said. Then he jabbed a finger back over his shoulder and Oprah blasted to life on the resurrected television.

"More," I begged, not caring about the TV.

Magnus looked down, nostrils flaring like a wild horse, eyes blazing, and that's not just some literary term. His eyes glowed with reds and golds amid the brown, and I felt heat emanate from him like he'd opened an oven door and was about to pull me inside.

"Undress," he commanded, pulling me to my feet. I shed my

clothes, cock springing up at him. He reached down and pulled on it and I started to come onto him while he guided my spurts like a graffiti artist with a spray can. My climax went beyond what that word conveys; it kept on until his black pants were full of my spatters. When he let go of me, I instantly stopped coming and went soft in both cock and body, stupefied by his incredible power.

I wasn't surprised that he picked me up and carried me away. Hefting me around the waist, he took me to the kitchen island, where he arranged me on my back. And then he got naked.

He was smooth beneath his ViaTel uniform, glistening like he'd been coated with come and giving off that maple sugar scent. His chest was well muscled, pecs rounded to perfection and sporting prominent nipples that begged a tongue. His thighs were thick and the hair between them dark, curly, and plentiful. The cock was still hard, like it never softened. I raised my legs, held them wide, and my pucker started an involuntary quiver. "Fuck me," I rasped and he grinned and growled and put it in. The pots on the rack above us chimed against one another as if to bless the union.

I broke into a pant as I accommodated the biggest dick I'd ever encountered. It snaked up into my gut so far I thought it was pressing my lungs because breathing became more and more difficult and he hadn't even started to thrust. As I received him, I fixed on his beautiful face, which now bore a determined look, like he was planning to do damage.

Finally I had the whole prick, body complaining from head to foot except for my crotch, which was afire with a need only this man could quench. "Fuck me," I begged, "please," and he began to thrust.

"Fuck me, take me, have me, eat me, fuck me, chew me, lick me, kill me, fuck me…"

I couldn't stop begging and the faster he went, the worse I got, wanting more, more, more. The pots above us set up a ringing among themselves like church bells gone mad. And then I heard the blender running on its own and the dishwasher started in, even the timer was going off, all while Magnus rammed his meat into me.

My own cock was hard again, never mind I'd already come buckets. I hadn't the strength to raise my arms, but it didn't matter. It erupted like some oil well, sending a white gusher a good foot into the air. Magnus licked his lips like he could taste me.

"Fuck me, fuck me, fuck me." I kept on because no matter how much I came, I was desperate for more. "Fuck me, fuck me, fuck me."

The pots kept clanging together, almost violently now, and then one fell, then another. Suddenly Magnus stopped but did not pull out. "You little shit!" he said, looking past me. I twisted my head to see an angelic-looking creature, a golden-haired man in a white tunic sporting wings on his back.

The creature spoke with calm amid the come. "Philip, I am Berthold, an angel sent to assist you in righting your life. The acts of Magnus demand I reveal myself and tell you he is not of this world. He is a fallen angel who seeks to corrupt you. I am here to save you from such a fate. You must be saved, Philip. Let me save you."

"Let me fuck you," Magnus said, resuming his thrust, which set off my climax again. The angel seemed like a nice guy, but at the moment I had little use for being saved.

"Fuck me, fuck me, fuck me," I started in again to Magnus, and he thrust ever deeper. Pots continued to clang and fall, rolling around on the floor. And then Berthold was around the island to stand beside me, which gave me a good look at his magnificent wings, big white lushly feathered things any bird would covet. They reached from his shoulders to his knees and I thought how wonderful it would be to have them around me. When my eyes met the angel's, I felt a sort of uplifting, my heart filled as much as my butt hole. I heard a beautiful distant choir and smelled fresh mountain air. Then the cock in me softened, as did my own, but I didn't care because I was elevated in some way, my insides tingling like never before, a good kind of tingle, whole-body pleasure. Magnus, meantime, backed away. The blender stopped running, as did the dishwasher. The timer quieted and the one remaining pot on the overhead rack was now still. "Fuck you," Magnus said before he disappeared.

Berthold, standing between my legs, raised his hands as if urging a congregation to its feet, then lowered them, which compelled my legs to follow. He righted me the same way, motioning, and I again felt the uplifting, like I was floating toward rapture. He handed me a big warm fluffy white towel, and as I stood and wrapped it around myself, I wondered where he'd gotten it, as none of my towels was that big and certainly not that soft. I was herded to the living room, Berthold never touching me, just motioning, and I found great satisfaction in doing his bidding. My little world opened up before my eyes, becoming vast and bright and filled with promise.

I was eased into the big overstuffed chair, towel tucked around me. The coziness was so pronounced I pulled my feet up to curl into myself while Berthold stood, hands together as if in prayer. I wanted to ask a million questions but couldn't get past the wings. "They're so beautiful," I gushed. The wings fluttered as if I'd ruffled them.

"You have much to offer," Berthold said, kneeling. The wings spread out as they touched the floor and I reached to pet them but he motioned to stop me. "You must regain your true self and value life once again," Berthold said and I noted how comforting his voice was, a soothing baritone that undoubtedly carried well in the heavenly choir. "You are a man of goodness and wisdom," he continued, "but you have been led astray. Wisdom and moral integrity were born into you and must be regained. My role is to help you toward this. You have strayed, Philip. You have attempted to cast off the life given you, and further, you have unknowingly embarked on a dangerous and decadent path. Together we shall set you right."

Here he paused and I felt warmth radiating from him, like he had the sun's energy inside, and I basked in his glow, my whole self lifting. Had someone asked me at that moment, I would have assured them I levitated.

"You are a man of beauty and light, Philip, but you have allowed others to pull you into their worlds rather than honor your own. You are a great artist. You must allow the inner man to emerge and rise up."

As he assured me of my greatness I found myself slipping into his thrall. He was like some Sistine cherub grown up, exuding heavenly innocence while embodying perfection. I couldn't help but reach out to him, and he smiled with indulgence even as he raised a hand to prevent contact. "We are allowed only limited human contact and nothing intimate," he explained.

"But you're so appealing."

"Are you aroused?"

My dick remained soft but the rest of me felt hard. "Sort of," I said.

He chuckled. "You and I must be above such indulgence. We have the work of life, which is far greater than physical coupling and is ultimately more rewarding."

"But I feel such longing."

"You long to be whole," he soothed, "and with guidance you shall be. Now I suggest a refreshing shower, after which you take up your brushes and paint. For a time you must remain solitary. Regain and renew."

"Will you stay with me?"

He drew me to my feet. "Angels are not allowed extended contact with humans, else we might become dependent. Our work is usually not in body, but when we must make ourselves physically present, it is limited. The rules are quite strict."

He saw me to the bathroom and I took the suggested shower and suffered no intrusions. Soaping myself, I had none of the usual inclination to work my cock. Instead I found myself thrilled to be attending such a remarkable body. Feet, legs, chest, hands, arms, all tingly with newfound life, as if I'd been reborn. I soaped with care, rinsed with delight, and toweled myself into a mood of pure joy.

Berthold was gone when I emerged, but the apartment seemed to have taken on a glow in his wake. Things seemed brighter and more welcoming, and when I glanced at the corner where my easel stood, I thought I heard that distant choir. The painting, neglected for weeks, beckoned to me, still life far from still. Colors seemed to dance on the canvas or was it just me projecting my newfound bliss onto the work? Hah! Projecting. Dr. Hardy seemed a million miles away.

Dropping the towel, I opened my paint box. Always an enjoyable gesture, it held even more this time, the tubes of paint sensuous in their promise. I opened cadmium red, squeezed a dollop onto my palette, and a tingle ran from the tube into my thumb and up my arm and down my front and into my legs and stomach and crotch. And that red dollop was so enticing, thick and bright. I picked up a brush but really would rather have run my finger through the stuff.

I'd never painted naked and found it wonderfully innocent, like I had truly been reborn as the artist. Unconfined, I was able to personally enter the canvas. The simple bowl of fruit had a soft peach shade in the background that I now saw as my flesh. How could I not have noticed this before? My cock even twitched, but not enough to demand attention. Rather, it was in sync with the whole of me, not dominating but, for once, adding to the complete man. I worked on an apple until it shone, then added yellow, green, and orange to my palette, savoring the tubes in my fingers and the inviting look of the paint.

How long I painted I have no idea, only that it felt more right than ever before. Like it was back before Robert and before Tim who was before Robert and before Alex who was before Tim and, well, before them all. And I saw how they had needed so much of me there wasn't enough left for my art. Berthold had come down to point me in the right direction. I didn't know where he'd gone, but he'd freed the artist in me and for that I was grateful. As I daubed yellow ochre onto a plump orange and felt a citrus tang on my tongue, the doorbell rang. I paused, brush in midair.

"ViaTel Cable," a familiar voice called. My cock began to fill.

How fortunate I was already naked. Magnus needed no invitation. He had his dick out when I opened the door. As I thrilled to the sight, something clattered to the floor and I saw, of all things, a paint brush. Kneeling, it was of little concern.

I couldn't get enough come. I swallowed prodigious spurts that kept on until my jaw ached, but I still sucked because I would never get enough of this cock or its issue. That the jizz still tasted of my favorite candy only made me more hungry.

Instead of fucking me on the kitchen island, this time Magnus laid me over the back of the overstuffed chair, spread me and speared me. I cried out a garbled welcome, realizing only then how deprived I'd been.

There were no pots clanging overhead, no appliances run amok, just our juicy fuck slap. When I came I fleetingly thought about it staining the chair, but such trivia is lost amid a bucket of come. And as before, I was compelled to beg. "Fuck me, take me, have me, lick me, kill me, suck me, fuck me." On and on as jizz continued to shoot out of me.

Limp from the climax, I slid to the floor when Magnus withdrew but looked up to see him now naked, cock still hard and beckoning, wagging at me on its own while he just stood. I lay enthralled at the sight. "Put it in," I gasped. "Fuck me."

He offered a leer that set me quivering. My cock was hard again and I held it as offering. "Please."

When he picked me up it was not gently. Like a lifeless body, I was hoisted back up onto the chair, but this time instead of his dick, I felt hot breath on my bottom. And then something snaked between my cheeks. Glancing over my shoulder, I could make out Magnus's head down there but the something slithering into me couldn't be a tongue because it kept going like a snake or lizard or some other crawly creature except this one was hot blooded, feeling its way along, licking my passage, prodding my every inch. I began to come on the chair again as the crawling creature went still deeper.

As I unloaded, I felt a rustle beside me and turned to find feathers engulfing my face, warm feathers, pungent sweet feathers, as if they'd just flown in from the great outdoors. They caressed me and I rubbed them like some cat against its owner's leg. And I heard myself purring, which caused the creature in my ass to nip my insides, which jolted me back to the rear action. And only then did I understand my circumstance. Magnus had my ass while Berthold addressed himself higher up.

"He's a filthy beast," Berthold cooed from somewhere within the wing. As it continued to caress me, he stated his case. "Magnus uses you to his own ends and will devour you completely if you do not resist. Cast him out. You are a better man than this."

I heard his message but I was coming again, the creature at my rear caressing the most sensitive inner region just as Berthold caressed the outer, only Magnus one-upped the angel in that he got me off. "Eat me," I told him and the feathers retreated.

Humping the chair, I came until I thought I'd pass out and when the climax relented and I collapsed onto the floor, Magnus ran his big toe into my mouth. I sucked with what felt the last ounce of energy yet still wanted more. But then a great wind swept over us, as if the shower storm had returned, only this time there were feathers floating like snowflakes. "Fuck me," I begged as Berthold rose up behind Magnus, wings outstretched, fluttering to create the storm. Magnus batted at them as if a mere mosquito was after him.

Magnus grabbed his cock and drew me up to get my mouth onto it. Desperate for more of his maple come, I began to suck but a wing got between us, engulfing him, and the television came on, as did all the lights. The CD player blasted Beethoven's Fifth as I tried to suck a demon's dick while the angel fought for my life.

A wing struck me and knocked me back. Lying on the floor, I

could only watch the angelic creature attempt to do in the ViaTel man. Berthold seemed to have it over Magnus as far as levitating, for he was off the ground for much of their tussle, but Magnus had strength and he flailed at the angel, dick still stiff, precome flying. I raised up, trying to catch the maple drippings.

"He's mine!" Magnus growled. "He shall fuck all his days and nights. My cock is his life!"

"It is his death!" Berthold cried, arm around his adversary's throat. The overstuffed chair, heavy as a sofa, skittered away as if in fear for its life and the sofa also retreated, pushing itself up against the wall, which caused the little canoe painting to start sinking again. Even the doorbell chimed in. "You seek only to satisfy yourself!" Berthold accused.

"Beware of condemning others when you are not so clean," Magnus returned, trying to unstick Berthold. "Philip, don't listen to this guy. He doesn't give a flying fuck about you. You're his charity assignment so he can obtain God's fucking grace. That's all you are to an angel, a means to an end. Ask him. He's no better than anyone, he just thinks he is because God sent him down here. Well, his motives are down here with me, down in this shit hole called life, so take heed, Philip. Look at your fine feathered friend and then look at the cock that is yours for eternity."

Still on the floor, I sat beneath the dripping prick, mouth open like some baby bird. Long strings of precome tantalized me while feathers rained down to such an extent I thought Berthold's wings would become threadbare. As the angel clung to the interloper's neck, the wings flapped and kept up the wind that brought back the familiar maelstrom only more so, like we were headed for hurricane territory.

"I shall save him from himself and from you," Berthold declared, voice straining. And then he let go of Magnus and the beast staggered back, turned upon the angel, and attempted to grab him. "Come here, you little shit. I'll show you charity. I'll fuck your angelic ass."

Berthold was too swift for capture and flew to the window, perched on the sill with wings outstretched like some gargoyle. He was magnificent, I'll give him that. The mighty wings on the heavenly body were impressive but then Magnus was running at him, cock in the lead. "I'll fuck you raw," he growled and I felt the carpet begin to bunch under me, undulating like an ocean, and I was lifted up, carried a couple feet and dropped as from a wave, then picked up again, propelled away from the fight until, after several such waves, I landed on the kitchen floor. There I remained, head spinning, as the battle continued without me.

Lying on the tile, I had nothing left, not even the will to sit up. I listened to thumps and crashes, to threats of fucking, to declarations of saving the poor wretch. The dishwasher was running again and the blender seemed to be trying to get going but couldn't sustain itself. The timer had gone quiet. I heard the doorbell ring a couple more times, then stop so abruptly I wondered if one angel had killed the other—or was it even possible for angels to die? Maybe Magnus was fucking Berthold or maybe Berthold had won, vanquishing the fallen, and he would soon come to raise me up again and lead me toward rapture. At this point I wouldn't mind being saved.

Suddenly I was thirsty. And ravenous. When had I last eaten? Getting to my feet, I felt as if my innards had been consumed. I rummaged in the fridge, found an apple and water, and began eating and drinking like a starving man. I then cautiously ventured into the living room.

They were gone, and in their wake my apartment was a disaster. The carpet was unstuck from the floor and bunched in waves. The canoe painting was on the sofa and the sofa was in the middle of the room while the overstuffed chair was at the front door, like it had tried to escape. Books were scattered, blinds were half-ripped from windows, and lamps were on their sides. Feathers were everywhere.

A "what now?" rattled around inside my head but I didn't let it land because nobody was there to answer except me, and I had pretty much nothing to offer myself. I didn't know if the battle was over or if they were simply between rounds, each side regrouping for the final melee in which they'd take down the entire building.

Finishing my apple, I was suddenly aware of my nakedness and hurried to dress in shorts and tee, wondering how long I'd been naked and, beyond that, how long I'd been in a combat zone. Time had gotten away along with everything else. Calm was welcome yet fragile, uncertain. Relief crept in but I didn't trust it. I tried the TV and found the cable working but maybe Magnus was just changing venues. Maybe the dishwasher would break and the Sears man would fuck me.

And just because I didn't at that moment feel like killing myself didn't mean Berthold had prevailed. What if I tried to kill myself right that minute? I could slash my wrists, except it sounded way too messy to prove a point.

Alone, I fell into an encumbered sort of limbo which led me to resist straightening the apartment. I sat amid the shambles for the rest of the day and at night avoided the TV. Instead I picked up feathers. They alone merited attention and I enjoyed their soft feel, so welcoming and warm. One by one I gathered them into a pillowcase because a bag—plastic or paper—seemed too crass for angel debris. But what then? Stuff something?

I then resumed half my life. For the next two days I showered, shaved, dressed, ate, drank, waiting not actively but passively for some sign as to the outcome of my personal angel war. I busied myself with cleaning the apartment while anticipation clung much like Berthold had to Magnus in that final round. Any minute I expected to hear "ViaTel Cable" and I found myself open to another storm of feathers and sex, but after two days I allowed that the angels had fled and worse, hadn't the courtesy to tell me who won the battle. Did I feel better for this? Yes and no. I was no longer determined to end my life, but what was left was far from improved. At this, anger began to rise, creating my own inner maelstrom, and in this unsettled state I had nowhere to turn but Dr. Hardy. Yet when I finally sat before him, I told him none of what had happened.

He attributed my melancholy to grief at Robert's leaving and I let him follow this path as it got us to the same place—abandonment. And when he got around to his usual bit about my moving on, I resigned myself to take his advice. "Are you painting these days?" he asked.

"No."

"Wouldn't it be rewarding to return to something so fulfilling? Something you can accomplish on your own? Don't look to others for your answers, Philip, not even me. It's all within you, awaiting your attention."

I sighed. None of this was new.

"You had a showing last year at the art co-op on Tenth Street, didn't you?"

"Yes."

"Well, they're having another. Perhaps you should go. Reconnect with other artists. Let their work inspire you, the atmosphere encourage you. View the larger world, Philip. Plus it will get you out of the house."

"I suppose I could go."

When I left Dr. Hardy that day I could feel his sense of accomplishment more than my own. He could go on about his life content that he'd repaired someone while I, the subject, had to dredge up the will to get myself to the gallery, which I did, even if reluctantly.

Ordinarily I loved entering the colorful storefront, but this night I dragged along a good measure of resentment that repairs were necessary. My life having been turned upside down, I prepared to approach everything like some elderly curmudgeon gotten up on the wrong side of the bed but, of course, that's impossible in the face of creative splendor.

The gallery fairly thrummed with energy. As always, it boasted every medium: painting, drawing, sculpture, pottery, textiles, mobiles, and even a couple of electronic pieces. And my favorites: art from found objects. Debris turned to pictures and sculptures and all manner of things, they were of wood, plastic, paper, cardboard, you name it.

I found myself smiling at a whimsical wire construction dangling like string and at child's blocks made of paper. There were lush woven pieces, indistinct shapes in rich purples and pinks that begged a touch and next to this, weathered steel constructions that appeared ancient. A series of bamboo dolls held out their little arms in welcome while a tall tempera-colored cardboard man leaned forward, as if bowing.

I saw people I knew but didn't linger because they kept asking about Robert or consoling me over his loss. Working my way along, I enjoyed Dr. Hardy's sense of the larger world. Yes, Doctor, you were right that one could not remain in the self alone while experiencing a riot of color and texture.

The back wall held three remarkable pieces by one artist, a Robin Marks, and here I was absolutely captured. All from found objects, the two outer works merited close attention and I found all sorts of bits—grass made of bobby pins, a tree of cardboard, a picket fence of ice cream sticks. Splashed with bold color, they cheered me and I allowed them a good amount of consideration before turning to the center work because I knew when I gazed upon it, I would be transported.

It was a plump feathered figure, neither bird nor man, yet possessed of life. Its wings were outstretched and angled upward as if taking off. I couldn't resist touching it and found the feathers quite real and lush. White, full, soft, and surprisingly warm, they brought back a thrill and then someone was at my side. I turned, half expecting Berthold, but it was a red-haired man who simply smiled.

"It's wonderful," I managed to say, and when he nodded I asked if he was the artist.

"Yes, Robin Marks. I'm pleased you like it."

"I'm Philip Krantz, painter, and this is the most original and welcoming piece in the entire gallery. I like your other two but this one, the feathers, it just captures me." I went on and on, unable to stop myself from gushing while also enjoying that budding tingle of attraction that infects the entire body rather than just the crotch. How long since I'd been taken with a man this way?

"You must forgive me for touching them," I said as I swept my fingertips over the feathers, "but I can't resist. I love the texture. It's like the wings are going to reach out and wrap around me."

"It's quite all right," he replied. "Your connecting with the work is my reward."

He had carroty red hair and green eyes, fair skin, an imperfect nose and jutting chin which gave him a homespun accessibility. I'd never cared for redheads, yet on him any other color would have fallen short.

I wanted to ask him where he got the feathers but didn't because I was afraid of the answer. Did he raise chickens or some other larger fowl? Pluck an angel? Had he seen battle in his apartment? Bagged a pillowcase full and made them into art?

Robin began to discuss his work and I sank into listening. His enthusiasm at scavenging bits and pieces around the city was enticing. I envisioned us trekking the streets together, sharing excitement at a scrap of wood or bit of wire. As he explained how he worked, I glanced at his feathered creature and arrived at a decision. Berthold had won the battle and nobody had told me because things didn't work that way. Part of the process was for me to come to conclusions on my own and thus reconnect with myself. I was taking charge of my life at last, valuing it as I engaged with Robin and embraced possibility. I turned to him and suggested we go for coffee.

"I'd love to," he said.

We beamed at one another and I couldn't resist a revelation. "You know, I have these feathers…"

Before Darkness Falls
Jay Starre

Lance was afraid. Very afraid.

He didn't consider himself a coward, but the dudes after him were insanely violent. Psychotic, in fact. Their threats were all too real.

The heat and remoteness of the Arizona desert where his cabin hid among saguaro and sand was no defense against these relentless criminals. A drug deal gone bad, and he was caught in the middle with few choices.

If he ratted on his connection, these guys would leave him be. But poor Danny and Hector would not be so lucky. He felt like vomiting when he imagined the pair with their heads bashed in, which just might be their fate—if he wanted to prevent the same from happening to him.

The two were just happy-go-lucky college dropouts who liked to get high on pot and had lots of friends who were willing to pay them for some of the good shit. It had worked for a while for all of them. But with all things illegal and unregulated, someone got greedy, or careless.

Now he owed his dealers a shitload of money, which he had no hope in hell of coming up with. And Danny and Hector, the ones who got ripped off and couldn't pay him for what he'd fronted them, were as broke as him. Ripped off. Who would have thought?

Trying to clear his head after downing four consecutive cups of coffee, he headed out to the one place where no one would disturb him. Less than a mile from his cabin, the wash was always deserted and usually safe from flash flooding this time of year.

He'd discovered the cavern with its caved-in roof when he was just a kid, and he'd fled there ever since when troubles in his life grew too unbearable. Like when his mom and dad died in a car crash, or when his boyfriend left him for some pretty twink from L.A.

Today brilliant sunlight splashed down through the opening in the ceiling to illuminate the dusty ochers and golds of the sand and rock that covered the cavern floor in jumbled disarray.

He liked the echoing quiet and the stark barrenness of the place. He liked the way he felt enclosed and safe by the rocky walls and the low entrance from the wash that no one could enter without him seeing them. He liked the way the huge rent in the roof let in the sun and the sky and let out his thoughts of despair and fear.

Dressed in heavy boots against the desert critters that might bite, cut-off jean shorts, and a tight khaki green T-shirt, he perched on a large boulder near the back where he could watch that entrance, even though there was no chance anyone would actually come through it. He took a deep breath and attempted to gather his thoughts.

It was no good. That giddy fear crowded in immediately and blocked all rational thought.

He stood up and paced, then tried a few yoga stretches in the hopes of calming himself. His muscles bulged and flowed, which always made him feel a little better. He had time to work out regularly with the money he made from selling pot at least, and getting high didn't seem to affect his ability to pump weights.

Today he was off the stuff. He was too freaked out and pot only made him more paranoid when he was already nervous. So when he first noticed the sky shimmering above him, he knew it wasn't a drug-induced hallucination.

Maybe he was just going nuts.

Then—

The pristine blue of the December sky broke apart in a blaze of golden light, a trumpet blast paralyzed him in his tracks, and an apparition emerged from the blazing tear in the heavens.

A dark figure. Wings opened up and spread wide, black as midnight and immense. Dangling from the slowly flapping wings, a figure shimmered in an array of opalescent navy blues, deepest purples, and darkest emeralds.

"I am the angel Jacob. I am a servant of the Dark Lord sent to greet you."

The voice was like a thunderclap and Lance cringed, now totally freaked out. His throat constricted in awe and fear as he made a croaking protest. "I don't believe in religion and God and the devil and all that shit!"

The angel fluttered downward so that he hovered directly overhead, the beating of those opalescent wings offering a cool breeze that wafted over Lance something like the breath of spring. In fact, he imagined he smelled spring, flowing water, sprouting grass, fragrant buds.

That thundering voice now grew more subdued. It still echoed eerily in the quiet of the cavern but was soft and liquid rather than booming and strident. "It doesn't matter what you believe. I am here to help you. You must make a decision. That decision will not only affect the course of your life, but the destiny of your soul."

"Fuck yeah. Don't I know it?" he managed to blurt out.

But now that his heart had stopped pounding violently in his chest and he'd managed to catch his breath, he was able to take a closer look at the floating figure above.

Winged, yes, but for all intents and purposes a man too. A long and slender body was encased in shimmering leather, a silver-zippered vest, long chaps that encased lithe thighs and calves and bulged at the crotch where another silver zipper gleamed. Hints of the same midnight emeralds and purples that shot through those immense wings glinted in the snugly fitting garb.

Odd dress, he thought briefly, but then bit back a hysterical laugh as he recognized how ridiculous the entire scenario was. He did not believe in angels. No, he did not.

But gazing upward, he dared a look into the flying being's face.

All that opalescent darkness shimmering around Jacob seemed to flow into the jet-black eyes and back out. All the more startling due to the fact the angel was blond, a dark-blond yes, but blond nevertheless. Above those black eyes, finely sculpted blond brows arched, while below a porcelain-pale face was dominated by a generous mouth with full lips and straight teeth. Wide cheekbones and a long straight nose and firm chin all lent a solidly human aspect to the otherworldly nature of the creature.

He tore his eyes away as the angel beat his massive wings and dropped a little lower. Now just above him that jock-strapped crotch hovered. He gasped and shuddered as he witnessed a definite bulge growing there. He imagined quite clearly an all-too-human cock swelling and lengthening behind the opalescent leather.

His own crotch stirred, so suddenly and so violently he actually jerked on his feet and thrust upward with his hips. Sweat broke out on his body in a sudden flush. He trembled all over as his cock strained against the buttoned fly of his cut-offs.

He fought for control and fell back onto his natural cynicism. "So what's the deal? Are you going to lecture me, give me some sage advice, or tempt me to sell my soul for a way out of my fucked-up situation?"

"No. I am going to offer you a few hours of something else. A few hours of divine sharing. No lecture. Just us—and some of what you need the most right now. We have until darkness falls."

Enigmatic it might have sounded, but Lance immediately understood what that offer of sharing meant, or at least he imagined he did. The bulge in that leather jock-strap hovered just above his face, only a scant foot away from his mouth.

Regardless, what followed was so far from anything he could have imagined, it was nearly impossible for him to reconcile what he had believed before with how he felt afterward.

Jacob smiled. It was so shocking in that dark glow that Lance toppled backward, stumbling over the uneven ground. He would have fallen except for the nearly instantaneous movement of the hovering angel.

Hands cupped his face and gently but firmly held him up. That dark jockstrap was in his face. And unzipped!

Cock, stiff and throbbing, reared above his lips and nostrils.

He smelled it. Ripe, rich, earthy, and absolutely irresistible.

"Smell it. Taste it. Suck it."

The command was a sibilant hiss that sent a wave of crazed need rushing through his entire body. He literally flopped and jerked on his feet as he emitted a desperate moan, then did the only thing he could, the only thing he wanted to do, the one thing he needed to do.

He opened wide, stuck out his pink tongue, and began to lap at the turgid shaft now pressing against his mouth and nose. He snorted in air, smelling rife male stench. He groaned as his tongue swept up across the pulsing shank and found the crown. He tongued the oozing piss slit, then with a whimper swallowed the head and sucked.

He was no longer standing on the ground!

The hands that cupped his chin were gentle, but somehow supported him as he floated several feet off the cavern floor and gurgled around the leaking knob sliding around inside his wet mouth.

The angel pumped his face, a steady thrust that quickly sought out his tonsils and slithered beyond. In what seemed a mere instant, Lance was deep-throating that angelic prick with slobbering greed.

It was absolutely amazing. He'd never been all that good at opening up to a throat-probing, but this time it was impossibly easy. He felt the smooth balls of the floating angel nestling against his chin, and the throb and pulse of all that fat cock between his lips, across his tongue, and deep in the tight cavern of his throat.

He reached up with trembling arms and embraced the angel's slim waist. Jacob's body swelled outward where the fullness of his hips and buttocks reared, while smooth leather pressed against Lance's sweaty flesh and damp T-shirt.

Angelic cock pulsed in his mouth in a matching rhythm to both the beating of his own heart and the flapping of those immense dark wings above. They rose higher as Lance gurgled and whimpered. As that thick pole throbbed in his throat, he felt his own cock throbbing down in his tight cut-offs, begging for release.

He was afraid to let go of the angel's waist, even though the need to release his aching rod was nearly overwhelming. He contented himself with smacking his lips and drooling as he sucked at the base of the stiff meat in his mouth, then snorting in air when it slid back from his throat to allow him a chance to breathe.

"There is more. Taste me. Explore me."

The echoing demand vibrated in his head and chest, yet the command seemed only to be an extension of what he desired. Yes! He wanted more. He wanted to explore! His mouth slid off the pulsing prick and journeyed downward. The angel's cock and balls spilled out of the opening in his leather jockstrap to hang in the air before him. Those nads were full and silky smooth as he lapped at them, emitted a choked moan, then sucked them in, one at a time.

Sucking on those round balls had him quivering and panting. He sensed the angelic seed within and all at once craved it with all his being. Perhaps that nut-juice would contain the magical answers to his own frightening predicament!

He banished the rush of mingled hope and fear and moved to explore further. He allowed the balls to slip from his wet lips and traveled lower. Beneath the dangling sack he discovered a strip of dark leather that snaked down and backward between the round buttocks.

Just as he began to lap at it, Jacob moved himself. It was a fluid shift, hardly disturbing their floating embrace. The hands that had maintained a gentle grip on his face slid away. They settled on the underside of the angel's knees and pulled up and back, while Lance's hands followed to slide off Jacob's waist and onto the satin-smooth flesh of his naked ass.

He glanced upward and gasped. Those black orbs beneath the blond brows had grown decidedly brighter. Now they were a liquid shade of deep brown. And there was more. Above Jacob's smiling face, the beating wings glowed with a brighter sheen, the emeralds, magentas, and blues less dark and more brilliant.

But even as he gazed at that subtle but magical transformation, his attention was drawn back to what reared in his face now, the angel's beautiful spread ass.

His own hands had slid over the bare mounds already. Firm, absolutely smooth, and as porcelain pale as the angelic face, they were wide open and exposed for his perfect view.

Between the pale cheeks, that leather strap snaked from the bottom of the jockstrap to the waistband of the leather chaps. It was a dark slash dividing the pristine mounds, hiding and protecting the hole behind.

The leather chaps encased Jacob's lithe thighs and outlined his lush butt cheeks. The dark leather only made those cheeks appear even paler, almost translucent. Lance moaned, suddenly desperate to taste the cheeks, the crack, and the trapped hole under that protective strap.

Floating in the air suspended by a gentle wave of air from beneath that seemed to swirl down and up from those beating wings, he feasted on that exposed ass. Jacob had both of his own hands behind his knees to pull them up and toward his chest, allowing free access to Lance's hungry mouth, lips, and tongue.

Free access to everywhere—except that hidden hole! He licked the solid expanse of round ass cheek, he tasted the all-too-human sweat that beaded there, he lapped at the tight strap that divided those lovely cheeks, he kissed gently, then licked with moaning greed all over.

His mouth settled on the strap right where he sensed the hole beneath. He sucked on it almost desperately. All at once he was again aware of his own trapped prick, straining against the fly of his tight cut-offs. It was trapped, and he could not free it! So was that hole, the doorway to the angel's secrets trapped along with it.

Sucking on that restraining strap, he groaned inwardly as he fought for the will power to tear it away, to free the hole and to take possession of it. His fingers slid to the base of the jockstrap and found a snap. He could release the strap if he dared! Did he dare?

"Yes! Do it. Free me and taste me!"

His fingers shook violently as they tore open that snap. The strap fell away. He pulled back and stared.

Hole! Pink and snug, twitching just slightly. He groaned aloud this time as he dove for it. His mouth attached itself to the puckered rim and his tongue stabbed at the tender center. The hole pouted and yielded and he was inside.

Now his cock surged in his shorts as it struggled for release. But he could not find the courage to drop his hands and let it out. Instead he devoured the pulsing maw, sucking, licking, probing, searching for the delicious secrets within.

It yielded totally. Jacob floated above him with legs spread wide and succulent asshole pink and dripping. It was everything, yet it was not enough.

"Come. You know you need to. Fuck your angel."

The sibilant hiss and the crude words rocked him to the core. He found himself crawling upward with desperate need. Then he was in the angel's arms, his crotch mashing against the spread ass crack, his arms wrapped around the slim but powerful chest.

He looked into eyes now turned honey-gold.

Gasping, he reared backward and looked up at the flapping wings. Emerald had turned almost golden, magenta almost pink, navy blue now nearly sky blue. The transformation was shocking.

Jacob kissed him. He felt the angel's tongue slither between his lips and he lunged against the floating body, driving his trapped prick directly against the hole he'd just been eating with such greed.

As that tongue delved between his gaping lips, he struggled to fuck that spread ass, thrusting and humping with a growing desperation. His prick was still trapped, even though the angel's hole was free and his for the taking. He wanted it! He needed it!

"You can take it. You must take it. You must."

The words reared up in his mind. It was Jacob speaking to him, or it was his own voice urging him to take courage and to move.

His hands dropped to his own waist. He tore at his cut-offs. They fell away almost miraculously, along with his skivvies. Except for his tight T-shirt and heavy boots, he was naked now. His prick, released from its confinement, lunged with a will of its own.

He buried it in the angel's pulsing hole.

Jacob kissed him as he fucked him. It was a near-violent collision, tamed only by the steady beating of those mighty wings and the updraft that cradled them as they writhed and humped against one another.

The angel's wet hole sucked in his prick, gripped it with pulsing possessiveness, then released it with gaping generosity. Lance fucked and fucked and fucked.

It was both liberating and frightening. He just couldn't seem to get enough, and on top of that something else was happening to Jacob, and to him.

The golden eyes were growing lighter, now almost green. The flapping wings above shimmered with hints of lightness, the odd feather transformed to snow white. Beautiful and glorious and wonderful, but there was more.

He was undergoing a nearly irresistible transformation of his own. Now that he was naked and exposed, his own ass felt equally vulnerable and exposed. As he pounded deep into the angel's willing fuck-pit, his own asshole began to pulse and twitch.

His muscular thighs fell wider apart. He reared up and wriggled, his ass cheeks opening, his hole growing more and more sweaty and slippery and loose. Eventually he found himself flopping between the angel's upended legs, his own legs wide open, his own ass wide open, his own hole yielding and greedy and hungry. The harder he fucked the angel's seething hole, the more his own hole gaped and yawned with a rising greed for attention.

Even though he had what he wanted, his prick pumping that sweet, angelic slot, it was not enough. He had to have more.

Jacob pulled away, his tongue sliding from Lance's mouth with a sloppy smack.

"Yes. It is time. Time for me to tell you my story. And time for you to surrender your greed."

Again, Jacob moved with such fluid ease it happened almost without a halt in their writhing, humping connection. Lance was turned around with Jacob behind him. The angel's lithe, leather-clad thighs slipped between his. That thick angelic prick slid between his powerful ass mounds and found his wet, aching hole.

It entered him so smoothly he could only rear backward and swallow. The entire length snaked into his gut, deeper and deeper until he felt those smooth balls slapping against his sweaty ass crack.

Then Jacob fucked him. He flopped helplessly in the angel's arms as cock gored him. It was not a gentle fuck, but for all its pounding intensity, it was far from violent. It was merely all-consuming.

He gave himself up to it. Legs dangling wide apart, he surrendered his hole to the driving heat ramming in and out relentlessly. His own prick remained hard and pulsing between his thighs, even as his hole grew wetter and more yielding to the angel's lunging greed.

Then Jacob spoke to him.

"I was once as you are now. Frightened and unable to make my choice, even though the choice was clear. The Archangel Erasmus had rallied against the Lord of the Heavens, defying what he claimed was the despotism of God's rule. Erasmus's voice cajoled with promises that rooted in our vanities and our greed. I fell under his spell. I joined him to defy heaven itself."

Prick slid in and out of Lance as Jacob spoke, possessing him as clearly and completely as he imagined the Archangel Erasmus possessed Jacob on that long-ago occasion.

He sympathized with Jacob's story, but his emotions were so tattered and torn, all he could do was flop helplessly in the throes of the exquisite fuck and try not to think, not to think of his own dilemma and his own fears and choices.

That's when he noticed the angel's final transformation. The sun had slipped off, no longer shining down through the rent in the cavern ceiling, and in fact it had obviously set. The sky above was growing dark.

When darkness falls, their time would be up, Jacob had told him earlier!

Suddenly Lance was desperate again. He reared back against the pounding prick, gulping at it with his greedy asshole. Although he hadn't the courage to speak aloud, inwardly he begged the angel not to leave him, not to abandon him to his miserable fate.

"I followed the wrong leader. I was banished, doomed to this existence. My fate is to repeat my own mistake with others, such as you, endlessly, until perhaps one day I will be redeemed. Lance, can you find it within yourself to redeem me?"

The flapping wings above him suddenly burst into brilliant snow-white glory.

He was almost blinded. Then he was released, finding himself on the floor of the cavern and gazing upward.

Jacob floated there, so beautiful it hurt his eyes to look at him. The dark leather that encased his lithe body was now pure white. The wings too. The eyes, once midnight black, were now brilliant emerald. The smile was exquisite.

"Thank you!"

Lance reached up, sobbing and shaking, his asshole quaking, his prick aching.

The angel released a shower of seed, his mighty cock spraying in gobs of shimmering light.

Lance groaned aloud as he too spewed. Orgasm rocked him to the core as those shimmering droplets rained down on him.

Darkness fell like a hammer blow. Jacob was gone.

❖

The jail cell was stark and bare, but clean enough. It had been a month since he'd been incarcerated and he was slowly growing used to the confinement and the boredom. An odd tranquility had settled over him even as he counted off the days of his eighteen-month sentence.

After Jacob had disappeared, Lance gathered his shattered wits and battered emotions and headed straight to the police. They struck a deal. He turned in the creeps who were threatening him, but refused to turn in Danny and Hector. The pair weren't bad guys, just young and foolish, kind of like himself.

So the cops hadn't let him off entirely. He was fine with that, though. He felt like he needed some kind of punishment for his mistakes. He'd imagined the jail sentence might help him redeem himself.

And last night that hope had been realized.

In the quiet of the night, Jacob appeared. Gloriously white, shimmering above his lumpy bed, a beaming smile on his face.

"I am now yours, Lance. Your guardian angel. I have been forgiven because of your actions. Shall we celebrate?"

Sheer exhilaration soon became sheer rapture as the angel gathered him up in his arms and made love to him. The jail cell no longer seemed a prison as they writhed lustily in sweaty joy from one end of it to the other.

That night had been blissful, and Lance had more of the same to look forward to. Now when darkness fell, the light of his angel would come to comfort him. He was no longer alone. He had made the right choice.

The Hate Patrol

Joseph Baneth Allen

I always love watching Reyn's skinny fingers as they move across the computer keyboard with the agile gracefulness of a concert pianist.

Even when Reyn twists the cap off a two-liter soda bottle, his long fingers always move with such a casual, yet deliberate elegance that whispers of a bygone era of Hollywood glamour where even lighting a match for a lady's cigarette was a carefully choreographed affair.

Reyn was also well practiced when it came to deploying the masterful touch of his fingers upon my body. I smiled a bit as I stretched in bed, recalling our most recent bedroom romp. As always, Reyn had proven himself a master of innovative play with his fingers, tongue, and feathers. With a few millennia behind him, Reyn has had more than enough ample time and experience to perfect techniques and to think up a few new ones.

In order to distract myself from tempting thoughts that would undoubtedly interfere with Reyn's attempt to hack into Assistant District Attorney Pamela Gambert's computer, I returned to attempting to read today's *Florida Times-Union.* Our paperboy Daniel Newsome had so thoughtfully tossed the paper into the dew-drenched yard earlier this morning only half-wrapped in its protective plastic sleeve. Dan was definitely not going to get his usual Christmas bonus this year if he continued to deliver my newspapers sopping wet.

I nibbled on a chocolate-chip muffin Reyn had brought up for me from the kitchen and placed the damp front, business, and sports sections of the First Coast City's finest fish wrap up on the window ledge beside our bed to dry out for later reading in the rays of the early morning sun. The metro section had been insulated by the other sections and was fairly dry. Good fortune had once again smiled upon my barely legal, eye-candy twink of a curly raven-haired paperboy with the mischievous blue eyes.

Even after all three local news affiliates had stories in their evening broadcasts on an assault that occurred last night off Lara Street in downtown Jacksonville, no detail-laced story graced the front page of the paper or the metro section. So I delved into the section's back pages in search of Amelia Lumb's daily "Law & Disorder" column and found that she had devoted four small paragraphs to what she described as a mugging that left the middle-aged male victim in serious condition at Shands Hospital.

I set the paper aside on the rumpled comforter. Nothing new was to be gleaned and teased out of those powder-puff paragraphs that the paper passed off as hard crime news. Any confirmation of Reyn's and my suspicions that the latest reported assault was the seventh in a string of late-evening attacks on gay men of various ages that had left four men dead and two others still recovering from being beaten to within an inch of their lives was going to have to come from whatever information Pamela Gambert was closely guarding in her locked computer files.

Prior hacking expeditions into her computer had yielded treasure troves of information Reyn and I had put to good use in keeping the cogs and grooves of daily life pleasant and well oiled for our fellow neighbors throughout Jacksonville.

Yet Reyn, it appeared, was just stymied with the lack of usable information forthcoming from the ADA's hard drive. By now his fingers had stopped doing their Fred Astaire and Ginger Rogers routine on the keyboard and were now performing a silent drum tattoo over the keys.

"ADA Gambert just may have become smarter than the average bear," Reyn said. He got up from his chair and stretched his arms outward from his body. His wings followed suit, their ivory-white feathers sparking as they caught and reflected the morning sunlight streaming into our bedroom.

Now that caught my complete attention—even as his wings folded back to reveal the full glory of his muscular, almost smooth, lean body. Whatever the attributes were that had made Gambert heralded as one of the toughest prosecuting attorneys this side of the St. Johns River, being computer competent wasn't one of them.

"Changing a password doesn't mean she's now become an uber-geek," I said. "More than likely Mike Ranieri changed it after reading some memo the city IT department e-mailed to all city employees."

I had worked for the city of Jacksonville for several years as an internal auditor prior to Reyn's arrival in my life. During that period I had encountered Mike out and about in city hall and the federal courthouse. Mike was a nice enough guy, but why he had mistakenly chosen to climb the city's career ladder as the assistant to an absolute bitch like Pamela Gambert was beyond any rational being's explanation and mine as well. It would be just like him to take immediate action on a techie compliance issue to please her—as if anybody could. Love was indeed wonderful, blind and strange, but in poor Mike's case, it had manifested itself into the form of a ball-busting dominatrix, and he its willing minion.

"New passwords are only part of the problem," Reyn said. He now arched his back, with his fingers reaching for the floor behind him, and I again found myself wondering how he managed to maintain perfect balance with his wings fully deployed behind him. "Her desktop now has tracking software installed on it. If I log into her computer from here, the city's IT department can trace my tracks through the Internet no matter how well I cover them.

"Entertaining some of Jacksonville's finest and answering questions as to how and why I'm hacking into an assistant district attorney's computer isn't my idea of spending my day. Had enough of explaining things to them on the night when we first met."

Like all guardian angels, Reyn had been watching over me since I had drawn my first breath outside the womb. He'd only physically manifested himself after a former corrupt city council president tried to kill me when I'd discovered how she had swindled travel funds out of the city's coffers.

"Oh, now that is a game changer," I said, mulling what we should do next. I sighed, pulling up my legs and cupping my chin in my hands, and rested my elbows on top of my knees. "Obviously she's become more than a bit suspicious due to our past activities, so, our next step should be to hack in from a computer at a different location than here and see what happens."

Reyn gave me a lopsided smile as he modestly stepped into the walk-in closet we shared. "Your former coworker Mike also took the extra caution of requiring two additional logins with separate passwords."

"Just peachy," I grumbled. I sat silently stewing over how to obtain the two logins and passwords we needed as I waited for Reyn to finish dressing.

He walked out of the closet about a minute later, wearing tan Lacoste chinos and a plain white, long-sleeved Lacoste polo shirt. A plain white Hanes T-shirt under the polo further concealed any of his sun-bronzed skin that might have peeked out of the polo shirt. He had tucked his wings back into the heavenly realm.

A pair of small silver wire-rimmed glasses now perched atop his nose. Contact lenses concealed his azure eyes and camouflaged them into ordinary brown ones. His wavy dark brown hair was now slicked down and pushed off his forehead. Somehow Reyn had even managed to find those clunky black clodhoppers he wore for shoes from where I had previously hidden them. His transformation into a computer nerd didn't surprise me.

Reyn usually went for the well-rounded geeky look when passing as an ordinary human to avoid being given the second glance individuals of his height—six foot seven inches—usually get from gawkers and passers-by.

"Angels and their natural abilities are bound by the physical laws that were woven into the universe at Creation's dawn," Reyn had once told me at the very beginning of our relationship. So physically disguising himself with a facade of clothes was less time consuming than outright changing his physical appearance.

Satisfied with his appearance after giving himself a once-over in the closet door mirror, Reyn came over and we embraced over a lingering kiss.

"I'm going to try my luck at Tokyo University's computer lab," he said when our lips and bodies finally parted. He gave me a wicked smile. "I'll try to be back after lunch."

He was gone before the pillow I lobbed at him could make contact. It bounced harmlessly against the dresser before coming to rest on the floor. Sure, he'd spend some time attempting to hack into Gambert's computer from some untended computer in one of the labs there, but when the hacking eventually failed to breach Mike's firewall, Reyn would be off to our favorite store in Tokyo—Akihabara, with its eight full floors of sublime anime goodness.

If karma smiled upon me, it would extract its revenge at Akihabara in the form of giggling pubescent Japanese schoolgirls who would encircle the tall "American" and shower him with all sorts of unwanted attention. Still, I wasn't going to count on karma to do my dirty work for me.

Getting out of bed and taking a shower to clean off the dried sweat from last night's activities was the first step in my brilliantly evil plan for getting back at Reyn for making a side trip to Akihabara without me. To get full and complete access into Gambert's computer, we needed those passwords. Mike had been, and still probably was, a creature of extreme habit. When I worked for the city, he had kept all his computer passwords neatly written on a small piece of paper he kept behind his driver's license in his wallet, and probably still did so.

I stepped out of the shower and began toweling myself dry. All I needed to do was nick Mike's wallet inside the Duval County Courthouse in front of a whole bunch of witnesses. No problemo there. I'd return it after memorizing the passwords, of course. Yet my presence and my history with local and federal law enforcement would draw unwanted attention. Like Reyn, I too would need to be in disguise, and for that I would require the services of our very own resident makeup wizard, Elsie Conley.

Elsie is an authentic old-fashioned Hollywood-era diamond with a heart and soul of pure blinding gold the good folks out in La La Land had seen fit to toss on their refuse heap many years ago. Reyn had first brought her to our home in the South Mandarin section of suburban Jacksonville about a year after we had started living here. When Reyn had first introduced me to Elsie, his eyes had flashed the resolve and defiance of those of a little boy daring his parents to say no to keeping the stray puppy dog he had brought home.

The silly boy needn't have worried. I had absolutely fallen in love with Elsie the moment I laid eyes upon her. Still, as much as Elsie reciprocated my feelings toward her back then and now, it just wouldn't do to show up in my adopted grandma's room wearing nothing but a smile on my face.

Once I had shimmied into a pair of boxers, I slipped on a robe and made my way down the stairs to the mother-in-suite where Elsie lived.

If Elsie suspected Reyn's true nature, she never let on. She appeared content to believe that he and I were just a wealthy, socially angst-riddled couple who relieved our anxieties by performing mitzvahs by dressing up in various disguises, which she created. Elsie's silence was her good-natured way of bribing us to keep her.

Speaking of mitzvahs and bribes, I stopped off briefly in the kitchen to whip up her favorite morning repast: a hot white chocolate mocha with toaster waffles topped off with a dollop of maple syrup. Empty hands are never a good way to approach a co-conspirator.

Elsie's green eyes crinkled up with delight when she saw me enter with the breakfast tray. Her domain is one of modern domestic comforts surrounded by framed posters of all the movies she had worked on as a makeup artist.

"Ben darling, are you trying to corrupt a sweet little old lady with your tray of goodies?" she playfully jested with a seductive wink. She set down the *National Enquirer* she was reading.

"Guilty as charged, Elsie." I laughed. She accepted the tray from my hands and I sat down beside her. "Reyn is off on an errand I'm afraid he's probably not going to have much success on. When he gets back, I want to surprise him by having the information he needs to enable him to successfully hack into ADA Gambert's computer."

As she daintily ate the breakfast I had prepared for her, I briefly told Elsie how I intended to go about what I needed to do. She gave my request every bit of the studied opinion it required.

"Old Man Number Five should do the trick nicely," Elsie said after a moment's thought. She finished the last bit of waffle and drained the last dregs out of her coffee cup before setting aside her breakfast tray. "Step into my makeup area and disrobe. We'll get started on your transformation once you're seated."

She motioned me over to the chair against the far wall where she nowadays performed her movie makeover magic and went over to the filing cabinet. Within a minute she had found the file of notes and photos she would consult throughout the process of turning me from my vibrant thirty-something self into a decrepit seventy-something old man.

We spent the next three hours on my transformation. Once Elsie had finished creating snow on my mountaintop, she enchanted me once again with tales of rubbing shoulders with Hollywood royalty during her heyday out and about in La La Land.

One of her favorite tales was about being rescued from being raped by a studio boss at the wrap party for *The Glass Bottom Boat.* Her rescuer was a tall, handsome lighting technician whose name she had never learned. Not only had he scrounged up a snazzy replacement dress for her, but had seen her safely home in a cab.

Her unnamed rescuer was even the perfect gentleman; he'd seen her to the door to her apartment and given her a chaste good-night kiss on the forehead before departing. She had never seen him again after she had closed the door to her apartment. "To this very day, I regret not trying harder to find and thank him again," Elsie said.

She never tired of telling the tale and I never got tired of hearing it. Elsie still had the dress—mothproofed and tucked away in her memory chest. All this had happened about some thirty years before I was born. Reyn perfectly matched the description of Elsie's actor in shining armor.

Angels always help more than just one person, and the amount of time they spend with an individual in their charge varies. Yet while I suspected it had been Reyn, my suspicions always remained unvoiced. Romantic mystery and magic are always spoiled by a bit of unnecessary knowledge.

"Good thing you're allergic to the makeup," Elsie said, as she finished retouching the makeup a bit on my face after I dressed in clothing appropriate for the Old Man Number Five disguise. She stepped back a few paces to admire her handiwork. "The red splotches add a nice realistic touch if anyone gets too up close and personal."

"Don't forget my watery eyes." I laughed. My fabricated pot belly shook a bit under my clothes. Applied makeup is just one part of any good disguise. Changing facial shape with rolled-up gauze to alter the shape and contour of the nose and cheeks is another. Chunking or bulking up the body with padding also works wonders. Elsie had truly transformed me into someone I truly hoped I never would be, and what she wasn't, when I reached her age.

"You better get going if you want to surprise Reyn before he comes back," she said, sitting back down on her sofa. "I think I'll nap for a bit."

Despite her fussing over ruining my makeup, I managed to plant a thank-you kiss on her cheek before going to snatch up the keys to the Santa Fe. I also pocketed the beat-up wallet holding the fabricated driver's license and other faked credentials for Old Man Appelt, as I liked to call this disguise.

Thankfully traffic along San Jose Boulevard was light as I drove downtown to the Duval County Courthouse. Akihabara's anime selection was going to hold Reyn's interest for only so long, and I wanted to get back before he returned. He never likes me going off on my own—especially if he has to intercede on my behalf.

Reyn doesn't scold, but he does spank if the situation warrants it.

I lost a little time having to take a detour around San Marco due to roadwork being done, but within minutes I was over the gaudy blue Main Street Bridge and had taken the off-ramp leading to East Bay Street. The bridge had been painted blue after a city-wide vote had been held to choose a new color for the bridge when it needed a new paint job. At least it looked better at night with the electric blue lighting added after Jacksonville had won its bid with the NFL to host Super Bowl XXXIX back in 2005.

I lost about another two minutes having to patiently wait for traffic lights to turn green before I could turn off East Bay Street and into the courthouse's rear parking lot facing the St. Johns River. Rummaging through the glove compartment while waiting for my turn to drive through the entrance gate, I found the handicap parking placard to place on the rearview mirror. If the need for a quick escape was in my immediate future, I wanted my getaway SUV to be parked as close as possible to the courthouse.

Luck continued to be on my side, and I was able to snag a handicap parking space about a hundred yards from the courthouse's main rear entrance. I hobbled out of the car with my quad walking cane.

After ambling inside, I emptied my pockets and put my wallet and car keys inside the worn green plastic basket provided to me by a friendly butch security guard. Hawkins was the surname on her gold name badge.

She placed my cane alongside the basket that held my wallet and keys on the conveyor belt and helped walked me through the upright metal detector.

"Now where are you going, dear?" Officer Hawkins asked once the x-ray scans had cleared me to proceed deeper into the courthouse. She handed me back my walker after I re-pocketed my wallet and keys.

"I'm picking up my wife in Room 100," I replied. "She gave me a ring. The civil suit she was a juror on is going to be dismissed. Elsie and the other jurors are just waiting to be released from the case by the presiding judge."

"Even for a person my age, it's quite a bit of a walk to the jury assembly room," Officer Hawkins said. "If you'd like, I could get a wheelchair and take you there. Save some wear and tear on your legs."

Last thing I wanted was an escort, so I smiled and patted her hand in thanks. "Elsie, my wife, is a jealous woman," I said with just a twinge of remorseful regret. "Otherwise I'd let you escort me to the jury assembly room, or anywhere else you'd like to take me."

I resisted the temptation to give Officer Hawkins a sly wink. She rewarded me with a boisterous laugh.

"Just holler for me if you change your mind," she said. I smiled and gave a little wave as I ambled down the corridor. My true destination was the courthouse's main lobby just inside the front Bay Street entrance.

Reyn and Elsie had long tried to get me to channel my natural improvisational skills into acting onstage as part of Jacksonville's community theater scene. Reyn desired me to have a performance outlet so that he'd get to spend less time pulling me out of the hot water I occasionally found myself knee-deep in. Elsie believed it was a pity I didn't perform for a broader audience. Truth was I absolutely sucked when it came to auditioning for roles before overly analytical casting directors.

Neither one of them fully understood that being able to con people into believing you're somebody else in real life is entirely different than pulling off the same trick on a well-lit stage.

Outside of a theater, no one expects the stranger beside them to be playing a real-life role in a disguise. Being able to improvise on the fly also adds to the illusion most people so willingly believe without sparing any additional moments on thinking.

When I stepped into the main lobby, I immediately spied a jittery

Mike Ranieri just stepping back inside from taking a cigarette break. My heart went out a little bit to him as I began walking on a clear and calculated path to bump into him. Once he had been a somewhat decent-looking guy—fit, but not overly firm.

Now he carried an additional thirty-plus-pound paunch he had gained through stress eating. Coupled with the loss of his straight auburn hair, he looked almost twenty years older than he actually was. He hadn't been a smoker prior to working for uber-bitch Gambert. Now his once immaculate hands were badly stained with nicotine.

If anyone was in need of a life intervention, it was Mike. Reyn's azure eyes had turned sorrowful when I had once inquired about the poor performance record of Mike's guardian angel.

"Nothing can be done," Reyn told me back then. "Mike freely chooses his hellish existence every day."

From Reyn's mournful manner, I decided to drop the subject. Heaven's rulebook for angels is a complicated tangle of bureaucratic lingo for a mere mortal, let alone an angel, to comprehend.

"Oh, I beg your pardon, sir," Mike said as he bumped into me. I stumbled forward in a headlong dive. He caught hold of me to make sure I didn't fall. Deep black circles under his eyes only added to the overall bleak condition of his haggard face.

I so badly wanted to treat Gambert to a cane dance.

"Just need to regain my breath," I rasped out in my best Old Man Appelt voice. "Can you help me over to a bench?"

"Sure, sure, it's the least I can do for almost making you fall." Mike acquiesced. He kept apologizing. I felt guilty. His wallet was already resting comfortably in the front pocket of my jacket.

"Would you like me to get you a drink of water?" Mike asked once I had seated myself on a nearby bench.

"No, no thank you. I'll be all right in a minute," I said. I gave him the best smile my artificially aged teeth allowed for. "You've been most kind and helpful. I should have paid more attention to where I was going."

"Not a problem," Mike said. He gave me a halfhearted smile before walking away. Poor guy still wasn't used to being complimented.

With his back turned to me, I quickly rummaged through his wallet and found the passwords where I had suspected they would be. I had to restrain myself from bursting out laughing and calling unwanted attention to myself. Reyn was going to blush later when I got around to telling him what they were. I was a bit pleased with Mike. It was a bit reassuring that at least he still had a tad bit of his cojones left.

My pleasure with Mike's salvaged manhood quickly soured when I saw him being approached by ADA Gambert. She had a laptop with her. From the looks of it, she had been locked out of it. Mike reached for his wallet and realized it was gone.

I was so fucked.

A panicked flight out the courthouse's revolving glass door wouldn't have the finesse I was going to need to extricate myself from this situation. My options for a strategic retreat began to dwindle as both Mike and Gambert exchanged a few frantic bits of conversation before turning to look my way.

Reyn walked by and took the wallet from my shaking hands before Mike and Gambert could set their eyes on me. Mild annoyance mixed with a hearty helping of pure amusement danced in his azure eyes. Sure, he'd come to my rescue. Only he was going to enjoy letting my short hairs get singed a bit.

I did my best to look pleasantly nondescript as Mike and Gambert approached me. "My wallet's missing," Mike said.

Gambert decided to take the more direct approach with her line of accusatory questioning. "Did you take it?"

"I'm nobody's thief," I said a bit indignantly. It was time to go on the offensive against their good cop, bad bitch routine. "He almost knocked me down here in the lobby. Now you have the gall to accuse me of something I didn't do!"

"Excuse me, Mr. Ranieri," Officer Hawkins said. She looked a bit winded. "A good Samaritan turned in your wallet. He said he found it on the men's room floor."

She smiled at me. "How ya doing, sugar? Resting a bit before you collect your wife?"

I used the opening Officer Hawkins had so kindly provided me with. I pointed a shaky hand at Gambert. "That witch accused me of stealing his wallet," I stammered, with just the right measured tone of indignation.

"Now, now, Mr. Appelt," she said. "I'm sure 'witch' isn't the appropriate word here. Is it, Ms. Gambert?"

I was definitely beginning to fall very much in like with her. Not only had Officer Hawkins remembered my false name, but she knew how to properly use words to bitch-slap dullards like Gambert. The assistant district attorney was beet red from embarrassed anger over the situation she now found herself in.

"Sorry for the mistake," Gambert managed to finally sputter out. She shot both me and Officer Hawkins a look of contempt before dragging poor Mike out of the main lobby along with her.

"How dare you make me look bad in front of people with room temperature IQs," we heard Gambert upbraid Mike. "Next time get some hard proof before you even think of accusing somebody of stealing in my presence. Not that a little prick like yourself could get hard about anything."

Officer Hawkins sighed. "Security's going to get a call one of these days that he's beating her to a bloody pulp. Hope she doesn't expect any of us with the room-temperature IQs to come running to her aid."

I guffawed in agreement.

"I better get back to my post." She sighed. "Remember what I said Mr. Appelt. Just send for me if you need any more help. Lucky for both of us some nice man like you turned in Mr. Ranieri's wallet. Otherwise our grand bitch of an assistant district attorney would have created a bit of a sticky wicket—as the Brits would say."

I returned her smile as she walked away. My angel had returned. Reyn was seated beside me.

"Time to get you home before you manage to stir up any more trouble," he said.

Before any words of protest could escape from my lips, Reyn embraced me and we jumped back to our room. Both of us were seated on top of our bed.

In angelic lingo, creating quantum tunnels to travel to destinations in the universe is called jumping. Trekkers who dream of cruising around the galaxy in warp-driven starships wouldn't like the side effects of jumping to get to a planet's surface. If not prepared for it, mortals like me can get severe bouts of nausea followed by dry heaving when we jump. Angels like Reyn aren't bothered by any side effects and can jump whenever they want to.

"You fucking bastard," I managed to get out before the extreme need to vomit forced me to run into the bathroom.

Reyn waited patiently for me to finish retching up the remains of lunch from my stomach. I spent a few extra minutes brushing the taste of bile out of my mouth and away from my teeth. My anger subsided a bit as the nausea finally faded. It's hard for me to stay angry at Reyn for more than just a couple of minutes.

"You were right to get me away from there," I conceded. I stepped out of the bathroom and stripped off my Old Man Appelt disguise. "Would you like the passwords? You can try again to hack into Gambert's computer at Tokyo University. Heck, you can spend an entire day at Akihabara. I won't mind."

"Nice try. Sure, I'll take those passwords, but we'll discuss your punishment later when I get back."

So I definitely was due for a spanking. Still, my little adventure at the courthouse had definitely been worth it when he turned several dark shades of shocked embarrassment over hearing the two choice passwords Mike had selected as his digital gatekeepers.

"I'll try one of Duke's computer student labs," Reyn said after he regained a bit of his normal coloring. "Then I'll bring the Santa Fe home. Be back in a bit."

He was gone before my last bit of clothing hit the bedroom carpet. I occupied myself by taking a long hot shower to erase all traces of the wonderfully effective makeup job Elsie had performed on my body. The red splotches caused by my usual allergic reaction had begun to fade away.

Reyn had returned by the time I finally wrapped a towel around myself and stepped back into our bedroom. Whatever he had downloaded from Gambert's computer must have been really bad. Normally if given the chance, he would spend hours wandering around the campus at Duke, admiring the college's Gothic architecture.

"Come and take a look at what Gambert is concealing," Reyn said. He motioned me to sit beside him at the old World War Two army desk that served as our computer table. Refurbishing it had been one of our more mundane joint projects. While I suspected the desk held another significant tie to his recent past century, I gave him the privacy of that memory.

Gambert's typed musings did not paint a pretty picture. She had speculated a serial killer was attacking gays foolish enough to engage in late-night cruising in the seedier sections of downtown Jacksonville.

Forensics had determined the killer used a lead pipe to beat his victims.

None of the victims were of a specific age range or racial type. Nor had they been raped or sexually mutilated. Angel bureaucracy prevented Reyn from interviewing newly departed for any useful information on identifying the killer. Coupled with the two surviving victims being in medically induced comas at Shands Hospital, Gambert's purloined notes would be all we had to go on.

Reading further, I discovered that forensics had speculated that the pipe was about a foot long. So the killer was getting up close and personal before bashing his victims' brains in. It also meant that this individual was skilled at concealing his weapon.

Lacking in her notes was a plan of action to warn the public and to bring the killer to justice. Gambert had responded negatively to several repeated requests from homicide detectives to enlist the help of Don Mueller—the region's Tallahassee-based FBI profiler.

"Letting Amelia Lumb play with this data dump is sorely tempting," Reyn said.

"Nothing would make me happier than seeing Gambert publically humiliated on the front page of the *Times-Union*," I replied. "Only down side is that poor Mike would get dragged down with her once the true nature of these murders and beatings is revealed."

Reyn sighed. I rested my head on his shoulders. "Let's do a little deeper mining into Gambert's data dump," I suggested. "Maybe we'll discover a behavioral pattern."

We spent the next few hours reading and rereading printouts of Gambert's files. The only break we took was to throw on sweats before having a late dinner with Elsie. After seeing that she was settled for the evening, we went back to our room to redouble our efforts at what seemed like a hopeless task.

Reyn used Google Earth to print out a map of downtown Jacksonville. He used Elsie's bingo markers to highlight each location where an attack had occurred. Immediately a possible behavioral pattern into the attacker's mindset leaped out at us.

"The Landing," Reyn and I said concurrently. All seven of the attacks were clustered around the downtown shopping mall—one of the more popular gay cruising spots in Jacksonville.

I grabbed a ruler and began measuring the distances. Each of the attacks had occurred roughly a half mile from the center of the mall. Using the Landing as a base, I drew lines from the mall to the bingo marker dots indicating the attack sites on the map.

A pattern resembling the spokes of a bisected bicycle wheel emerged. With the mall abutting the St. Johns River, figuring out the location of the next attack was a pretty simple task. All I had to do was measure out the two-block distance between each of the lines on Reyn's map, and draw the next line out in the spoke pattern. If Reyn and I were correct, the next attack was going to take place at the city's waterfront parking garage. It was a pattern that should have jumped out and bit the Duval County sheriff detectives in their collective ass.

Only Gambert had prevented them from seeing it, much less looking for it.

Now that we knew the how and where, all we had to do was to continue to follow the pattern to see where it led us. So our next step was to figure out when. With Reyn's help, I proceeded to write the estimated time each attack occurred with the location each victim had been found at. All the attacks had occurred between Thursday and Sunday, between eleven at night and one in the morning.

We went on to assume that Gambert's notes were accurate with their notations about splattered blood found on the outer walls of the buildings where the victims were found. That section of her notes definitely boosted our working theory that the killer stalked his victims as they left the Landing.

The mall's outdoor stage hosted local and regional bands on Thursday through Sunday evenings. Mall management believed free outdoor music concerts boosted sales for its restaurant and retail tenants.

"Check to see if there's any one particular band that played the night of each attack," Reyn said.

"Already done it," I replied. My laptop had been broken out hours ago. "Pale Gringo has played at the Landing each night an attack occurred."

Reyn raised an eyebrow.

"An alternative Latin band—or so their website states," I replied to his silent inquiry.

"So our killer is either a band member or he simply follows the band," Reyn concluded.

"Pale Gringo's next show is on Thursday." I looked up from the monitor. "That gives us about three days to get ready."

"Meantime, there is a small disciplinary matter I must take care of." Reyn took the laptop away from me.

I playfully eluded his reaching hands.

"Now, Reyn, you'd still be hacking away at some dark, dank computer lab at Tokyo University if it hadn't been for my ingenuity."

"No, I'd still be at Akihabara getting cruised by horny Japanese schoolboys."

The edge of the bed brushed against the back of my legs by the time Reyn had "caught" me. It was at that moment that he made the mistake of attempting to bend me over his knee. He compounded that mistake by opting to remain in his human form. With his tall body in somewhat of an awkward position, it was much easier to flip Reyn on to the bed. I pinned his hands over his head as I straddled him.

"Naughty man," I teased as my lips brushed against the nape of his neck. Reyn arched his back and moaned in pleasure as my tongue began probing his left ear. "Wanting to waste your time on inexperienced twinks who won't even kiss, much less reciprocate unless you force them to."

I removed his T-shirt. My tongue teased his nipples erect before tracing a trail from his soul patch down to the treasure trail below his belly button. I pulled down his sweatpants to reveal the now fully erect prize I was after.

"Worst off all, twinks gag." I had his pants down far enough so that they wouldn't be an impediment. "I don't."

My tongue teased the full length of his cock. Reyn moaned and writhed under me as I continued to remind him why I remained the only current person who could spank his monkey to a satisfactory conclusion.

We spent the next few days scoping out the first floor of the city's waterfront parking garage and reinforcing my self-defense training. Our plan was relatively a simple one. I was going to dangle myself as bait by walking to the parking garage after Pale Gringo's Thursday evening's performance at the Landing.

With luck, the predator we sought would get a very nasty surprise when he tried to get a piece of me.

Reyn worked with me so that I could move easily with the body armor that he insisted I'd be wearing Thursday evening. His ability to protect me from physical harm during this venture would be limited. I'd be knowingly and willingly jaunting off into danger. The rulebook he was governed by was quite clear. Reyn could help me only if I was in danger of immediate death. He could only stand by and helplessly watch if I was getting the snot beat out of me.

At times heavenly guidelines for life with a guardian angel sucked.

Elsie modified a shirt and pair of pants so that they'd easily conceal the Kevlar I was wearing underneath. Steel-toed sneakers were going to be my footwear of choice that evening. The only visible flaw in our plan was that my hands and head would be unprotected.

I made arrangements for Dan to stay with Elsie Thursday evening while Reyn and I were out. Dan always enjoyed hearing her Hollywood stories as much as I did. He was not, I learned, a Pale Gringo fan.

I made a mental note to myself to ask him later why he hung out at a popular gay cruising spot in downtown Jacksonville. Dan perhaps was not so much the innocent as Reyn and I liked to believe.

My stomach remained largely settled when Reyn jumped me over to the Landing early Thursday evening. He gave me a quick kiss before parting company with me. I knew he wasn't going to be far away.

No single individual stuck out as the killer Reyn and I were hunting as people continued to mill around the mall. I did some casual window shopping as I waited for the zero hour to arrive.

As the time grew near for Pale Gringo to take the outdoor stage, I leaned against the railing near the waterfront. From where I was I could see just about everyone who stayed for the concert or just ambled by.

My estimation of Dan's musical tastes went up a bit when the five assorted members of Pale Gringo took to the stage with their guitars and violins and began performing shortly after nine o'clock. Dan was right. Apart from the relative coolness of their bright pink velvet neo-Gothic flamenco guitar player outfits, their music sucked raw eggs.

For the next two hours I kept wishing that wearing earplugs had been an option. The Landing always kept their outer courtyard well illuminated for the evening performances. I had plenty of light to scan the crowd in front of me for anyone who looked like they were scoping out a potential victim.

Only a few rent boys approached me at various times throughout

Pale Gringo's musical nightmare. I waved them away each time. Reyn expressed amusement at their attempts to solicit twenty bucks from me the few times he walked by to check up on me. I discreetly flipped him off.

The Landing's lights dimmed a bit as the five members of the horrific alternative Latin band thankfully announced their last set. As people began to meander back to their cars, I casually strolled back to the garage. No one in particular had caught my attention until I felt the hard, rounded muzzle of a gun pressed against my back.

"Just keep walking, Ben."

I didn't bother to turn my head to confirm what the voice had already told me. Mike was the one holding the gun on me.

I had already been careless by letting him sneak up on me. No sense in compounding the error. I was still safe and alive. Reyn could only act if I was in grave mortal danger. Still, I hated feeling like an absolute schmuck over the ease with which I had been taken.

My inner calf muscles tensed as I pondered an escape attempt. I had been a good sprinter when I ran track at Lejeune High School. Pity I had been absent the day Coach Williams had taught bullet dodging.

Mike must have been reading my body language.

"Running's not going to be an option for you, my friend," he informed me. "Yeah, I figured you'd be wearing body armor. Fortunately, I sprang for the more expensive CZ 75 C 9 millemeter compact, Satin Nickel semi-automatic. The clip contains even fancier cop-killer bullets."

"There are still people around," I pointed out. "Kill me and they'll finger you as the trigger man."

"Yeah, and I can kill them just as easily as I can you. So just keep on walking to the garage. Angel boy ain't charging to your rescue this time." Mike prodded the gun harder against the small of my back. My heart had already leapt into my throat. I complied by picking up my pace a little bit. "He's got to play by the same rules Gambert does. All he's going to be able to do is watch as you commit suicide. Then he'll have to go back to the heavenly realm and I get rid of two thorns that have been in my side for a long time."

Playing stupid about Reyn's true nature was probably going to get me dead a whole lot quicker. I knew Reyn was somewhere out there in the night, between the mortal and heavenly realms, waiting to help me. I had to give him that chance. Nothing was going to be lost by being honestly dumb about Gambert. Maybe being blond might buy me enough time to figure out a way out of this sticky wicket.

"Funny, Gambert never struck me as the angelic type," I said as we continued walking along the sidewalk on East Bay Street. "I always had her pegged more as a sadistic bitch."

I decided to try goading him into hitting me. If I could do that, Reyn would have an opening to rescue me. "I always had you pegged as a bottom pig. Tell me, is she any good with the strap-on? Or did she already have one of her own?"

"Nice try," Mike snorted. "Gambert's my own personal demon. A perfect beard, if you like. An obedient bitch too. She grabs her ankles real nicely in human and demon form when she's told to. Everybody's heartfelt sympathy prevented them from seeing who's really calling the shots.

"I've got that bitch all trussed up in a French maid outfit at my condo. She knows all her holes are going to be fully abused tonight after our business here is finished. Even you were blindsided by my little charade as a submissive bootlicker. You'll have to admit, Mr. Appelt, I'm better at role-playing than you are. I'd suggest modifying your voice a bit to a higher pitch than the one you used—only you're not going to have a next time."

"Ouch," I mumbled. So he had seen through my disguise at the courthouse.

Gambert being a demon meant Reyn and I still had a shot of surviving this night. I prayed Reyn was already on his way to bind and collect her. Reyn's ties to the mortal realm would be severed upon my ascending into the heavenly realm. I was Reyn's anchor. Likewise, Mike would need Gambert alive and kicking if he wanted his perverted murder spree to continue unchecked.

We now were approaching the street entrance to the parking garage. My luck was continuing to head further south. Nary a soul was in sight anywhere inside or outside the garage. Mike nudged me forward again with the tip of his gun.

"Keep walking," he said. "We're going all the way to the top."

"You didn't have to beat five men to death just to smoke Reyn and me out," I said. I felt physically sick that the past interventions Reyn and I had carried out caused the deaths of five men, and probably the eventual deaths of the other two now on life support at Shands.

I had a vague notion of how he intended for my "suicidal" death to occur. By playing for time, I was hoping Reyn could accomplish what I had hoped he was now doing. "Surely you could have thought up a less violent way to get our attention."

"Oh, Ben, you're still thinking of me as Gambert's lapdog." Mike giggled. "I enjoyed it. Licking freshly splattered blood and brain matter off my skin was ever so invigorating. I may continue on after you're gone. I'll need some kind of outside hobby to deal with the pressures of climbing the career ladder all the way to the governorship."

My urge to vomit almost won out. We had now reached the top floor of the parking garage.

"All Reyn and I ever did was help clear innocent people falsely accused of crimes they didn't commit," I retorted. I risked looking back at him. "No sane person could justify what you've done."

"Ben, Ben, silly Ben. Haven't you figured it out yet? I'm a fucking lunatic." Ben giggled again. "Now be a good boy and walk over to the edge."

Not having a better game plan, I complied. I was quickly running out of time. Walking slowly over to the edge, I decided to use public nudity as another stalling tactic.

"Shouldn't I at least strip off the Kevlar before I jump?" I offered. I began unbuttoning my shirt. "Spare you and the DA's office any embarrassing questions about a body wearing bulletproof armor when it washes up along the riverfront."

"Nope. You've got nothing to tempt me with," Mike said. He started squeezing the trigger. "So don't bother. Just jump."

He definitely knew how to hurt a guy whose time on Earth was just about expired.

"Mike, put down the gun!" Reyn roared. He had jumped to about ten feet away from us, and he had brought company. Gambert was with him.

Her legs and arms were bound in iron chains. A snug gag had been fitted between her bloodied lips. The French maid outfit she was wearing had been ripped in various places, exposing skin. Mike had obviously made a fatal error in ordering his pet demon to remain in human form.

Reyn stood beside her. His wings were erect in full angelic glory. He placed a restraining hand on Gambert's shoulder, lest she try to escape. He pointed his sword of living flame at Mike.

"Even trade," Reyn told Mike.

Mike betrayed no emotion for a moment. "Nah. The bitch is worthless to me now."

He brought up his gun and fired. Reyn couldn't save her. Gambert's body pitched backward just as the bullet exited the back of her skull. Dark blood mixed with fragmented bone and gray brain matter stained the pavement.

Now that Gambert had been terminated in her human form, Mike swung the gun around to me.

I took the only option now available to me and jumped over the side.

Reyn caught me in his arms just as I was beginning to fall past the seventh floor. Nasty bruises were going to grace the back of my body due to the Kevlar. Even angelic rescues were bound tightly by the mundane physical laws of force equaling mass multiplied by acceleration.

Reyn carried me upward, past the open eighth floor of the parking garage and well beyond the range of Mike's gun. Mike stared at us for a moment before swallowing the gun barrel and pulling the trigger. Another mess of blood and bone stained the pavement.

Reyn carried me away from the lifeless shells that had once been a demon and her human captor. He was holding me tightly in his arms as he walked across the St. Johns River. A perfect swath of moonlight from the quarter-moon that hung high in the sky shimmered in the dark night waters. Neither one of us was feeling romantic now. Too much death had brought us to this point.

A commuter would undoubtedly discover the bodies of Mike and Gambert sometime in today's wee morning hours. Officer Hawkins would be able to clean up in the office pool over who snuffed out whom first when the sheriff's office released its final report to Amelia Lumb and other members of the Northeast Florida press corps.

Still, when I finally looked up at Reyn, only love mixed with relief showed in his azure eyes. I reached up and cupped his face in my hands.

"Let's go home, beloved," I said.

Our lips touched as Reyn jumped us back home.

Divine Intervention
William Holden

Father, why have you forsaken me?" Haniel sat in the darkened corner as his appointed slept nearby. His wings were folded against his back, exposing the black tips and shades of gray as they led to the layers of white feathers underneath. "Did I not serve you well in the kingdom of heaven? Did I not bathe you when dirt covered your body? Did I not coddle you when you needed lavish touches? Please, Father, speak to me. I fear Nathan will soon wake and I must understand why you have done this to me."

"Haniel, my beloved son, you are indeed one of my favorites and yet you continue to question the roles I choose for you. I have no more abandoned you than I have my kingdom."

"Then why, Father, did you send me to earth to guard over this man?" Haniel glanced toward the tiny cot that Nathan called his bed. "Father, you know of my ways. You yourself have embraced me and taken pleasure from my body. Yet you send me to earth to watch over a priest. A priest, Father, who has taken his vow of celibacy." He could feel the pull of Nathan's mind, yet he pressed on, desperate to have answers. "You know my desire and urges for men are strong and ones I cannot deny for long, and yet you place me here with this man where pleasure is forbidden. How am I to think this is not punishment?"

"Haniel, you must have faith in yourself and in my love for you. It is a journey the two of you will have to make together. Just remember, Haniel, the one rule all angels must follow."

"Yes, Father. No angel shall show themselves to their appointed without falling from your grace."

"You are one of my most beloved sons, and one of the most

beautiful. Do not let yourself get carried away as you have so many times in the past. Tread lightly this time, Haniel."

"Father, please..." Haniel felt the shift in the air as God's presence left him. The pull from Nathan grew stronger. Haniel stood and walked over to the edge of Nathan's bed. He looked down upon the sleeping man and watched the rise and fall of the thin linen that covered his otherwise naked body. A noticeable stir between Nathan's legs caught the corner of Haniel's eye. He watched the movement of Nathan's cock pulse beneath the thin linens. Haniel's hope rose and without pause he leapt up above the bed and descended, slipping into Nathan's body.

Haniel felt Nathan's body stir as he entered him. The smell of the man's night sweat caught within the fibers of the sheet surrounded Haniel and gave rise to his own unmet needs. These temptations of the human flesh only strengthened his determination to lead the priest astray, sending both of them down a path of sexual release and pleasure. Haniel knew the priest would not go down this path of his own volition. He also knew that he could not be imprisoned within a celibate man. He would have to use every power given to him to evoke the priest's desires—even if it meant going against the words of his heavenly Father.

Nathan's restless mind became invaded by visions of the flesh. An erect nipple protruded through a blanket of blond hair. The nipple expanded and twisted. It blurred and became the recesses of a man's armpit. Sweat formed on the hair and dripped down the side of a naked torso, leading to the profile of a round ass covered in a light dusting of golden fuzz. The impure thoughts clouded his usual dreams of peace and tranquility. Nathan tossed and turned within his bed. His sweat-dampened body stuck to the thin sheets.

In Nathan's mind, a young man lay naked on a stone cliff overlooking the ocean. Nathan thought the young man looked familiar, but could not place him. The warm breeze glided over the young man's sun-soaked body, rustling through the golden hairs that covered his stomach and chest. Nathan could smell the warmth of the man's body as the wind carried his scent through the salty air.

Nathan took a couple of steps closer and felt a chill around his body. He looked down at himself. He stood naked. The wind battered his tender balls and cock. His cock, slow to rise, swayed between his legs. A thick string of precome clung to the tip of his cock. The young man reached out and cupped his hand to capture Nathan's release. He brought it to his face and drank from it as if taking the blood of Christ from a chalice. The stranger's flesh shimmered in the morning light. He turned and met Nathan's gaze.

"I've waited a long time for you to notice me." The young man's voice carried over the roar of the ocean. "Do you like what you see?" The young man slid his hand across his abdomen, grabbed his stiffening cock, and milked his own precome. It fell in thick rivulets into his navel, spilling down his side and onto the slate-colored stones.

"Go to him," Haniel whispered in Nathan's mind. "Reach out to him and allow yourself to feel the pleasures gifted to you from heaven."

Nathan's trembling hand reached out toward the man's raised arm. Their fingertips touched. Nathan closed his eyes as he resisted the young man's pull. Something within him snapped and he found himself being pulled down with the gentle guidance of his tormentor. Their bodies touched, leg against leg, shoulder against shoulder. The warmth of the young man's body against his sent a shiver down Nathan's spine.

"We...I shouldn't be here. This isn't..." Nathan's words were stopped as the young man placed his finger upon Nathan's lips. He could taste the young man's sun-dampened skin. Nathan caught the young man's eyes. They sparkled in the light of the sun. He felt the young man edging closer to him. The heat of their bodies entangling each other in a desire Nathan could not explain. He closed his eyes to the sight as he felt the soft, gentle lips of the young man upon his own. Nathan trembled as he felt the young man's body pushing into him. He gave in and leaned back against the stones letting the young man's naked body fall upon his own.

Nathan tossed and turned in his bed as the heat of his dreams swelled within his groin. Haniel continued to assail Nathan's mind with visions. It had been a long time since Haniel had felt the warmth and bliss that can only be witnessed by an angel from a human's sexual fulfillment, and he wasn't about to let up.

The cool, damp surface of the rocky cliff chilled Nathan's overheated body. He felt the young man's erection, wet with precome, press against his leg. Nathan glanced down between their bodies and became mesmerized by the folds of skin hiding the young man's cock. The golden hairs covering the man's balls blew in the brisk breeze.

Nathan wondered what it would be like to hold them in his hands, to fondle them, to lick them. His cock bounced against his stomach at the thought.

A surge of electricity ran through Nathan's body as the young man ran his hand down Nathan's abdomen and into the mass of dark pubic hair. Precome flowed from Nathan's cock and fell into the young man's hand. Nathan's heart pounded in his chest as the young man grabbed his cock and started stroking him.

"You have to stop," Nathan groaned. "Please, you cannot do this to me. It's against God's wishes."

"How can something so pleasurable be so wrong?"

"Oh, God," Nathan moaned. He fell back against the rocky surface as he felt the head of his cock slip into the young man's mouth. He gave in to the sin. His head swooned with emotions he never knew existed as he allowed the young man to pleasure him. His groin began to ache. His cock swelled as he felt the young man's grip tighten around the pulsing veins.

Nathan wanted to close his eyes to block out the sinful pleasures that invaded his body; yet he couldn't look away from the sight of the beautiful young man taking pleasure from his body. A body that had never before known such emotions, senses, and desires. He stared at their nakedness as the head of his cock expanded further. His piss slit opened wider as a rush of liquid heat filled his cock. A thick, white jet of come shot out from his cock and landed across his neck and chest. His body hitched. The young man stroked. Another rush burst through his groin as he came a second and third time. Nathan's head hit the stone surface with a thump as a final rush passed through his body.

Haniel, not expecting such a jolt, was almost thrown from Nathan's body as he awoke from the dream. He felt Nathan's blood racing through his body, warming his skin and coating it with a thin layer of sweat. Nathan sat up in the bed and looked at himself in the mirror. Haniel saw the innocence in Nathan's reflection and found his desire grew even greater. Nathan's eyes, Haniel's eyes followed the contours of Nathan's chest and stomach. Thick streaks of white come clung to Nathan's salt-and-pepper chest hair. A pulse softened from between their legs. Nathan threw off the covers and saw his cock stiff and wet. Haniel embraced the moment of pleasure and willed Nathan to touch himself outside of his dream. Shame rushed through Nathan's mind, blinding Haniel's vision and shattering the will he tried to invoke.

"For I know my transgressions, and my sin is ever before me." Nathan rose from the bed and knelt before the mirror. "Father, forgive me my sin and help me cleanse my mind. The temptation of the flesh is upon me and has darkened my soul."

Haniel winced at the words of Nathan's confession, and thought how sad it must be to fear the pleasures of the body, the same body that God had given man. Nathan's words subsided. The room fell silent around them. Haniel listened to the prayers running through Nathan's mind as he prepared his thoughts for the Sunday morning service.

Nathan carried a heavy heart as he rose from his prayers and stood looking at himself in the mirror. Haniel looked through Nathan's eyes at Nathan's nakedness. His nipples were dark against his pale complexion. He wanted Nathan to run his hand over his torso so he could feel what Nathan felt as his fingers grazed his skin. Nathan's long cock fell from a mass of black curly hair and hung between his legs. His legs were well toned and coated with the same coarse hair that covered his crotch. Haniel struggled to hold back his desire as Nathan showered to clean himself of his sin.

Haniel felt the weights of burden lift from Nathan's mind as they stood before the mirror dressed in his full-length cassock. *If only it were that simple*, Haniel thought. He knew that Nathan would not be leading the service, that they would simply be present in the eyes of the congregation, their Lord, and hopefully Adam with his angel, Michael. Nathan's sexual awakening had only just begun.

The chapel of the monastery was modest in size compared to most in the city. Its one-hundred-fifty-year-old stone structure held no more than fifty people, yet the small space felt comforting to Haniel. The quaint, intimate spaces of worship were more to his liking than were the massive Bible-thumping buildings that rose within the other parts of the world. Frankincense and myrrh filled the air as Haniel and Nathan took their seat among the empty choir stalls.

Haniel looked out across the nave as the congregation filled the chairs. Relief swelled, as did his groin as he noticed Adam sitting in the front row staring in their direction. Adam's long brown hair fell just below his collarbone, slicing jagged edges of darker browns across his neck. His smooth skin expressed a youthful innocence, yet his features were masculine and rugged for twenty-two. Haniel, with a little coaxing, turned Nathan's gaze from the altar. They caught Adam's stare. Haniel felt Nathan's body tense as he realized who the young man had been in his dream. Adam nodded and smiled at Nathan. Haniel's wings fluttered, sending a ripple of nerves through Nathan's body. Though Haniel couldn't see Michael, he felt his presence. He knew from the energy that filled the air that Michael was on board with his plan.

The music from the organ filled the air and reverberated against the walls. The congregation rose. Nathan stood. His eyes remained fixed on Adam. Haniel and Nathan's gaze fell from Adam's face and washed over his tall, slender body. Haniel's wings fluttered with excitement; Nathan's lips trembled as they noticed the bulge in Adam's pants. They watched as Adam looked down. He lifted his head slightly and winked. Dimples formed on his blushed cheeks. His left hand held the hymnal. He slipped his other hand into his pants pocket and moved up and down on his swollen cock. Against Haniel's wishes, Nathan looked down at the hymnal as the congregation began to sing.

Let all mortal flesh keep silence
And with fear and trembling stand
Ponder nothing earthly minded
For with blessing in his hand...

Haniel felt Nathan's body quiver from the assault of Adam's eyes. The built-up energy released from Nathan's tremors vibrated throughout Haniel's being. The tips of his wings shivered. The tug-of-war of emotions—guilt, desire, anguish, and pleasure—battled for control of Nathan's mind. Adam continued to fondle himself in the front row of the congregation while his deep tenor voice tossed the notes of the song into the air. Haniel no longer had to push Nathan into stealing glances. His eye moved in Adam's direction of his own free will.

The song ended and everyone took their seat. Nathan looked to his right as he sat down and noticed Adam with both hands in his lap, cradling his crotch. Haniel took the opportunity to play with Nathan's emotions, flashing images of his dream through his mind. Nathan remembered how Adam's balls were covered in golden blond hair and how each hair moved in the breeze. Nathan touched the spot on his leg where Adam's erect cock had been. As if reading Nathan's thoughts, Adam extended his left pointer finger and drew small circles over the bulge in his pants.

Haniel felt something change in Nathan. His body became consumed with guilt. Nathan looked away from Adam and closed his eyes to concentrate on the sermon. Haniel nudged Nathan. He tossed thoughts of Adam's naked body through his mind. Nathan's body trembled. Sweat seeped out of his pores as his mind fought against the images. A need stirred between Nathan's legs. He opened his eyes and without looking around, he stood up and headed down the hallway to the cloister.

Nathan paused by the door to his room and took a deep breath. He opened the door and froze at the sight of Adam lying on his bed with only the thin sheet to cover his body. He looked away from the sight and noticed Adam's clothes piled up at the foot of his bed. Adam's white briefs lay on top of the pile. His groin stirred with unwanted desire as he stared at the white material that had just moments ago held this young man's cock and balls.

"I've waited a long time for this moment." Adam's voice drifted in soft, sensual tones across the room. "Do you like what you see?" Adam lifted the sheet off his body, exposing his nakedness to Nathan.

Nathan remembered the soft voice from his dream. The scent of Adam's body filled the air. The warm muskiness penetrated Nathan's senses. Haniel pushed Nathan forward. He took a step toward the bed. Haniel's wings fluttered with excitement. The vibrations echoed in Nathan's ears like the pounding of distant drums. Memories of the dream haunted his mind. His cock stirred beneath his cassock.

Haniel inhaled the sweet smell of sex in the air. His wings blossomed, his feathers twitched as he looked upon Adam's angel lying incased in the young man's body. Michael's body glowed with a white light. Waves of dark hair spotted with flecks of gray covered Michael's chest. His nipples were dark spheres hidden within the thick curls. Haniel's eyes full of greed stole glances down Michael's body. He followed the thin trail of hair as it spread out across Michael's crotch, cushioning his semi-erect cock. Haniel pushed forward and sent Nathan to the edge of the bed.

"Adam, you shouldn't be here. You must leave my room immediately. If someone saw us together…"

"No one saw me come in. I was careful." Adam raised his arms behind his head and winked.

"How did you know which room was mine?" Nathan's eyes stole toward the blond hair that lay damp within Adam's armpits.

"I followed my instincts."

"You must get dressed and leave. The way you feel about me is a sin. You must know that."

"You don't believe those words any more than I do, especially after last night."

"Last night?" Nathan's mind flowed with images of his dream.

"The dream. We were together on the cliffs. It's where you gave yourself to me."

"You can't possibly know my dreams." Nathan's mind was a whirlwind of confusion. He bent down and picked up Adam's underwear. "Get dressed." His fingers caressed the soft ribbed fabric. The scent of Adam's crotch held in the fibers of the cotton surrounded him. He hesitated before handing them to Adam.

"You don't mean that." Adam sat up in bed and grabbed Nathan's hand. "I know you're scared…"

"You don't know anything about me. Please, I beg of you, leave."

"You still don't understand, do you?" Adam stood up and pressed his body against Nathan's. "You and I were placed here together for a reason. It's God's will. He has sent his angels down to guide us in our journey through life. Do you think it is not fate or God's will that we shared the same dream last night?"

"Whatever angel you are speaking of, it is not an angel of heaven." Nathan's fear and desire turned to anger. "You, my child, have been struck by the dark angels of Satan and their unholy ways."

"Tell me that you did not enjoy what we shared together in our dream." Adam leaned in and placed his lips upon Nathan's.

"No. This is not right." Nathan pushed Adam away and turned his back to his nakedness. "Get dressed and leave. You have sinned against the church and our Holy Father. Your soul is lost to God, for you have turned your allegiance to Satan. You shall no longer be welcomed into this church."

Haniel looked at Michael with a sense of loss. He tried to coax Nathan to turn around, in hopes that the sight of Adam would weaken him again. Nathan stood strong against the invisible force that seemed to be a part of him. Haniel watched with a saddened heart as Adam left the room, and with him, any hope for Michael.

"Get out of me," Nathan shouted. "I command you, the messenger of Satan, to leave my body in the name of the Father and of the Son and of the Holy Spirit."

Haniel in a fit of rage flew from Nathan's body and stood before Nathan. His wings stretched and fluttered through the air as he tried to regain his composure. He stood before his appointed. "Do you have any idea what you have done?"

Haniel watched as Nathan fell to the floor in front of him. Nathan's eyes widened and his mouth was agape as he stared at Haniel in his heavenly body. "You're not what I expected." Nathan's voice trembled. "You're beautiful and your presence is one of peace. How can you be a messenger of Satan?"

"I am Haniel. I am your guardian angel. I am one of God's messengers, not Satan's."

"How can that be? You place unholy thoughts in my head and have steered me away from God's work. How can you be one of God's creations?"

Haniel's desire grew despite his agitation as he felt Nathan's eyes upon his body. It glowed with a brilliant white light that shimmered around him. His black hair fell to his shoulders and hung over his eyes. Haniel saw Nathan's gaze follow the toned contours of his smooth, sculpted torso. Haniel heard Nathan gasp when he noticed Haniel's cock hanging thick with need between his legs. His crotch was barren of any hair just like the rest of his body.

"You have forced me to show myself to you out of your own fear and hatred for what you do not understand. I have gone against God's rule that no angel shall be seen by man, and still you fight against me." Haniel knelt down in front of Nathan. "If you forsake me, all hope for your own soul will be lost."

"I don't understand any of this. If you are a messenger of God, then I am sorry for any hurt I have caused you."

"I am not the one you should concern yourself with. The young man should be your priority."

"Adam? What does he have to do with any of this?"

"Everything in this world is connected. For every action there are repercussions; a ripple that can cause great harm to people, people who are not directly connected to the action. Angels are what connect everything on this earth. Every person on earth is sent an angel. It is the angel's responsibility to guard them, to protect them, and to help them on their journey through life. When a human forsakes their angel, whether intentionally or not, their angel is cast from the body and brought back to heaven and reassigned."

"What happens to the person?"

"When humans are not protected by God's messengers, Satan sends up one of his messengers to fill the empty space. When this happens, that soul is lost from goodness for all eternity. They will spend their remaining years on this earth in sadness and anger. They will take what is not theirs, they will do harm unto others, and when they die, they are sent to Satan to become one of his messengers of darkness."

"Haniel, I do not forsake you. Please do not allow yourself to be taken from me."

"That is not up to Haniel." A voice echoed around them.

"Father, I know you are angry with me for disobeying you. Please, you have to understand, there is more at stake here than my misdeed. A young man is about to descend into darkness, and the only one who can help him is Nathan. I had to show myself to him or lose both, and I could not let that happen."

"Father?" Nathan questioned.

"Yes, it is the voice of our Lord." Haniel reached out and grasped Nathan's hands. "He is right. It is not up to us. I have broken the rules and I must accept my fate."

"Please, Father, if you can hear me, do not blame Haniel. It was I who bid him to show himself. If anyone is to be punished, it should be me."

"Haniel, do you think you can save Adam?" The voice of the Lord echoed around them.

"Adam?" Nathan questioned.

"Yes, Father, if we can get to him in time. I can feel Michael's pain and remorse at being cast out."

"Go, and if you can save the life of Adam and that of Michael, than I shall overlook your transgressions against me."

"Thank you, Father. I won't let you down again."

"Adam? What about Adam?"

"Don't you see? Adam acted on his angel's guidance. He believed in the goodness of God and knew that he was brought to you through God's love."

"I don't understand."

"You threw him out. You crushed his hopes and beliefs in the good of mankind by not accepting him for who he is. His strength in love is waning because of you. He is close to casting out his angel, and if that happens, we will have lost him to the darkness."

"I didn't mean…I didn't know."

"We have to get to him before it's too late."

"How can we find him?"

"I know where they are. I can see them. He didn't go far. He wanted to be close to where he feels all this started—the chapel." Haniel flew up over Nathan and entered his body.

Nathan stood up and ran out of his room. The service had ended and the chapel stood empty except for Adam, who knelt by the altar. He was still naked, his clothes folded up next to him as they had been in Nathan's room.

"I don't know what I did to deserve this pain. I thought I was doing what God asked of me. You've played with my heart and my head and I cannot let it continue. I want you out…"

"Adam, please wait." Nathan ran to him and sat down beside him. He reached out and touched Adam's chin. Tears fell down Adam's cheeks. "Adam, please don't do this. I was wrong."

"I thought it's what God wanted. It felt so right to want to be with another man, to want to be with you."

"It is what God wants. I was the one who hurt you, not your angel, and certainly not God."

"You know of the angels?"

"Yes, they have spoken to me, as has our Father. What you feel for me is real, just as real as the two of us sitting here together. I thought my feelings for you were the work of Satan, unholy and sinful. If I'd only known how wrong I was, I would never have sent you away." Nathan brushed away Adam's tears with his thumb. "You are a beautiful young man, and I was a fool to think you were not a gift from heaven."

Nathan leaned in and placed his lips upon Adam's. Nathan opened his mouth to Adam's tongue and tasted the salty tears that had fallen between his lips.

Nathan broke their kiss and stood up. He could see the look of confusion on Adam's face. Nathan smiled and unbuttoned his cassock. It fell to the floor. He kicked off his shoes and slipped his underwear down his legs. His cock bobbed out in front of him as he stood naked before Adam.

Haniel and Michael's wings spread open and vibrated from the passion of the two men they watched over. As Nathan dropped to the floor and laid his body next to Adam, Haniel and Michael came together in a tight embrace.

Nathan moved his hand over Adam's body, exploring the pleasure of the young man's body without guilt. He moved further down and felt the heat and wetness of Adam's cock. He rubbed the precome over Adam's shaft and anxiously stroked the pulsing cock that grew in his grip.

Nathan rolled over on his back and pulled Adam on top of him. Nathan felt Adam's hand grasp his cock. The young man's hand was smooth and gentle in its strokes. Nathan raised Adam's hips up and positioned himself beneath Adam's ass.

Nathan looked at Adam and saw him smile and nod. Nathan guided his cock over the center of Adam's ass and pushed the head of his cock against Adam's tight hole. Nathan watched with growing desire as Adam winced, then smiled as the large head slipped through the tight, tender muscles. Nathan pushed Adam further down onto his cock, sending showers of pleasure through his own body. Nathan's cock swelled within the warm, dark recesses of Adam's ass. He reached between them and felt his cock sliding in and out of Adam. His head swam with emotions and pleasures he never knew existed. He knew he needed more. He didn't want to be blind to the beautiful sight of what was happening between their legs. He wanted to see what he was feeling, to touch their sex, to taste it.

Nathan kissed Adam as he pulled Adam off him. His cock fell to his stomach with a heavy, wet smack. Nathan stood up and turned Adam around. He leaned Adam over the altar and spread his ass cheeks. His fingers glided up and down Adam's crack. He played with the wet hair that covered the small opening.

Nathan slipped a finger into Adam's ass as he knelt behind him. He moved his finger in and out of Adam's ass, watching the contractions of the tight, puckered hole. He pulled his finger out and ran his tongue along the crack of Adam's ass. He inhaled the musky scent that surrounded him. He tasted his precome mixed with the flavors of Adam's ass. Nathan felt the movement of Adam's ass muscles against the tip of his tongue. He paused then slipped his tongue deep inside. The warmth blanketed his tongue. He licked and teased the soft inner walls, smearing his spit and precome over his lips and cheeks. He pulled his tongue out and licked the wet hole one last time before gliding his tongue up Adam's crack. Nathan kissed Adam's back as he stood up.

Nathan leaned in and kissed the sweat off Adam's neck as he slipped his cock inside him. He leaned back and spread Adam's ass cheeks. He watched as his cock moved in and out of the magnificent hole he had found himself in. His balls began to tighten. A knot of intense heat filled his groin as he watched the soft blond hair of Adam's ass sticking to his hot, wet shaft. He pushed harder into Adam. The sound of the bodies slapping against each other echoed through the empty chapel.

Nathan pulled Adam up against him and wrapped one arm around Adam's chest while his free hand grabbed Adam's cock. Nathan thrust in and out of Adam's ass as his hand massaged and stroked Adam's cock. Nathan could hear Adam's breathing getting heavy. It came in short thick bursts.

"Oh, God, I'm going to come." Adam moaned. "Yeah, fuck me, stroke that cock."

Nathan felt the pressure of Adam's orgasm building in his grip. Adam's body tightened against Nathan's as the first wave of Adam's come raced out of his cock and showered the red altar cloth with thick, white streams. Nathan felt the warmth of Adam's come covering his fingers. He stroked Adam's cock harder and faster, sending ribbons of white come over the floor and Adam's crotch.

Nathan felt Adam's hand covering his. He relaxed his grip on Adam's softening cock and allowed his hand to be taken by Adam. The warmth of Adam's tongue glided over Nathan's skin, as Adam licked his come from Nathan's fingers.

"I want to receive your offering," Adam groaned as he pulled himself off Nathan's cock and turned around.

Nathan held on to Adam's shoulder as Adam knelt in front of him. Nathan stroked his cock as the intense pleasure consumed him. His breaths came in short bursts as he reached the final barrier. He looked down as the first wave of his orgasm forced thick streams of come out of his cock. The thick, white liquid sprayed across Adam's face. Nathan watched as Adam smiled. The sight of Adam taking his come was more than Nathan could take. He pumped his cock harder until another thick stream of come ripped through his shaft and fell over Adam's lips. Nathan's legs gave out and he collapsed on the floor in Adam's arms. Nathan licked his come from Adam's lips and chin, savoring his own warm, salty flavor.

Haniel and Michael embraced the passion and heat of the two men and basked in the remains of their intimate pleasure. Haniel looked up toward heaven and spoke. "Father, have I been forgiven for my transgressions?"

"Yes, my son, all is forgiven. You and Michael shall watch over these two men and protect them at all costs. Their love will be looked upon as sinful and they will need the both of you to support them and guide them through their journey together. Go and enjoy what the two of you have set in motion. Take part in their pleasure and know that I am satisfied."

The Adorable One

Jay Lygon

Fallen angels are demons, so when you think about it, calling on angels is the same thing as summoning a demon. It just sounds better when you're trying to justify to yourself what you're doing, and I'm sure Archangel Michael did a lot of soul searching before he called on me.

Truth is, it pissed me off that when Michael made a celestial booty call, he acted as if I'd been summoned into the divine presence of Himself instead of merely a fellow angel. Not that Michael wasn't divine. Every bulging muscle was chiseled as if from granite. Even his nipples could probably cut diamonds. But his conceit that his Lord of the Host somehow outranked my Lord didn't make me want to drop important business to get up into his any time soon.

While Michael was the essence of masculine perfection in the Western aesthetic, my beauty—it wasn't vanity if it was the truth—was the Eastern ideal: softer eyes, golden brown skin, small dark nipples, a lithe build, and no body hair, but I was no twink. First off, I existed before time, and second, I could kick ass like Jet Li in a berserker rage. All angels were warriors. Don't let a slight build fool you.

For a while, I ignored Michael's call. He didn't seem to understand that there was some serious shit going down in my part of the world. Iran, Iraq, Afghanistan, they were all my turf. I and the other Adorable Ones, the angels of Zoroastrianism, had our hands full.

After a few years of being ignored, you'd think Michael would get the hint that I had better things to do than him, but he was horny, so he kept at it. Annoyed, I kept putting him off, until it got to the point where I needed to blow off some energy. That's when I summoned him.

Michael didn't return my call; he just materialized in front of me.

He had some nerve barging into my presence like a marine storming Baghdad. As if he could inspire shock and awe in me. Only he would show up at a fuck buddy's place wearing full armor that gleamed like the sun.

Because I knew it pissed him off like nothing else, my gaze made a languid trip from his blazing eyes to his groin while I smiled like the serpent of Eden. His flimsy angelic kilt tented.

"Ready for battle, I see, oh Chief of Princes," I said.

The heavenly realm surrounding us was heavy on the harem fantasy theme. Michael still got into that. Lots of pillows and rugs scattered across the floor. Flimsy sheer drapes hung from vaulted ceiling arches that faded away into the nighttime sky. A huge carved couch that humans called an opium bed stood behind me. To make my intentions painfully clear, the low table before the couch was set with the minimum of food and drink required by the ancient rules of hospitality.

"You have some nerve, Sraosha." Michael sheathed his sword, the metal one, as an excuse to turn away from me. With the glow of celestial light behind him, all he accomplished was to show me a silhouette of his cock jutting underneath his kilt.

"If you're that offended, leave." I peeled off my tunic and baggy trousers to remind him why he didn't want to. "Maybe I should have called on Atar instead. You know how hot he is."

It was a stupid joke, since my fellow Adorable One Atar was the embodiment of sacred fire, but Michael had no sense of humor, so he didn't laugh. He almost looked hurt. Behind all those bulging muscles was a touchy ego. For an archangel, Michael was a bit stupid, which suited me just fine because it was so easy to push his buttons.

Michael's hands clenched in and out of fists as his chest heaved. His gaze followed my hand down to my cock. He licked his bottom lip as I stroked myself. Soon, he gripped his hard-on.

"Take off your frilly angel dress and let me see that cock," I said.

"It's not a dress!"

Button, pushed.

His face flushed as he huffed. Still, he unclasped his gold breastplate and let it fall onto the thick rug at his feet. He posed for me after he peeled off his kilt. Maybe he was stupid, but oh, what a body. His pecs popped as his biceps peaked into mountains. He turned to show off his back. Muscles ripped across his broad shoulders. Dimples above his meaty ass deepened as he flexed.

Showing off always calmed him down. He turned back to me with a triumphant grin.

I yawned.

He glowered.

Button, mashed hard.

"Take off your sandals while you're at it, Michael. Were you born in a barn? Oh, that's right. You weren't. I was thinking of Himself's new favorite right-hand man."

Fuming, Michael lunged. Instead of sidestepping the charging bull, I let him slam into me. If he thought he could knock me over, he was wrong. He gripped my wrist as he tried to shove me back. Muscle ground against muscle. He grunted from the effort.

I pushed my hand forward, then suddenly yanked back. You'd think after a couple thousand years he'd learn that trick. He toppled forward. I grabbed his gold forearm gauntlet and twisted his arm behind his back as I shoved him face- down onto the couch. Before he could react, I shoved my thigh between his legs so that his ass cheeks parted. His hole puckered.

I smacked his butt. Those solid glutes barely moved under the blow, but his alabaster flesh reddened.

"You cocksucking fucker!"

That probably would have sounded more menacing if Michael's mouth hadn't been full of purple silk pillow.

"Is that any way to talk to your daddy, boy?"

He bellowed as he writhed out of my hold. Each deep breath raised his shoulders. He lowered his chin and glared.

It might have seemed as if I simply stood there waiting for his next charge, but my weight subtly shifted in preparation. Poor Michael, he was always about brute force where my fighting style used his bulk against him. East meets West. Push meets string. He howled as he sprang. I flowed like water around a rock. He crashed to the ground. When I dropped between his spread legs, my knee pinched the inside of his thigh against the rug. He screamed.

"Why don't you just beg me to fuck you, Michael? It would be more dignified."

I slapped his ass again much harder.

He wriggled out from under me and staggered to his feet. His eyes were full of hate. It had been thousands of years since I'd seen him in battle, but that's what I remembered most, how his eyes shone, the grim set of his square jaw, and the solid upward curve of his cock.

Humans didn't like the idea of bloodlust angels anymore. They made us pretty in their pictures, and we were, but not the goddamned lobotomized eunuchs they depicted. Humans would have been mortified that Michael, among others of the host, got a hard-on for violence. I used that trait to make him crazy. He'd never admit it, but he really got into that.

I rose with far more grace than he had. A slight, mocking smile pulled at the corner of my mouth.

Too quick for Michael to react, I pinched the head of his cock to milk a drop of precome out of him. As I backed away, I licked the slick drop off my fingers. My tongue ran over my lips.

"The angel's portion."

My foreskin pulled back to reveal my cockhead as I stroked myself. "If you want a taste of me, you'll have to work harder."

He eyed my hand. I slid my hand up my chest to play with my nipple. Dumb with lust, he breathed heavily and watched in silence. My hand stopped moving as I pumped into my fist. Every flex of my Adonis belt and twitch of my hips made him grunt. He grabbed his cock to mirror my moves. I stopped.

"If I wanted a mutual jerk-off with a beautiful being, I would have stood in front of a mirror instead of calling on you," I said.

Button obliterated. The countdown to ignition had begun.

He tackled me from the side. We crashed down on the table and sent food flying. I rolled; he followed. I shoved against his bulging muscles as he tried to pin me. He grunted as I slipped out of his hold time and again.

When Michael sprawled over my back and twisted my leg in a painful hold, I went limp. I'm not evil, but I'm not above dangling temptation before an archangel to make a point.

"I submit!" I called out as I lifted my ass.

He let go and scuttled across the floor.

The scent of sweat got in my nose when I landed on top of him, wrapped my legs around his, and forced them apart. His skin was too slick to hold on to for long, but those seconds of grinding my ass against his cock and jamming my hard-on into his gut got him as worked up as I wanted him.

He pushed me off and immediately came after me.

Panting after escaping a headlock, I knelt up and beckoned him to try again.

"Come on, avenging angel. Show me what you got."

He crawled across the rug and gripped my thigh before he caught his breath. I grabbed a handful of his hair and shoved his face into my sweaty armpit. He took his sweet time snuffling around before he got serious about pulling away. His hand slipped off my leg, but I still had a handful of his hair, so I forced his head down between my knees until his chest pressed to the rug.

Michael made a big show of flailing around to get up from his hands and knees, as if that would make me ignore his tongue on my balls. Once he'd licked every drop of sweat from my sack, I yanked his hair until his lips were a whisper away from my cock. He strained to get it into his mouth as I held him back. Afraid I'd end up with a handful of hair ripped out by the roots if I didn't let the greedy fucker suck me, I shoved my cock into his mouth.

My hand slid down his spine toward his ass. He arched as he tried to get my fingers into his hole. I moved my hand under him. His balls were a hefty handful. I lifted them, then let them drop. He yelped.

"Slow down, or I'll come in your mouth," I said.

He nodded and backed off a bit. As a reward, I stroked his cock until he started fucking my grip. That's when I pulled my cock out of his mouth. He almost pouted as he looked up at me.

"Well?"

Michael tried a sorrowful look, then a defiant one before he rolled onto his back and pulled his knees to his chest. He preferred to get fucked from behind, but after a couple thousand years, he finally figured out that what he wanted wasn't how he was going to get it from me.

His hole tightened and relaxed as he held up his legs and stared at the ceiling. Somehow, that was more humbling than being on his knees with his ass up in the air.

No matter what position he was in, Michael was perfection. More Hercules than Ganymede, his thighs, meaty butt, and the cluster of muscles leading from his chest to his groin were the height of the Greek ideal, which was kind of funny considering that their pantheon didn't include angels. On the other hand, they'd made ass-fucking an art, so it was hard to get too angry about Olympian slights.

"Look at me, Michael."

I didn't know which sight turned me on more—his wince as I shoved my cock into him, or his pink-brown hole gripping me just below my cockhead. He made those little sounds he always did while I let him get used to my girth. When I got tired of the whimpers, I pushed deep into him.

Michael gasped.

I pulled back slowly, then slammed back into him. His pecs bounced along with the rhythm. Slowly—it always took him a while—he relaxed. I saw it in his face first as his grimace melted away. I've seen everything under the heavens, and nothing is as beautiful as an angel blissfully grinning while being sodomized. The surrender flowed through his body down to his grip on my cock.

Each of my hard thrusts shoved him a fraction of an inch across the floor. I had no idea if Michael liked it that rough. I'd never asked and had no intention of finding out. He kept coming back for more, so the rug burns down his back must not have bothered him too much.

"Jerk off for me." I gripped his thighs hard enough to leave bruises.

He spat on his hand and grabbed his cock.

I pushed his knees closer to his chest and pounded that perfect ass until I was close. Then I backed off to make it last.

Michael's head lifted. One grunt and he shot a load into his chest hair. Another spurt flew over his head as he squeezed his balls. That was all it took to send me over the edge. I pulled out of his ass and jerked off onto his stomach. The puddle oozed over his abs.

I let go of his legs and sprawled over him. He wrapped a big arm around me. We stayed like that for a while. Then I got bored.

"We both have duties." It was my kind way of telling him to go away.

He held on tighter as he caressed my cheek.

We kissed a bit but I didn't exactly encourage him. We were fuck buddies, not lovers. When he finally got the message and got up to collect his armor, I reclined on the couch.

His eyes were wide and full of hope when he finished buckling his breastplate. "I could stay a bit longer."

No, he couldn't.

Michael couldn't meet my eyes. He sucked at this part. Why did he have to make it so painful? I wished there was a way to unsummon an angel. All I could do was let the silence stretch until he remembered his pride.

He kissed me again, lightly, as he squeezed my arm. "Bye!"

Then he was gone, much to my relief.

With a sweep of my hand, I dismissed the harem fantasy décor and replaced it with a gleaming high-tech interior. I padded over to the wall of computer monitors to search for anything of interest. The world, it seemed, was getting along just fine without me at that moment, so I poured a glass of red wine and sank onto my couch to enjoy the lingering pleasant peace of a decent fuck.

It might take Michael a couple hundred years to get over his ceaselessly breaking heart, but eventually, he'd call on me again. Then I'd take a few hundred years to decide if he was worth the trouble. That was the way it had always been between us, and would be for all eternity. If only he'd learn to quit hoping for more. One thing was certain, though—no matter how awkward our partings were for him, he couldn't stay away from me. Never had, never would. Among the multitudes of the hosts, I alone was his personal demon.

White Knight
Mel Bossa

Ever since Joshua was a kid he had a thing for circles. It was the completion of a line that got him. The endlessness of a thought. The satisfaction of knowing movement does not cease.

Today was his twenty-eighth birthday.

"—jerk took my only Saturday off and gave it to Cal"—one of the paramedics was shouting over the sound of the sirens—"but I don't give a damn. Hey, avoid Saint-Urbain, they're still coating the right lane."

Today would be the day Joshua died.

"Yeah, they've got three witnesses. Said the guy was freebasin' or somethin', swingin' that gun around—"

Thus completing the greatest of all circles.

"The gun went off, and shit man, this kid here was just standing there. Talk about bad timing—"

The end must have been near. Joshua could foresee it in the subtle change in the paramedics' voices. When they had lifted his limp body into the ambulance, past the four a.m. crowd of glassy-eyed, dry-mouthed onlookers, the medics' pitch had been hitting the high notes and their cadence had been hurried. But as the ambulance rolled down Montreal's wet streets—sirens blazing—the medics' tone was clearly deflating with every turn the ambulance made. Their words had become practical and overripe—syllables sitting inside their mouths for too long.

Rotten. This whole deal was.

Joshua worked at picking up on the trail of sounds the world was leaving for him; when they shut the sirens off, then he'd know he was definitely a corpse. There would have to be some kind of cue, because his body had ceased feeding him signs of life. Where there had been an enormous stabbing pain in his chest, now was only muted sensation, a mild tremor that was impossible to distinguish. He bent his will (did he still have one?) to isolate a clear physical reaction, but there was none.

A ricochet bullet. Happy birthday, Joshua.

"Shit, we're losing him again—"

Zap. Pain. A kaleidoscope of white and yellow. The medic had used the defibrillator twice. Or was it three times?

"Clear."

Lying flat on a stretcher, bloodless, eyes opened, fists closed. This was it? This simple, blurry transition? One moment smoking a cigarette outside the club, then dead?

"—fucking disaster this city is. Ride the alley all the way up." The medics were in a jiff, it seemed. Construction maybe.

With every pothole the ambulance tore over, the stretcher jumped under Joshua and his thoughts wandered like leaves torn from a tree. His consciousness drifted backward, leafing through the pages of his existence. Memories, clearer than the most lucid dream, assailed his mind.

A carpeted basement. A summer party. Music. The clean scent of Christopher Saint-Pierre's flannel shirt and the feel of Christopher's tangled blond curls against his bare stomach.

Christopher. His one and only love. Christopher. Talented, tortured, and reckless. Dead now for seven years.

No, Joshua, I'm here. I'm right here.

They were strangers once, young, inexperienced, but so eager and so willing. Nearing the end of the school year, Christopher and he had (at last) been *properly* introduced by a mutual friend, a plump, fast-talking, brown-skinned girl named Rosario—a mother now perhaps—and the two boys had spent the evening exchanging quick, assessing glances. Though they had grown up in the same neighborhood and even shared some classes, he and Christopher had never exchanged more than a few banalities. No matter, because they hadn't needed words. They'd had their eyes to speak all of their clumsy, secret desires. And for months, Joshua had dreamed of that party, that chance to spend some time alone with the boy whose name was etched into his skin, blood letters carved with an X-acto on his inner thigh, safely hidden from any suspicious adult. Christopher was two years Joshua's senior, smoked Camels, wore red Doc Martens boots (fourteen holes, yes sir), carried fake ID and a tattered paperback book inside the pocket of his worn out black jeans. He was by far the most exciting thing for miles and miles. After all, this was the burbs.

"Is it true your mom left you at school one morning and never came back?"

Though he hadn't seen Christopher for years now (miserable, nightmarish years), he remembered every detail of Christopher's face; the aquiline nose, the thin, arched eyebrows, and those lips. Lips that seemed always ready to smile. Lips whose gifts could bring bliss or torment, depending on Christopher's mood and drug of choice.

That long-ago evening—the commencement of their roller-coaster on-and-off relationship—he and Christopher had escaped the party and were in the laundry room, alone, door closed, sitting side by side, feet dangling over the old, yellowed appliances. Joshua had heard rumors about Christopher's unconventional upbringing (people said he'd pretty much raised himself, fed and clothed by his older brother), and now that Joshua's blood was pumped with spiked Sprite, he could finally speak to Christopher in a calmer manner. He'd been wanting to be alone with him for eight months. Eight long, never-ending, agonizing months. They only had gym together, and most of the time, Joshua spent that time trying to keep from getting an erection. When he was around Chris, his cock had its own agenda.

"Yeah, so what if my mom left?" Christopher asked, passing the bottle back to him. "My mom wanted to be something else. Only assholes don't ever change their minds."

Joshua mulled over that statement. Christopher was definitely—what was that word he had learned this week?—an *iconoclast.* Yes. Christopher was an iconoclast. A free thinker.

"I'm so done with high school," Christopher said, leaning his head back on the cupboard, turning his electric gray eyes to Joshua. His eyes were the color of volcano ash, but seared hotter than molten lava. "Too bad you still got two more years to go."

Joshua had been good with keeping a safe distance all through the school year, but this sudden proximity was more than he could take. "What are you gonna do now?" he asked, feigning nonchalance. "Gonna go to college?"

Christopher's thigh brushed his, and slowly, like hot air rising, a smile warmed his angular features (of course, after that first night, they'd gone through five years of romantic warfare, and Joshua had suffered so intensely, he'd sometimes wished he'd never met Christopher), but tonight, between life and the void, lying on this cursed stretcher, he remembered that laundry room smile—seductive, offered with no expectations.

"What am I gonna do now?" Christopher asked, echoing the question back to him.

Joshua nodded, cheeks searing, heart pounding, cock swelling to the point of burn. "Yeah, what—"

"I'm gonna lock this door." Christopher slid off the washer, staggered to the door, and turned the flimsy lock. He leaned up against the door, his stare bold and challenging, yet laced with affection. "You know what I think?" He raked his fingers through his disheveled locks. "I think you like me."

Joshua's face blistered. "I don't know—"

"Hey wait," Christopher whispered, taking a step forward, smile waning. "I'm not setting you up."

Joshua dared a glance upward. If Christopher didn't touch him, he'd explode in his shorts.

Christopher neared him cautiously. "You wanna piss your parents off?" He stood a few inches from Joshua's taut body. "'Cause if you let me do what I wanna do to you, there's gonna be—"

"That's fine."

"Fine?" Christopher threw his head back, revealing a slightly protruding Adam's apple, and roared a laugh, but soon, his features tensed. "I don't know how to say this any other way, but damn, Josh, you're fucking beautiful, and behind all those good-boy manners, you've got an animal itching to claw out."

Abiding by no rules, thinking of no consequences (and it had been like this from that moment on), Joshua leaned his chin against Christopher's chest in an effort to stem his raging hormones. Christopher groaned, bending to his mouth, skimming his lips with his.

"Gimme your hand," he breathed, cupping his fingers around Joshua's, tugging his shaky hand to the bulge in his jeans. "See what you do to me? Josh, I really want you to touch me. It's okay."

Through the wooden door, over the sounds of laughter and bottles clacking, Eddie Vedder's voice seeped through. "Someone will come in here." Joshua's heart thundered furiously, his stomach tight and soaked with liquid fire. A sweet pain. A fantastically impossible pleasure. "I don't know what to do," he admitted meekly.

"Okay then, lie back." Christopher pushed on his chest, caressing Joshua's thighs, scalding his skin through the fabric of his jeans. "I'll take the lead, but don't stop me," Christopher said, cheeks flaming. "Don't fucking stop me."

Never. He would never stop him. He couldn't if he had tried. Christopher's nature was an avalanche.

Christopher fumbled with the plastic buttons of Joshua's cheap shirt, popping them one by one, from top to bottom. His fingertips paused on every newly exposed inch of Joshua's skin like a blind man deciphering a lost love letter, and when the shirt was undone, Christopher brushed it off his shoulders, the cool air hardening Joshua's nipples. He wished he was hairier, bigger, so much more of a man, but Christopher's gaze was shrouded with such passion that Joshua felt empowered, desirable; and earnestly, but yet softly, Christopher lowered his mouth to his left nipple, kissing it, his tongue flicking the pebbled flesh. Hot and wet, Christopher's mouth moved over Joshua's skin, leaving trails of saliva along the fine down below his navel, and when Christopher reached the edge of the belt, Joshua heard himself moan, "oh fuck," and wondered if he had come already.

"Don't stop me," Christopher said. It was a plea. His eyes were veiled with urgency and his body was hard, pressing.

Joshua, whose hands had been chained to his side by some invisible moral shackles, broke free. "I won't Chris, I won't," he said, daring to touch Christopher's face.

The touch lit a pyre inside Christopher's steel eyes and he jerked Joshua's belt open. "Pretend you love me," he whispered between shallow pants, "just fucking pretend you love me."

Joshua didn't have to pretend, but years later, during their tumultuous love affair, Christopher had never believed he was worthy of anyone's love. No, Chris preferred the feel of the metal prick digging into his flesh. The elation of drug-induced dreams.

"I wanna kiss you," Joshua said, inaudibly, heart fluttering from his admission, his confession. Was kissing gay?

"No, no, just this. Just this." Christopher drove his hands deep into Joshua's cotton undies, his fingers circling Joshua's erection.

"Don't come," Christopher murmured into his ear. "Please." There was something compelling in Christopher's caresses, a mad, ravenous need. "Do you believe in me? Do you think I could be somebody?" His mouth found the tip of Joshua's dick and Joshua held back a cry.

"Yes," he groaned, kissing Christopher's shoulder. "I believe in you."

Christopher unfastened his flannel shirt and yanked his T-shirt over his head and then pulled open his jeans, sliding them down to his white knees. He didn't wear underwear, and seeing Chris naked, Joshua understood what communion meant. He could fathom a life now. He could imagine happiness. The length and width of Christopher's cock was all he would ever need. His gaze roamed over Christopher's belly, over the brown fuzz shooting downward from the navel, the smooth, barely chiseled chest, the small mole below his right nipple, and he reached for Christopher's shoulders and pulled his weight on him. Their chests collided and he banged his head back on the cupboard, but felt no pain. His hands tore at Christopher, digging, searching, exposing. He jerked his own jeans down, swinging them off his legs, until he was free of every layer of material that stood in the way of Christopher's skin. Naked now. And the music still played. But the threat of being discovered had vanished.

Christopher pushed into his thigh, where his name had been carved. "Touch me," he implored. And Joshua did. He grazed his fingers along the head of Christopher's cock, spreading the wetness over the slit. His own cock jumped with tension, his balls churning with pleasure and pain. Christopher pressed his hips to his, crushing his erection against his, cupping Joshua's scrotum, until his fingertips reached the puckered anus. "Don't stop me," he pleaded again. "Don't fucking stop me, Josh." He lathered his index with spit and, his face pushed into Joshua's neck, slid his fingers inside Joshua's virginal ass. The burn was exquisite; it nearly drove Joshua insane. He could no longer control his limbs or breaths. He spread his thighs wider, allowing Christopher deeper entry and rocked his hips against his fingers—from the pleasure he took from them, he thought he would die.

Christopher stroked himself, mouthing silent prayers. When his fingers reached what seemed to be the end of Joshua, that sweet sore place that connected with every single nerve in Joshua's body, Christopher bent his mouth to Joshua's cock and sucked on the head.

Joshua's body stretched from head to toe, and he closed his eyes, clutching Christopher's hair, letting the powerful orgasm build inside his balls, swelling like a dangerous tide, until it had nowhere to go, until it rushed up his belly and erupted out of him, hot, salty.

"Oh God," Christopher grunted, touching his reddened lips. "I'm sorry."

Sorry? Joshua, listless from the climax, frowned and hesitantly touched Christopher's cheek. "No. Don't say that. Ever."

But many times over the years, that word had been the only thing Christopher could say genuinely.

You're right, baby. I wasn't there for you, but I'm here now. I'm here, Joshua.

Summer had ended and Christopher hadn't gone to college. Instead, he had followed Adrian, a foul-mouthed, handsome doctor's son, and gone to London. There, Christopher had written him on three occasions; short, incisively clever letters full of false angst and well-disguised boredom. Christopher enjoyed the rain. The promise of another life in a land as gray as his eyes. But life had delivered no such thing.

Christopher Saint-Pierre was gone now. Gone.

Though in this instant, this moment between life and hereafter, Joshua could almost recognize his scent. In the ambulance. Was the medic wearing Cartier's Declaration?

No, baby, it's me. It's Christopher. Look at me.

The ambulance came to a grinding halt and Joshua reestablished a connection with reality. He was twenty-eight years old. On his way out.

I'm here. You're not alone. Joshua, I'm here.

"You're kidding," one of the medics growled. "Take a right. Oh man, this is a nightmare."

Baby boy. I'm here. See me. Please, see me. I've come back for you.

Three years later, Christopher had left London to come home, bringing with him fog and gloom. Chris was bartending, making in excess of five thousand dollars a week, but his coke habit was the ogre that needed to be fed, and their lives had been wrecked come the seventh month of their live-in arrangement. When Chris had thrown all of his clothes into a duffel bag and slammed the door behind him, Joshua had sat with his head against the door, holding himself down. How could he live without Chris? Then the letters had come again. This time, they had been cutting at first, accusing, tense with theatrics—notes from a junkie in search of ease, of peace, but mostly money. Determined, Joshua hadn't given in. No, he had loved that man until his love, like bleach, had burned through Christopher's wounds, cleansing him all the same. Joshua worked long days at the call center as a supervisor, and his nights were spent checking his e-mails, scotch in hand, hoping to get news from Christopher.

"I saw him at the Pulse club two nights ago," some acquaintance would say, passing him on the street. "He didn't look too good."

And Joshua would smile reassuringly though his heart ached. "He'll be all right. You know him. Just a bad patch."

Then one morning, Christopher showed up on his Montreal apartment doorstep. He'd gained some weight, but lost the humorous gleam in his eye. He leaned on the door frame and reached his hand out. "I wanna come back, Josh," he said carefully, yet confidently. Confidently, because Chris had always took his affection, his patience, for granted.

I know I did. You loved me like no one else could. But, Joshua, your face was the last thing on my mind before I closed my eyes. Feel me. My hands are on you again.

"Well, you can't. You just can't." Joshua shrank back from the doorway, inwardly praying for the strength to resist Christopher's persuasive stare. "My life is on track, Chris. I got stuff—"

"Look at me. I'm clean. It's over. Josh, baby, lemme in"—Christopher stepped over the threshold—"don't do it to me, don't make me beg," he said, dropping his bag on the hardwood floor.

Joshua turned his back to him and walked to the bedroom, heart in his throat, legs wobbly. With one piercing gaze, Chris had managed to pop the seams of his soul once more. How could Christopher knock on his door and demand entry after the torment he'd put him through? No, he wouldn't concede. Wouldn't let—

"Have you stopped loving me, Josh?" Chris stood in the bedroom doorway. A bloom of heat covered his face. "Have you?" He stepped into the room, eyes feverish. "Because if you don't love me, tell me now and I'll know it's the end of me—"

"Stop it." Joshua sat on the edge of the four-post bed. "Don't say those words again, and please don't look at me like that." Though his eyes remained fastened to the carpet under his bare toes, he could feel Christopher's stare licking his skin. "You hurt me so much, Chris—"

"Then hurt me back," Christopher breathed, nearing him, palms turned up.

Hurt him.

"Be quiet," Joshua said, fists clenched, anger soaring high up into his chest, into his voice. "Just shut up." His hands groped Christopher's shirt before he could stop himself. Under his palms, Chris's heart jumped and he smirked.

"I told you you had an animal—"

"I said be quiet." Joshua's voice shook. No more gentleness. No more. He shoved Chris back against the dresser. He wouldn't tear him, but he would make him cry, and he didn't care if it was from pleasure or pain. When Chris's mouth formed a word, Joshua silenced it with a deep kiss, pulling Christopher's blond locks with one hand, jerking his pants open with the other. "So many nights, Chris," he groaned. "You stole years from me—"

And I'm gonna give them all back to you. My lips are on your skin. My breath is eternal and it's yours.

Brusquely, Joshua turned Chris around and pinned his hands flat on the dresser. "Are you gonna stop me?" he asked, breathless, wild. "Are you gonna give in to me?" For once, could Christopher Saint-Pierre bequeath him with this gift?

Control.

Joshua yanked Chris's pants down, exposing his pale ass—the round buttocks he'd loved to squeeze when he and Chris had been intertwined, locked in a sweaty embrace. But Chris's ass didn't feel the same because time had robbed him of the map to Christopher's lean body, turning it into a strange land under his fingers. No matter, he didn't need the map anymore and he wouldn't take that road anyway. He held Chris's stomach, his face pushed into his neck, binding him to his chest, his heart drumming against his ribs, snuffing the breath out of his throat while the scent of Chris's skin steadily intoxicated his senses; and for a moment, he wanted only to hold him, touch him gently, confess to him all of his pain, but Chris moaned a little, reaching around to cup his cock, forcing Joshua to forget all of his delicate desires.

Then Joshua closed his eyes and spoke into Chris's ear. "Tell me it's the first time," he said, knowing there was no first times left in the world.

"Yes." Chris's knees bent and he leaned forward on the dresser. Joshua slipped his hand inside the open collar of Chris's white shirt, caressing his chest, and between two pulses, in the vanity mirror, their eyes met. "I can't think. I can't explain anything anymore," Chris said, kissing Joshua's forearm, staring at their reflection. "Put me back together."

Joshua didn't know how. Never would. But his body could try. He got to his knees, crushing them into the carpet, sliding his hands along the outlines of Christopher's thin thighs—they had been bulky once, but the drugs had taken almost everything from Chris.

But never you, Joshua. Never you, baby boy.

Joshua, kneeling, looked up, seeing what was his and what he was entitled to. Too long. It had been too long since he'd tasted the salt of Chris's skin, and he was so thirsty for it, he feared he'd never be quenched. Chris spread his ankles and tore his shirt loose, exposing his nakedness, his vulnerability, and Joshua touched Chris's hips with earnest hands, bringing his mouth to Christopher's white moon ass. Unknown to him. All of it. This caress…this intimate, almost obscene possession, but still, he kissed Chris's inner thigh and Chris shuddered, his hands slipping off the dresser. At once, Joshua knew he would bring Chris there. Would own him.

Joshua licked the tender skin of Chris's thigh, slowly making his path up to the dark meeting of the ass cheeks, and something base awoke inside him. A visceral instinct of territoriality, no, he wasn't sure what could sooth this madness. "Wider," he said, pushing Christopher's legs apart. The tone of his voice was unfamiliar. "Tell me no one ever did this to you."

Chris leaned forward, offering all of himself, his silence beckoning Joshua to ignore the unwritten rules they'd obeyed for the last five years. The only sound was the sound of their hurried breaths and Joshua's tongue grazing, tasting Chris's thigh, then his ass, up to the small of his back. He wanted to tease, but could barely restrain himself. He glided his lips down, moving slowly, though now his desire had betrayed him—he moaned and shivered with every flick of his tongue as if he was the one being licked. Though he'd never been rimmed, he could feel it on his own orifice: the softness of the tongue, the pressure of it on the lining of the anus, and he stroked himself, needing the release, yet knowing it could never compare to what Chris was feeling. With the tip of his tongue, he forced entry into the small, wrinkled orifice and clutched Chris's thighs, leaning him back into his face. Chris let out a cry, a lament, and Joshua caught sight of his fingers curling white around the dresser's edges—Chris was falling apart under his touch, and the notion excited Joshua further, sending his mind on leave, feeding the primal instinct in him. He licked the rim of Chris's anus, flicking his tongue in and out, always deeper, a little harder, until Christopher began mumbling promises, pledges, and divine incantations. Nonsense words, but beautiful nonetheless. How he loved to hear Chris come. The noises he made would be the soundtrack to his life.

Do you hear me now? Do you feel me, Joshua? It isn't over, baby. I'm here.

"Jesus," Chris said, looking down at the trickle of semen on his hollow stomach. He wiped it with his shirt and tossed the shirt in the corner. "Shit."

Chris was eloquent and poetic, but never after sex.

Joshua, still on his knees, grappled with his pants.

"You've changed," Chris said. His luminous gray eyes paused on Joshua's face, hovering like dust in the sun's first rays.

"Yes, well"—yes, he had changed, and because of Chris, the imposed loneliness, the fear of losing—"I guess I—"

"Look at me," Chris said, gently. "When you look at me, I know who I am."

That night they had slept side by side for the first time in five years and Joshua had woken in the earliest hours of the day to find Chris's sweaty, tangled curls splattered on his pillow.

And then he'd stared at the man he loved until the tears ran freely.

I remember that morning, baby. Our last.

April, seven years ago, Joshua had sauntered up the stairs—late again but who cared—on his way up to the main call center. "Josh here," he answered his cell phone, pausing on the last landing to catch his breath. Didn't want to sound like he'd been jerking off between calls—

"Mr. Gavins?"

His vision blurred and he reached out a hand in time to save himself from crashing into the wall across from him.

"I'm calling from Hotel-Dieu Hospital. You're listed on Mr. Christopher Saint-Pierre's ICE list."

They were going to go to Paris in June, survive on bread, Miller's work, and Merlot.

"I'm sorry, Mr. Gavins, but Mr. Saint-Pierre was in an accident."

Chris was going to stay clean. They were going to see about a small press over there. Chris had sent them some samples. They had said, "Canadian iconoclast, huh." They were going to print a column.

"It was a boating accident. Mr. Saint-Pierre drowned. He was pronounced dead on arrival. Are you family? We've been trying to reach…"

The voice faded into the edges of the world, sinking into the linings of the universe. The sadistic, cruel universe.

After the funeral, Joshua had shaken hands with strangers—men who'd loved Chris, men who'd had the luck of being in the right place, the right city, while he had stayed back, left behind by the man whose eyes held the answers to every question he had ever asked himself. And Joshua had smiled, pretending he knew who Chris was, knowing they would never know either.

I still have your answers, baby. See me. Feel me.

"Do I turn the the sirens off, or what?"

"There's no response. He's gone, man. Call it."

Joshua, look at me.

"Four thirty-three a.m."

Now Joshua's mind opened, blossoming wide, soaking up the vivid light that bathed his thoughts, his secret, dark chambers. What was that space inside him, that cavern of emptiness filling him inch by inch?

The pain is gone, baby. That's what you feel. You feel the possibilities it's left behind. You are a recipient, an empty vessel, and if you want it, Joshua, I can replenish you. Do you believe in me still?

Yes, Christopher, Joshua thought, felt, said, though in no voice, no particular, or possible way, I believe in you.

The sirens had been turned off.

"Almost looks like he's smiling."

Look at me. I am no longer ill, or weak. I am as I was when we touched the first time and shall always be. I've fought battles to come back to you, and I am here.

I am here. Your man. Your lover. Your knight.

I won't stop you. Joshua's soul unhinged. I'll never stop you.

I want you to touch me, it's okay.

A carpeted basement. A summer party. Music.

The clean scent of Christopher Saint-Pierre's flannel shirt and the feel of Christopher's tangled blond curls against his bare stomach…

A Coin in the Well

Nathan Sims

Jodie's heart fluttered in his chest, he was so nervous. Pulling the coin from his pocket, he kissed it and tossed it down the well's deep shaft. Not for the first time some twisted part of him wondered what that tumble into the earth might feel like. He envisioned falling like Alice, head over heels past cabinets and pianos and teacups. His teenage brain toyed with images of what he'd be offered to eat at the bottom of the hole and what might potentially grow…

Jodie sniggered and returned his attention to the well. He didn't hear the coin hit bottom. He never did. All he heard was the familiar, distant roar of the underground river at the base of the well. Somewhere past his childhood into adolescence, his parents had no longer found his fascination with the well charming. Now, as he turned eighteen, it was a source of consternation for them, not to mention a waste of good money.

"You could buy a car for what you've thrown down that ridiculous well," his father would say while his mother shook her head and talked of tithing ten percent.

Jodie didn't care. He knew the well was as good as its reputation. After all, from childhood on it had made many of his wishes come true, most recently the leads in the spring musicals both his junior and senior years. And Jodie had no doubt that tonight it would bring his one true love into his waiting arms.

The well wasn't looking her best these days. One side had caved in a couple of years back. Its stone lay crumbled in a heap. No one knew quite how it happened, nor had they cared enough to repair it. Jodie had thought he might try rebuilding it himself, but he'd never had a gift for building things. So like the rest of the town, he'd left the well in disrepair.

He leaned over the edge and looked down into its depths. The moonlight didn't penetrate past the first few feet. The darkness within was thick and complete.

Jodie stood and brushed off his jacket where he'd leaned against the stone. He'd bought it especially for tonight. It was a deep red, and he had it zipped a quarter of the way up with the white T-shirt beneath showing starkly by contrast.

He liked to think he looked like James Dean in the ensemble. All he needed was a cigarette and the image would be complete—except that he didn't smoke. Maybe he should take it up. Maybe then he'd look cooler.

Jodie fancied himself leaning against the edge of the well, the tip of a cigarette glowing in the night air as he raised it to his lips and drew off its shaft. He wondered what Ray would think as he walked up through the clearing and found him there smoking a cigarette with his deep red jacket and white T-shirt on.

The image passed. Ray was a football player and probably wouldn't want a boyfriend who smoked. He was too health-conscious for that.

Well then, maybe he could buy some glasses and, with a little curl at the front of his dark hairline, he might pull off a passable Clark Kent. He already had the black hair, so black there was a hint of blue to it. Ray wouldn't be able to resist Jodie dressed up like his favorite superhero—no matter how lame said superhero might be.

Jodie rolled his eyes. The things we do for love.

"Ugh!" he exclaimed, stamping his foot. He checked his watch again. Where was he? Jodie's note had clearly said 9:00 p.m.!

Meet me at 9:00 and I'll make all your wishes come true.

He'd even put a heart after the period with a slight curl where the two humps met at the top. He'd signed all of his notes to Ray the same way, with that same little heart. Over the last three weeks he'd sent twelve such notes to Ray.

They'd started off innocently enough, hinting that Ray had a secret admirer and giving voice to Jodie's secret feelings without fear of embarrassment. But after observing how Ray responded to the first few notes, he grew emboldened.

The football player hadn't rushed to his teammates like Jodie guessed some of the other jocks might have done. In fact, he hadn't shown the notes to anyone, not even Jodie, his best friend since grade school. He'd simply tucked each one away in his binder as he found them in his locker each day after third period.

Sometimes during sixth period, Jodie would watch him pull the most recent note out and study it as Mr. Watson droned on in world history class. Out of the corner of his eye, Ray would catch Jodie looking at him and quickly slip the piece of paper back into his notebook and out of sight. Later when he would ask Ray what he was looking at, his friend would always avoid his eyes and tell him it was nothing.

Ray's discretion made Jodie love him all the more. It revealed another side to his best friend that Jodie had always suspected was hidden away somewhere. Ray could appreciate the feelings of his secret admirer enough not to show the notes off to the entire world in an unbridled fit of machismo. He understood it was a confidence meant for his eyes alone. And Jodie would have happily kept it that way for weeks, if not months, to come. Unfortunately, necessity made that impossible.

The day Jodie decided to reveal his identity to Ray was the day he almost got caught sliding a note through the vent on his best friend's locker door.

Jodie was Ms. Baumgarten's student aid third period, and the computer teacher always had papers to send to the office or other odd jobs that took Jodie away from her classroom and out into the hallways. This was fine with Jodie. It gave him the perfect opportunity to slide his anonymous correspondence into Ray's locker.

That particular Wednesday, two days ago now, he'd approached the locker casually, not even checking to make sure if anyone was around, so overly confident had he grown over the last few weeks.

"What are you doing?"

Jodie spun around, his heart in his throat. The janitor Ronnie Butterman stood just a few feet away—or as he was known by most of the student body, Ronnie Buttman.

Ronnie still lived in the house he'd grown up in, the one his parents had left him in their will along with a comfortable inheritance. Despite his modest fortune, he'd been the high school's janitor for years now. When anyone asked him why, he'd wave noncommittally and say he liked to keep things neat and tidy. Rumor had it Ronnie actually worked at the school because it gave him easy access to the teenage boys, the ones he would pay to let him suck them off under the bleachers on the football field.

Everyone in town (Jodie included) rolled their eyes when they saw him swish down the sidewalk or sashay through the grocery store pushing his cart. The man (if you could call him that) was a joke, a buffoon, an unnamed illustration in Pastor Reed's sermons at least twice a year. He was everything Jodie swore he'd never be when he grew up.

"I was just…"

"Putting a love note in your boyfriend's locker?" Ronnie winked at Jodie.

"What? No! I was running something to the office for Ms. Baumgarten. That's all," Jodie sputtered. He slipped the note back in his pocket, glancing around to ensure that no one saw him talking to the janitor. The last thing Jodie needed was to be seen in the company of the town queer.

"Mmm-hmm," the janitor said knowingly. "Oh well, if it's nothing juicier than that, office is that way." The janitor flipped his hand palm-up and extended a languorous finger down the hall.

"Yes, I know." Jodie ducked his head and walked past the janitor.

"Oh by the way," "Buttman" said and Jodie turned back to him. "When you do decide to write those little love notes, let me know. I've got lots of experience."

Jodie blushed and hurried down the hall. How could he have been so stupid, almost letting himself get caught like that? He was so busy berating himself as he rounded the corner, he didn't even notice Ray standing in front of him until they'd nearly run into each other.

"What are you doing here?" his best friend asked.

Perfect! Could this get any worse? It was all over. Ray had no doubt overheard their conversation, and by now he'd figured out it was Jodie writing the notes and putting them in his locker. Jodie's heart thudded in his chest.

Desperate, he said the first thing that came to mind, "What are *you* doing here?"

Ray glanced down the hallway distractedly and said, "You mean besides watching you get hit on by the janitor? That guy is such a creep."

"Seriously," Jodie said, feeling relief rush through him from his head down to his toes. Ray hadn't overheard them. From the way he was eyeing his locker, it was obvious his only concern was staking it out. Little did he know he'd just caught his secret admirer red-handed! "I was on my way to the office when he stopped me."

"I don't know why they let him keep working here," Ray said, his focus still on his locker. When he realized Jodie hadn't left, he looked back at him and said, "Welp, guess I'll see you at lunch, then."

"Guess so," Jodie replied and walked away. Ray continued to hide around the corner, waiting to catch his unwitting secret admirer slipping that day's note into his locker.

That had sealed the deal for Jodie. He'd almost been found out. Better to do it on his own terms, he decided, than let it happen accidentally.

So the next note, Thursday's note, had invited Ray to meet his secret admirer face-to-face. The bit about "wishes coming true" had been a nice touch if Jodie did say so himself. It was obvious where he was referring to yet still held an edge of mystery to it.

"Joe?"

Ray stood ten feet away. The moonlight made him look even more handsome. He wore his peach pullover shirt tucked into his jeans (Ray was the only person he knew who could pull off a peach-colored shirt). His white sneakers glowed in the moonlight. His light brown hair gleamed.

How many times had they stood at this very spot together? How many futures had they charted out over the mouth of this well? How many times had Jodie nearly blurted out that any future without Ray in it was no future at all?

"What are you doing here?" his best friend asked. Even in the park's dim light, Jodie saw his green eyes scanning their surroundings, expecting to find his secret admirer stepping from the trees any moment now.

"I'm here to meet someone," Jodie explained. "What are you doing here?"

"Me too!" Ray replied.

"Huh," Jodie said, leaning against the lip of the well, showing off his dark red jacket to best effect. "What do you suppose the chances of that are?"

Ray stammered. He was so nervous. It was adorable. Jodie just wanted to grab him and kiss him.

"Wouldn't it be funny if we were here to meet the same person?" Jodie asked.

"Yeah hilarious, but I doubt…" Ray trailed off. Jodie saw the wheels turning. "Hey, have you been getting notes?"

"Notes?"

"Yeah, from a secret admirer."

"Secret admirer?"

"For about a month now I've been getting these notes," Ray reached into his back pocket and pulled out a piece of paper. He unfolded it and handed it to Jodie. "Someone's been putting them in my locker."

Jodie looked at the note. He pretended to study the words and the looped heart at the end. After so many years, how could Ray not recognize his handwriting? He supposed hope blinded everyone to reality sooner or later.

"All your wishes, huh?" he said handing the note back to Ray.

"Yeah," his best friend chuckled.

"Pretty tall order."

"So, did you get notes too?" Ray asked, sliding the folded piece of paper back into his pocket.

"No, I didn't get any notes."

Jodie crossed his arms over his chest. Standing in the park ready to confess his feelings, Jodie felt suddenly very cold. His heart pounded in what felt like an empty tomb. For the first time he thought he knew what stepping out into nothingness and falling down the well might actually feel like. Like plummeting with the sick feeling in your gut you might never touch down again. And if you did hit bottom, what would end up broken? Swallowing anxiously, Jodie took the leap.

"I sent them."

"You what?" Ray smiled that smile he had when he hadn't gotten the punch line but didn't want to let on.

"I sent them."

Still that same smile. Why couldn't Ray just hurry up already?

"I don't…"

"It was me. I sent the notes. I was your secret admirer." Jodie stepped toward his best friend, as if drawn by Ray's gravitational pull. "I'm the one in love with you." His best friend didn't say anything so Jodie added, "Me."

Ray was silent a moment longer, then burst out laughing. Playfully, he shoved Jodie, who stumbled but caught himself before he fell. The football player continued to laugh.

"You jerk!" Ray said when he finally stopped chuckling. "That was a good one! That's gotta be your best yet. 'I'm in love with you.' You had me going there."

"It's no joke," Jodie said quietly. This time he didn't move closer to Ray but kept his distance.

A final laugh escaped the football player and then he subsided into silence.

"I am in love with you," Jodie repeated the words. They escaped into the night air and vanished, so he sent others out after them. "I always have been, I guess. For as long as I can remember."

In the darkness Ray's eyes were impenetrable now. Just a few feet away and his face was a shadow of mystery. The ground felt unsteady beneath Jodie. Or was that just his legs? He held his breath waiting for the other boy to speak. All he heard was the distant roll of water in the riverbed beneath the ground.

"Say something," Jodie finally said.

"I don't know… How is this possible?"

"I'm gay, that's how," Jodie quipped.

"I know that," Ray replied.

"Well, we've never talked about it."

"I figured you'd talk when you were ready."

Jodie shrugged. "Guess I'm ready."

Ray sat down hard on the well's lip. The moment had played out so differently in Jodie's head. By now Ray should be putting his arms around him, kissing him, telling him he felt the same but had never had the words to express it, not sitting on the edge of the well with his eyes trained on the grass.

"So…you're in love with me, huh?"

It felt as if his best friend was casting blind in the dark. Jodie couldn't begin to guess what he might be thinking. Better to guard himself than be too vulnerable, he decided.

"Despite your affinity for D.C. over Marvel, yes. I've learned to look past that. Please note how I'm growing."

"Growth will be when you finally concede that Superman can kick anyone's ass in the Marvel U."

And that did it. The tremors Jodie's revelation had set in motion dissipated as Ray offered steady ground beneath their feet. Jodie accepted it gratefully.

"I never denied that. But what's the point of having a character without vulnerabilities? It's boring."

"Kryptonite." Ray jumped on the well-worn flaw in Jodie's argument.

"Kryptonite-schmiptonite." Jodie rolled his eyes, slipping comfortably into their well-trod conversation. "Anyone would be vulnerable to radiation. I'm talking real flaws, real vulnerabilities. I'm talking about taking him to the brink where you think he might lose everything, where you're scared he might actually die."

"He did die!"

"No, he didn't! His heart slowed to practically nothing, but he didn't die. That's my point! How can a man of steel die?"

The argument ended where it always did and the two lapsed into silence.

Then Jodie went on, "See, that's what I'm talking about. Who gets you better than me? Who's going to do your James Cameron marathons with you?"

"You like them too," Ray argued.

"*Titanic*? *Piranha 2*? I wouldn't sit through those for anyone but you."

He took a step toward Ray.

"Who else would watch *District 9* with you at least once a month? And every Keanu movie ever made?"

Another step.

"Who else is going to play Halo with you until three a.m. on a Friday night? Who else cheers louder for you in the stands than me?"

And another step.

"No one."

He stood before Ray, who was still seated on the well's edge. Jodie held his breath. He wanted desperately to reach out and touch him, to feel the other boy's flesh beneath his fingertips, to finally know how it felt to touch him in more than a passing fashion. How many sleepovers in Ray's basement or in his own bedroom had he spent watching his best friend's chest rise and fall in the dim light? How many times had he wondered what it might feel like to touch those nipples, or to play with the soft tuft of light brown hair in the center of his chest, or to lay his head over Ray's heart and listen to its steady beat? Too many to count, he was sure.

Finally, his best friend lifted his head, smiling. He shook it slightly and said with as much kindness as he could muster, "But I'm not in love with you. I'm not gay."

"How do you know?" Jodie asked.

"Well, how do you?" Ray countered. "Maybe you're straight and don't know it. Maybe you just haven't met the right girl yet."

"That's cause she doesn't exist. There's only one person for me." He leaned in close to Ray and said quietly, "Just like there's only one person for you."

Ray rose from the well and stepped away from Jodie. "Look, Joe. I'm flattered. I really am. But I'm not gay."

"You care about me, don't you?" Jodie asked.

"You know I do. You're like a brother to me. You're my best friend."

"Best friends fall in love all the time. It's a well-known fact."

"I think I should probably go," Ray said, turning to leave.

Jodie's dream was slipping away. His ever-faithful well was failing him. Desperate, he grabbed Ray and pulled him close, kissing him.

"Joe!" Ray shoved him away. "Get off me!"

Jodie toppled backward again. Before he could catch himself, though, his foot connected with the well's crumbled wall and he plummeted into blackness.

"Jodie!" he heard Ray shout from above.

Before he could think to scream, his body plunged into the underground river. The frigid water shocked Jodie and he sucked in, swallowing hard. He surfaced, hacking water as he struggled to find his footing.

"Are you okay?" Ray's voice could barely be heard over the rushing river. Jodie coughed, trying to purge the last of the water from his lungs.

More moonlight filtered down the well than he'd expected. He could see the riverbank ahead of him. He forded the water and clambered up onto dry ground.

"Jodie, can you hear me?" Ray shouted, desperately. Above him, Jodie saw his best friend's silhouette at the mouth of the well.

"I'm here," he answered.

"Jodie, is that you?"

"I said I'm here, didn't I?"

"Are you okay?"

"I fell down the well, Ray. How do you think I am?"

"I'm so sorry!" Jodie heard the panic in his voice. "I didn't mean—you just came at me, and I didn't know what to do so I pushed you away! And I'm so sorry!"

"It's okay, Ray. I landed in the river," Jodie said, finally catching his breath. "Just go for help."

"Are you gonna be all right till I get back?"

"Hurry!" Jodie shouted and Ray's silhouette disappeared from the mouth of the well.

He shivered in the darkness and hugged his legs to his chest, trying to keep warm. This was just great. Of all the ways he'd imagined this evening ending, freezing and alone at the bottom of the well was not one of them.

A sparkle drew his eye. The ground surrounding him was littered with coins all catching the moon's light, which just now appeared overhead through the well's mouth. He'd never imagined there was so much money down here. The ground was barely visible beneath the blanket of coins. Everywhere he looked, the riverbank shimmered. Who knew so many people had tossed their hopes and dreams down into this pit over the years? Praying the well's reputation might hold true one more time. Praying it might make their deepest desires reality. Cold and wet, he chuckled ruefully. Hopefully, they'd had better luck with their wishes than he'd had with his.

What had possibly made him think Ray felt the same way he did? Ray wasn't in love with him. He never had been. He never would be. He was straight. Jodie was alone, not just in his feelings for Ray but in his desire for men. He'd held on to the fantasy that he'd actually found someone who felt the same as he did, who understood the thing that made him different from all the other kids at school. The mockery, the bullying, it had seemed easier when he'd believed Ray felt the same way, that they'd shared this bond. The past ten years since he'd figured out he was gay had seemed manageable with the thought that someday he and Ray might proudly walk the halls of their school hand in hand like all the straight couples did, or go to prom and have their picture taken in matching tuxes. He'd fantasized the image so often he'd convinced himself it was true.

Now, alone at the bottom of the well, he saw how ridiculous he'd been. His fantasies of ending the evening in Ray's arms seemed so juvenile now. He felt miserable. More than miserable, he felt foolish. How could he have been so naïve? All that time he'd spent creating a delusion that his best friend was in love with him, all that energy, and what had it gotten him? Nothing but a trip to the bottom of this stupid well. And no Ray. He was such a fool.

He looked around him, his faith in the well dissolved. And no longer believing in it, he hated it. He hated the false hopes it had given him. He hated the way it had led him to believe that it could bring his dreams to reality only to dash them. He hated the fool it had made of him. His dad had been right. He'd wasted good money throwing it away down this stupid hole.

Jodie picked up a coin nearby and studied it a moment. "Since it didn't come true," he observed, "guess I'll take a refund."

He moved to pocket the coin when a voice from the darkness startled him saying, "Actually, this one's yours."

From the shadows a hand appeared, holding a coin in long, powerful fingers. An arm, then a sturdy, handsome face followed the hand into the light of the moonlit coins. Past the face came two shoulders. Attached to them were wings made of white feathers extending out several feet in either direction.

A serene smile shone in the glimmering light. The stranger held out the coin and asked, "You want it back?"

❖

Jodie huddled by the river's edge. "Who are you?"

"Don't be afraid," said the winged stranger, sitting just a few feet away.

"What makes you think I'm afraid?"

"You're shaking."

"I'm soaking wet and sitting forty feet underground. You'd be shaking too. Who are you?"

"Who do you think I am?"

Jodie couldn't help being reminded of Angel, the winged mutant from the X-Men comics he loved so much. The being's blond hair fell in distracted curls around a startlingly handsome face. His thick, muscular frame didn't escape Jodie's wandering eye either. And then, of course, there were those wings.

"I'll give you a freebie." His new companion winked. "I'm not him."

"Who?"

"Warren Worthington, your superhero from your comic books."

"How did you know…?"

The stranger raised an eyebrow as if to say "isn't it obvious?"

"Angels don't exist," Jodie replied. He tried to sound confident, but his chattering teeth and careful positioning as far from the being as possible belied his efforts.

"And yet here I am." The wings rose as his companion shrugged. For a moment Jodie was drawn to the miracle of his feathers sparkling in the moonlight. But only for a moment.

"Maybe it's hypothermia. Maybe you're a hallucination."

The stranger shook his head. "Despite every evidence to the contrary, you're willing to believe that your best friend is in love with you and yet you don't believe what's right before your eyes."

"How did you…? Oh, that's slick. You overhear our conversation and I'm supposed to be all 'oooh, you're an angel!' Please! For all I know you're some whack-job with a feather fetish. And what 'evidence to the contrary'?" Jodie asked, registering his comment. "How was I supposed to know he wasn't gay? I mean, I'm obviously gay—"

"Obviously."

"And despite that fact he's hung around me all my life, even though he knew I was gay. So why couldn't he have secret feelings for me he hadn't admitted to yet? I mean, I waited ten years to tell him how I felt. Why couldn't he do the same?"

The being smiled resignedly and said, "I guess you were right."

"About what?"

"Hope does blind everyone sooner or later."

Jodie froze. He remembered thinking that while he'd studied the note Ray had given him (his own note in his own handwriting), but he hadn't given voice to the thought. So how did the stranger know what he'd been thinking?

The being raised an eyebrow and said, "Think I overheard that one too?"

Jodie looked away, studying the coins littering the floor. There was no way the winged creature could know what he'd been thinking, unless…

"Fine, you're an angel," he snorted. "Don't you have a job you should be doing? I mean other than the oh-so-important task of sitting at the bottom of a well sticking your nose in people's business, of course. Shouldn't you be off guarding someone or something?"

"This is my job."

"What, spying on people?"

The angel smiled and said, "How else do you think your wishes came true?"

"What are you talking about?"

"Curly in *Oklahoma*? Billy Flynn? *Chicago*?"

Jodie studied the angel incredulously.

"What?" his companion winked. "You thought maybe I liked spending time in this dark little hole?"

"So you grant wishes." Jodie chuckled, masking how unnerved he felt over finding this stranger knew so much about him. "I thought you were an angel, not a genie."

"I've never known jinn to live in a well." The angel glanced up at the moon overhead. Something caught Jodie's eye. A scar ran from below the angel's right ear, down his jaw, to end on his neck. It was white and puckered and the sole blemish on his otherwise perfect skin. And there was certainly enough skin visible for Jodie to make that assessment.

He marveled at the beautiful physique: broad, dimpled shoulders; the plump muscles of the angel's chest; a ripple of abdominals ending at a swatch of cloth covering his loins. Again he was reminded of a host of superheroes soaring through the air doing battle with their equally generously drawn nemeses. Looking at his winged companion sitting just a few feet away, it was impossible not to believe that his every hero-fueled fantasy had sprung to life fully realized. The uncomfortable cling of wet boxer briefs under his khakis grew even clingier—in a not entirely uncomfortable fashion.

The angel had turned his attention back to Jodie. A knowing smile curled one corner of his lips. A flush of heat spread across Jodie's face and he glanced away.

"The scriptures speak of giants," said the angel. "Did you know that?"

Curious, Jodie looked back at him. His companion was looking him straight in the eyes. There was something deep and mysterious in the way the being appraised him, like a hungry secret lingered between the two of them just waiting to be revealed. It made Jodie's mouth go dry.

"It's true. The scriptures say that giants were the progeny of angels and humans. Angels bedding humans."

The words lay thick between them. Still, the angel stared at him, and Jodie found he couldn't look away. Distantly, he heard the sound of the river roaring by just inches from where he sat.

It wasn't the first time he'd heard the story. Back when he was younger, when he'd not yet turned his back on the church for condemning homosexuals to hell without once considering there might be one sitting quietly, faithfully in their midst, he'd read the scripture himself. In the privacy of his room, he'd imagined what that might be like, floating through the air sharing flesh with a heavenly being, the brush of feathers against naked skin.

"Is…is it true?" he finally asked.

The angel let the silence linger. His look pressed deep inside Jodie's eyes, deeper still into his soul. Jodie felt a throbbing in his chest, his heart pounding madly. His companion opened his mouth to speak but let it resolve into a smile instead. It was the kind of smile that turned the heat up on Jodie's body, despite the cold, damp clothes covering him. Finally, the angel licked his lips and spoke.

"I like your jacket."

Why were they talking about his jacket? Hadn't they just been talking about humans and angels and sex? He struggled to keep up.

"Thanks," Jodie replied.

He glanced down at the coat he'd bought especially for tonight.

The river water had caused the dye to bleed through and stain his white T-shirt red. In the dim light, it looked like he'd been wounded.

"A coat of many colors," the angel observed.

"What are you talking about?" Jodie asked, raising the sleeve. "It's burgundy."

"To your eye, maybe," the angel said, studying the fabric. He leaned his head to the side. In the pale moonlight his scar gleamed. Jodie couldn't take his eyes off it, its very imperfection making the angel more perfect. "But I see every color that went into making that burgundy dye," continued the angel. "The variations of yellow and blue and red all mixing together in a symphony of color to create the perfect shade of burgundy." His eyes drifted from the jacket back to Jodie's eyes before adding, "All for Ray."

Jodie blushed, reminded of his best friend. Not ten minutes ago he'd confessed he was in love with him and now here he was with a hard-on for a practically naked angel. What was wrong with him? How could he abandon ten years of love for Ray over this angel…no matter how perfect a specimen of male flesh he might be? Perfect areolas, ripe for sucking. Perfect mess of blond hair, looking like he'd just risen from bed or, better yet, might be headed back to it again. Perfect bulge hidden behind a loincloth just tempting Jodie to reach out and—

No. The angel was confusing him. That had to be it. The shock of falling down the well and the being's presence had to be screwing with his head. He couldn't just abandon his affections for Ray in a few minutes' time. If he could do that, then maybe Ray hadn't meant much to him in the first place, and maybe everything he'd been taught in church about gays and their hedonistic ways was true.

Not for me it's not, he decided.

He picked up a glittering quarter and flicked it off the end of his thumb. It went sailing through the air. The angel caught it.

"What's this for?" the angel asked.

"You still owe me a wish."

The being revealed the coin still palmed in his hand, the one he'd shown Jodie when he'd first fallen down the well. "What is it you wish?"

"Get me out of here."

The angel studied him for a moment, then shook his head and

handed the coin, Jodie's original one, back to him. He was taken aback by how warm it was.

"I'm sorry," the angel said. "I can't do that."

"Why not?"

"I can only fulfill wishes that are in the best interests of those requesting them."

"And me getting out of here isn't in my best interests?" Jodie gestured to the deep chasm above his head leading back to the surface.

"Not when it means I would lose my chance to talk to you." The creature rose for the first time. Towering over Jodie, he was easily seven feet tall. He stepped across the expanse between them and squatted down in front of Jodie, his white wings stretching out as far as possible, his feathers glittering like a million diamonds in the moonlight. A startling earthy smell mingled with the rich scent of incense crept into Jodie's nostrils as the angel said, "I've watched you for so long now, watched you come to this place and pin all your hopes and dreams on a coin tossed down a well. You don't know how long I've longed for this opportunity to talk to you, to share just a few moments with you. How could I possibly let this go by without taking advantage of it?"

The angel gently brushed the side of Jodie's face. A tingle lingered on his flesh where the fingers had been. He closed his eyes, reveling in the sensation, his thoughts and his body falling instantly back under the angel's spell. "I couldn't let it pass," his companion continued, "not when it means I would lose the chance to show you the error of your ways."

"What error of what ways?" Jodie asked, struggling to remain focused on the being's words.

"Isn't that obvious?" the angel replied, pulling his hand away. "The error of being gay, of course."

❖

Jodie would have sworn the river water had soaked all the way to the bone, the icy shock that jolted through him as he listened to the angel's words was so powerful.

"You what now?" he asked.

"I'm here to convince you that being gay is wrong."

Wait a minute. One minute the angel was flirting with him. The next he was calling Jodie wrong for being gay. It made no sense. Why was the angel teasing like this? Was he testing him? Irritated, Jodie's defenses went up.

"What, are you going to start quoting scripture now?"

"Would it work for me to start quoting scripture now?"

"No."

"Then I won't."

Jodie barked a laugh and rose to distance himself from the being. "So what will you do? Love the sinner but hate the sin?"

"I doubt—"

"I should probably tell you I don't believe in God."

"That's not true."

"Yes, yes, it is," Jodie lied. "Why would I believe in a God that made me gay but convinces his followers that I'm evil?"

"Well, there's your first mistake."

"What?"

"Believing the Father made you gay. Of course He didn't. He doesn't make mistakes."

Jodie bristled. "I'm a mistake?"

"Of course," the angel said but then amended, "Or would you prefer *anomaly*? 'God doesn't create anomalies.' There. Does that sooth your ego?"

"Not much, no."

The angel stood and stretched. Despite his frustration, Jodie couldn't take his eyes off the muscles reaching and pulling beneath his skin. His attraction to the angel only made him angrier. How had they gotten from the angel's look and touch to Jodie being a *mistake*? None of it made any sense.

The angel continued, "The Father designed the world to function in male and female pairings. It's everywhere. It's how the species flourish. As nature evolved, though, it created aberrations." The angel looked at him and with a gentle smile said, "You're one of those."

"So, I'm a fluke," Jodie replied.

"An abnormality, yes," the angel offered.

"And because of that God hates me."

"The Father doesn't hate you," the angel replied.

"Oh no, He only tells His followers to stone me, that's all."

"Yes, well, they did enjoy their stonings, didn't they?" the angel said as he casually pushed coins with his toes through the sand on the riverbank. "But that doesn't mean He wants you dead."

"Well, that's a comfort. He doesn't want me dead. He only wants to punish me."

Instantly, the angel's mood changed. If Jodie couldn't still see it in the sky overhead, he would have sworn the moon had passed from view and his companion's face was now cast in shadow.

"You have no idea what punishment is," the angel said. "Watching your home destroyed, going to war with your brethren, hearing their screams as they tumble from grace into eternal damnation, having your world turned on end and knowing there's nothing you can do to stop it." The angel's eyes were fixed on the water flowing through the riverbed a dozen feet away, his thoughts a million miles (and for all Jodie knew a million millennia) away.

"You humans think you were the first to unleash 'shock and awe.'" He ran a distracted finger down the scar running along the side of his face. "Until you watch your entire reality be obliterated, you have no idea what those words truly mean."

Jodie had never thought of it like that before. Growing up, any time he'd heard the story of the fallen angels in Sunday School or during a sermon, it had stirred images of some great battle from his comic books, the pages filled with winged soldiers swooping through a city of gold, fiery swords inked in their hands and vibrant blood staining white feathers red. It had never occurred to him to consider what it had done to those who experienced it firsthand, the pain and anguish it had caused for both those who'd been banished as well as those left behind. The whole thing made him feel juvenile and naïve. His previous moment's anger ebbed.

"I'm sorry," Jodie said.

At first he didn't think the angel had heard him, but then a weary smile spread across those lips. He turned from the river to look at Jodie and said, "Yes, well, if not for that, you wouldn't be here."

Confused, Jodie asked, "What?"

"How do you think your universe came into existence? Your scientists call it the *big bang*, yes? We call it *The Hour of Great Rebellion*, the day the Father banished a legion of the heavenly host from His presence forever."

"You're saying…"

"The Father is the eternal optimist," the angel said. "Only He could take the blackest day in Heaven's history and turn it into a cause for celebration with the formulation of you, His favorite creation."

Jodie's mind swirled. In the few minutes he'd been down the well, everything he understood, his entire reality, had been turned inside out. He tried to tell himself none of it could be true, that it was all some illusion. Yet on some deeper level that he couldn't quite discern, he knew that wasn't so. It was all true. And that fact terrified him.

Since walking away from the church, he'd convinced himself the Bible was just a myth and the truth of God was no more found in its pages than in the Koran or any of the other holy books that promoted themselves as the one true path to God. If that were so, why hadn't God come down here and told them which religion was legitimate? Why had millions died over the centuries arguing the point, when it could all be resolved with one single visit? He'd steeled himself with this defense even as his mother pleaded with him to return to church, crying and arguing with him until finally she relented at the urging of her husband to just let the boy make his own choice.

But now, here, in front of him, stood living proof. Proof there was truth to the scriptures. Proof they weren't just the prejudiced ramblings of a small-minded patriarchal society. Proof angels existed and hell was filled with the fallen. And if those were true, what about Jodie and the punishment those scriptures warned was waiting for him? The word *abomination* tolled like a death knell in his ears. Frantically, he dismissed the thought.

"Don't you see? That's why I'm here," the angel was saying, gripping Jodie by the shoulders. Through his wet shirt, the skin of his arms tingled like his face had when the angel brushed it with his fingers. His body stirred at the touch. Even at an innocent touch, Jodie couldn't control his body. What was the matter with him?

"I'm here because He loves you," his companion said. "He doesn't want to see you suffer, to spend your life alone and miserable. He wants you fulfilled and complete."

Desperately, Jodie clung to his hopes. "But who's to say I'll end up alone or miserable?"

"The first time you tell a boy you love him and what happens? You end up down a well."

"No, Ray didn't mean—"

"Of course he didn't, but what happens when they do? What happens when it isn't someone that 'loves you, but isn't in love with you'? What happens when you end up face-down in an alley, beaten and broken, your blood on the outside rather than the inside?" The pain was apparent on the angel's face. Tears welled in his eyes as he asked, "What happens then? God doesn't want you dead, Jodie, but man does. What kind of a life do you think you'll have hiding who you truly are for fear of retribution, for fear what others might do to you?"

The mocking and jeering he'd faced at school came back to him; the years of name-calling and bullying; the alienation; the strong memory of a middle-school boy forcing him to walk across a classroom in front of a crowd of fellow students just to prove he "moved like a girl."

He'd survived it all. He'd told himself if he could just hold on past high school it would get better. Everything would be better once he was away from here, someplace else where people would accept him for who he was, someplace far from his small, close-minded town.

"And what makes you think it'll be any different out there?" the angel asked, unnerving Jodie by reading his thoughts again. "What, you'll move off to some city where gay is okay? You don't think they'll be there too?" the angel asked leaning over and picking up a handful of coins. "You don't think the ignorant and the bigots live in cities too? They'll be there just like they are here. It'll be no different."

He tossed the coins into the air and whispered a word in a language Jodie had never heard before yet spoke to something deep in his soul. Rather than tumble back to the ground, the coins hung suspended in the air before Jodie, each one spinning on its axis, together forming a perfect ring. At its center an image appeared.

The vision was of Jodie walking down the street, briefcase in hand. He looked older—ten, maybe fifteen years older. His hair was graying prematurely and he'd inherited his father's pooch. He trundled along the sidewalk at the end of a long day. A group of young men walked past, laughing at something—possibly Jodie, possibly something else. Whatever it was, it set the Jodie in the vision on edge. Clearly the mockery and jeers that he'd believed would pass with time had continued on into adulthood. His older self pulled the collar of his suit coat close around his face and hunkered down, pressing toward a brownstone where he took the steps to the front door.

Safe on its other side, he opened his mailbox. A package tumbled out into his hands. The mutinous envelope lay exposed in his quivering fingers. He glanced around anxiously to ensure that no one was there, then slipped the padded envelope into his briefcase and climbed the stairs to his third-floor apartment.

Behind his locked door, he tore into the package and pulled out a DVD case. On its cover were two naked men, fondling one another as they kissed passionately. A shuddering sigh escaped older Jodie's lips as he traced a finger across their oiled torsos. He licked his lips hungrily.

Jodie watched his older self shuffle through his empty apartment to the living room and flip on the television and slip the disc into the DVD player's waiting slot. He laid the case on top of a pile of similar cases casually stacked beside the television. Apparently visitors were rare enough that he didn't need to worry about hiding his collection. Jodie watched in horror as his older self sat down on his couch and the movie began. A cat jumped up to greet him but he shooed the beast away and began to unzip his pants.

"No," Jodie said, unable to stand another moment. He rushed at the image, batting away the coins. They tumbled to the ground, motionless, the image gone.

This couldn't be real. Where was the life he'd always imagined? Where were the friends? The boyfriends? The husband? Where was the family he'd promised himself waited once he escaped this backwoods burg he called home where being different meant being bad? Where desiring something that wasn't the norm meant you were a monster and vilified?

Tears welled up in his eyes. This was it? This was all there was? A miserable, lonely existence lost in some city with no friends and no one to love? This was what awaited him?

"It's not too late," the angel said. "You can still turn your back on this path you're headed down. Please. Just turn around."

"I don't understand," Jodie said through his tears. "They're not all lonely. They're not all that way. I know they're not."

"How would you know that? From movies? Television? What's your own personal experience, Jodie?" the angel pressed. "I mean, who do you actually know that's gay?"

Instantly, the janitor "Buttman" came to mind.

"You think Ronnie expected to turn out that way?" his companion asked. Jodie was so preoccupied that he didn't even notice the angel was reading his thoughts again. "You think he didn't want a family? Companionship? Love?

"He left town for a while. Did you know that? He moved away in hopes of finding everything you hope to have someday. But eventually, he came back. He saw the truth. He knew there was no hope for a future in that life, no chance to create something real and have it grow into family and friends. But not before he found himself alone. Not before he realized the lie he'd told himself. And one day…one day, when he couldn't take it anymore, he found himself standing on a chair with a rope tied around his throat." The angel left the thought unfinished.

Jodie gulped down a staggered breath of air. He didn't need to hear the rest. He knew firsthand the tickle of that rope as it brushed against his neck and the desperation it took to put it there. He knew the suffering that led to thinking that was the best answer, the only answer. That feeling nothing was better than feeling only pain and rejection.

"There's another way," the angel was saying, "for him and for you. The Father has something else, something wonderful in store for you if you'll only let Him." The angel was at his ear whispering, his breath warm against his skin. "Won't you let Him?"

Jodie closed his eyes. After what he'd just seen, it was hard not to listen to the angel's words, hard not to believe that taking a different path, living a different life might not be for the best after all. Sure, he'd have to learn to adjust, but at least he wouldn't stand out anymore. He wouldn't be different. He wouldn't be a freak. A queer. A faggot. He'd be normal. He'd be accepted. He would fit in. He wanted so desperately to fit in.

"All you have to do is say yes."

Yes to a God he'd loved as a child sitting on his mother's lap reading stories from his picture Bible. Yes to a God he'd desperately clung to when he faced the pain and rejection of his peers who'd branded him as different. Yes to a God he'd felt comfort him in those dark times of loneliness and suffering. Yes to a God who wanted nothing more than to comfort now, to make him feel happy, complete, and loved.

Yes.

He swallowed past a lump in his throat that refused to budge. He opened his eyes to turn and face the angel and say the word, to fall back into the loving arms of a God who wanted nothing but the best for him. A streak of light flashed across his teary-eyed vision. The moon still hung above. The coins all around him shimmered.

So many hopes, so many dreams, all tossed down this well in some vainglorious attempt to control fate. To dictate the outcome of life. To find happiness and joy. Jodie had spent years believing it was possible, that he could simply make a wish and everything would be all right. But it was all a lie, wasn't it? Ray's rejection of him had proven that. No matter how hard you wished, life didn't always give you what you wanted.

The light from the coins danced before his eyes. It was cold and white and utterly lovely. He wondered how many of those wishes had actually come true. How many bets had been wagered down the shaft of this well and yielded a return? He'd seen it happen in his own life on more than one occasion. But was it really hoping blindly for a twist of fate that made your dreams come true? Or was it the one making the wish that made it happen?

Would he have gotten the leads whether he'd come here and made the wishes or not? Did it all just come down to believing in yourself, and choosing to make it so? And would that translate past high school to his life? Could he make the life he wanted come true? Could he have the love and the family and the joy he dreamed of? Could he live a life unashamed and proud of who he was? Jodie liked to think it was so. Jodie had to believe it was so.

Still superstitious, though, he felt the need to hedge his bets. The coin the angel had returned to him sat in his palm. He lifted it to his lips.

"What are you doing?" the angel asked.

Jodie whispered to the coin. It was his wish, his heart's desire. It was his prayer for the future.

"What are you doing, Jodie?" the angel demanded behind him. "You can't really think this will work, can you?"

Jodie looked at the angel over his shoulder and replied, "Guess hope blinds everyone sooner or later."

Cold and alone, Jodie stood at the bottom of the world and threw the coin as hard as he could into the river, one arm propelling the coin forward, the other stretched out behind for balance. The coin skipped across the surface several times and vanished from sight into the river's depths before being swept downstream by the current. Jodie watched it disappear, his arms still outstretched. He raised his face to the moonlight. He felt like an eagle, ready to take flight from this dark hole back to the surface. Back to where life waited for him. His life. His way.

A weight slammed into him. It drove him off the riverbank and into the water. He plunged beneath into its icy depths, the angel clinging to his back, forcing them both to the riverbed. The weight of the angel vanished as a hand gripped his shirt and yanked him to the surface.

"You stupid sack of meat!" the angel roared. He backhanded Jodie, his head slamming to the side.

"You think you can deny the Father's wishes? You think you can turn your back on Him?"

Another stinging blow across his face. It rocketed through his jaw and up into his head.

"He gave you everything! Everything we should have had! He chose you over us. He turned His mourning into dancing just by creating you. He forgot all about us, about my brethren. He abandoned them to the pit without a second thought all because He had a new toy to play with. You! He loved you so much He gave you a universe, and what do you do?"

The angel plunged him back beneath the surface. Jodie barely had time to gulp down air before he submerged. The creature shook him. A flurry of bubbles escaped his nose until there were no more. His body cried for air. He struggled to break the creature's grip, to resurface and fill his burning lungs. He shook his head, forcing himself not to breathe, not to inhale the water surrounding him. His vision blurred and started turning black. The angel jerked his head back to the surface. Jodie dragged precious air past his lips into his body.

"You turn your back on Him," the creature was shouting. "You foster your own gods from those ridiculous comic books you read! You create your own religion of sexuality and perversion and tell Him you'd choose communion with a man over His eternal, perfect love! You who don't even know what love is! You who claim you're in love with your best friend!"

"I am," Jodie screamed.

"Yet you can't take your eyes off me, off the flesh of my body."

The angel shoved his free hand beneath the surface of the water.

Jodie felt fingers grip his groin and squeeze. Kneading fingers began to work at his flesh till, unbidden, Jodie felt himself thicken and grow.

The angel sneered at him. "Even now, like this, you're aroused by me! So depraved in your desire that the one who could destroy you arouses you. You disgust me!" Gripping Jodie by his belt and the collar of his jacket, the angel lifted him over his head. "You disgust the Father!" And as casually as he might have tossed one of the coins dotting the bank, the angel threw him. Jodie landed with a splash in the water. Before he could struggle back to his feet, he found himself surrounded by air. He looked up to see a wall of water on either side of him, the damp riverbed beneath him revealed. Arms outstretched, the angel had parted the river and was walking toward him.

"You're a worm! A maggot! You're dust from the corners swept up and breathed life into. You are nothing!" the angel screeched.

"Better a maggot then a hateful, vengeful God!" Jodie leapt to his feet. He wiped water from his face and tears from his eyes. "This is the God of love? This is the God who wants the best for me but lets others bully me and revile me and hate me just for being who I am? You can have Him!" he yelled. "I'll burn in hell before I spend one more minute worshiping a God like that!"

The angel's rage dissipated instantly into pained embarrassment. The walls of water gave way and the river flowed back into its bed. "Jodie, I…"

Before he could say more, though, a length of rope tumbled down between them and splashed gently on the surface of the water.

"Jodie!" he heard a voice shout from above.

"Dad?"

"Do you see the rope, son? Grab it."

"It's got a loop tied in it," Ray shouted, his silhouette joining Jodie's dad's at the mouth of the well. "Slip it around your chest and we'll pull you up."

Jodie grabbed the thick rope.

"It's not too late, Jodie." The angel was at his shoulder, grabbing the collar of his jacket, turning him so they faced one another.

"Let go of me," Jodie said, trying to pry free from the angel's grasp.

"Don't turn your back on the message just because of the

messenger," the angel said, holding fast. "I made a mess of it, but you can still choose the right path. You can still find God."

"I said, *let go*!" He twisted and pulled himself out of the jacket, leaving it in the angel's grip. He threw the loop over his shoulders and beneath his arms, wrapping it around his chest.

He looked at the angel one final time, his heart hard and full of venom, and said, "Go to hell and take your God with you."

Jodie tugged on the rope and was jerked up out of the water toward the moonlight overhead.

"Please, Jodie, please don't do this," the angel shouted from beneath him. "Please!"

Jodie ignored the angel's pleading and the God in whose name he spoke. He kept his eyes on the mouth of the well as it grew larger and larger overhead.

❖

The angel watched the boy's father and best friend pull him from the well. He looked at the burgundy jacket in his hands, the one the boy had abandoned to be free of him. He lifted it, enjoying the colors as they blended and danced in the moonlight. He released the jacket and watched as the river carried it downstream into the blackness and far from view.

The angel cocked his head to the side, watching the boy approach the surface.

At first the change was subtle. It started with the scar on his jaw and spread out from there as the skin on his face blackened and cracked like parched earth gone too long without water. Or skin cooked too close to a flame.

The metamorphosis journeyed past his face and down his throat to his chest and beyond. The locks of golden hair on his head crumbled away to nothing, revealing a bald scalp covered in angry blisters, cracked and oozing. The tips of his wings turned black as his feathers dissolved to carbon and blew away across the water's surface, carried on the breeze of the rushing river until nothing was left but the stubs on his back where glorious wings had once sprouted when he'd been part of the heavenly host.

The being forded the river back toward its bank. As he did, a chain shimmered back into view attached to a clasp around his neck. The chain snaked its way across the shore to vanish in the shadows of the cave from which he'd emerged.

He bent to crawl back inside and glanced up a final time. The boy's legs were now kicking their way over the edge of the well's broken wall and back onto the grassy lawn of the park.

"Wait. No. Stop," he said quietly, mockingly. "Jesus loves you, Jodie. And I do too." But the boy was beyond hearing now, beyond caring. Forever.

Satisfied with his efforts, the fallen one wheezed something like a chuckle and climbed back inside his prison.

Exalted Thoughts

Nic P. Ramsies

When Alix was a young boy he loved to hear Brother Dominic tell the story about the night he was found on the front steps of the Home for Little Angels. And Brother Dominic, the headmaster of the Jesuit orphanage, enjoyed telling the story almost as much as Alix liked hearing it. In fact, he delighted in telling any story and had over the years gained a reputation for enhancing his tales. So every time Alix asked, Brother Dominic happily retold the tale of that dark, wet night that Alix came to live at the orphanage. A careful listener would realize the details of the story never changed at all when Brother Dominic told the tale. And an even more attentive listener would see a look of wonder on Brother Dominic's face that matched that of the children listening to his story for the first time. And such was the case on that Saturday afternoon when an eight year-old Alix brought four of the other orphans to Brother Dominic's office and asked for him to once again tell the story.

Brother Dominic was sitting behind his large, old wooden desk grading papers. He looked up at Alix, a slender boy with graceful movements, dark hair, and even darker solemn eyes, in the doorway, ran a hand over his balding head, and removed his reading glasses. "All right," he said in a tone that falsely implied he didn't want to tell the tale and slowly rose from his seat before he flashed a quick smile and winked at Alix and then followed him to the main entryway. For Brother Dominic, as Alix knew, liked to tell the story on the stairs across from the very front door where the event occurred.

The four other boys, all of whom were under seven years old and new to the orphanage, were already sitting halfway up the large stairwell. Brother Dominic sat in the middle of their semicircle and closed his eyes as if to recall the story from some distant part of his memory. Alix sat on the last step at Brother Dominic's feet.

"I was working in my study on lesson plans for the next day," he began the tale in an overly excited voice. "Everyone else was already in bed and Mrs. Smith had gone home for the night. It was very late and I was very tired." Brother Dominic faked a yawn and stretched his arms, then playfully messed the hair of the boy sitting next to him. "I was ready for bed. So I got up from my desk, turned off the light, and went into the hallway. I checked the door to make sure it was locked. I looked outside through that very window, but it was sleeting outside and very dark. So I started up these very steps to my room."

"What happened next?" Alix asked.

"You, young man, could tell this story yourself." Brother Dominic smiled. "I was halfway up the stairs when I saw my shadow projected in front of me on the steps. This light was shining on my back. It was so bright. I could feel its warmth as if it was the sun. I turned around and the windows on either side of the door were filled with an impossibly bright, golden light." The boys all looked at the front door set in a frame with a ceiling-to-floor window about a foot wide on each side of it. "In fact, the entire front wall was full of the light, as if it was able to penetrate the very wood of the building." Brother Dominic paused, looking at the door, recalling the event itself. "I made my way slowly back down the stairs to the doorway."

"Were you afraid?" asked Steven, one of the little boys who was hearing the story for the first time.

"I was afraid, a little bit anyway. I wasn't sure what could cause such a light, but I trusted in God and made my way to the door. I tried to look outside through the window but couldn't see anything because I was blinded by the pure gold light. I put my hand on the doorknob, said a little prayer, and opened the door. As soon as I opened it, the light was gone." The sounds of five little boys in awe filled the air. Brother Dominic nodded, affirming they had indeed heard him correctly. "Outside it was dark. There wasn't even a streetlight or moon overhead. A light icy rain fell from the sky. It was pure darkness, as if I was deep in the woods. If it hadn't been for the light, I wouldn't have opened the door and I never would have seen the little basket." Brother Dominic wondered what would have happened if he hadn't found the baby that night. Would Alix have been able to make it to the morning? "And there on the top step wrapped in a blanket in that basket was our Alix."

"Don't forget the feather," Alix said sternly.

"Yes, the feather. Resting on top of him was a small feather. I have yet to identify what type of bird the feather came from, but I have it still in my drawer in my desk."

"Can we see it?" three of the boys asked in unison as everyone but Brother Dominic stood up to race off to his office.

"No, it's lunchtime," Mrs. Smith, the orphanage's cook and Lady Friday, responded before Brother Dominic could answer. "Go wash up. Off with all of you now," she said as the boys dragged themselves up the steps to wash up. "You shouldn't tell them that tale. It isn't right to fill their head with foolishness. Especially *poor* Alix."

"Why, Mrs. Smith, you know the tale is as true as I do," Brother Dominic said, crossing his arms on his chest, ready for the old, familiar banter.

"True, perhaps, but embellished like a fancy embroidered sweater, Brother."

"Not so. I saw the light and I have the feather."

"Off with you too, Brother. Now wash up for lunch."

While Mrs. Smith would never accuse Brother Dominic of lying, even he knew she didn't believe the story about his finding Alix. The bishop, with whom Brother Dominic was often at odds, dismissed it as car lights and an overtired monk with a too active imagination. Despite the fact that Mrs. Smith always fell in line with whatever the bishop said, she made a fabulous apple pie and was wonderful with all of the children. Still, Brother Dominic knew in his heart of hearts that it had been a miracle and that Alix was a gift from God.

Over the years, the orphanage had been unable to place Alix in a permanent home. And while this wasn't completely uncommon, it was rare, especially for a child with Alix's disposition. He was calm and quiet; thoughtful in his ways and mindful of adults. But each time Alix was sent out on a Friday for a weekend visit with a prospective family, he was returned the following Sunday night with a fantastical tale of horror avoided and what's more, a single feather of the variety found in his basket.

Alix climbed a tree and fell. We found him unconscious on the ground with this next to him. He ran into traffic and was unhurt but found unconscious with this feather clutched in his hand. We turned away for one minute and he was gone, we found him next to the river, wet and unconscious with this feather next to him. It seemed each visit contained a potentially life threatening event that put the family off and returned Alix to the orphanage and, more importantly, to Brother Dominic.

Brother Dominic had a drawer with eight feathers from seven weekend trips, all the same except for the size. He knew the exact order the feathers had appeared, as they increased slightly in size as Alix aged. Brother Dominic felt guilty each time Alix was returned because he was secretly happy about it. He didn't want Alix to leave. Of all the boys he had taught, helped raise, and lived with at the orphanage, Alix was somehow special to him. Brother Dominic was sure Alix was meant to be here with him at Little Angels.

As Alix got older, fewer opportunities for his finding a family appeared, as most people wanted younger boys, until finally when Alix was ten everyone quietly accepted that Brother Dominic would raise him at the orphanage. Alix excelled at his schoolwork, and when he reached eighth grade he was sent down the street to the Catholic high school. Alix helped Mrs. Smith with the younger children, did yard work and helped Brother Dominic with every task he was assigned and many he wasn't. Never getting into any trouble. He grew into a kind, thoughtful young man who was obedient and empathetic to those around him. Except regarding the questioning of issues of faith, Alix was a perfect boy. This made the problem of placing him an even odder sign to Brother Dominic. He was sure God had sent Alix for a reason. He just wasn't sure what that reason was. Was Alix a test of his faith or of that of the church? The answer remained to be seen.

"Brother Dominic, I don't understand why the church fathers believe homosexuality is wrong," Alix stated when he was in the 11th grade. "Didn't God make each of us in his image?" Brother Dominic nodded. "Isn't God love?" Again Brother Dominic nodded. "Can't a person be a good person and be gay?"

Brother Dominic removed his glasses, "Alix, God is always right. The church fathers are human and therefore not infallible, not perfect." Brother Dominic paused waiting for Alix to mull over this idea.

Alix nodded. "The fathers mean well, but they are not God."

Brother Dominic smiled. "Yes, Alix, they usually mean well."

"Someday when I am older, I'll become a Jesuit and help the church fathers understand their mistakes in interpreting Jesus's message."

"That's a wonderful goal, Alix. Perhaps someday you will do that, or perhaps you'll find you want to be a doctor or a lawyer. There's plenty of time to figure it out."

Brother Dominic feared the day that Alix would push this question, perhaps demanding to know what his views on the subject were. For Brother Dominic was himself gay, and as Alix grew older, he believed the boy was gay too. But for now, Brother Dominic would provide as little information as Alix demanded for each question on church law and try very hard to not influence the boy with his own interpretations of God's words.

But the day Brother Dominic feared eventually came when Alix was in his second year of college and home for the winter holiday break. Alix had grown into a tall, thin but muscular twenty-year-old with dark wavy hair and eyes so dark they appeared black in all but the strongest light. "Brother Dominic," Alix said as the two men were placing the donated Christmas presents under the tree for the little children to open in the morning, "is it wrong that I have romantic feelings for other men?"

The question hung in the air between them until Brother Dominic answered, "Does it feel wrong, Alix?"

Alix pondered the idea, "No. It feels right." Then after a pause added "It feels like truth. Like love."

Brother Dominic nodded. "God is love, Alix." He grabbed his hand. "No matter what, don't forget that God is love. That truth will eventually win out."

Releasing the boy's hand he added, "But best not mention this to Mrs. Smith or the bishop. They both already believe we Jesuits are heretics."

Both men laughed and returned to placing gifts under the tree, but Alix's thoughts were on Rob, his roommate at college, and Brother Dominic's thoughts were on Alix's future and what trials lay ahead for him.

❖

Rob grew up in Iowa and looked the part. He had piercing blue eyes and short, sort of curly blond hair that one could easily imagine had been cut using a mixing bowl as a pattern. He was average build and average height and could easily be lost or overlooked in a crowd. Rob was quick to smile and laugh at a joke, but kept himself slightly apart from everyone around him. Rob wanted more than anything to be who he was and to be accepted for just that; perhaps this was because he was estranged from his family or perhaps it was because he was engaged in an internal struggle. His family didn't accept him anymore because of his choices. He missed them more than anything in the world but wouldn't lie to win back their love.

Rob and Alix had roomed together for their freshman year and again for the fall term of their sophomore year. The two young men shared many interests—in books, nature, bird watching, silly movies, and reinterpreting the meaning of the Bible—and grew close over time. Neither of them truly fit in with their classmates but neither minded so much. They studied together, talked about the Bible and God, and even went to a few parties before they discovered they'd rather stay at the dorm and watch a movie.

Rob's family were members of the First Congregation of Jesus Christ Crucified, a very popular fundamentalist Christian church in the Midwest. When Rob was eight he began spontaneously preaching to the congregation. By the time he was nine, everyone believed God was speaking through him and he gathered a following. People came from other states to see him preach the word of God, have him lay hands on the young, sick, and elderly. The church prospered and his family became semi-famous in the Bible belt—blessed by both God and with material things. Rob's future was bright and the path he was on was clear and well lit.

One Sunday when Rob was seventeen years old, as he preached God's word to the congregation both in the newly constructed temple and over the Internet, broadcast to believers in all fifty states and Canada, he felt a golden light burning inside him and he said, "Jesus loves everyone." The audience replied with a hearty *Amen* and he continued, "God is speaking to me right now and he says Jesus loves everyone, including his gay sons and daughters. Jesus wants us to embrace the homosexuals and stop persecuting them."

The congregation went stone silent. Rob repeated himself: "Jesus loves everyone, including his gay sons and daughters." Before he could say anything else, he was ushered off the stage and the choir sang an uplifting gospel song.

The church's minister met repeatedly with Rob and his parents in an attempt to get Rob to stand up in front of the congregation and say that Satan had deceived him. That the words he had thought came from God were actually from Satan. Rob refused. Rob's parents attempted to convince their son that this was what had happened, but Rob refused. He knew God had spoken to him in the past as well as this time. It didn't matter if the minister didn't like what God said, Rob wasn't going to lie to make the minister or his parents happy.

Suddenly Rob found himself alone for the first time. He was cast out of the only community he knew. The small town that had once embraced and loved him was cold to him. He wasn't allowed to attend services. His parents stopped speaking to him. Rob prayed, but he didn't get a response from God. Still he refused to change his story. He applied to colleges and received a scholarship. Everyone was relieved when he went east to attend college.

Just before holiday break their second year of college, Rob had told Alix his story. He told Alix that God had spoken to him and what was more, that God had stopped. Rob said he felt close enough to share this with him. Alix agreed he felt close to Rob and thanked him for telling him and trusting him with the story. The truth Alix didn't share was that he felt so close to Rob that he believed he was falling in love.

"Maybe God is still speaking to you, but what he is asking you to do is so difficult you have blocked his words out of your mind," Alix offered as a solution.

"Maybe, but God took everything from me, and still I believed in him." Rob shook his head. "Maybe I'm wrong."

"Maybe it's a test. God likes tests. This could be a test to see if you truly love God and if you are willing to do what he asks of you no matter what you lose."

"Maybe God did send you to me," Rob said, stroking Alix's face, and locked eyes with him.

"God did," Alix said before getting up and walking over to his suitcase. Despite his strong feelings for Rob, the sudden intimacy made him uncomfortable. "Are you sure you won't come home with me for the holiday? Brother Dominic would be happy to have you with us."

"No, I'll stay with Janet and her family. But thanks."

❖

And so in late January, Alix returned to school and to his dorm room where he hoped Rob would be waiting. It was the start of the spring term, and Alix had made up his mind that he was going to tell Rob he was in love with him. Truth always won out, Brother Dominic had told him this his entire life, and Alix believed it. He believed God had sent him to Rob despite what the church fathers and the Christian fundamentalists said. God was love and Jesus loved everyone and truth would win out.

"Hey," Rob said as Alix entered their small room. "How was your break?"

Alix put his bags down, took off his jacket, and closed the door behind him. "Good. Listen, I have to say this before I lose my nerve."

Rob sat on the bed, "Okay, go ahead."

Alix took a deep breath, then exhaled. "I missed you."

Rob smiled. "I missed you too."

"No. I *really* missed you. I think…no, I know I'm falling in love with you." Alix stood there staring at Rob; waiting for his response, holding his breath.

"I know. I'm falling in love with you too." Alix smiled and laughed as Rob walked over to join him by the door. "I just wasn't sure if you felt the same, I mean…" He shrugged and hooked his thumbs into the belt loops of Alix's jeans.

"I do," Alix said and pulled Rob into his arms and kissed him softly at first, then harder, exploring the soft wetness of his mouth with his tongue.

Rob pulled the collar of Alix's shirt aside and licked his neck, starting at the base and working his way up to his ear, where he nibbled on his lobe while he ground his crotch into Alix's. Both of them were rock hard. The two men pulled apart and Rob gestured toward the bed. Alix locked the door and they both sat on Rob's bed, where they held hands and started kissing again, slowly at first then harder and deeper. Alix felt tingles inside his body and he wanted to be in full contact with Rob's flesh. He tugged at his clothing and they both removed their shirts, shoes, and jeans.

Rob's cock was hard, so Alix grabbed it and the two of them tumbled onto the bed. Alix licked Rob's nipple, then sucked on it as Rob squirmed under him. Rob bit into Alix's neck and Alix groaned. He'd never felt anything like this before. He wanted to force Rob's legs open and enter him. He wanted to be inside Rob, but more importantly he wanted to take Rob. Alix could feel power building inside him and he was sure if he didn't expend it, he would explode.

As if Rob knew what Alix was thinking, he said, "There's lube in the nightstand drawer."

Alix rolled off Rob, opened the drawer and removed the lube. "I've never done this before."

Rob laughed. "I have. You're doing fine."

Alix kissed Rob again as he poured the lube into his hand. Rob lay on the bed, pulling his legs up to give Alix access. Alix kneeled on the bed and quickly found Rob's hole and worked it in small circles with his finger before he slipped one inside. Rob moaned and jerked his ass toward Alix. Alix pumped his fingers in and out while stroking Rob's cock with his other hand. Alix wanted to consume Rob; he couldn't get enough of him fast enough to satisfy himself. He pulled his finger out of Rob's hole and squeezed a generous amount of the lube over his hand, then coated his own hard cock with it. He positioned his cock at the mouth of Rob's hole and pushed inside.

Rob sighed and exhaled as he felt the pressure of Alix's cock and the tight pulling of his anal flesh. Rob held his breath and bore down, meeting Alix's gentle inward thrust, and swallowed Alix's cock with his ass. Rob exhaled as every nerve ending in his body became electrified. He looked directly into Alix's eyes and held his intense gaze. As Alix gradually increased the power of his thrusts inside Rob, sending shock waves of intense pleasure through him, Rob noticed a golden light glowing from Alix's skin.

Alix continued to pump his cock deep and hard into Rob. He could feel the power building inside him. The smell of musk and sweat filled his nostrils and he never wanted to stop pounding Rob. Alix grabbed Rob's legs, holding him firmly in place, and thrust deeper. He was sure he would come at any minute. Rob started to pump his own cock in time to Alix's thrusts.

Just as they were about to both come hard, there was a tearing sound as if flesh and bone were metamorphosing into something new. Alix thrust again deeply into Rob and there was a popping sound, followed by the sound of wings flapping, and Alix screamed as he came deep inside Rob. A flood of memories came over him, centuries of lives lived, of messages delivered, of choices made and orders followed, and it was all so very clear again. Clear as when he had agreed to do it.

As Rob came, his come squirted onto his hand and chest. Both of their bodies shook with the overload of sensation. Alix gave a final thrust, then both men stopped.

Rob looked up at Alix. "You have freaking wings."

Looking into Rob's eyes, his cock still inside him, Alix said, "I am the eighth archangel, Jeremiel, God's exaltation." His wings rustled as he pulled out of Rob and lay next to him. "I am God's answer to your prayers. I am here to help you complete your calling."

"You're an angel?"

"I am the inspirer and awakener of exalted thoughts that raise a person toward God."

"I have a calling?"

"Yes, to spread Jesus's message of love and correct the injustice done in his name. I chose to come here to earth and be with you and help you to fix the mess Christians have made."

"I fucked an archangel?"

"Technically an archangel fucked you. But yes. I am still Alix, but I am also an angel."

"I'm in love with an angel and I'm on a mission from God?"

"Yes. You are."

Rob put his head on Alix's chest and Alix wrapped his wings around them both.

Angel on Break
Mel Spenser

Chapter 1

Why does it always have to rain on days like these? Micah wondered.

It was early morning, and he stood at the window looking down on the parking lot. Behind him the life support machines hummed. Sarah had gotten steadily worse in the last twenty-four hours. He knew it was almost over, and he waited patiently, as he had done many times before.

At ninety-three years old, Sarah had outlived her husband, siblings and children. Now it was just she and Micah waiting it out.

They had been together continuously all of those years. He was there when she was born, and had not left her side. It had been a long run. The longest he'd ever had.

Finally, he heard the unmistakable death rattle. He sighed and turned toward the bed. He closed the small space between them and stood looking down at her. She opened her eyes.

"You," she whispered.

"Yes."

"I knew you existed. But no one ever believed me."

"I've been beside you the whole time," he said. "But now you don't need me any longer. It's time for you to move on."

With a gentle movement that started at her forehead, he passed his hand a whisper's breath over her face. And she moved on.

"Well done, Micah."

He glanced at the other angel, Paschar, who had not been in the room seconds earlier. They stood on either side of the bed looking down at Sarah's body.

"What next?" Micah asked. "Where are you sending me?"

"This has been a long one for you, Micah," Paschar said. "Almost a hundred years. You need a rest."

"That would be nice," he admitted. "How long do I get?"

"Let's leave it open for now," Paschar said. "I'll contact you when I find a good match. Since people are living so long now, we try to get the best possible fit. What do you plan on doing on your time off?"

"I'm going to get laid," Micah said. "A lot."

Chapter 2

As Micah walked out of the hospital, he turned up the collar on his long trench coat to keep the rain off his neck. San Francisco at that time of year was cold and wet. He didn't like the weather, but it did make it convenient to blend with the humans until his wings receded. He paused for a moment, and then continued up the sidewalk, away from the hospital and Sarah, and toward his brief freedom.

He'd known this day would come eventually. The stint with Sarah had been a long one. He'd never left her side and had watched over her, even intervening to save her on more than one occasion. He'd done a good job. Not many guardian angels could say they were with someone for nine decades. As she got older, he had begun planning what he would do if he had some time to himself. One of the first things he planned on doing was getting laid. Ninety-three years was too long to go between fucks.

He'd been amazed at the advances in technology during Sarah's lifetime. Her era was really one of the most exciting he'd witnessed in the long line of people he'd been charged to protect over the centuries. And he'd kept up with each astounding invention. Especially the Internet.

The only catch to his newfound time off was that he would be earthbound until called again. Between wards, the guardian angels were forced to walk with the humans. They became subject to human needs and functions. It was supposed to give the angels a taste of what it was like to be human. To walk around in their shoes, so to speak. The good part of this was the food and sex. The only thing he would miss would be the use of his invisibility and the ability to fly.

Now it was necessary for him to get to a safe house. They were set up in major cities for angels in waiting and provided everything that they required. He had to get some better clothes if he was going to attract any potential lovers. Putting his hand in the pocket of the trench coat, he felt the coins they had left him. Just enough money to get him where he needed to be.

With that thought in mind, he went down the subway steps to catch the BART. Twenty minutes later, he emerged on Market Street in the Castro.

Chapter 3

He walked up a side street, looking at addresses as he went. Finally spotting the correct one, he hurried up the steps to the door of a white Victorian and knocked. He saw a flutter of the lace curtain over the window and then heard the lock being undone. A tall thin man opened the door just enough to place his body in the opening.

"Yes?"

"I'm Micah."

The man smiled and opened the door wider, gesturing for Micah to enter.

"Oh, we've been expecting you. I'm Gavin, the owner." He stepped back, as Micah came inside. "Welcome to my inn.

"I have a room ready for you at the front of the house overlooking the street. You'll see that it has a nice bay window with a lovely view."

The man indicated the closed door not ten feet from the entrance. "In fact, here is your room."

He reached out, turned the knob, and pushed the door open. He allowed Micah to enter first, and then followed.

"We always want our special guests to be as comfortable as possible. Everything you need is here at the inn. Food, shelter, TV, music, and a laptop with wireless. Everything," he said again. "Well, except for clothes. You will need to go pick some out. Which reminds me…"

Gavin pointed to a wallet, credit card, ID, book, necklace, and key sitting on the nightstand.

"Those are for you to use."

Micah picked up the ID. It had a picture of him grinning like a fool with the name "Mic Dolenz." Somebody obviously had a warped sense of humor.

Mic picked up the necklace. The circular silver pendant was inscribed with the words *Angelus Custos*. Guardian angel.

"Latin?" Mic asked.

"It's what we're going with these days," Gavin said, shrugging.

Mic picked up the book, *Rector pro Angelus in Effrego*. Guide for Angels on Break.

"You should read that," Gavin said. "To help you avoid any pitfalls."

Mic set the book down and put on the necklace.

"Thank you, Gavin," Mic said, holding the pendant between his fingers. "For everything."

"No trouble at all. It's what I'm here for." As he walked to the door, he added, "Meals are served in the dining room. Right up those stairs." He pointed somewhere over his left shoulder. "Please make yourself at home and enjoy your stay with us," he said, backing out of the room. He left, pulling the door shut.

As soon as he was alone, Mic crossed the room to the desk and turned on the laptop. As it booted, he looked at the room while taking off his coat. He glanced over his shoulder to check his back in the full-length mirror. Much of his wings had receded, but they still had a good bit to go before the process was complete. He'd always liked his wings. They were a scarlet red. Pity they had to be hidden.

He sat down at the desk as the computer finished coming up. He was impatient to get started. He didn't know how much time he had. Sure, Paschar had implied that he'd get a long time off, but he just didn't know when he'd be called.

He had already done some research and knew of two sites to start with. He liked the sound of AngelCrunch.com more than HeavenlyPassions.com, so he decided to try that first. He clicked on through all the disclaimers and then stopped when he realized he had to create an account for himself. Damn. And here he thought he was prepared. He hadn't even thought about what to call himself.

Sitting at the computer, staring out the bay window, he racked his brain trying to think of something. He ran all sorts of names through his head, dismissing each one for being too cute, too desperate sounding, nerdy, or just plain vulgar. Finally he typed *AngelonBreak*, and found that it was available. A few moments later, he was in.

Immediately, he was hit with candid photos of chests, abdomens, asses, and cocks. Apparently, there were a lot of horny angels out there with little time to spare, so they'd cut to the chase fairly quickly. Surely he could find something here, he thought as he scrolled through the listings. He shifted in the chair as he started getting an erection.

He stopped and clicked on BigIsaiah's profile. By the look of it, BigIsaiah was definitely big. More like huge. One of the pictures within the profile showed BigIsaiah's erect cock next to a universal remote control for comparison. Mic raised his eyebrows, cleared his throat, and involuntarily clenched his sphincter. He decided to move on.

A profile called RedwingedBear caught his eye. He thought it must be another angel with red wings like himself. Although he knew he wouldn't get to see them, the thought of another angel with red wings was intriguing. He clicked on the profile. *Holy crap*, Mic thought as he sat back in the chair. The picture showed a very large and very hairy man standing in a doorway with his hands on the doorsill overhead. Even though the guy was big, his cock was pretty much hidden in a thatch of hair. Now Mic understood what was meant by Redwinged. The guy was nude except for a pair of white work socks that peeked over the top of Red Wing work boots. Another photo showed the guy in a recliner, his legs spread advertising his goods, with the soles of his boots pointing toward the camera. Mic had seen enough. Clicking out of RedwingedBear, he scrolled past several more suspect profiles: FeathersAndFur; CherubCub; RubMeRyan; DevilishChub; and Cloud9_69. That left him with a half dozen to seriously look at.

Moving down the page, he came to a picture of a nice torso. *Not bad*, he thought. He clicked on AtomicAngel's profile. Now, this was more like it. AtomicAngel was gorgeous. Nice pecs and abs. Stylish brown hair with that tousled look that said he'd just gotten out of bed and was ready to get back in again. Mic didn't see a thing wrong with him. Plus he was versatile. Making his decision, he quickly sent off an e-mail to AtomicAngel, promising to add a picture before the day was over.

Excited at the prospect of hooking up with AtomicAngel, Mic logged off. He stood and went to the mirror. He glanced at his back and saw that his wings had completely receded. He found a T-shirt in the dresser drawer and put it on. Grabbing the wallet and keys, he headed out to buy some clothes.

Chapter 4

Carrying shopping bags full of clothes and supplies in each hand, Mic bounded up the steps of the inn later that afternoon. He was struggling to locate the key when the front door opened abruptly. Gavin was looming over him, smiling.

"I just happened to be walking by the door," Gavin said. He took several steps back to allow Mic to get inside with his packages. "I see you've had success shopping."

"Yes," Mic said. "Yes, I did."

"Did you get everything you need?"

"Yes, thank you," Mic said, edging away. He was anxious to get to his room so he could log on to see if AtomicAngel had responded.

"Dinner is ready," Gavin said.

"What?"

"Dinner," Gavin said again. "Upstairs." He gestured toward the ceiling, smiling at Mic. "You really should eat something. Miles knocked himself out tonight with the menu."

"Okay, sure," Mic said as he finally got the door to his room open. "Let me set these things down and I'll be up."

Gavin might have been saying something else, but Mic had already shut the door. He tossed the shopping bags on the bed and practically pounced on the laptop to turn it on. He started pulling clothes out of the sacks while he waited impatiently for the computer to boot.

Once the computer was up, he quickly logged onto the site. Yes! He had a message. Well, he had about a dozen. He hoped one of them was from AtomicAngel. He opened the mailbox and looked anxiously at the screen. There he was, halfway down the list. He clicked on the message to open it and read the short note.

Hello AngelonBreak,

You must be new here. Upload a pic and we'll see what happens from there.

AA

Mic felt excited. He'd already heard back from his first choice. If things worked out, he could be fucking by tonight. Then he realized he didn't have a camera. Shit. He sat looking out the bay window for a few moments, thinking. Gavin! He imagined Gavin had a camera that he could use.

He left the room and took the steps two at a time to the next level of the inn. When he burst into the dining room, conversation stopped and the two men sitting at the table looked at him.

"Oh," Mic said. "Sorry about that."

"That's quite all right," the blond at the other end of the table said to him. The guy was obviously checking Mic out. "No problem at all. Join us."

"Thanks," Mic said as he took one of the empty chairs.

"Tea?" Gavin asked, materializing next to Mic.

"Uh, yes, thank you."

Gavin poured tea from a pitcher, then disappeared into what must have been the kitchen.

"So what's your name?" one of the guys asked.

"Micah. I mean Mic."

"Oh no you don't. You're not getting off that easy. What's the whole name that he gave you?"

Mic sighed and said, "Mic Dolenz."

"Like from the Monkees?" the other guy asked. "Gavin sure has a bent sense of humor."

"Gavin?" Mic asked. "He comes up with the names?"

"Oh, yes," the blond said. "Gavin sets up everything. He has a love for anything retro Hollywood and pop culture. Tell him your name," he said to the other guy.

"Shekinah. Otherwise known as Shecky Greene."

"I'm Tabbris. Tab Hunter."

Gavin drifted back into the room with a tray and set it on the buffet behind Mic.

"Gavin?" Mic asked.

"Yes?"

"Do you have a camera that I could use?"

"Certainly. I will fetch it for you."

Less than an hour later Mic was back in his room with Gavin's camera. After taking a selfie in the mirror, he uploaded his picture to his account, then sent an e-mail off to AtomicAngel.

He was really hoping that he'd get a response. Yes, it had been a long day, but it was still early. And he was more than ready to get laid.

After he took a shower, he checked his email. AtomicAngel had responded. He suggested that they meet at a place called Lime on Market. Mic sent back a note and got ready.

When he walked into Lime about an hour later, he was blasted by the noise. It was a crowded happy hour, and the music was loud. He made his way to the bar and ordered a drink. Once he had it, he turned and looked at the crowd. He tried to spot AtomicAngel somewhere within the bright pink club.

"Are you Mic?"

Mic turned to see AtomicAngel in the flesh. He was smaller than Mic imagined he would be. Mic didn't care, though, because he was even cuter in person.

"Yes. Nice to meet you."

"My name is Perry," he said. "Have you been out long?"

"I just got released this morning."

"You didn't waste any time."

"No," Mic admitted. "I was pretty anxious."

"I know the feeling. When I was released, I did the same thing."

"How about you?" Mic asked. "Have you been out long?"

"About three months."

"Man, this place is loud," Mic said.

"Did you want to get something to eat?"

"I'm not really hungry."

"You want to get out of here?"

"Yes."

"Let's go, then," Perry said, leading the way.

They left the club and walked up Market together.

When they arrived at the inn, Mic glanced through the door

window, hoping that Gavin wasn't hovering in the foyer. His hands shook as he tried to get the key in the lock.

Once inside, he opened the door to his room and let Perry enter first.

"This is nice," Perry said, looking around. "I haven't been to this particular safe house…"

Perry was turning toward Mic as he was talking. Mic must have had a look of desperation on his face, because Perry added, "Okay, then. Let's get started, shall we?"

They stood facing each other for a moment. Then Mic reached out, grabbed Perry's wrist, and pulled him close.

Perry's arms went around Mic's waist. They looked at each other briefly before Mic leaned down and kissed him. Perry gave a small sound, his hands moving up Mic's back.

Mic turned them and pushed Perry up against the door. Removing Perry's arms from around his waist, Mic lifted them and held them by the wrists against the door on either side of Perry's head. While holding Perry's wrists firmly, Mic angled his mouth over Perry's. He deepened the kiss, tongue probing Perry's lips until they parted.

Mic nudged Perry's feet apart with his, and wedged a thigh between Perry's legs. When Perry leaned into him, he felt Perry's erection straining against the denim of the jeans. He rubbed his own already hard dick against Perry's hip.

Perry made several little sounds while kissing that drove Mic even further toward the edge. He broke the kiss and looked down at Perry's flushed face and lips swollen from being kissed. Mic dipped his head down for more.

As they kissed, Perry began lightly struggling against the hold that Mic had on him. It only served to rub their aching cocks against one another.

Mic pulled back and said, "I've got to have you."

They were both breathing hard. From inches away, Mic's gaze roamed over Perry's face and hair before making eye contact. Neither said anything, yet they stayed in the same position, Mic holding Perry against the door with his body, and still gripping Perry's wrists.

Perry arched slightly and pressed his crotch more firmly against Mic's thigh.

When Mic let go of Perry's wrists, Perry's arms momentarily stayed up against the door on their own while they continued to look at each other. Then Perry reached up and pulled Mic's head down for another kiss.

When they parted again, Mic leaned down, resting his forehead on Perry's. He was breathing hard, trying to slow himself down.

Perry's hands began working the button on Mic's jeans. Mic helped out and soon the jeans, as well as the rest of the clothes that they were wearing, were scattered on the floor.

Perry led Mic to the chair and said, "Sit down and let me take care of you first."

Mic sat down, leaned back in the chair, and let Perry take over. The first feeling of a warm wet mouth on his cock almost made him come. It had been such a long time, a stiff wind would have made him pop off. However, if he did, he wasn't too worried. It wouldn't take him long to be ready for another round.

He closed his eyes and concentrated on what Perry was doing. Mouth sliding up and down on his dick. Fingers lightly tugging his balls. It was so good. He gave a little moan.

Then, abruptly, there was no longer a mouth on his dick. When there wasn't any indication of a mouth coming back to it, Mic frowned and opened his eyes. He raised his head to look at Perry.

Perry was still kneeling between Mic's spread legs. However, he had a strange look on his face.

"What's the matter?" Mic asked.

Perry didn't answer. There was a curious look on his face, and his head was slightly cocked as if he was listening. Mic didn't hear anything. It seemed that it was something only Perry could hear.

Then Mic realized.

"Oh shit," Mic said. "Not now."

Perry, apparently done listening, turned his attention back to Mic.

"Sorry. Gotta go," Perry said, standing.

"Wait! Can't we finish?"

"No can do," Perry said, as he backed away toward the middle of the room to give himself some space. "You know as soon as we get the call, we have to leave. My new assignment is about to be delivered."

Already, Perry's wings were unfurling. Mic watched as purple feathers sprouted and grew along the underside of them.

"Sorry to leave you in this condition..." Perry started to say.

Perry stood flexing the large wings as they filled in. Mic watched as his body morphed from its human form to angel perfection.

"Yeah, I know," Mic said. He was resigned to the fact that he was going to have blue balls.

Mic watched as Perry ascended to the high ceiling of the old inn and hovered for a moment. Then, in a flash of light, he was gone.

Mic laid his head back on the chair and closed his eyes. He had no choice now but to finish it himself. Not very satisfying.

Chapter 5

The next morning at breakfast, only Tab was present.

"Where's Shecky?" Mic asked.

"Gone. He got the call just as he was sitting down to eat breakfast," Tab said as he buttered his toast.

"There seems to be a lot of that going around," Mic mumbled, walking to the buffet.

"How'd it go last night?" Tab asked.

"It didn't. He got called right in the middle of it," Mic said as he loaded his plate with food.

"Ouch. Sorry."

"Yeah, well," Mic said. "There's always tonight."

"You might give the Café on Market a try," Tab said. "Just beware of the groupies."

"What?"

"Wingwankers. They are like those humans who hang around with vampires, only they prefer angels."

"I'm not following you."

"Fangbangers," he said. "You know...they have sex with vampires. Supply them with blood."

"Huh?"

"Anyway," Tab said, waving his hand that was holding the fork, "Just make sure that whoever you hook up with is another angel. Not some guy pretending to be one, or worse yet, a demon."

"Oh, yeah," Mic said, finally comprehending. "We're forbidden to lie with humans. I know that."

"Yes," Tab said. "Ever since the Nephilim. And you know what happened that time."

"Noah and the floods."

"Exactly," Tab said. "Except nowadays, it's the angel that takes all the punishment. Still, some of them do it." Tab shook his head as he picked at his food. "The temptation is just too great."

"But it's forbidden," Mic said again.

"Yes, well, Lucifer is always looking for recruits," Tab said matter-of-factly, taking a bite of his omelet. "Look for the pendant." He pointed at the necklace around Mic's neck. It matched his own. "Just be careful out there."

❖

Despite his best efforts, Mic still hadn't secured a date for the evening. He had made contact with several guys on AngelCrunch, but none really caught his eye. He was anxious, sure. And about ready to pop, actually. But he wasn't that desperate. Yet.

Screw this, he thought, getting up. He went to take a shower. It wasn't long before he was heading down Market in search of some fun. What bar was it that Tab had suggested? The Café, that was it.

It was Friday night and the place was packed by the time he got there. Surely he'd have some luck here. He got a drink and walked around for a bit. He was cruised several times, but since he had mostly been looking at necks for the pendant, he'd missed several opportunities.

Mic made it back to the bar and saw a cute guy sitting on a stool. Mic had noticed him earlier, but then had lost track of him. Now there he was a couple of feet away.

"Loud in here, isn't it?" Mic asked.

Obviously taken by surprise, the guy quickly turned and looked at Mic.

"What?" the guy asked, leaning in close.

"I said, it's loud in here, isn't it?" Mic said again, trying to be heard above the din.

"I can't hear you. It's too loud." He looked at Mic's pendant. He cocked an eyebrow and Mic could tell that its significance registered with the guy. He got up from the stool and began walking toward the door, indicating for Mic to follow him. When the guy headed downstairs, Mic was right behind him.

"Hey, where are you going?" Mic asked.

"Let's go outside where we can talk."

Mic followed the guy to the parking lot to a dark spot next to the building. Although standing only a couple of feet away from him, Mic couldn't make out the guy's face too well in the half-light.

"This is better," the guy said. "My name's Val. I haven't seen you before. You must have just been released."

"Yeah," Mic said. "Yesterday."

"Ah," Val said, smiling. "Fresh."

There was something about Val's smile that seemed sinister. Mic was getting a bad vibe. He started to take a step back, intending to walk away. However, he didn't get far. Before he knew what was happening, Val pulled him close, trapping his arms behind his back. Then Val kissed him. But it wasn't really a kiss. Val's mouth was sealed over Mic's. Val was strong and, caught by surprise, Mic was unable to struggle. Aware of every sensation, Mic was overcome with visions of hell and suffering. He felt himself weakening as his life force began leaving him.

However, as quickly as it began, it was over. Abruptly, Val released Mic. Actually, it was more like Val was pulled off and tossed aside. The instant their lips parted, it was as if the spell was broken. Everything came back clearly for Mic as he quickly regained his strength.

"Nice try, Valefar," Tab said.

Valefar, who had landed on the ground, sat up and glared up at Tab through his bangs.

"Fuck you, Tabbris," Valefar said.

"The last I heard, you were in L.A.," Tab said.

"I have better results up here."

"I wouldn't count on it. I'll be here for a while, and I'll put the word out," Tab said. "Hunting won't be so easy for you now."

"You can't be everywhere at once."

"Neither can you," Tab said. "We're just angels, after all. Although one of us is fallen."

Tab pushed Mic toward the street, leaving Val sitting on the pavement. "Let's get out of here."

They left the parking lot and started walking up Market toward the Inn. “What did I tell you about being careful?” Tab asked.

Mic didn’t answer. He was still too shook up over what almost happened.

“Did you even read the book?”

Mic had to hurry to keep up with him.

“What book?”

“The guide,” he said. “I know Gavin must have left a copy of it on the nightstand with everything else that you needed,” Tab said, irritated. “Gavin doesn’t make mistakes.”

Tab stopped abruptly, and Mic did as well.

“And the pendant,” Tab added. “What did you think that was for?”

“So we angels could identify each other.”

“The trouble is, it allows for those to identify you who you don’t want,” Tab said. “Valefar could have easily been a human. But he’s not. He’s a fallen angel looking for recruits.”

Mic realized how close he had come to blowing it. Forever.

“Thanks for helping me back there,” Mic said.

“Don’t mention it.”

“Why did you do it?”

“I had someone that I cared about make that fatal mistake,” Tab said. “I didn’t want the same thing happening to you.”

They walked back to the inn in silence. They walked up the stairs and Tab used his key to let them in. He followed Mic into his room.

“I knew Gavin gave you a copy,” Tab said, indicating the book on the nightstand. “Like I said, Gavin doesn’t make mistakes.”

Mic studied Tab’s profile for a moment. Tab turned his head and Mic gave a sharp intake of breath when their eyes met. Pale blue eyes looked back at him. He hadn’t realized Tab was so good looking. How had he missed that?

“Hey, wait,” Mic said as Tab turned to leave.

Tab stopped and looked at him expectantly.

“Do you have to go?” Mic asked.

“So am I your consolation prize?” Tab asked.

“No, I didn’t mean that. I didn’t realize…”

“I’m not the one having trouble getting laid,” Tab said and started to walk away.

"Will you wait a minute?" Mic put his hand out and touched Tab's sleeve. Tab looked down at Mic's hand, and then back up at his face. Their gazes locked for an instant. Mic could swear he saw interest in Tab's eyes. Then the moment was broken when Tab glanced over his shoulder.

"Looks like you've got mail," Tab said, indicating the laptop.

When Mic turned to look at it, Tab left the room.

He just wasn't getting anything right. He began pacing while removing his clothes. He had the opportunity to be with a hot guy, and here he was, back in his room, alone and frustrated.

When he had removed everything but his shirt and boxers, he turned on the TV. He stood idly watching the news while he undid his cuffs and unbuttoned his shirt.

Mic heard a knock on the door. Frowning, he walked to it and looked through the peephole. Tab was standing on the other side of the door, looking down the hall. Mic yanked the door open.

"What do you want?" Mic said.

Tab looked up at Mic, uncertainty on his face.

"You," he said.

They stood facing each other in the doorway. Finally, Mic reached out, grabbed him around the wrist, and pulled him into the room, pushing the door shut.

Mic backed up and took Tab's hands, leading him further inside. Standing by the bed, Mic helped Tab off with his jacket and laid it on the chair. Then he undid the buttons on Tab's shirt.

Tab stood still while Mic undressed him, making Mic feel as if he was opening a present. When he parted Tab's shirt, he stopped to look at Tab's smooth skin and pale nipples.

His hand shaking, Mic traced his fingertips over Tab's skin. Tab shuddered at his touch. Mic pulled Tab to him so that their bare torsos were touching. As they kissed, they removed the rest of each other's clothes.

Mic backed Tab to the bed and urged him to lie down. Tab lay on his back, and Mic kneeled between his spread legs. Mic leaned forward, running both hands up Tab's front and then back down the slim sides. Resting his hands on Tab's hips, Mic looked at the man spread out in front of him.

Mic's gaze rested on Tab's dick. He took the hard cock in one hand. Leaning over, he propped himself up with the other hand and took Tab's cock in his mouth. Tab's hips lifted off the bed and his head pressed back into the pillow when Mic licked the head.

As Mic sucked him, Tab's hands bunched up the sheets. Mic got lost in the feel of his lips and tongue sliding over Tab's cock. He closed his eyes and let his mouth slide over the satiny skin of the tight head. Mic breathed deeply as he continued to practically worship the rigid flesh that he held in his hand.

Mic finally released Tab's prick and looked up at him. Tab was looking back with hooded eyes, his lips slightly parted.

He lay down on his side next to Tab. Mic watched his hand as he ran it over Tab's chest and stomach. He ran his palm over the pink nipples, causing them to pebble. Then he rolled them between his fingertips until they were tight.

Tab rolled on his side to face Mic. He began flicking at Mic's nipples with his tongue while he lightly tugged on Mic's balls and stroked his cock.

Mic ran his hand along Tab's back, cupping his ass. His fingers teased along the crease until he found Tab's hole. Tab shuddered when Mic found the pucker and probed with his finger.

Tab reached across Mic and picked the lube up off the table. He squeezed some into Mic's hand, then draped his leg over Mic's hip. While they kissed, Mic slipped a greased finger into him, getting him to relax and open up.

Mic gently pushed Tab onto his back, encouraging Tab to raise the leg nearest Mic, knee bent. Holding Tab tightly around the chest, Mic scooted over until the head of his cock lined up with Tab's hole. Tab reached down, wrapped his fingers around Mic's cock, and guided it in.

Mic felt resistance at first. When he tried again, Tab relaxed, and the head of Mic's cock slid in.

Mic paused long enough for Tab to adjust, and to help himself maintain control. He pulled out slightly, and then pushed back in further, spreading the lube with his cock. Finally, Mic pushed until he was in, his balls snug against Tab's ass.

He leaned over and kissed Tab. As they kissed, Mic began moving his hips, sliding his cock inside Tab's tight heat. Mic's movements became more urgent, and as his hips moved faster, he reached for Tab's stiff cock and stroked the hot flesh.

Tab tensed right before he came. As come shot out of his dick, his ass gripped Mic's cock tighter. Mic pulled out and stroked himself off with a firm grip as he came on Tab's ass and balls. Then Mic leaned over, and they kissed as their tremors subsided.

Tab rolled over on his side, facing away from Mic, and they spooned. Pulling Tab close, Mic placed little kisses on his shoulders. Then he paused and looked at Tab's back. There was a jagged scar below Tab's shoulder blade.

"What happened here?" Mic asked, as his fingertips lightly traced the scar.

He felt Tab tense.

"Val," was the only answer Tab gave.

❖

Mic opened one eye and looked at the clock on the nightstand. It was close to nine in the morning.

The previous evening came rushing back. He noticed that he was sporting some serious morning wood. Then he thought of Tab, and how it would be a great idea to start the morning with a bang.

He rolled over with the intention of waking Tab up, only to find the other side of the bed empty. He felt around on the bed, then he sat up and looked around the room, panicking. Tab's clothes were on the chair, but Tab was not in the room. Tab must have been called away in the night. He lay back on the bed with his forearm over his eyes, trying to get his emotions in check. He wasn't going to get used to this.

Then he heard the toilet flush and the sound of water running in the sink.

"Hey."

He looked up to see Tab standing in the doorway of the bathroom. The relief was overwhelming.

"Hey, yourself," Mic answered as Tab walked toward the bed.

"Feeling better this morning?"

"Much."

"Did you have any plans for today?" Tab asked.

"Nope."

"Do you want to do something together?"

"Yes," Mic said, taking his hand.

"What?"

"Everything," Mic said. He pulled Tab down unto the bed, rolled them both over with Tab under him, and kissed him. "But first I want to do this."

Gift

Felice Picano

This is what I know about drowning: some persons can hold their breath longer than others. No one can hold it longer than five minutes seventeen seconds underwater without a special apparatus. Of course there may be someone in the Guinness Book of Records. But I've not met him.

This is what I know about Kevin Mark Orange, age seven and three-quarters. He vanished at 2:15 p.m., a Thursday afternoon. As it was late April, it rained twice that evening, obliterating any footprints or tire marks.

That, at least, is what anyone knows who listened to the 6:30 p.m. local ("K-RUF—We're soft on you!") television news that also showed two photos of Kevin, one taken a month ago, with his chocolate Labrador, named Bre'r Bear, and one taken over a year ago with his little sister Jean-Eartha Orange, no age given.

This is what I called and told to Sheriff Harold ("Hal") B. Longish, one hour after that broadcast. "I know where Kevin Mark Orange is. I don't know the name of the place exactly. I can't take you there, because I'm only a kid and can't drive. I never met that boy in my life. I don't know anyone who does know him. I can't tell you how I know. I just *do*!...*But* I can draw you a map."

So, of course, after wasting another hour, the sheriff and his deputy arrived. They were naturally doubtful. So I said immediately, "Sheriff Longish, your deputy had a left-hand upper molar pulled this morning. And also your mother's cat named Harlequin ran away for the sixth time yesterday night and she called and begged you to look for it."

"How in tarnation!" his deputy, a woman named Sheryl Jamison, asked.

Sheriff Lognish looked at me and said, "Sher, this lil' critter may actually be the real thing."

I laughed and said, "I *am* the real thing."

"How old are you?" the deputy asked.

"Nine years, four months, and two days yesterday," I replied. "I learned everything I know outta that series of books," pointing to the encyclopedia that Granny-Mama had left to her by a cousin twice removed. "And online my I.Q. is one hundred and fifty-three."

They looked at each other awhile and at that moment I realized she had aborted his male fetus in the second trimester, one year and six months and fourteen days ago up at a clinic up outside Tallahassee, even though they never were married and in fact were supposedly happily married to other people.

He sat down, she stood behind him, and he said, "Boy, draw me that map."

So I did, with magic markers on the plastic board hanging at my side.

"That wide oval," I explained, "is Lake Pishimere, that lil' pond-like mostly dried-up thing about four miles down the route 208 from where Kevin lives."

"We've got people looking not far from there," Sheryl Jamison said, and picked up her cell phone and speed dialed.

"What are those three exes in a row?" Sheriff Longish asked me.

"Those are beached and wrecked flat boats from ten-odd years ago."

"Hugh?" Sheryl spoke into the phone. "You at the dried-up lake, right? You see any wrecked boats there?"

"He took Kevin on a path between the last boat and the blackberry bush in full bloom," I said, drawing a line to show it.

"Go as far as the blackberry bush," Sheryl directed into the phone, "then turn north."

"He was assaulted on the flat rock there." I drew it kind of smushed in. "He pulled down Kevin's pants and did it to him three times."

"Oh, Jesus! Be my Savior now," Sheriff Longish said in a plummy kind of praying voice, and Sheryl added, "Amen, Lord."

"He dragged him a little further up and strangled him there," I said, dotting the line now, "using the elastic from the underwear he took off Kevin. He left him there, where thc two old cypress trees are rotting away in still water."

"Lord, hear my prayer," Sheriff Longish chanted.

Sheryl Jamison amened that, then repeated my directions into the phone.

Eight minutes and thirteen seconds later, she got a report that they had found the boy—just like I'd said.

Granny-Mama brought the two of them beers from the icebox and they all gathered around me and kneeled for a prayer, holding hands all around and stuff.

"He just knows things!" Granny-Mama explained to Sheryl Jamison over a piece of that morning's fresh-baked cheddar corn bread. "You know. Where things is gone missing to. Who's going to ring on the telephone. He predicts all the elections on the TV. He's got A Gift, you see."

"It's the Lord's compensation," Sheriff Longish said, still using his holy voice. That way he didn't have to say anything pitying about my physical condition, all twisted up as I am, and in a wheelchair and barely able to do the normal stuff for myself that most anyone can do.

It wasn't until three days later that the sheriff came to visit again. This time he was alone. He asked, "You see it happen? That kid Kevin being…you know, and all? In your mind's eye, I mean?"

"I sorta did. Yes sir. And by the way, sir, as we are speaking, I'm seeing in my mind's eye your eldest boy, Drew Longish, age sixteen years, four months, and twelve days," I added, "at home, right now, smoking maryjane and sucking his best friend, Tommy Thorn's, dick."

I thought Sheriff Longish was going to smack me hard, he got so red in the face, almost purple, and his fist just got all stony. But he just stormed off and tore hell out of the dirt in front of our house driving away—I guess in a hurry to get home and catch a look.

Granny-Mama had been listening behind the door and she came out and we laughed at what I'd told him. We agree, Granny-Mama and me, on most things. All kinds of things we hear, and things I see. We don't care what those folks are doing. But them others do care a lot, don't they?

"Be a while before that sheriff comes by again," I said.

"I thought you kinda liked him?" Granny-Mama said.

"I did. Kinda." Nice-looking man. Big hands. "But he'll be back. Know why?"

"Because he never axed you who simonized and kilt that lil' boy," she answered.

Granny-Mama may not know her words right—she can barely read—but she can be smart.

❖

He did come by again, that Sheriff Longish, two weeks later, with this pretty little blondie woman all dressed up tight as she could be in a gray suit for men, except it was specially tailored for her. Right off I knew she was going to be trouble for me. You see, they carry dark spots on them, all those who are going to be trouble. It sorta stains their clothing like moss or something, alive and growing, nasty. Hey, I thought. This is interesting. No's one been trouble for me in a long time. Not since Granny-Mama took me outta that hospital ward in that awful place near Stark. I was kind of excited, you see. It gets kind of boring around here. And she was something new.

"So! You're a Fed-er-al-ay!" I said to the blondie woman. "F.B.I.?"

She looked at the sheriff and he looked at her. On the drive over here, he'd wondered if his stick is too fat to fit into her pussy thing. He don't much like her attitude toward him and he hoped it would hurt like hell should he ever get the opportunity.

"That's right," she said to me. "So you must know why I'm here."

"You're here onaconna the serial killer…Underwear Man," I added, giving the secret name her unit up in Birmingham, Alabama, called him, because of how after he's done sexually molesting his children of both gender victims he always strangles them with the elastic of their unmentionables, just like he did with Kevin Mark Orange.

"Now, this is a top secret operation," Sheriff Longish said to me. "So everything you hear and say is among only us three. Understand?"

I said I understood. Anyway, he was okay today. He'd calmed

himself down before he got home that other day and he'd stopped "to think." Which meant he'd allowed Tommy Thorn some time to get the hell out of the Longish house before he went in himself. The weed smoke was covered over with "Summer Rain" air freshener and Drew Longish was extremely occupied at that time doing his trigonometry homework, for which he only got a C+ and that only because he cheated from Suzanne Hillyer on the last pop exam. His father didn't even notice the dried jizz on his son's hairless chest, visible if he'd carefully looked through the half-unbuttoned shirt. I guess he was so relieved not to have caught the two of them *in flagrante*, as the newspapers write it.

The blondie lady said there had been five others in her state and one up near Pensacola. The time between the crimes was getting shorter, she said. She knew I wanted to keep some other lil' innocent kid from being done in. Would I help? Would I tell her whatever I saw?

I said I would, though I didn't give half a crap for any of those lil' kids, in Alabama or Florida, for that matter. I did it for Sheriff Longish. Told him what I'd seen was an ordinary feller. Good looking. Very ordinary feller, just like everyone else, except he favored pale blue shirts for everyday use.

I then asked to see blondie's revolver and she showed me as she asked all kinds of questions that I gave her indefinite answers to, whether I knew them or not. Looking at her gun I knew then that a forty-seven-year-old black woman named Mariah Gregg who took in colored's laundry for food money had been caught in a crossfire and had died two years, one month, and nine days ago with this very weapon up in Dunwoody, Mississippi, in an unrelated case.

While she took a call on her cell phone out on the front verandah—as Granny-Mama grandly calls that lil' porch—Sheriff Longish stayed with me and told me, "You're not one hundred percent accurate, you know."

"If that's what makes you feel good to believe, you go on ahead," I told him back.

When blondie stepped back inside the house her suit was even tighter on her than before, and her stains was actually standing up to look at me.

"The Underwear Man has struck again," I told the sheriff, before she could say a word. "This time it's a girl missing."

He looked almost angry. “Why in hell didn’t you say something?”

“Just got the message this minute,” I lied. “I guess it come in along that cell phone call.”

He looked at me funny. But she took control of the situation. “Is she still alive?”

“Yes ma’am.”

“Can you tell where they are?” she asked.

“Where’s she been snatched from?” Sheriff Longish asked.

“Lake Geneva Village Mall.”

“She’d been left inside a ‘cerulean’ Chevy Cobalt sedan,” I added. And rubbing it in, “I told you he favored light blue.”

“You got a map in your mind’s eye yet?” he asked me, kinda roughly.

I was going to say maybe I do and maybe I don’t and what’s it to you, when blondie asked, “What else can you tell us?” Being all nice to me.

“He’s gonna let her go,” I told blondie, ignoring the sheriff.

“What? Why would he do that?”

“Onaconna she’s peed herself bad. He hates peeing like that,” I said.

“Weren’t there urine traces on the others?” Sheriff Longish asked her.

“Nothing substantial or long standing, no. Maybe at the moment of…”

“He hates the smell of it,” I repeated.

“You go,” Sheriff Longish told blondie. “I’ll stay with him. Just in case…”

“Hold on!” She called on the phone: “What make and color is the vehicle?” she asked, and when she was answered, she did something with her lip to show I was right. “Jackson, we think he’s ditched the child. Headed south on…”

“Southeast,” I corrected.

“Headed southeast on…” She looked at me for confirmation. “Is it 207? The road from the Lake Geneva Village Mall?”

I nodded yes.

Twenty minutes later, they found Liza Beth Morgan, aged six

years and four months, sitting on the side of the road, unharmed, hysterical, covered from the neck down in her own urine. They didn't find Underwear Man, as he was long gone.

"You just earned yourself a government commendation," blondie said to me.

"What good is that piece of paper? It ain't money, is it? You can't eat it, can you?" Granny-Mama would wonder aloud later on when she saw it arrive by special delivery mail. But blondie already had something else on her mind involving me. I could tell, because the stains were getting bigger and nastier.

❖

Granny-Mama couldn't understand why I would agree to it.

"They'll give you plenty of money, if'n I do," I explained. "Enough to get that big screen Hi-Def television you been after. And then some."

"The kind they show in the newspaper?" She'd tacked that ad over her bed like it was some movie star.

"I'll make sure they get you that very one," I told her.

She thought a bit and said, "Well, then, all right. What about you?"

"I guess I'll have to take my chances," I told Granny-Mama.

"You're a lucky child. Nothing bad can happen to you, if you will it so," she insisted.

I got doubles of Rocky Road for dessert then, messy as I can be with it, onaconna she was already contemplating watching *Wheel of Fortune* on that big TV.

Next day they came out in three big white vans with turning TV mesh dishes on top and seven other vehicles, KRUF, KTAK, and even the big TV station from Gainesville, this being the biggest story from the area since the student murders a quarter century ago.

I was dressed just like we'd discussed in pale blue shirt, with dark blue pants and even blue running shoes, although I'll never run in them. My hair had been barbered by a pretty woman from the TV station, and blondie and me had rehearsed exactly what I was going to say, like it was a play or something.

"Are you *sure* about this?" Sheriff Longish kept asking me, every chance he could get me alone, which wasn't too often. So I had to reassure him. He didn't like it one bit, and he was right not to. Not with those stains on even her shoes and fingernails now.

After they'd all gone, they left me a videotape so Granny-Mama could watch as much as she liked. She thought I was as good as a TV actor-person.

"Shouldn't he have protection?" Sheriff Longish asked blondie twice, once all the vans and other TV vehicles had gotten their interview and "statement" from me and were tooling off up the road.

"You planning on sleepin' over?" I asked him.

Blondie and me laughed at the look on his face.

Nothing happened for two more days and so we moved into what blondie called "phase two," i.e., getting me out in the public, away from here where Underwear Man would think there were sharpshooters behind every copse of red leaf.

This was exhausting but kinda fun. "Phase two" made me a celebrity—the psychic kid who knew all about the serial killer. It got me out in a local Wal-Mart, at another, this time higher-end, mall outside of Gainesville, and in a county hall meeting in the First Baptist Church on Highway 225 up near Lawley.

It was while driving home from that event that I saw Underwear Man for the first time in person. It was outside Dan Deavens Elementary School, and he was the crossing guard for all the little kids. Wearing a pale blue shirt with the white plastic stripes across his chest and his back and a pale blue cap. And of course his stains were all but three-dimensional, they were so many and so strong. I almost gave him away then, laughing at how much sense it all made. What better place to find kids? To find out which ones to take? What better way to gain their trust than wearing that uniform? He was even younger looking and better looking than I'd seen in my mind's eye. With big blue eyes to match. The kind of boy who'd model underwear for those Sears flyers that Granny-Mama would keep stuffed in her bathroom drawer and think I didn't know about.

He was very careful in holding all the kiddies back safely as we passed them by. They all knew who I was by then because of the TV and newspapers and they yelled and waved. And so did he. Our eyes locked as we slowly drove by. "Hello, Underwear Man." I mouthed the words to him. Then we were gone.

How he finally got me was kind of a surprise. But by then he'd been on the hunt over a year and seven months, so he'd gotten pretty good at it. I'd been left alone less than a minute in the disabilities restroom the following afternoon, when blondie, who was guarding me, was distracted by what sounded like shots—actually fireworks he'd planned—going off outside the back window, and she stepped away briefly.

"Your face is very nice, but otherwise you ain't very pretty!" he said to me, just before he applied the chloroform hanky. That had been my fear, of course, because all the others had been so very pretty, head to toe pretty, pretty like he was, pretty like he must have been as a lil' child when he was being sexually molested.

Later on, when we was alone, and he was doing it to me, he kept on saying "So soft! So soft!" about my skin and body. "So soft!" Which was a nice compliment.

It hurt at first a lot, but then I thought about Sheriff Longish and that made it better. Of course I could have just peed myself all over to stop it, but I wanted to see what it felt like. Sex, I mean—having heard and read so much about it.

He'd read and heard by then too about the name the F.B.I. had given him and why. So even though he had my underwear ripped apart with his teeth when he began biting me to do his molestation and he was really ready to use it around my neck, he restrained himself. Taking a great deal of effort to do so, so he wouldn't be ever caught that way again.

"You'll have to leave, now they know where you are," I told him.

He was crying by then, the fit having passed. "I know," he said.

"You should go to Mexico," I said. "Unless you don't like dark-haired kids."

He looked up at me and smiled. "That was just what I was thinking."

This is what I know about drowning: some persons can hold their breaths longer than others. No one can hold it longer than five minutes seventeen seconds underwater without a special apparatus. With all my conditions, I certainly can't. So when Underwear Man pushes my wheelchair into the pond. I'll just gulp as much water down as I can all at once and hope my body doesn't try to struggle. That'll happen in six minutes. He's cleared the pathway of all debris down to there and is walking back up to come get me. Sheriff Longish will blame himself for a while. But he'll get over it.

They say that drowning is the easiest death. And after all, my work here is done.

INTERCESSION

'NATHAN BURGOINE

Curtis was in the kitchen. I knew it the moment I woke and stretched, feeling the satisfying cracks and snaps of my back and the low ache in my balls that comes from a good night's work. That I could feel Curtis's presence before I could see him was something I was having trouble getting used to. Among the many effects of our new triad was my ability to know where he and Luc were. Curtis felt like a warm wind, Luc felt like a cool mist, but if they could feel me, neither of them had said so.

It was well into the day, and Curtis glanced at me with a wry smile when he saw me walk in.

"Good morning," he said, then made a show of checking his watch. "Barely."

"Best kind," I said, and reached for the coffeepot. Since I moved in, Curtis had been slow to let me add my tastes to his home—he has something against hanging posters of naked men where people can see them—but the coffeepot was non-negotiable. He drinks tea, and Luc only has the one taste, so the coffeepot was all mine.

It had done its job, but it had done its job three hours ago and shut itself off an hour after that. I reached for the switch, but stopped. I poured a cup of the cooled coffee, then winked at Curtis, holding the mug.

I called heat to my hand—not open flame, just heat—and then guided it effortlessly into the cup. It swirled, rising almost to a boil, in moments. I barely felt any effort at all. A trace of brimstone drifted in the air.

"Lovely," Curtis said, waving his hand. Then he smiled at me. "Someone had fun last night."

The hot liquid was magic on my tongue, and I felt the heat of it spread through me. Say what you will about demons, but we love our heat.

"Would you believe I picked up some twins and fucked them both in the entrance hall?" I jerked one thumb over my shoulder.

Curtis winced, though there was a smile behind his dark eyes. "Of course I believe you," he said. "They were very…vocal." He frowned at the open doorway. "You're going to mop in there, right?"

I laughed, walked around behind him, and drew him into a bear hug. He leaned into it, chuckling to himself, and I kissed the top of his head, willing a little of my allure into the touch. Curtis isn't tall, and I enjoyed the sensation of wrapping myself around the hot young man. He has an "aw-shucks" to him that I just want to corrupt over and over. I rubbed my free hand on his chest.

He shivered. I enjoyed making him shiver.

"You're insatiable," he said.

"By definition," I agreed, pressing my dick against the small of his back.

He tipped his head back, and I kissed him, taking his mouth with my tongue the way I knew he liked. I slid my hand down the front of his shirt, across his chest, and let my thumb graze one nipple. His throat made that little moaning sound I'd gotten familiar with in the last few weeks. I smiled, knowing I was turning him on.

He broke the kiss with some effort. "Sorry, Anders."

I raised an eyebrow and put my lips at his ear. "You got something better to do?"

"Not better." He sighed, sliding out of my arms. He had to adjust himself in his khakis, which made me grin. "But I'm meeting with the other coven heads today." His smile was tense, and his eyes didn't quite meet mine.

"Be careful," I said, even though I'd said it before. Our triad depended on all of us remaining intact. My freedom depended on the other two as much as on me.

Easy math.

He nodded. "I know."

"They chose the middle of the day so Luc couldn't go with you, and they chose a church so that I can't go with you," I reminded him.

"I know," he repeated. "But if I'm going to make this work, I have to meet them, declare us a coven, and then we're off-limits by their own laws."

The wizards, the weres, the vampires, the demons, all the magical communities had one thing in common: three. It took three wizards to make a coven, three vampires to make a coterie, and three demons or three weres to make a pack. Curtis, Luc, and I had been on our own, defenseless against the rest of the mystical world, eking out a living on the nights of the full moon when we knew they gathered and we were more or less safe.

Curtis had suggested we form a triad of our own, by mixing the rituals of our kinds. We'd had to do a bunch of magic crap for Curtis, share Luc's blood and let him bite us both, and then we'd enjoyed some spectacular fucking—I count myself lucky that Curtis's runner's legs just love to be wide open for my dick, and Luc doesn't mind rolling over and taking one for the team. A bond had formed, just like Curtis had hoped.

The vampires had honored it as a coterie. They'd had no choice—the first time Luc had bumped into some other bloodsuckers, he'd asserted dominance so strongly it was a thing of fucking beauty. They'd fallen all over themselves getting out of his way, and he'd barely put any effort into it. Something about us three wasn't just like a coterie, or a pack, or a coven—it was bigger, badder, and better.

I hadn't had a run-in with any demons yet—and I had to admit I was looking forward to it. We demons function on a fundamental principle: look out for number one. The pack comes a very close second, but it's really all about using the pack to gain the freedom to enjoy your own chaos. I'd never had a pack. When I came into my powers, I'd broken the rules: I liked fucking men. That didn't perpetuate the demon bloodlines, and that was an abomination in their eyes. So I struck out on my own, hiding, gleaning souls from the men I fucked when I could, and staying out of sight of the more powerful demon packs, who'd enjoyed kicking my ass whenever they'd found me.

I couldn't wait for some payback, but so far the other demons seemed to be hanging back. I'd sometimes catch a glimpse of a demon here or there, but mostly they just watched me.

They were likely waiting for a sign of weakness. Since we formed our triad, I hadn't felt weak even once. I figured the other demons could wait till hell froze over. The world was full of hot guys who needed my attention. If the demons didn't want to chat, I was cool with that.

But Curtis had been "invited" to talk with the wizards. He picked up his glasses and tucked them onto the V of his shirt.

"Good luck," I said. I liked the freedom we all now had, and it depended on all three of us. It was worth putting up with Luc's annoying personality, and it was certainly no hardship fucking Curtis. In fact, strictly speaking, we only needed to fuck whenever the moon was full, to maintain the bond. I'd yet to go more than two nights in a row without getting inside him.

What can I say? The man likes my dick.

Curtis glanced at the coffeepot and said, *"fervefacio."*

It boiled. He smiled at me. "I used to be terrible at fire sorcery." He picked up his keys and winked at me. "All my magic and sorcery is stronger now. I think the covens don't know what they're getting themselves into." I could feel the false note in his bravado, however. He was nervous. He didn't want to go alone.

It was an interesting sensation to feel his emotions so easily.

When Curtis was gone, I finished my coffee and poured another scalding cup and drank that down, too. I stretched, the whole—well, half—day ahead of me like an open buffet. Once I was sure Curtis had left and was well on his way, I went outside and found a natural shadow—cast by the large oak that grew in Curtis's front yard—and stepped through.

❖

It took a while to find a natural shadow near the church wide enough to step out of, but there was a maple on the street that was casting its shadow beneath itself, and I stepped out, repelling the attention of the people on the street with a reverse of my allure. Chilled, they glanced away, checked their watches, or happened to notice something somewhere else just long enough that my sudden appearance from the shadow was unseen.

It was a short walk to the church, and I couldn't quite get within a block of it. It was hallowed, and must have had a sizeable congregation.

It was old enough to have built up a real barrier, and I sighed, spotting Curtis's Mazda on the street. He was already inside. I must have lost more time to the shadow-walking than I had intended.

As I'd expected, I couldn't quite feel Curtis inside, the barrier was too strong for that, but I still wanted to be close. I didn't trust the covens at all, and their leaders would no doubt be trying to figure out a way to twist our triad to their use.

Demons don't have a great history with the wizards of the world. There are magics that can force us to act on their behalf, though it takes a lot of power to manage it, and we'll tear the throat out of a wizard who slips up even slightly in the attempt.

"I'm surprised you're this close."

I turned, wary, my fists curling and building heat—and then stopped. The man beside me seemed young, barely past his twenties, with a smooth skin, pale blue eyes, and hair so blond it might as well be white. He wore a simple yellow dress shirt and black pants. He was beautiful, but in a nearly fragile way, and even looking at him made my eyes water.

Unless I was mistaken, he was an angel.

I felt heat coil inside me, but kept my voice even. "What do you want?"

The angel seemed surprised. "What do we ever want?"

"Blood? Vengeance? Murder?" I offered.

"Those are your desires, not ours," the angel said.

I shook my head. "So your kind insists, but there's a lot more stories about your sort than mine, and the victims pile up just as high." I smiled. "Or higher."

"Our motives—" the angel began.

"Don't mean shit to the dead," I interrupted.

"You don't wish to listen to me." The angel spoke sadly.

"Not a fan of dogma," I said.

"How about redemption?" the angel asked, eyes filling with a slightly golden hue that hurt just to look at. "Could I interest you in some of that?"

❖

I fucked the college kid in the alley behind the bar, a rough and quick rutting that he had been dreaming about since the first time he'd seen me two weeks ago and I'd nabbed him in my allure. His jeans down at his ankles, I had him spread-eagled against the wall, and jerked his hard dick in time with my thrusts. When he came, I breathed in a slice of his soul, and his entire body jerked with a second, spontaneous orgasm as my seed flooded the condom.

I cleaned myself up quickly and left him still mumbling "Holy fuck" over and over to himself as he leaned against the wall. The life energy I'd drawn from him buzzed on my skin and made me feel larger and more awake as I stepped out from the alley and into the night street. He'd feel tired for a few days, and far more likely to give into temptations, but I'd not taken enough to really damage him.

"You never answered my question."

I turned and saw the angel in step with me.

"That was a clue," I said.

"Since your joining with the vampire and the wizard, you've changed," the angel said.

"Really," I said. "Hadn't noticed."

"I can feel it in you. You are more than merely a demon now. There is…potential."

I stopped walking and glared at the angel. "There's potential for me to fuck you up if you don't leave me alone." I let the fire light my eyes, and the angel stepped back at the scent of brimstone.

"You can be cleansed," the angel said, voice trembling.

"What?" It came out in a whisper, when I'd intended to growl.

"There is a way to fill the shell, if you turn your back on the ways."

He vanished into a shaft of moonlight, leaving me shaken and pissed off.

And scared.

❖

I watched Curtis in the dark for a while, my demon eyes adjusting to the night. He lay on his back, mouth slightly open, sheet loose around his chest and right arm above his head. He had a runner's build, lithe and lean, though his wide shoulders saved him from seeming small. I really enjoyed fucking him.

When I turned to leave, he spoke.

"You're home early," he said, voice rough from sleep.

"Didn't mean to wake you," I said.

He sat up, and I turned back to him. The sheet pooled in his lap, and he rubbed his eyes. "I went to bed early," he said. "Long day."

I'd forgotten. "How did it go with the coven heads?"

He sighed. "A lot of pontificating, warnings, and double-edged words. It boiled down to them telling me that as long as I keep myself off their radar, they'll leave me alone." He shrugged. "I can live with that. Truth be told, I don't think they want to test me. I think they've spoken with the vampires."

I smiled at that, but Curtis saw through it.

"What's wrong?" he asked. "You're upset."

I didn't like that he could tell. I shrugged and moved to his bedside, then sat next to him.

"What do you know about demons?" I asked. "Where we come from, I mean."

He looked at me for a moment. "Not much. In your case, as an incubus, you're sort of a half-breed, aren't you? A human mother and a demon father?"

I shook my head. "I wasn't conceived with a demon father. We're shelled by the demon when he fucks a pregnant woman."

Curtis shifted. "I'm sorry. I don't know what that means."

"The demon takes the soul of the unborn child and implants a kind of seed within the shelled remains of the child. If mother and child survive—which they rarely do—the child is born incubus if male, succubus if female." I spoke without inflection. "It's why we cannot approach places of faith. We are born without soul, and must feed on the souls of others to remain strong."

"That's…" Curtis's voice faltered.

"Awful?" I offered.

"I was going to say 'not your fault.'"

I turned to face him, surprised. A warmth spread through me that had nothing to do with hellfire. "You're an odd man," I said.

He swatted the back of my head. "You want to sleep here tonight?"

It was a casual question, but I could feel the worry and fear in him. His discussion with the coven heads had him more freaked than he'd admitted.

I slid my hand down his stomach, and under the elastic of his boxers.

"Just sleep?" I asked, and gave his neck a quick flick of my tongue.

"Eventually sleep," he said, and tugged my shirt over my head, going for my nipple with his mouth.

I rolled onto him, and we worked our way out of our clothes. He rubbed his hands on my hairy chest—a favorite of his, I knew—and I allowed a little of my allure to surface, to heighten his sensations. When I finally rolled him onto his stomach and took the bottle of lube and a condom from the beside drawer, he spread himself the way he knew I liked to see him, and I spent a good long time getting him ready for me. When I finally pressed inside him, he made the little moaning sound far in his throat. I smiled in the dark, and took him.

❖

My eyes opened. The angel sat on the back of Curtis's desk chair, impossibly balanced, and lit from within with a pale pearlescent light. I turned my head, but Curtis remained asleep, his naked body tucked beside mine.

"You could be like him, if you were only to seek it."

"If one of your kind ever makes sense, do you explode?" I kept my voice low.

The angel smiled only slightly. "Can you find it in yourself to turn away from the path of the demon?"

I closed my eyes and breathed. Did I want that? Did I care?

"What would that do to me?" I asked.

When he didn't answer, I opened my eyes. The angel was gone.

Carefully, ensuring I didn't wake Curtis, I slid from the bed, pulling the sheet over Curtis's body, and left the bedroom, pushing the door nearly closed behind me.

"You're home."

The cool breeze sensation preceded Luc's speech. I turned to the vampire, who was dressed in a perfectly tailored navy shirt and gray pants. His French Canadian heritage gave him a dark coloring that hadn't faded completely with his nocturnal life. We'd known each other a very long time. I'd only recently learned to tolerate him.

"Curtis spoke to the coven heads today," I said, by way of explanation.

"Ah," Luc said. "That explains the worry."

I raised an eyebrow. "You can feel it?"

Luc frowned at me. "You cannot?"

"I can. I'm just surprised…"

"Our bond, I assume." Luc shrugged. "It did not go well?"

I grinned. "They warned him not to make a scene."

"They're afraid of him, then." Luc's lips curled, and there was a hint of fang. Like any predator, fear was definitely a state of mind Luc enjoyed in his enemies.

"That was my take," I said. I took a deep breath. "You think they'll challenge him?"

Luc's fangs flashed again in the dark hallway. "Absolutely."

"We'll have to watch his back, then," I said.

"If we wish to retain the freedom we have acquired, yes." Luc regarded me. "You two are intimate quite often."

I smirked. "We fuck."

He nodded. "You fuck. You are not draining him, are you?"

I shook my head. "No. I don't have to. Only on the full moon, and that's more like sharing, since we're trying to match what a demon pack does." I grinned. "I can't help it if he likes my dick, though, can I?"

"There is no accounting for taste," Luc said. He had the slightest of smiles on his face, and I wondered how different he felt since the triad had formed. "I go to feed. I will be back in a few hours. If you do go out this evening, and bring home a companion or two, I ask you use your bedroom, rather than the entrance hall." He paused at the end of the hallway. "And if you do continue to wander about, should I return with someone, might you trouble yourself to put on some clothes?"

I grinned at him and scratched my bare stomach. "No promises."

"Of course not," Luc said, affecting a heavy sigh—a good trick for a guy who doesn't breathe. Then he left.

❖

I sat at the kitchen table, having put on a pair of shorts in case Luc brought someone back, though I'd never admit it to him. I held out my hand, palm up, and brought the hellfire to my skin. It danced on my palm with deep blue flames, so hot even I felt the heat, and so much brighter and stronger than it had ever been before. The room filled with the scent of sulfur.

"Can you give up the way of the demons?"

I'd almost grown used to the way the angel just appeared. I didn't look at him, still gazing at the fire that danced on my palm.

"Hellfire, soul eating, shadow walking, allure…" I trailed off the likely culprits. "Fucking." I finally looked at him. "Give up all that, and get what?" I snapped my fingers closed, snuffing out the fire with a quiet rush of air.

The angel regarded me. "Everything."

I sighed. "So that's the deal? I don't nab anyone with my allure, no soul sucking, keep the fires off, and stick to the light, and what? I'll get fixed?"

"Reject the ways of the demon," the angel repeated.

"Fabulous." I sighed. "Thanks for the clarity." I looked at the hallway, thinking of Curtis and the little noises he made when I'd slowly pushed myself inside him. What would it mean to our triad if I rejected my demon abilities and tried to "go clean"?

Would I even need the triad? Would I be free?

I shivered and turned back to the angel.

He was gone, of course. I went back to bed, ignoring the slight hunger already flickering inside me.

I woke up with Curtis curled around me and ran my hand down his bare back, trailing a finger between the cheeks of his lovely runner's ass. He shifted and woke, lip curling into a sleepy smile.

"Again?" He rubbed his cheek against my chest hair. "Can we at least have breakfast first?"

I wanted him, but I remembered the angel and said, "Breakfast."

Curtis seemed more confident today, and moved about the kitchen in his usual manner. He wasted no movement, organized as he collected the ingredients for the omelets he was making. Being able to alter the world with words must make you act like that. Watching him move, so contained and precise, I wanted to throw him against the counter and make him moan and beg me to fuck him.

He caught me staring at him and said, “You keep looking at me like that, and I won’t make it through breakfast.” He started beating the eggs, and watching his slender torso bend over the bowl, I felt a stirring in my chest. I forced myself to go to the coffeepot and pour a cup.

We ate and spoke of nothing important. It was an odd routine we’d picked up whenever we shared breakfast. He would tell me stories about his parents—now dead, murdered by the coven heads as a lesson to him—or I would tell him about my travels throughout the world before settling here.

“What are your plans for the day?” Curtis asked, finishing the last of his tea. He smiled lazily over the cup at me, and I realized what plans he was hoping I’d have.

I’d have liked nothing better than to take him up on it, but didn’t trust myself not to use my allure to get him riled up.

“I need to go out,” I said.

He sighed. “Okay. You’re not bringing more of your tacky stuff, are you?”

“You didn’t care when Luc brought his shit here.”

“Luc’s furniture was mostly beautiful colonial pieces. He didn’t have a collection of 1970s porn posters,” Curtis said.

“They’re classic,” I said, rising. I put my coffee cup in the sink.

“They’re tacky,” he said, watching me. “Hey…when’d you get the tattoo? Or is that more of your allure thing?”

I turned my head to look over my shoulder, spotting lines that I couldn’t make out on the back of my shoulder blade. I shrugged. “I can alter myself quite a bit,” I said, dodging the question, since the truth was I hadn’t done it on purpose and had no idea when it had appeared.

“It’s hot,” he said, and rose himself. He came up behind me and slid his arms up my chest, running his fingertips in my chest hair. “Have a good day,” he said.

I put my hands over his for a moment. “I’ll be back in a while.”

He let go, and I went to my room. I spent a while in my bathroom, looking over my shoulder at the mirror.

Across my shoulder blade, there was a stylized tattoo. It was tribal, more lines and sharp curls rather than anything realistic, but fuck me if it didn't look like a feathered wing.

I took a hot shower and scrubbed myself, feeling myself shake under the spray. When I turned the water off, my hand was trembling.

Was it possible?

I got dressed and left the house.

❖

I walked, stepping past the large tree on the front yard of Curtis's home that was my usual entry into the shadows. The sun was warm, with only the barest breeze, and I set my feet toward the river promenade, where I could walk and lose myself in my thoughts.

There were many people out running, biking, and rollerblading along the promenade, and more than once I caught myself reaching for my allure when a hot man passed. I clamped it down firmly, feeling a little more sure of myself every time and feeling the deep ache in my gut starting to take hold.

I hadn't felt this way since before the triad, when I'd been forced to cram all my feeding into the three nights of the full moon, when the demons were off reinforcing their bonds. I knew it would only grow worse, and I wondered how long I'd have to deny myself before the angel's promise would come to pass.

And what was the point? I'd fed off souls since I'd become an adult, more years ago than I wished to consider. I enjoyed it. Fuck, did I enjoy it. I had aged more than most demons did, given my inability to go wild with my urges. I looked like I was in my late thirties or early forties, depending on how long it had been since I'd fucked and sucked. But I'd never had a soul of my own, and didn't know what would happen to me if I reclaimed one.

Would I become human again, a state I hadn't been since before my birth?

No allure. No hellfire. No shadow walking. No delicious fucking *souls*… In exchange for freedom from the need and from reliance on the others? Was that preferable? Yes. It was.

What would it do to the triad? I tried not to think about it. If the triad collapsed when I was redeemed, then Curtis and Luc would be no worse off than they had been before. Luc knew how to survive. He'd been doing it longer than I had. And Curtis…

I paused, looking out over the river. I was nearly at the lake now, and heard seagulls screeching above me. I didn't feel like being in the crowds and turned off the path, starting down one of the streets of the rich residential area.

Curtis was bright, and powerful even before the triad. He'd adapt.

I'd be free. No hiding from the other demons…

It was as though thinking of them made me notice, just in time. Three of them were surrounding me, two male, one female, and all three had moved up to me without my noticing, probably bending their allure backward.

At that last second, though, I saw them, and as they burst with demon speed toward me, I twisted, leaping ahead. Only one of the men managed to graze me with his fingers, each one nearly blue-hot with hellfire. My shirt smoldered with four burned lines, the flesh of my side glistening with four rakes that had drawn blood.

I could have burned hotter than them. They were a small pack, only three of them—the bare minimum needed—and their attack wasn't planned well, even if I had been surprised. The street didn't have anyone on it at the moment, but at any time someone could appear.

I could have fought them, ignited my hands and torn them apart. I had the right, now that I had a triad, and I certainly had the desire. But there was a flicker of pale white light out of the corner of my eye, and instead of leaping at the three demons, I curled my fists at my side and glared. The three crouched low in the street, regarding me with wary eyes, waiting for my counterattack, knowing they'd failed to get the jump on me as they'd planned.

"Go away, and I might not kill you," I said.

"You smell weak," the woman said, her lips curling. "You barely noticed us in time."

I stared, and she glanced away first.

"I'm only going to give you one more chance. You barely wounded me. You're not strong enough to kill me."

Her eyes flicked back up to me. "What makes you think we were here to kill you?"

I froze.

She laughed, seeing that I understood, and then stepped back into a shadow and walked, vanishing. The other two demons followed suit.

The angel's voice was calm and full of compassion.

"Deception," he said. "A distraction, I imagine."

I could have walked the shadows and been home in moments. Instead, I started to run, not turning to look to see if the angel was going to come with me or if he'd already disappeared.

❖

They'd broken down with hellfire whatever magical barriers Curtis had crafted on the rear entrance, and the ruin of the door was still crackling and burning. I ran through, leaping over the wreckage, and saw the living room was covered in burns and scorches, the couch tipped on its side, and some of Curtis's artwork had fallen from the walls. The room reeked of sulfur.

Near the door, I saw a body, mostly fallen into ashes, surrounded by puddles of melting ice. Sorcery. Curtis had killed the demon, which meant I might not be too late.

"Curtis!" I yelled.

"Kitchen!" came Luc's strained voice, loud and angry. I was surprised. I hadn't known the vampire could move about during the day.

I ran through the hall and skidded to a halt at the entrance to the kitchen. Luc was curled at the edge of the basement stairs, trapped at the first step by the sunlight that flooded the room, unable to come out any further. A demon lay at his feet, however, a huge tear in its neck, and Luc's chest was covered with fresh blood. The demon's body was beginning to crumble into ash, the shell collapsing into its soulless form.

Curtis was being held by a tall, muscular blond demon, who held the wizard tight against his chest and was whispering in Curtis's ears. Curtis was still as I'd left him, in just his boxers, but his eyes were drowsy and his skin was sweaty and pale. A cut bled over his left eye and a bruise blossomed on his stomach. On either side of the demon holding Curtis, three more demons stood, allured into strong, muscular bodies. I hesitated, unsure.

There'd been nine of them. Luc had handled one, and judging

from the torn clothes on two others and the way a third was holding his wrist, Curtis had managed to deal some damage too. But now they had him, and it was obvious they'd been draining his soul.

As I watched, the blond holding Curtis met my gaze and trailed his hand down the front of Curtis's boxers. Curtis rolled his head from side to side. The blond demon's eyes turned inky black, and he inhaled, lines of Curtis's soul drawing into him, visible as distortions in the air like heat over pavement.

"Let go of him," I snarled.

The blond narrowed his eyes, which cleared to a startling green. "Your union with the wizard and the vampire cannot be tolerated." He licked Curtis's ear. "Though I certainly see why you enjoy the taste of him. Wizards do have that extra spice."

The angel appeared. Given that no one else moved at all, I realized he was somehow keeping the rest of them from seeing him.

"Let him go," I repeated.

"You must reject the demon ways," the angel said. No one heard him but me.

How was I supposed to stop them without using my allure, or my hellfire, or my strength? I growled in frustration.

"Just leave," the blond demon said, and his hand rubbed beneath the cloth of Curtis's boxers. Curtis leaned back against the demon, shivering. "And you may live as you lived before."

They would drain Curtis until he died. They would burn the house down, and Luc would also perish. But I would be alive. I wasn't sure I could defeat them, even with my demonic abilities bettered through our triad.

I could walk away.

The angel looked at me. No one noticed.

Curtis's head rolled to the side, and his eyes fluttered. The blond demon licked his neck. Curtis made the soft moaning noise in the back of his throat. I felt anger rise throughout me in a hot rush.

They would not have him.

I moved with all the speed I could draw from within, and was across the room in a blur, my fist slamming into the throat of the blond demon, igniting with a blazing blue flame, and I threw him back into the wall of the kitchen, which cracked from floor to ceiling with the impact. I caught Curtis in my left arm and turned on my heel, lifting my free hand and igniting it as hot as I could make it. The six demons finally caught up, stepping back, but forming a tight circle around me. The blond demon gagged and twitched, his throat burned and crushed, then fell still.

"Anders?" Curtis's voice was weak.

"Take him and go," Luc said from the shadows of the stairwell. One of the demons turned and hissed at him. Luc rose, but could not step into the light.

"No," I said, and holding my hand up, warding the demons off with the blue flame, I pressed my lips to Curtis's forehead and tried something I'd never tried to do before in all the years I had existed.

I breathed soul into him, and took nothing in return.

Even as I felt him stir, the flame on my hand began to dim a little, and the ache inside me grew. Still, I maintained, even as the demons began to shift, their eyes narrowing, sensing my weakness. Blue flames sparked on their fingertips, which grew and curled into wicked claws. The room was choked with the scent of brimstone.

"Stop," Curtis said, and I broke our contact. I felt weaker, but I could stand. Curtis shifted in my arm, still shivering.

"You can't take us all," one of the demons said. "One of us will kill him before you can kill all of us."

"Willing to bet it will be you?" I grinned.

Curtis took a deep breath and said, *"Tempestas, niger tempestas."*

The demons frowned, tensing, but nothing seemed to happen at first. The loud crack of thunder surprised all of us, except the angel, who was still just watching me, pale eyes shining. The wind began to whip through the broken back door and rain began to pelt against the windows.

The demons, not caring about the rainstorm, leapt forward in unison.

I pushed Curtis behind me and shoved my flaming fist into the first demon to arrive, but the next three all connected with their blows, slicing me open and burning me with their hellfire. While the first fell and began flaking away into ashes, I twisted, keeping myself between Curtis and the demons, and ducking the blows of the other two. I moved at a blur, just a fraction faster than the other demons, but it wouldn't be enough. Another set of burning claws sliced across my chest, and I staggered, nearly falling over Curtis behind me.

"Tempestas," Curtis kept saying, curled behind me and shivering. *"Niger tempestas."* His voice was weak, and I knew what I'd given him was already running thin.

The room grew dark as the storm grew heavier, black clouds forming in the sky. Rain fell in torrents, and lightning flashed only a bare moment before thunder boomed through the house.

I twisted away from one of the demon's outstretched claws, barely twisting my face away from the blue flames, knowing it would take me into the path of another and not sure I could withstand another attack.

Curtis, I thought.

But the other demon flew backward away from me, and I had time to blink before I saw Luc sink his teeth into the neck of another.

"*Niger tempestas,*" Curtis said once more, then his voice fell silent behind me. A storm of black clouds and heavy rain.

To cover the sun.

Demons are fast. Vampires are faster. The tide turned in that moment, and soon the flaking bodies of the demons littered the floor. I shivered, looking down at myself. I felt cold; my chest was covered with blood, and ragged cuts of burned flesh crossed my body.

Curtis coughed. I kneeled beside him and tried to wave away the worst of the hellfire smoke. He was very pale.

I gathered him in my arms, and Luc knelt beside us. "He is dying," the vampire said.

"You must turn away from the demon ways," the angel repeated.

"I had to save him," I snapped at the angel, and then turned back to Curtis. I was so cold. I had almost nothing left. Curtis's eyes had rolled up in his head.

I kissed him and gave him everything I had.

"Yes," the angel said, and then I was gone.

❖

The scent of coffee woke me up. I saw Luc, a tray balanced on one hand, standing at the door to Curtis's room. I blinked. My eyelids were heavy, and though I wanted to turn my head, I couldn't quite seem to turn the thought into action.

"You're awake," Luc said.

"M'alive?" I said. My throat was dry.

"That predisposes being awake," Luc said, and put the tray on Curtis's desk. "Can you sit up?"

I finally managed to turn my head. Curtis was beside me, up on one elbow, a small white Band-Aid over his left eye. He was still a little pale, but he smiled at me, putting one hand on my shoulder.

The two of them helped me sit up, and then Luc picked up the tray and set it across my lap. I winced, looking down at my chest. I was bandaged, and blood had seeped through the fabric in a few places. I shivered. Demons healed fast. I must have been in worse shape than I'd known.

"You should eat something," Curtis said, sitting up beside me.

"I'm still waiting on the carpenter," Luc said. "They charge an exorbitant amount to visit at night."

"My wallet is on the table," Curtis said.

Luc turned, standing at the door for a long moment, watching. "I feel it worth mentioning that I have never before been able to wake in the middle of the day," he said. "Also, I fear the wizards will not consider the sudden appearance of a storm 'staying off the radar.'" He let that sink in, then stepped through the door, closing it behind him.

I looked down at the tray. There was coffee in a mug and a bowl of tomato soup, with a box of crackers. I picked up the mug and took a sip. It was lukewarm and weak. I spat it back in the cup and coughed.

"That's horrible," I said.

Curtis laughed. "In his defense, I don't think Luc's ever made instant coffee before."

I leaned against him. He put his arm around my shoulder.

"You saved my life," Curtis said.

"If you died, where would I be?" I said, and nudged his shoulder with my chin. "Takes three of us to keep this thing going."

Curtis chuckled. "Give me a couple of seconds, and I'll go make you some coffee."

I picked up the cup and felt heat build in my hand. The weak coffee boiled.

Curtis sucked in a breath.

I looked at him, taking a swallow. Weak hot coffee wasn't great, but it was tolerable.

"What's wrong?" I said, putting the cup down.

"Do that again," he said. "Heat up the coffee…no, actually, don't. Can you call some fire?"

I frowned, but held out my hand. Pale white flames danced into being, almost golden at their tips. I stared at my palm, mouth open.

"It doesn't smell," Curtis said. "No brimstone."

I closed my fingers against my palm, snuffing the pale white flames.

"What does that mean?" Curtis asked me.

I shook my head, so tired. The ache was still there, deep inside, the urge to drink souls. And I could feel the shadows calling to me still. I knew I could alter myself with will. I was the same, and yet… I hadn't crumbled to ash when I'd released all the soul I'd stolen into Curtis. I looked into Curtis's dark eyes and felt a tightening in my chest.

"I don't know," I said, and closed my eyes, leaning my head on his shoulder again. "Can we worry about it in the morning? I'm really fucking tired."

He took my hand and slid it down his stomach, pushing my fingertips just under the elastic of his boxers.

"Just sleep?" he teased.

I felt my dick stir. I opened my eyes a slit.

"You just lie there," he said, lifting the tray and lowering it off the side of the bed. He shifted the blanket off me, sliding himself down between my legs, and gently tugging my underwear down. My cock rose to attention. "I'll take care of you. Least I can do for saving my life."

"Can I bring my posters?" I grinned down at him.

He licked his lips. "Ask me again in the morning." Then his mouth was on me, and I closed my eyes and leaned back, feeling better already.

North of Kabul

Max Reynolds

You hear people talk about "better angels" all the time, as if they know that not all of us are A-list angels out here, that some of us might have been slackers in the angel corps.

It's not something we're supposed to discuss. Sure, you've got your seraphim and cherubim and archangels. But the rest of us are supposed to be on the same level, a kind of socialism of angels, if we're talking terms of venery. You've got your exaltation of larks and you've got your socialism of angels.

Except, of course, you don't. We're no more egalitarian out here (it's out here, not up there, by the way) than people on earth, which should be a shame, but isn't.

Frank Capra and other saccharine film makers notwithstanding, we all get our metaphoric wings in different ways. (Tinkling bells on Christmas trees have nothing to do with it, however, and we don't actually have wings, although we do like the concept.) And contrary to the Vatican's preaching, we aren't all male, nor are we some kind of non-sexual eunuch with a male moniker, either. That's just medieval fantasy that got codified into dogma sometime around the Renaissance because the Church has always been looking for ways to protect itself from what goes on under the cassock and deflect attention with mysticism. One does have to wonder where all those blond angels with flowing locks came from, though. Ever see an angel portrayed with dark brown or black hair? They are always of the golden tresses and seriously feminized. As if Italian Renaissance priest portraitists had seen blondes somewhere. Even then the angel hierarchy was being established with angel hair being like gold and angels being a golden class.

If you've spent any time in the study of angelology—not that anyone seems to have actually done so since the Renaissance—you know that we are basically messengers. We bring tidings of great joy, as in the Christmas carols and gospel of Luke, and we also bring vengeance, as we did in Egypt to Pharaoh's first born. We are extensions of God—we perform tasks for God and we are both not human and not God. Think of us as the essence of spirituality, which explains why a lot of people who aren't religious still believe in angels.

Angels also do protection, which is what we have become known for most in the twenty-first century. We're guardians, because God really cannot be in all places at all times but likes to be hands-on.

So why the long preamble about angel status, you probably want to know. Because I'm not one of the A-list angels and likely never will be, since angeldom is a lot like MI-6—getting your license to be God's messenger is like getting the license to kill in that British agency. It doesn't come easily.

I haven't been an angel for long. We're appointed, not made, you see, and I was appointed soon after my earthly death. (Living a good life means you're more likely to get a good job in the Afterlife, by the way, in case you were considering remaining a total asshole because you thought there *was* no Afterlife. We angels are big on getting you to redirect, if not outright repent.)

Before I was an angel, I was a physician for Doctors Without Borders. I had been doing some especially hellish work in the inaptly named Democratic Republic of Congo when I got macheted to death one night while trying to rescue three young girls—not even teenagers, really—who had been raped and beaten in the bush behind the camp where we were in the Luvungi area that has become one of the rape capitals of the world.

At my memorial service they said I had died a hero, but that wasn't my intent—I wasn't expecting to die and had hoped to continue the work I was doing, debilitating and soul-ravaging as it was. To be honest, what I'd been doing—repairing bodies that had been torn apart with sheer animal savagery by people purporting to be human beings and to have a pristine political objective—was more important to me than anything. I didn't want to leave it. I also didn't want to leave Alain, a French physician assistant with whom I had fallen in love while working in that hellish place.

His name means handsome, and he was. He was *my* angel at that bush camp. Had it not been for the long nights in the tent with him, I should have gone mad, I think, from the endlessness of the brutality. There's nothing like war to make one hate men to the core of one's being. But Alain was possibly the sweetest man I had ever met, while also being incredibly strong and brave. I had seen him risk his life more than once, seen him save more than a dozen lives that would otherwise have been lost, and feeling him nearby in that sweltering hellish heat and stench at the camp catapulted me forward into every day and allowed me to stay there. Because as much as I believed in what we were doing, I often lost faith; Alain never did. And he seemed always to be able to sense when I was wavering, when I was thinking about a flight out, back to London, out of this seventh circle of hell and the images I would never be able to erase from my mind.

At those times he would just glance his hand over my shoulder or brush up against me as he walked past and flash me that gorgeous smile and whisper,

"Continue ton excellent travail por Dieu, Simon." Keep up the good work for God, Simon. And I would. For Alain, though, not God. More than once I felt God had abandoned all of us there. And yet I propelled myself forward. Because I could not bear the thought of Alain thinking me a coward. Nothing back in London held the same power over me as he did.

And then they killed me.

I had a particularly gruesome and bloody death. Of all the ways one could die, being hacked to death is definitely in the top five of how you do not want to leave the mortal coil.

They'd been there still, you see, in the bush. There's nothing as dark as rainforest jungle dark. In a starless night there is nothing but blackness. We had to conserve the torches for emergencies, and while I knew that screams from outside the camp of the sort that I was hearing from my tent was emergency enough, I didn't take the time to search out the light and as a consequence, met my end.

Two of the girls were already dead when I reached them. As it turned out, my being killed likely saved the last one's life as it deflected attention away from her and she was still able to walk, so she ran to the camp where Alain and another doctor with whom I worked and who was great friends with Alain and me, Lisette, those two were able to keep her from bleeding to death. But by the time they got to me, I was done for. Already gone. Alain was torn to bits, seeing me like that—my head was nearly taken off and I'd lost an arm and part of a leg and my guts were all over the place. Mercifully, they'd gone for my head first, so I bled out rather quickly from the slash on the carotid. I wouldn't have liked to feel the figure-eight of the blade in my guts, of that I am certain.

But poor Alain—his sweetness that had been all over me night after night in our tent, the way we had worshiped each other's bodies—that same passion poured out on the ground around my body as he lamented to God in French and Swahili and his broken English and he tried somehow to save me, even as he knew I was already gone. Over and over he told me how he loved me, which was heart-breaking to witness, as there was nothing I could do to comfort him. Lisette came out with a torch to find him, hearing his anguish and she, too, was broken by the scene. It was, in a word, dreadful.

You never get used to carnage, I find. Not even in the Afterlife. I wish I could have saved them both seeing me like that, having yet another image of destruction in their minds to pore over. If I could have saved my own life, I would have. I just couldn't let that little girl die in front of me. It was just one more thing I simply could not let happen. When it came down to her or me, I chose her.

That was the aspect of my death, combined with my other good works, it seemed, that propelled me into the Afterlife stratosphere. It's difficult to explain in human terms how God chooses angels, but suffice it to say I had good street cred when it came to the idea that I could be a guardian. I like to think it would have happened even if that young girl had died, but God is a bit more justice oriented than that, I've discovered.

You get a bit of a respite between death and your first assignment. I think you're supposed to be reviewing your life and then discarding it for good and all and moving solidly forward into what the Sylvia Browne contingent calls "The Light."

I seemed to have been a bit of a slow learner on that one. I wasn't really ready to discard my memories, particularly not my memories of Alain, for whom I could still feel a great wash of love and also—and I was pretty sure I was supposed to leave *this* behind—desire. So picture me, all ruggedly angelic since I had my head back on and my arm and leg and I was a pretty good looking sod back on earth, even if I did look more like a North London laborer than a surgeon. So there I am—very much *not* a golden-tressed, feminized Renaissance angel of yore, but a black-Irish looking (thanks to my mother's strong genes) lank of a guy wandering around lyre-less and thinking about the great sex he'd had with the Frenchman back on earth.

This wasn't the plan, I am sure. And I started to get the feeling—because everything is sensation and intuition on the Other Side—that I was supposed to be moving on, moving on, moving on.

And yet Alain held me to earth. Held me with memories of his remarkable smooth skin—the bush makes you terribly desiccated—with the burnished golden tan and his light brown hair that glinted with streaks of gold from the sun. And he had the bluest eyes you can imagine. Not that light, kind of eerie blue that one can almost see through, but a deep, Mediterranean blue. Azure. And of course his cock was divine, with a capital D.

God, I loved that body. You can't do all that you want in the bush, because you'd likely die of some hellish parasite, but we got it on just fine and I must say, it was a satisfying kind of sex that I hadn't remembered having before. I'd led a reprobate life personally—I'd saved all my goodness for the surgical theater and pro bono work here and there on the East End. I had fucked my way through a good portion of North London, Hackney, Kensington, Earls Court (yes, I liked them dark, too), and even Docklands, if you can imagine. If you know London, you know how expansive my repertoire was, then. So when I gave all that up—the nights doing a dark back room at an Earls Court club with my dick out for all and sundry, the elegant evenings that led to cultured light S/M in some high-rise flat, the occasional rough hand job in an alley off Covent Garden because it really was intense, that kind of almost-getting-caught, almost-public sex that I'd learned as a teenager and never seemed to lose the taste for—when I gave all that up, I was ready for a higher consciousness to take over. I wasn't giving up sex, mind you, I was just giving up the rapaciousness. I was hoping to transcend the carnal and just focus on the good works for a time and try and get my head on straight. Which is how, when Natalie, a nurse I knew at the hospital who I'd seen around town doing just about everything carnal as well, asked me if I wanted to do a tour in the Congo and said, *sotto voce*, "I have pictures to convince you," I said yes. I didn't want to see the pictures.

So all of this was going through my angel consciousness after my murder. I tried to get with the Afterlife consciousness, but I seemed to be drawn repeatedly back to earth and the carnal and of course, Alain. You think you'd be able to choose to protect those you loved once you've been granted angel status, but the Afterlife is as fickle as the life you've just left. So I was not able to watch over Alain and Lisette and Natalie and that little girl.

Instead, I was sent to Afghanistan.

❖

There's no training for being an angel. You're just expected to assume the position, as it were. For the most part, that works. The fabulous thing about higher consciousness is it just floods you. You're immersed in it and it's all rather elegant the way you just appear here, there, and everywhere, which is likely how that wing metaphor got started, I'm sure. People sense their angels, of that I am certain. So some artist somewhere along the line thought, "my angel must have wings" and there it was. Because it's not in the Torah or the Bible, the wing bit. But we do get around. And with amazing ease. Stephen Hawking, should he become one of us, will be so pleased to be able to move again with such blissful freedom.

Sod all how I ended up back in hell, though, almost immediately after I'd been slaughtered in Congo. That seemed a level of irony I wasn't prepared for. But one does as one is told, and God sent me to protect and serve in Afghanistan, which was not at all what I was expecting, but something told me that it had to do with my not letting earth go and putting my old life away and becoming all shiny and new and heavenly creature-ish.

I'm not sure what I was expecting, exactly—as I've already said, I wasn't an A-list angel, more like a solid B, but it still seemed a bit unfair how I ended up *there.* And yet once I got to where I'd been sent and saw who I was protecting, it all made sense. It just didn't make the assignment any easier. It sort of seemed like rather than helping me to divest myself of the worldly and especially those I loved at the end, it was guaranteed to immerse me in earth-ness, rather than angel- or God-ness.

Timothy Rankin was the leader of a small outfit north of Kabul. I never understood military rankings when I was alive, and nothing in the angel repertoire taught me what they meant in the Afterlife. I just knew he was an American, he was, like I had been, thirty-five. He'd been married to a woman right out of high school and thus had a teenaged son, but he'd been divorced since the boy was five and had been, it seemed, on his own ever since, which seemed unlikely for a man as solidly good-looking as he was.

Which made me think, of course, that he was gay.

As I noted before, we're intuitive beings, we angels. Our cognition is beyond the human realm, so we discover things with an immediacy that can at times be breathtaking. I know it was the most difficult thing for me to adjust to, since I was human once, rather than a graded angel—one of the archangels or seraphim or cherubim, that born-to-the-breed level of angel hierarchy. The *all-knowing* part of angeldom threw me. And then I arrived at Rankin's makeshift quarters and I realized why I was there.

He'd given up. He was ready to die. Except we weren't ready to have him. This wasn't like what had happened to me. I was, apparently, expected to give my life for that child. And I did, willingly, as it happens, and surprisingly without fear.

That was not where we were with Rankin. He had more that he was supposed to live for, and I realized that I was getting better at the angel thing, because I didn't resent that as much as I might have done—that he was allowed to live on while my life had been snuffed out right quick at thirty-five, which is, let's face it, young, no matter how hard one has lived. And there had been Alain… But I digress and I am trying to move forward and Rankin is clearly supposed to help me get there just as I am supposed to keep him safe.

Except, of course, that's not what he wants.

There are limits to angel life. We can't read minds, intuitive as we are, because we are not God and the last time an angel mistook himself for God, he—Lucifer, that would be—ended up in the fiery pit. So we check our hubris before it checks us.

As I said, we can't read minds, but we can sense with that heightened level of consciousness what is happening with someone we are entrusted to. And as soon as I saw him, I knew Rankin was looking six ways to Sunday for death at the hands of a sniper or IED or just the opportunity to toss himself on a grenade to save his men.

What I didn't know was why.

❖

One night, when Alain and I were lying in the tent, exhausted beyond all imagining from an especially gruesome day where we'd been brought several child victims—very young, these four little girls were, about five or six—who had been chopped at with machetes and one had been raped. It was hard work, saving them, and part of us couldn't help but wonder if it had been the right thing to do, that's how bad it was.

It's hard to explain how much you need sex in a war zone. Just the knowledge that a man's hands can be for something other than mayhem is important to remember. You have to remind yourself often that you, too, are capable of something other than brutality. I needed to touch Alain after days as bad as that day had been. I needed to be kissed and stroked and licked and sucked and made to feel that there would somehow be an end to the hideousness at some point. That one day there would be no more screaming, no more wounds, no more blood and vomit and God knows what all else everywhere one looked.

You can be reminded of life with a kiss. Trite, I know, but the trite is so often also true. I was thinking when I first saw Rankin that what he needed most was to be brought back to life with a kiss.

Was that why I had been sent to him? To be some kind of angel lover who would work some kind of somnambulist magic on him in the dark of night that would remind him there would be something else soon that was worth living for, that there was a world beyond war and carnage and mayhem?

❖

When I was a boy back in London, I recall when I had first gone to Westminster Abbey. I was on some truancy, as I recall, with some mate of mine that I had a fancy for, because I was one of those—born gay, there were no dalliances with women for me. I always knew it was men I wanted and early on, too. The boy was named Rupert, and he was dead handsome and I had hope I could figure something out with him that would seem all innocent and let's-just-try-this-shall-we?

Part of my teenaged wooing, since teenagers are notoriously bad at this, was to take him to Poets' Corner at Westminster, because it's romantic but still manly and I could point out that the great war poet, Rupert Brooke, was memorialized there. And maybe I could quote some lines about forever England and he would want to get close to me.

As it turned out, I hadn't been to the war poet's memorial before and I was not prepared for the effect it had on me and I was fighting back tears when I read along the bottom the quote from Wilfred Owen: "My subject is War, and the pity of War. The Poetry is in the pity."

We were what, Rupert and I, fifteen, sixteen? And there we were, talking about the lost generation of young British men who died in World War I, at best a decade older than we were then, and most, just a few years older. Instead of being a sexually charged afternoon, it put a pall on us, because we weren't of the suicidal Goth class of kids. We were bad boys who liked a bit of fun, and this was not it. We were shaken. And I remembered that day a long while after. I had never wanted to die in the trenches—literal or metaphoric—but that had been my fate, to die in wartime. I just hadn't known it then. Or perhaps I had intuited it. All I know is that imagining all those beautiful young men dead in the mud and mustard gas had brought about tears to my teenaged eyes that I didn't yet know I had to weep.

It resonated now, that line of Owen's, as I looked at Rankin, sitting stock still on the edge of a big outcropping of rock. It was dead quiet in the lowering sky of autumn afternoon, and chill beyond belief. But he sat there, a cigarette in his hand but not smoking—the thing unlit—and staring out with that glassy dead stare I had seen too often in Congo. I tried to see what it was he saw, but there was nothing. There was the valley and the mountain range. The sky and the tops of the mountains disappeared into each other, it was that close to early dusk.

I could hear the other men nearby—the encampment was around the rocky bit and down a piece, I could tell. The sounds were loud and life-affirming and all I could think was that Rankin had had to get away because there was too much life there with the other men, and he wanted to be closer to where he could dream of death uninterrupted.

I came up behind him and sat down above him on the rock face. I saw then that he had a small diary on his lap and that the cigarette was actually a pen. He'd been writing, but had stopped. I felt the smell of death fairly coming off him and had a moment of human-style panic that I would not be able to fix this, I would not be able to save him from himself. That whatever message I was supposed to deliver would be garbled and indistinct and just screw the guy up worse than he already was.

I had half a mind to just tap him on the shoulder and remind him about Lucifer, because suicide is so close to hubris—we think God has deserted us or worse, don't care. I think it was Alain who turned me spiritual. I have him to thank for my role as middle-grade angel, I suppose. I know I had him to thank for re-infusing me with life. I had him to thank for reminding me that all touch is not brutality and that men can love more easily than they can kill, most days.

But what was I to do with Rankin? There should have been a manual with the angel job. *Really.* God was a little too trusting.

I started with something I'd have never done in life. I read the journal.

I was right about him. He was indeed gay and not the least bit torn up about it. He liked men. His journal was in part an erotic treatise to the men he served with. He loved their bodies, the sound of them, the harsh smells that came off them, and the sudden fear and humanity that came over them. Like me, he had been distanced from his love of men by the brutality of war, but his comrades had brought him back, as Alain had brought me back.

And then he'd met the man in Kabul, in the old part of the city, the part with the romantic winding streets and the bazaars and the little close-together shops. The part of the city where no one carried cell phones and you never saw cars, just the occasional donkey. The part of the city that seemed like a different time—a time when there was not a war on and where the two men were not, by virtue of who they were, on opposite sides in that war.

Suddenly, I knew the reason for the death wish that had come over him. He'd fallen in love with the wrong man, it had ended savagely, and the memory was eating him alive.

I wondered what he'd been thinking, detailing the affair as he had. He must have been mad with first passion, then grief to cling to each detail with such reverence. I tried—and failed—to imagine what it would be like to fall in love in this barren-seeming place. I tried to imagine the risk both men had taken and failed again. Perhaps I was more of a C angel than a B. I had to get this right.

When Christ is in Gethsemane in the final hours of his life on earth, just before he is turned over to the Romans by the kiss of Judas, he is almost fully man, distanced from his God-self. He actually begs the Father not to kill him, not to force the sacrifice from him. "Father, let this cup pass by me." But it doesn't pass and in the homoerotic life of Christ, the kiss comes and then the long dying with his beloved mother and his disciple John at the foot of his cross.

I would have liked this cup to pass by me, to be sure, but I knew this might be my one and only mission in the Afterlife—save this one man from dying. Remind him about the importance of living. Get it right for all the things I had gotten wrong for years before the Congo.

❖

Rankin had met Shamir while on an excursion in Kabul. We think of Afghanistan as nothing but mountains and rock and people living a life entrenched in maybe the fifteenth century, but Kabul is a big city—nearly three million people live there—and it's a bustling metropolis, just not of the sort we're used to in the West. It's no bush outpost like where I was in Luvungi. But there is a taint of violence that hovers over the city that one can almost taste, it is that close to the surface of everything that happens there.

Shamir dealt in rugs and antiquities in the old part of Kabul, away from the buses and cars and modernity. He was an elegant man, as Rankin described him—tall and lean, dark and bearded as all Afghan men were. Rankin himself was tall, but muscular from carrying the huge sacks and weaponry of war. Battle had made him rugged, if rugged he had not been before. His hair was a sandy brown-blond and his eyes were a greenish color that seemed to change to amber in the light. He looked like what he was—a soldier. It was hard for me to imagine he had ever been anything else.

Rankin had gone shopping for something to send home to his son, whose birthday was approaching. And he'd gone into Shamir's shop.

It had been a day filled with longing. He'd begun the day stripped bare with fellow soldiers, bathing, and had felt a wave of desire crest over him with such force he knew he had to get out and away. I couldn't tell if the other members of his team knew he was gay or not, but he knew and that was what mattered. He'd banked his desire for months, but an extended deployment had kept him from the release that he usually sought in bars, stateside, and like his fellow soldiers ached for women, he ached for men.

So he was primed for Shamir, really. He just didn't know it in time to protect himself and Shamir from what was to come.

The air in the shop, as Rankin wrote about it, was redolent with scents he couldn't define and he'd felt a wave of panic as he'd gone deeper inside and felt himself surrounded by rugs and those scents and brass and ceramic objects that he didn't recognize and he'd turned to leave and Shamir had come up to him and touched his shoulder, asked in Persian, then in a heavily accented English, if he was all right and if he needed to sit, to have some tea.

Shamir had taken him back to a room beyond the rugs where a big samovar steamed and had poured him a thick tea, which he had shown Rankin how to drink with a cube of sugar between his teeth. There had been some biscuits of a sort that tasted vaguely like violets and Rankin had felt faint—something he hadn't felt since his first day facing fire. There was a danger lurking in that room beyond the shop and Rankin had staggered up from his seat and tried to leave, but Shamir had stopped him. At first, Rankin had thought Shamir was going to kill him. But instead he had come very close and breathed the violet-scented breath against Rankin's face and Rankin had gotten suddenly aroused, which had terrified him.

Who knows how we men sense who wants us and who doesn't? I had known right away that Alain had wanted me as much as I had wanted him the day we had left the camp to drive for supplies. We'd ended up in a sweaty and somewhat awkwardly teenage embrace that had led to an even more teenage-style rub-off in the back of the Land Rover, but it had been spectacularly hot and neither of us had been the least bit embarrassed by the initial fumbling with buttons and zipper and cut and uncut dicks. That I could still remember that first time so vividly meant I was not moving forward into my angelhood, but perhaps that was the point—Rankin's story was to take me to the next phase of my consciousness as an angel. Which meant I had to understand what he had experienced and figure out how to help him forgive himself.

It wasn't going to be easy. That first day in the shop had led to stolen meetings whenever Rankin could leave camp. It was crazily self-destructive and yet the passion they felt for each other consumed them—or that is how Rankin described it. Like a flamethrower, he'd written. And I believed him because I knew that feeling for another man. I could still feel it, even though I knew I wasn't supposed to, that I should be beyond that, now.

Rankin had written, *What am I doing, I ask myself daily, sometimes hourly? How did I end up involved with a Tarjik from Kabul when we know we can't trust them and we know we're the invaders and we know that any day they might toss an IED in front of us and we'll all be incinerated—if we're lucky.*

I don't know what will happen to me if I get caught. I've always been such a stickler for rules and I can't even count how many I am breaking every time I go to him in the city. I end up discharged and Justin loses everything. Everything I have done for my kid is gutted and he'll never forgive me. I don't know if I'd forgive me.

When I think about the hours I've spent in the back of that shop, I want to knock myself in the head. And yet, I can't get enough of Shamir. Is it the exoticism? Am I just really a good-ol'-boy racist trying on a man with Eastern promise? Or is it just that he is so elegant and kind and the sex is mind-blowingly good and I want to fuck him night and day—just not here and under these circumstances and in this place, at this time, because something always tells me every time I enter that shop that today could be the day we die.

But it wasn't Rankin who died. It was Shamir.

The man was married and had a young son. His wife had no idea who he really was, any more than Rankin could be sure. Shamir had led a similar life to Rankin's—done what was expected of him, but not liked it. He'd finally used the excuse of the war to meet foreign men and he'd come to know which ones were interested and which ones weren't. The tea in the back room was his regular gambit—something about showing a man how to secure the sugar cube between his teeth led, inexorably, to fingers in the mouth and hands on the dick.

Shamir loved to suck cock and take it, and Rankin loved to give it, and they spent as much time sharing the heat as they could. But even in the bustle of Kabul and the streets that seemed so anonymous, Rankin knew he stood out and that too much time spent there would become suspicious to someone. Which it did.

Afterward, Rankin replayed what happened again and again. He wrote about it continually. But it never gave him that fake thing, closure, that people always give so much credit to. It only inflamed his grief and made him more determined to die. He had survivor's guilt, like many soldiers. Only because he'd been lucky enough never to have lost one of his own men, he had it about Shamir.

We'd had a long afternoon of nonstop fucking. I don't know who wants it more, him or me, but we go at it like we just discovered sex yesterday. He's so dark and his ass is tight and high and just grabbing it makes me want to come. It's insane how hot I am with him. And he's never been with anyone for any length of time—so this is new for him, getting to know one man and feeling that kind of pleasure. I love showing him a different side of globalization. It's as if all the conflicts, all the mistrust from his side and mine disappear when we're together. I don't get how this happened, but it's good. It's more than just the heat and the sex—I feel something with him that I'm not used to feeling. He's softened me up. I don't know if that's good or bad, though, given why I'm here. I guess time will tell. If I get my head blown off because I'm remembering my dick in his ass, then I guess it's on me. As long as I don't get any of the guys involved, I don't know that I really care. It all seems worth it right now. But then we're in this place out of time, aren't we? It's not like it can happen outside of this place, this time. So for now, it's what it is.

Rankin had spent the afternoon with Shamir and then had gotten ready to leave. The shop was closed, but they heard the door open. They were dressed, but there was no good reason for Rankin to be in the room beyond the shop. He had flattened himself against the wall behind the curtained doorway instinctively, like the soldier he was.

A man had called out in Persian, and Rankin had seen the look on Shamir's face. *"My brother-in-law,"* he'd whispered, the color drained from him. He'd grabbed Rankin's hand and pressed it to his lips. It had been an impossibly romantic gesture and Rankin had noted it as such.

But he'd also been intolerably afraid. How *I* should have felt that night in the bush.

"Where are you, Shamir?" the man had repeated, this time his voice edged with anger.

"I was getting some tea, Hamid," Shamir had said and left the room without a glance back at Rankin. The soldier had looked around for someplace to hide and had slithered behind a pile of rugs, feeling suddenly like he was on patrol, at night, alone.

There had been a flurry of angry-sounding talk, then a muffled sound, and then the door had opened and shut with a bang. Rankin had eased out from his hiding place and called softly to Shamir. All he'd heard was a murmur in response. That's when he'd felt the adrenaline course through him like fire. He'd run from the back room into the shop to find Shamir on the floor, bleeding from a wound in his chest. The knife was still there and Rankin had seen enough on three tours to know there was no coming back from that wound. He was mad with fear and anguish and he dropped to the floor beside Shamir, touched his hand to Shamir's face. Tried to talk, but didn't know what to say. He knew better than to ask Shamir not to die. He knew that Shamir would be dead in minutes. He knew that it was his fault. He knew that he should be stabbed on the floor with his lover.

"He's been watching me," whispered Shamir, his voice so faint Rankin expected the life to flow right out with the words. "He said I had disgraced his sister, that people thought I was consorting with the enemy, but that he knew what I was really doing. He would kill me to make it seem that I was merely an informant, not the dreadful thing I was. He—" Here Shamir had stopped speaking and the glassy look of impending death had come over him. Rankin had held his hand, kissed his face, finally been unable to help himself from begging him not to die. *It was all his fault, he'd made this happen, he should be dying there, too.*

And then it had been over. Shamir had died a quick death, a brave man's death, and Rankin had slithered like the coward he felt out of the shop and onto the street and had staggered back to the camp, Shamir's blood still warm on the leg of his uniform. The murder had been a month ago and Rankin had been reliving it day and night ever since. He'd written that he'd let a sniper's bullet whiz past him and hadn't ducked, hoping it would take him out. He'd written that he'd stood outside the camp—having volunteered for lookout every night for a week—hoping to be killed in the Kabul darkness.

But he hadn't been killed—yet—and now I was here to make sure he got a life lesson in the importance of staying alive.

It had grown dark as we sat on the outcropping of rock, both of us reliving the affair with Shamir and his monstrous death. There really wasn't anything left for me to do but to touch him and let him feel me. I was pretty sure now that this was what was expected of me. The cup had not passed me by; this was a job I had to see through and see through right.

And so I leaned over Rankin and put both hands on his shoulders. I leaned close to his left ear and let him feel my breath on him. I thought about what words I should say to him, but I wasn't sure. Would my breath be enough? At this point, I thought not. I was pretty sure he needed a full ghostly apparition-type jolt. So I gave it to him.

The breath on his ear became a light kiss and then the words flowed, but they were whispered, so soft that they could easily be mistaken for the wind, so clear they could not be mistaken for anything but a directive from the Other Side. *You cannot die, you must not die, you have a son and a country and men who love you now and men who will love you later and men who will remind you of how much you have to give and how God would have taken you if it were time and it is not time. Life is still here for you. Don't squander it.*

I had no idea if he'd heard me, or if he had, if what I had said had registered with him or if it was even enough. I kept my hands firmly on his shoulders for a good minute before I let go. I was afraid to look in his face, afraid that glassy, already dead stare would gaze back at me still.

It did not. The face I saw was transfixed with both fear and awe. Rankin knew he'd had some kind of revelation, he just wasn't sure what that was. But he didn't have the look anymore.

He picked up the journal and began to write in a flurry of words.

All this time I have been sure I should have died with Shamir, that it was somehow an insult to him that I did not take my own life right there, with him. He was no more culpable than I. But I see now that the tragedy was that he had to die at all. That those crowded little streets in the old city were indicative of how far from this century it is here, no matter how many cell phone towers there are, how many planes fly out of Kabul airport every day. There was no place for us, here. But this was Shamir's country and he was living his life the best he could, given the constrictions of the old city and the traditions that go with it. His time was up because his time had not yet come. There was no place for him ever in this part of the world. He would have had to leave with me. But Hamid wasn't going to let that happen, either.

It has to be enough for me that I loved him and that I was with him till he took his last breath. Now I have to breathe for us both. I've been looking at this all wrong—to honor him, I have to live, not die. I have to make sure his life had meaning, that someone remembers his beauty and elegance and the heat we generated together.

He put down the pen and closed the book. He got up, stretched, and stuck the pen in a pocket, stuffed the journal in his jacket. Dark was descending and he could hear the men getting louder as the world around them grew quieter. He disappeared down behind the rock and into the warmth of his battalion.

Was that it? Was I done? Had I finished the task as expected? I thought so. Rankin had been almost gone when I had first seen him and now, just hours later, he was back to life. It had taken so little—I'd only had to remind him of how important life is.

We're not supposed to ache after we die. I'm sure of this. So why was I aching and torn with longing for my earthly life in that moment? Why was I yearning for Alain with an almost palpable ache? I closed my eyes, wondering what I would see when I opened them again.

There he was, in front of me. Still in the bush, still working hard. *So this is the plan for me, then—to travel the earth reminding the living of why they are lucky to be alive, to forgo counting their losses and just give in to counting their blessings? I am to be the traditional angel, the messenger from God.* I could do this, I could get good at this. I was pretty sure I could do what was required of me and get to the next plane with less struggle than I had feared. I was already feeling more confident, but not *too* confident. I knew what I had to do next.

I walked up behind Alain. He was standing by our old tent, just staring. The camp is never fully quiet, even at night, and now, at dusk, it was still alive with sound. He looked as if he were trying to hear something specific, something that was out of the range of ordinary hearing. I brushed against his arm, like he used to do to me all the time.

I leaned in and whispered in his ear, *"Continue ton excellent travail por Dieu, Alain."* It was what he had always said to me: Keep up the good work for God.

He turned slowly toward me. I don't know if he thought he saw something or not. I reached out and touched his face lightly with my fingers. He reached up to touch where my fingers should be. Then we both closed our eyes as memory flooded us. And when I opened mine, he was gone. This time, I understood, forever.

Angels Don't Fall in Love
Todd Gregory

"Angel..."

I wake up in the middle of the night whispering his name. When my alarm goes off at seven in the morning, for that brief instant I imagine that he is there with me in the bed, that he never left, that his warm body is lying there next to me, and when I open my eyes his round liquid brown eyes will be looking into mine with that curious sexy mixture of innocence and awareness. But my eyes open, as they do every morning, to see the other side of the bed empty, a vast desolate waste of cotton sheets and woolen blankets. My heart sinks again, down into that blackness, the darkness of despair, loneliness, and missed opportunity. For I have known love, I have known passion, I have known joy.

And lost it.

I first laid eyes on Angel one night wandering home from the bars at about two in the morning. I'd had more than my fair share of drinks that night, and was giving up and going home. Staying out didn't mean meeting the man of my dreams, or even just a warm body with a forgettable name for the night. It just meant more alcohol, more disappointment, standing alone in a corner of the bar, not approaching anyone, nobody approaching me. Before going out that night I'd made a promise to myself that I would break the cycle. I would not stay out ordering more drinks thinking that maybe in five minutes the right guy would walk in. The drinks would only cloud my judgment and distort the way guys looked, making them look far better than they would in the cold light of morning, when I would ask myself, what were you thinking? It was a tired old game, and one I didn't feel like playing anymore.

He was standing, leaning against a lamppost on Royal Street just a block from my apartment. He was smoking a cigarette dangling from his lower lip. His hair was that dark shade of black that looks blue in the light. There was a mustache and goatee, and he was wearing one of those white ribbed tank tops that cling. His jeans were several sizes too big and were slung low across his hips, exposing black boxer shorts. There was a tattoo on his right arm, a cross in outline with beams of light radiating from it. In the flickering light of the gaslit lamp he seemed to be a large presence, but when I got closer I saw that he was maybe five-five, five-six possibly. His eyes were amazing, round liquid pools of brown with golden flecks in them, like the sad eyes of a Madonna in a Renaissance painting by a forgotten master. They were framed by long, curling lashes that looked dewy in the light.

"Hey." He nodded as I started to walk past him.

"Hey." I nodded, but stopped walking when I saw him cast his eyes down at the cracked and tilted sidewalk, but a shy smile starting to spread across his face. The smile ignited the lights behind his eyes; he seemed to radiate light and purity. "How ya doing?"

He shrugged, the smile staying in place. "On my last cigarette." He took one last drag and tossed it into the street.

"Drag."

"Ain't it though?"

I wanted to touch his arms, brown with wiry muscles underneath. I wanted to taste his full red lips. He was probably a hustler, I thought in a bright flash of clarity, or looking for a drunk trick to rob. But the eyes, those amazing eyes…it couldn't be. Even if he were, he was welcome to the twenty-odd dollars in my wallet. I wished in that instant I smoked, so I could offer him a cigarette to replace the one he just finished. How to ask him to come back to my apartment? How to initiate a seduction of this beautiful Latin apparition? My tongue seemed incapable of making a sound. "My name's Mark," I said, sticking out my hand.

"Angel." He shook my hand, and when our skin touched I felt an electric pulse course through my body, burning the effects of the alcohol out of my bloodstream, unfogging my brain, making my cock stir and start to come to life inside my pants. I wondered if he felt it too. He must have, there was no way it could have just happened to me. It couldn't have been that way. It just couldn't. He cast his eyes down again, then looked up at me through those dewy lashes that curled and framed his eyes. "You live nearby?" He had a slight accent.

"Uh huh."

"Can we go there?" He reached out and touched my arm, sending chills down my spine. He smiled at me.

"Um, sure." I smiled hesitantly at him, wondering if this was the stupidest thing I'd ever done. I'd never picked someone up off the street before, and then I laughed at myself. Like you couldn't pick up someone dangerous in a bar? But there was something about this scenario, the possibility of danger, the chance this pretty boy might be dangerous, that seemed to make the entire thing even more intense, more erotic, hotter. My cock was growing to full size now inside my pants. "It's just up the street a little ways." I started walking.

He fell into step beside me, reaching out and taking my hand. His hand felt warm and soft, and I felt that electric charge yet again. Not quite as intensely, but I still felt it. The little hairs on the back of my neck stood up. My nipples hardened and became sensitive. The fabric of my T-shirt rubbing against them as I walked felt like feathers being brushed against them, making them harder and more erect.

I slipped my key into the door and opened it, reaching in to turn on the overhead light and the ceiling fan, then stood aside to let my Angel in. He smiled at me. "Beautiful place."

"Thanks." I felt the fear again in the pit of my stomach. Was I about to be robbed? Beaten? Murdered? But he was smaller than me, and when he turned those innocent eyes toward me again, I banished those thoughts once and for all. He stepped toward me almost shyly, hesitantly, and bit his lower lip. I leaned down and brought my lips against his. They were soft but firm, tender but strong. He tasted slightly of stale smoke and spearmint. He brought his arms up and around my back, pulling me closer. I slid my own arms around him and down his back. I put my hands on his ass. It was round and hard, solid. I longed to see it bare, unfettered from his clothes.

"You seem very sad," he whispered, his lips brushing against my neck.

I shook my head. "No, I am not sad now."

"It is still there." He tilted his head back, looking me right in the eyes. "In your eyes."

Again, I shook my head. What was there to tell? About the lover who'd left me a few months earlier, ripping my heart out? About the nights going to the bars hoping to meet someone, drinking myself into a stupor? The nights when I had hoped to find someone just like him, only to be disappointed? Instead, I kissed his neck, flicking my tongue out and licking his skin in a circular motion.

"Madre de dios," he whispered. "That is so nice."

I slid my tongue down to where his neck met his shoulders. I kissed him there in the hollow of his throat, squeezing his ass harder. His back arched.

He pulled his head back and smiled at me. "Do you want to fuck me, papi?"

"Very much," I replied, and kissed his lips again. I could smell his cologne—Calvin Klein Escape—and luxuriated in the velvety smoothness of his skin. He moaned a little as I continued kissing on his neck, squeezing his hard ass with both hands. His hands came up and pulled on my hard nipples. I slid my arms around him and lifted him up, his legs coming around my waist. I could feel his erection through his jeans, hard, insistent, urgent. He bit one of my nipples through my T-shirt, not hard, just enough to send another jolt of arousal through my body. We stood like that for an eternity, it seemed, him gently grazing my nipples with his teeth and lips, my cock becoming harder and harder. He slid down off me at last.

He grabbed my hard cock through my jeans, gripping it loosely. I let out my breath in an explosive blast.

I reached down and undid his belt, then his jeans. They fell down to his ankles. He stepped back from me and sat down on the couch. He took off his clunky boots, revealing white socks, and then stood up and stepped out of his pants. His legs were muscular, covered with wiry black hair. He reached down and pulled his tank top up and over his head in one motion. There was a trail of black hair from his navel down to the waistband of his boxer briefs. A few straggly hairs pointed out from his round nipples. There was another tattoo on his left chest; a halo. He smiled at me. I kicked off my shoes and then he was on his knees before me, slowly undoing my belt, my pants. He slid them down my legs, and I lifted one foot, then the other as he pulled them off me. He leaned forward and put his mouth on my cock through the cotton underwear.

I closed my eyes and tilted my head back.

"You like that?" he asked softly, barely audible over the sound of the air-conditioning blowing air through the vents.

"Yes, Angel, I like."

He slid his thumbs beneath the waistband of my underwear then jerked them down. My cock slapped against my lower belly once it was set free of the cotton restraint. I could feel my underwear sliding slowly down my legs as his tongue run along the underside of my cock. He licked it, always stopping just before his tongue reached the head of my cock, and then started back down the shaft. He took my balls into his mouth, gently applying pressure, just enough to make me moan but not enough to give pain. It felt incredible as my balls slid around inside his mouth, brushing up against his teeth, his tongue manipulating them from side to side. Then his mouth moved to my inner thighs, kissing, biting softly and gently, going from the top to just inside the knee and then back up and down the other leg. I was moaning. It had never felt like this before. No one had ever taken the time.

His tongue slid back up to the base of my cock and then back up to the head, and then he slipped it inside his mouth. He started sucking gently on the head, the whole time swirling his tongue around it, into the slit and then back to the outside again. Goose bumps rose on my skin. I was starting to tremble just a little bit. Then he took the whole thing into his mouth. I started moving my hips back and forth. I put my hands on his head. My cock slid slowly, gently, into and out of his mouth. He gagged once, and I felt his body react to the reflex, his stomach clenching, his shoulders coming forward. I slid back but he grabbed my ass and pulled it back forward, down into his throat, the whole time his tongue working and sliding around it.

"You wanna fuck me, papi?" he asked again, smiling up at me, stroking my wet cock with one hand.

"Yes." The word escaped my mouth, barely above a whisper.

He stood up and slid his boxer briefs down, stepping out of them. His own cock was swollen and hard. I reached for it, kneeling down to take it into my mouth. I licked the head and he moaned as I slid my tongue along the slit in the head, then slid it down the shaft until I reached his shaved balls. I reached up and took a nipple in each hand, pinching them gently, pulling on them. A gasp escaped his lips, and his body went rigid. He stepped back away from me, and turned, getting down onto the floor on all fours.

There were two matching tattoos on his back, on each shoulder blade, mirror images of each other. They were wings, outlined in blue ink but colored in with reds, greens, and yellows. They were the most breathtakingly beautiful tattoos I had ever seen, the work of a real master. I stood there staring at them as he arched his back, lifting his beautiful hard ass up into the air.

"Fuck me, please," he whispered. "Please."

I got down to my knees and pulled a condom out of my pants pocket, tearing the package open with my teeth. I slid it over my cock, feeling the latex gripping like a second layer of skin. I spat into my hand and ran the wetness over my cock, and took it into my hand and guided the head into his hole.

He gasped when he felt the pressure, his entire body going rigid for just an instant, and then he relaxed, and my cock slowly started to slide into him. Even as he relaxed and opened up for it, I could see the tense muscles in his back and shoulders. I reached down and began to knead his shoulder muscles, digging my fingers in ever so gently, moving them with slightly increased pressure. He moaned and gasped as I got deeper inside him.

I stopped when he cried out, my cock only about halfway inside him. I moved my hips backward, slowly sliding out of him. His entire body was rigid. I stopped when only the head was inside him, and then began to slide it inside again. I began moving my hips in a circular motion, to try to loosen him up a bit. He moaned, his hands becoming fists.

"You like that, Angel?" I whispered.

"Oh, yes, papi, I like that." His voice came in a half-whisper.

Once again, I was a little more than halfway inside of him when it stopped, meeting an obstruction. I leaned down and began kissing the back of his neck.

"Oooooooh…"

I pulled back a little, then slid forward again.

A little further.

I pulled back again, and this time he opened completely for me. My cock slid all the way in, my balls slapping against him. I grabbed his shoulders and pulled him back, and he moaned. I sat there, fully inside him, holding him, until he began to move his ass back and forth. I released his shoulders and pulled back again, sliding almost completely out. He was gasping by now. I moved slowly, enjoying the feeling of him tightening and gripping my cock as it moved in and out of him, the pressure against my balls when I got all the way in. I closed my eyes briefly, opening them again to stare at the wings tattooed so vibrantly on his back. They almost seemed alive, moving with the rippling of the muscles of his back, as though they were trying to take on a life of their own, to unfold and spread, the brilliantly colored feathers shining in the light from the chandelier overhead.

His body began moving back toward mine as I slid into him, slowly at first, then faster, trying to drive me deeper inside him. I teased him with my cock, pulling it out, just leaving the head inside, sitting there like that for a few seconds until he started moving his ass back, trying to get me back inside. I moved my hips from side to side, around in a circle, and his moans grew louder and faster. Beads of sweat formed on his wings. Finally, I had enough of teasing his ass, and I started moving faster, matching the rhythm he was creating, driving deeper into him, trying to reach his core, the center of his very being. My cock seemed to grow harder and thicker and longer as I fucked him. The feathers of his tattoo seemed to glisten and glow from the sheen of sweat forming on his back. I was sweating myself, sweat forming at my hairline, my bangs growing damp, the hair under my arms becoming slick. Sweat rolled off my face, splashing onto his beautiful back.

This was how it was meant to be.

I could feel my balls working to start pumping out hot sticky fluid, but I wasn't ready. I wanted to keep fucking him, to keep pounding away on his beautiful ass, watching as the wings slowly took form, flexing and moving, propelling us upward into the air until we were floating in the clouds, far above the twinkling lights of the French Quarter.

He grunted and gasped as his body shuddered as he came.

My entire body arched, went rigid, as the condom filled with my own come, spasming and convulsing as my cock emptied itself, my body shaking, the goose bumps coming out on my skin.

Afterward, we stayed together, my cock inside him, for a few moments, as we returned to earth and reality.

He slid away from my cock and faced me, his face and hair damp with sweat. He smiled, his liquid eyes looking up into mine.

I stood and took his hand, kissing it, and then led him back to the bedroom, leaving the puddle of his come on the hardwood floor. We didn't speak as I gently pushed him onto the bed and lay down beside him, curling my arms around him, pulling him to me. We kissed once, tenderly, without passion, a sweet kiss, like one shared by two teenagers who have just discovered the ecstasy their bodies are capable of experiencing.

It felt so right, holding him there in the bed.

"I love you, papi," he whispered, his lips brushing against my throat.

"I love you, my Angel," I whispered back, pulling him closer.

I woke to daylight streaming through my bedroom window, alone in my bed. I called for him, walking the length of my house, hoping he would still be there. But he wasn't anywhere. He was gone. He'd even cleaned up the puddle he'd left on the living room floor. It was as though he'd never been there at all. I sat down on my couch, naked, and hugged myself. I felt alone, more alone than I ever had in my life. Tears came to my eyes. "Damn you, Angel," I whispered. Somehow, I knew I would never see him again. It was too, too cruel.

There was a note on the coffee table.

Papi, I cannot stay here with you, much as I would like to. It is forbidden. But thank you for giving me such joy. You won't always be sad. Angel.

"Forbidden?" I said aloud.

And that's when I saw it, lying underneath the coffee table. I reached down and picked it up, held it up to the light, and smiled to myself. It was all I had left of him, my Angel, and I vowed to keep it forever.

A long green feather with hints of gold and red.

Contributors

Joseph Baneth Allen grew up in Camp Lejeune, North Carolina. His nonfiction has been published in *OMNI*, *Popular Science*, *Final Frontier*, *Astronomy*, *Florida Living*, *Dog Fancy*, *Pet Life*, *eBay Magazine*, and many others. He was also a feature, military affairs, and political journalist for two daily North Carolina newspapers. His short story "The Bone Box" was published in Todd Gregory's highly acclaimed *Blood Sacraments* anthology. He now lives with his family in Jacksonville, Florida, where he continues to write fiction and nonfiction.

Mel Bossa lives in Montreal and is currently at work on a new novel. Bossa's first two novels, *Split* and *Suite Nineteen*, are available from Bold Strokes Books. Mel also published a short story in the anthology *Men of the Mean Streets.*

'Nathan Burgoine lives in Ottawa, Canada with his husband, Daniel. Previous short stories appear in *Fool for Love*, *I Do Two*, and *Men of the Mean Streets* (fall 2011). He has nonfiction works in *I Like It Like That* and *5x5* Literary Magazine. Anders, Luc, and Curtis made their first appearance in *Blood Sacraments*. You can find 'Nathan online at n8an.livejournal.com.

Dale Chase has been writing male erotica for over a decade with more than one hundred stories published in various magazines and anthologies including translation into Italian and German. Dale has two erotica collections currently in print: *The Company He Keeps: Victorian Gentlemen's Erotica* (Bold Strokes Books), and *If The Spirit Moves You: Ghostly Gay Erotica* (Lethe Press). A California native, Chase lives near San Francisco and can be found online at dalechasestrokes.com.

Todd Gregory has published numerous short stories in various anthologies and magazines. His first novel, *Every Frat Boy Wants It*, was a best seller for Insightoutbooks, as was his anthology *Blood Sacraments* (also nominated for a ForeWord Award for Best Horror of 2010). His novella "Blood on the Moon" was in *Midnight Hungers*, and his anthology *Rough Trade* was a finalist for a Lambda Literary Award. His second novel, *Games Frat Boys Play*, will be published in June 2011. He is currently adapting "Blood on the Moon" into the novel *A Vampire's Heart.*

William Holden lives in Cambridge, Massachusetts, with his partner of thirteen years. His writing career spans more than a decade, with over forty published short stories in erotica, romance, fantasy, and horror. He has served as fiction editor for *RFD Magazine* and has written various encyclopedia articles on the history of gay fiction and literature. He is co-founder and co-editor of *Out in Print: Queer Book Reviews* at www.outinprint.net. His first collection was nominated for a Lambda Award. He can be reached by visiting his website at williamholdenonline.com.

Jay Lygon may live in the City of Angels, but he's not wearing a halo. If you want to find out how hard he bites, find Jay's short story in *Blood Sacraments* (Bold Strokes Books), or the *Bonded* series (Torquere Press). Even the gods aren't safe from his sacrilegious touch in the *Chaos Magic* series (Torquere Press). He can be found on line at www.JayLygonWrites.Com.

Jeff Mann's books include three collections of poetry: *Bones Washed with Wine*, *On the Tongue*, and *Ash: Poems from Norse Mythology*; two books of personal essays: *Edge: Travels of an Appalachian Leather Bear* and *Binding the God: Ursine Essays from the Mountain South*; a novella, "Devoured," included in *Masters of Midnight: Erotic Tales of the Vampire*; a collection of poetry and memoir, *Loving Mountains, Loving Men*; and a volume of short fiction, *A History of Barbed Wire*, winner of a Lambda Literary Award. He teaches creative writing at Virginia Tech in Blacksburg, Virginia.

Felice Picano is the author of nineteen books, including the literary memoirs *Ambidextrous*, *Men Who Loved Me*, and *A House on the Ocean, a House on the Bay*, as well as the best-selling novels *Like People in History*, *Looking Glass Lives*, *The Lure*, and *Eyes*. He is the founder of Sea Horse Press, one of the first gay publishing houses, which later merged with two other publishing houses to become the Gay Presses of New York. With Andrew Holleran, Robert Ferro, Edmund White, and George Whitmore, he founded the Violet Quill Club to promote and increase the visibility of gay authors and their works. He has edited and written for *The Advocate*, *Blueboy*, *Mandate*, *GaysWeek*, *Christopher Street*, and was Books Editor of *The New York Native* and has been a culture reviewer for *The Los Angeles Examiner*, *San Francisco Examiner*, *New York Native*, *Harvard Lesbian & Gay Review*, and the *Lambda Book Report*. He has won the Ferro-Grumley Award for best gay novel (*Like People in History*) and the PEN Syndicated Fiction Award for short story. He was a finalist for the Ernest Hemingway Award and has been nominated for three Lambda Literary Awards. A native of New York, Felice Picano now lives in Los Angeles. His most recent book, *True Stories*, presents sweet and sometimes controversial anecdotes of his precocious childhood, odd, funny, and often disturbing encounters from before he found his calling as a writer and later as one of the first GLBT publishers. Throughout are his delightful encounters and surprising relationships with the one-of-a-kind and the famous—including Tennessee Williams, W.H. Auden, Charles Henri Ford, Bette Midler, and Diana Vreeland.

Nic P. Ramsies is an East Coast native with a passion for tiaras and ball gowns. He is a recovering Catholic. The second oldest in a family of six, Nic was the first boy in his small rural Pennsylvania town to *not* get his prom date pregnant. Voted most likely to take a boy to bed on the first date by his high school senior class (and they thought that was an insult), Nic has worked hard to live up to this title. While he is definitely royalty, no one would call him a queen. His name ultimately says it all. His erotic writing has appeared in the anthologies *Rough Trade*, *Sex Buddies*, and *Bad Boys*.

Max Reynolds is the pseudonym of a well-known East Coast writer and academic. Reynolds's stories and novellas have appeared in numerous anthologies, including *Men of Mystery*, *FRATSEX*, *Rough Trade*, *His Underwear*, *Porn! Dirty Gay Erotica*, and *Blood Sacraments*. He is currently at work on an erotic vampire novel set in Mexico.

Jeffrey Ricker is a writer, editor, and graphic designer. His writing has appeared in the literary magazine *Collective Fallout* and the anthologies *Paws and Reflect*, *Fool for Love: New Gay Fiction*, *Blood Sacraments*, *Men of the Mean Streets,* and *Speaking Out*. His first novel, *Detours*, will be published in November 2011 by Bold Strokes Books. A magna cum laude graduate of the University of Missouri School of Journalism, he lives with his partner, Michael, and two dogs, and is working on his second novel. Follow his blog at jeffreyricker.wordpress.com.

Nathan Sims grew up knowing he wanted to be a storyteller. Somewhere along the way his storytelling turned from the written word to the stage and he spent many years acting, directing, and teaching before returning to his first love: writing. He currently lives outside Washington, D.C., with his partner. His fiction can be found in various anthologies, magazines, and online. He is currently at work on his first novel, *Wish Bone*.

Mel Spenser is the author of three books, as many novellas, and several short stories, in the genre of contemporary and paranormal erotic romance. Chosen by readers, Mel's first book, *Miss Me?* won the Night Owl Romance Award for Best Gay Erotic Romance for 2008. Having grown up in the Midwest, Mel has lived all over the U.S. and currently lives in Houston.

From Vancouver, Canada, **Jay Starre** has written for numerous gay men's anthologies over the past dozen years. His imaginative and stimulating stories can be found in anthologies such as *His Underwear*, *Full Body Contact*, *Kink*, *A View to A Thrill*, and *Wired Hard 3*. His short story "The Four Doors" was nominated for a 2003 Spectrum Award. Two of his erotic gay novels, *The Erotic Tales of the Knight Templars* and *The Lusty Adventures of the Knossos Prince*, have been published recently.

Editor of the Lambda Literary Award finalist *Tented: Gay Erotic Tales from Under the Big Top* (Lethe Press 2010), and the forthcoming *Riding the Rails* for Bold Strokes Books, **Jerry L. Wheeler** has appeared in many anthologies, including *Law of Desire*, *Best Gay Romance 2010*, *Bears in the Wild*, and *I Like It Like That.* Be sure to catch his book reviews on the web at *Out in Print* (www.outinprint.net).

About the Editor

Todd Gregory is a New Orleans–based writer who survived Hurricane Katrina and its aftermath with the help of prescription medication. He has edited the anthologies *Blood Sacraments*, *Rough Trade*, *His Underwear*, and *Blood Lust* (with M. Christian). Todd has published short stories in numerous anthologies and his works have been translated into German.

Books Available From Bold Strokes Books

Pirate's Fortune: Supreme Constellations Book Four by Gun Brooke. Set against the backdrop of war, captured mercenary Weiss Kyakh is persuaded to work undercover with bio-android Madisyn Pimm, which foils her plans to escape, but kindles unexpected love. (978-1-60282-563-5)

Sex and Skateboards by Ashley Bartlett. Sex and skateboards and surfing on the California coast. What more could anyone want? Alden McKenna thinks that's all she needs, until she meets Weston Duvall. (978-1-60282-562-8)

Waiting in the Wings by Melissa Brayden. Jenna has spent her whole life training for the stage, but the one thing she didn't prepare for was Adrienne. Is she ready to sacrifice what she's worked so hard for in exchange for a shot at something much deeper? (978-1-60282-561-1)

Wings: Subversive Gay Angel Erotica, edited by Todd Gregory. A collection of powerfully written tales of passion and desire centered on the aching beauty of angels. (978-1-60282-565-9)

Suite Nineteen by Mel Bossa. Psychic Ben Lebeau moves into Shilts Manor, where he meets seductive Lennox Van Kemp and his clan of Métis—guardians of a spiritual conspiracy dating back to Christ. But are Ben's psychic abilities strong enough to save him? (978-1-60282-564-2)

Speaking Out: LGBTQ Youth Stand Up, edited by Steve Berman. Inspiring stories written for and about LGBTQ teens of overcoming adversity (against intolerance and homophobia) and experiencing life after "coming out." (978-1-60282-566-6)

Forbidden Passions by MJ Williamz. Passion burns hotter when it's forbidden, and the fire between Katie Prentiss and Corrine Staples in antebellum Louisiana is raging out of control. (978-1-60282-641-0)

Men of the Mean Streets, edited by Greg Herren and J.M. Redmann. Dark tales of amorality and criminality by some of the top authors of gay mysteries. (978-1-60282-240-5)

After the Fall by Robin Summers. When the plague destroys most of humanity, Taylor Stone thinks there's nothing left to live for, until she meets Kate, a woman who makes her realize love is still alive and makes her dream of a future she thought was no longer possible. (978-1-60282-234-4)

Accidents Never Happen by David-Matthew Barnes. From the moment Albert and Joey meet by chance beneath a train track on a street in Chicago, a domino effect is triggered, setting off a chain reaction of murder and tragedy. (978-1-60282-235-1)

In Plain View, edited by Shane Allison. Best-selling gay erotica authors create the stories of sex and desire modern readers crave. (978-1-60282-236-8)

Wild by Meghan O'Brien. Shapeshifter Selene Rhodes dreads the full moon and the loss of control it brings, but when she rescues forensic pathologist Eve Thomas from a vicious attack by a masked man, she discovers she isn't the scariest monster in San Francisco. (978-1-60282-227-6)

Conquest by Ronica Black. When Mary Brunelle stumbles into the arms of Jude Jaeger, a gorgeous dominatrix at a private nightclub, she is smitten, but she soon finds out Jude is her professor, and Professor Jaeger doesn't date her students…or her conquests. (978-1-60282-229-0)

The Affair of the Porcelain Dog by Jess Faraday. What darkness stalks the London streets at night? Ira Adler, present plaything of crime lord Cain Goddard, will soon find out. (978-1-60282-230-6)

Who Dat Whodunnit by Greg Herren. Popular New Orleans detective Scotty Bradley investigates the murder of a dethroned beauty queen to clear the name of his pro football–playing cousin. (978-1-60282-225-2)

The Company He Keeps by Dale Chase. A riotously erotic collection of stories set in the sexually repressed and therefore sexually rampant Victorian era. (978-1-60282-226-9)